ADMIT ONE

JENNA HILARY SINCLAIR

Published by
Dreamspinner Press
4760 Preston Road
Suite 244-149
Frisco, TX 75034
http://www.dreamspinnerpress.com/

Admit One

Cover Design by Mara McKennen

ISBN: 978-1-61581-097-0

Printed in the United States of America
First Edition
November, 2009

eBook edition available
eBook ISBN: 978-1-61581-098-7

I dedicate *Admit One* to my husband Ralph. He's not only loved me and encouraged me in my writing for years, but he listened to me read this novel to him (yes, the whole thing!) and provided invaluable editorial commentary. I will always remember him settling into our big green chair and saying, "What did you write today?" Sweetheart, thank you so much for all your help. I love you.

Many thanks also to Dusky, Beth, and Elke for their friendship and excellent editing. Dusky is a "prose pro" at ferreting out even the tiniest writing mistakes; Beth often provided super-fast, comprehensive edits when I needed them most; and Elke pinpointed a subtle plot problem just in time for me to fix it. I wouldn't dream of writing without their steadfast support and expertise. Thank you, friends!

Any remaining errors or miscues are mine. I hope you enjoy reading *Admit One*.

CHAPTER 1
GOOD REASON

THE first time Kevin and I had sex, he followed me in his Camry to the Holiday Inn Express where I was staying. I watched his headlights in the rearview mirror, checking to see.... I don't know what I was checking. What did I think he was going to do—stop, jump out, and shout, *Look at us, we're fags*? But his car remained steadfastly, securely behind me.

Usually I would have gone to one of the rooms in the back of the bar with him; it was so much safer. But I'd gone without for months. It was late, I'd been drinking and dancing since I'd walked into Good Times hours before, and I was desperate for a warm, male body to stand in for my own hand. I needed more than a stand-up quickie, and I was willing to take risks I shouldn't have. My judgment evaporated with my need.

I'd told him my room number, and he came up to the third floor five minutes after I'd let myself in. We didn't talk. I didn't want to talk. I barely knew his name. When he'd given me the eye and the last dance of the night, he'd passed the test. He looked healthy and clean, if unexpectedly good-looking for someone who would be willing to go with me; he talked like a sensible on-the-make gay man and not an ax-murderer on the prowl for unsuspecting homos; and he was shorter and lighter than I was by three inches and thirty pounds. I thought I could at least hold my own against him if things turned nasty.

I got down on my knees right there in front of the door, pulled out his cock, and got to it. He was hard even before I slipped him into my mouth, and it didn't take long to suck him off. When he gripped my shoulders and erupted against my working tongue, I moaned. He was real. Whoever he was, he was real and he tasted like a man, and half of what I'd come to Houston for slotted into place.

We stayed like that for a span of seconds, each of us fighting for breath, and then he hauled me up and kissed me. I hadn't expected that, didn't want it, didn't often get it from my pickups, but in my surprise, I didn't fight it. His arms went around me too, strong for all he was slender, as if he knew me and cared, and I clutched at him mainly to keep from falling full against him. I thought he might have liked tasting himself in my mouth, that he got off on it. His tongue in my mouth was sweet, like he'd been drinking bourbon and Coke.

Kevin pushed me backward until I sprawled on the bed, and in a sex-drenched, raspy voice, he growled, "Get undressed." A shiver of unease swept through me at being told what to do; I don't go in for that sort of thing. I'm an ordinary man with ordinary tastes. But, God, I wanted him on my cock, and so I did it, got my clothes off while he took off his. And though I hadn't expected this either and wouldn't have asked him to get naked just for a suck-off in an anonymous hotel room, it was great to see his whole body revealed along with the sturdy-looking cock that had been in my mouth.

He wasn't buff; with his long legs, he looked more like a greyhound who could run sprints. A black-haired sprinter with a generous sprinkling of chest hair. He was very masculine in a controlled, clearly defined sort of way, just the way I liked my men. When he got on the bed and moved forward to taste me, my eyelids fluttered at all that man-skin bent in service to my needs.

It was a good orgasm, what he gave me. What I took from him.

Afterward, without asking, he flopped down onto the bed next to me and closed his eyes. I thought about asking him to leave, but I didn't have the energy. We fell asleep next to each other.

Around four o'clock, I got up to take a piss, and on my way back to the bed I put out the light. We had sex again in the dark, where I couldn't see him and he couldn't see me, just right, humping against each other until his hand fumbled down between us and held us together. He smelled of the smoke from the club. When he rubbed against me with his thumb, I jetted within a few seconds, not giving it up loudly, only sighing, and he followed me not long after that.

The clock showed eight-thirty when I woke up. Kevin was coming out of the shower with a towel wrapped around his hips. He looked good to my eyes, though maybe a little pale, as if he didn't see the sun often. I eased my left arm under the sheet where it couldn't be seen.

He picked up his briefs from the floor and pulled them on, then sat down on the bed and started working his socks on.

"Good morning," he said in his hoarse voice.

"Sure."

He finished with the socks and twisted around to look at where I was still flat on my back. "What do you say we go get some—"

"I have to leave soon," I said.

His eyebrows rose. "Leave?"

"Deadline to meet. Sorry."

He got the message: I wasn't interested in anything else. His name was Kevin and he gave good head, period. If I'd given him a false message because we'd gone to a real hotel room and not some rent-by-the-hour dive or the backseat of a car, well, I was sorry. My life was punctuated by infrequent one-night stands, driven by my free choice and forced through hard experience, and that was just the way it was.

I watched him dress the rest of the way and put his wallet in his back pocket. He paused and looked down at where I lay with his spunk crusted dry on my belly. Then he came closer and leaned over me, and I tensed. I was surprised when he kissed me, a closed-mouth kiss with nothing much behind it, merely a brief pressing of lips. He had more to give than I did, that was for sure.

"So long, Tom," he said. And then he left.

I took my time after that and started the hours-long drive home at noon.

There wasn't supposed to be a second time when Kevin and I had sex. When I went back to Houston five months later, he wasn't on my mind. Getting my rocks off, yeah, that was on my mind, and the only reason I ever went to Houston. Work had been stressful, I hadn't been sleeping well, and the walls of my small house were starting to close in on me. So I'd taken off for the weekend when normally I would have been able to hold off for another month or two. As always, I went carefully, alert to those around me as I walked toward the bar, and I would always, always be careful of how I left it.

I was at the bar, working on my second beer. I'd already walked around, seeing what was on display that night and figuring what my chances were of getting somebody to suck off a middle-aged man without much to recommend him. I didn't have any illusions about myself. Next to the youngsters strutting their stuff, next to the gym-queens, next to the noses that'd been fixed with surgery and the skin that'd been coaxed and creamed, I was nothing. I was an unassuming man with a degree, a passion for my job, and a need for sex. Before I entered the meat-market fray again, I needed another drink, and so I was up on a barstool, staring without really looking into my glass of Miller Lite.

That was when I felt a tap on my shoulder. My eyes flew up to the mirror behind the bottles of Jack Daniel and Jim Beam, and I saw a familiar face behind me. Blue eyes, a definite chin, close-to-the-skull short hair, heavy eyebrows….

It took a few pounding pulses of the music for me to remember who he was. When recognition dawned and I moved to swivel around and face him, he said, "I'm Kevin, remember?" in the husky voice I'd heard before.

"And I'm—"

"Tom. With the souped-up Mazda."

It was my only indulgence. Everything else I kept reined in tight, but I did enjoy driving that car. "Right," I said. He looked like he'd come from a late night at work. His long-sleeved, button-down blue shirt probably had been accented by a tie a few hours earlier, and his pants were of a fine weave that went best with a suit jacket. Kevin, I guessed, was a businessman who worked in downtown Houston.

"Mind if I…." He nodded to the empty seat next to me, and I realized he was remembering how we'd parted before. He was quite obviously trying not to push and, just as obviously, inexplicably wanting to spend some time in my company.

I don't know why I said, "Okay." Maybe it was that almost sixteen years had passed since I'd been twenty-two. Lately I could feel a sort of weariness all through me; I was always tired. The way I lived made me tired. Maybe it was the easy way he'd left me before, not making a fuss. Maybe it was the nice smile he had.

Or maybe I was flattered. What the hell, I thought. A beer wasn't going to change my world.

He sat and ordered a Michelob, and for a while neither of us said anything. The noisy activity of the bar went on behind and around us, and I wondered how far outside my boundaries I was willing to go. Kevin looked good in the remains of his work wear. He had neat, capable hands.

He was halfway finished with his beer when he asked, "You have a football team you support?"

In the heat of a Texas spring, football season was long gone, but it was the perfect safe subject. We talked. The words came from me in fits and starts at first, and both of us were impeded by the music, which wasn't designed for two late-thirty-somethings to talk over. But eventually we got into a rhythm. We ripped the Cowboys and destroyed the hapless Texans and paid homage to Bill Belichick and the Patriots. Kevin knew his sports way better than I did, but I held my own as we argued the merits of the three-four defense and whether Ben Roethlisberger was worth the contract he'd gotten. By the time we'd exhausted football, the bartender had us on our fourth drinks. On the TV set up high in the corner, an ad came on for Hillary Clinton, and that got us started on her and the presidential race. Kevin was a Democrat, but then again, I doubt there were many gay Republicans around us looking for action that Friday night.

I kept telling myself to get up off the barstool and go circulate, that Kevin was just shooting the shit and that's it, but I didn't leave. Talking with Kevin was like the safe conversations I had at home, where I was plain, unthreatening, unsuspected Tom, and it was curiously nonsexual. That was all right. At least for a little while, I could avoid an everyday reality of my life: that I lived alone and had to travel across the state to find someone willing to have sex with me.

That curious bubble of unreality that I stayed in for a few hours with Kevin—drinking and watching the TV and talking—didn't burst until I got up to take a piss. On my way back a line dance started, one I knew, one I liked to dance to, and when a stranger's hand reached out to pull me onto the floor, I didn't resist.

I looked over at where Kevin was, and though he was looking at me with his chin up, he didn't make any other kind of move. Fuck him, I thought, only then realizing I'd issued a challenge that he wasn't about to meet. If he wasn't interested, fine.

Fifteen minutes later, though, the music changed to the occasional slow and sultry number that caught jeers from the crowd at the same time that it drove most of them to the floor. One of the much older men who'd been dancing near me took a step in my direction, but then it was Kevin who was right in front of me.

"May I have this dance?" he asked, perfectly serious. He stood there with his arms out, poised as if to embrace me.

Even in a gay club, I didn't like to cause a scene, and I would have moved closer to him for that reason alone and not because I wanted to. But I did want to. There was something appealing, even arresting, in the tilt of his head as he asked and didn't insist. There was sweet seduction—something I'd always been able to resist before—in the way I knew him when I didn't know anybody else around me. His arms closed around my shoulders, my hands rested on his trim waist, and it looked like we were dance partners. I was suddenly blazingly conscious that we'd had sex before. He moved the same way he had in bed, with a certain grace that seemed to come from the confidence I lacked. Fred Astaire he wasn't, but he didn't need to be. All he needed was to touch me the way he was doing, with a man's surety and a sense of claiming that he didn't deserve and I wasn't willing to give, but that nevertheless had me hot in seconds.

We moved slowly to the notes of the song, and his eyes asked me if we were going to have sex tonight. I guess he read the answer in my face and in how our steps in the dance matched. Even though I never repeated my sex partners, at least not since I'd entered the working world, I was going to this night. I tore my gaze from his, looked around, and cynically thought that there wasn't anybody else waving their hands, asking for the privilege of getting me off that night, was there? So Kevin it was going to be. I looked back at him too soon, within seconds, and watched while a sort of sigh escaped his lips. He pulled me closer and I flowed into him; I could feel he was getting hard. I was too.

We stayed together for that dance and every one after that.

We went back to his hotel room a little past one a.m., me following him through the humid coastal air in my little Miata with the top down. The city-flavored wind felt good on my face and helped me focus through the booze-fog as I drove. I was surprised when we arrived at a Marriott Courtyard hotel not too far from the La Quinta where I was staying that time, but if he was as cautious as I was and didn't want to take strange men back to his house, I had no place to complain.

Being with him that night was good. Basic, uncompromising sex between two men who wanted it and wanted it right then. I'd forgotten some things from our first encounter—for instance, how he liked to kiss. How he hitched in his breath right before he flooded my mouth and then again when I filled his. How afterward he acted totally comfortable next to me, as if it weren't awkward at all between us, two mostly-strangers in bed together with the sharp taste of jism against our tongues. Watching him adjust the bedding over us so naturally, hearing him say *You don't have to leave. Let's go to sleep*, made me suddenly remember the things I used to want, and I fell asleep not-quite-satisfied.

We repeated ourselves in the morning, only more deliberately. Before I came close to the end, he flipped around and presented himself to me, his cock a couple of inches from my face, and though sixty-nine isn't my favorite, I did that. We weren't even close to coming together, but Kevin kept working on me once he'd finished.

Like each time before, he flopped over onto his back when we were done. A few minutes passed while my breathing evened out, and then the room became silent. Someone down the hall left their room and the door slammed shut, like a small explosion. I followed the sound of their footsteps in the hallway as they came closer, passed the room I was in, and then went down the open stairwell. Outside, someone leaned on the horn of their car, and from further away came the wail of an ambulance siren. I took a cleansing breath and licked my lips. Time to get up and start my own day. The big, anonymous city was all around us, an impartial judge who didn't blame me for my weakness in how I'd spent the night.

Next to me Kevin stirred and turned over onto his side. Even in the dim light I could see the twinkle in his eyes.

Lying there next to me, naked, he extended his hand in an unmistakable gesture. "Hello," he said. "I'm not sure we've properly met. I'm Kevin Bannerman. Pleased to meet you."

I took his hand and shook it because I was smoothed out, at least for the moment, still riding the echoes of my coming, and because I was amused. "Hi, I'm Tom."

"Tom-without-a-last-name?"

He was pushing, but I answered anyway. "Tom Smith."

There were those skeptical eyebrows again, rising. "Really?"

"Really. My forebears had no imagination."

"Okay, Tom Smith it is. Not Tom Jones."

"Nope, neither one of the Joneses."

"I can guess you're not a libertine."

"Or a singer. You wouldn't want to hear my voice."

"What do you do, then?" he asked easily. "I'm a banker. A commercial lending officer."

I stiffened, and he noticed. I didn't give out personal information.

"Tom," he said gently, "I'm only making conversation."

"I'm a teacher," I admitted, shocked at myself for saying it. "A high school teacher."

He nodded, understanding changing his expression to sympathetic. "Oh, I get it. That's a tough one when you're queer."

"You've got that right." I rolled over and sat up abruptly, pulling the sheet around me, trying to get it over my shoulders. I was on the left side of the bed, as with all my encounters. With the air conditioning on, it was cold in that room now that we'd stopped going at each other.

Kevin stayed where he was. "You must like what you're doing to stick with it."

"I do. The kids make it worthwhile." Fierce pride raced through me in a second, there and then gone. I was a good teacher.

"I make loans to small businesses, usually with revenues less than twenty million dollars."

“Those are small businesses?” I said without turning around.

“In this economy they are. How about you?”

“No, I don’t need a loan.”

He sat up next to me. I thought he might have wanted to put a hand on my arm, but he didn’t. “What is it with you, anyway? Why are you running scared?”

I wasn’t going to explain anything. Besides, most of it was pretty obvious. “I just prefer to keep things compartmentalized. Each thing in its own place.”

“You might be taking it too far, but I guess I won’t argue with you. Look, unless you’ve got another deadline to meet, how about we grab some breakfast?”

I wasn’t immune to his charm. His passing reference to how I’d lied the time before to get rid of him was said gently, without rancor and without blaming me. I stretched under the expanse of white that covered me and nodded. “IHOP?”

“I think there’s one a few miles up the freeway.”

“Over by Rice University, right.”

He gave me a speculative look then, as if trying to figure out if Rice was significant to me.

We showered and got dressed in an awkward dance, carefully not intruding into each other’s space. I wasn’t happy to be putting on the same clothes again, my work clothes from the day before, but I thought I’d have the chance to change soon enough. Kevin got into a pair of crisp, expensive-looking jeans, the kind with a crease to them that I couldn’t afford on my salary. A light blue golf shirt with some sort of crest over the breast pocket and a brown belt finished him off. He looked like he was ready for a tee time on the most exclusive country club course.

We went out to eat, getting the morning’s issue of the *Houston Chronicle* outside the restaurant and sharing the sections between us over eggs and pancakes. He ordered Rooty Tooty Fresh and Fruity—I think deliberately, to get a rise out of me. He sure looked at me devilishly over the top of the menu as he gave the order to the waitress. Kevin could put a world of meaning into those eyes of his.

Breakfast was easy, and I found myself relaxing. We finished and paid and then stood outside on the sidewalk under the cloudy haze that so often is the sum total of Houston's spring weather. The cars and trucks on Highway 59 whisked by, stirring up a continuous artificial breeze, making me thankful that I didn't have to contend with the pollution and the traffic of Texas's biggest city all the time.

"So, you headed home today?"

I shook my head. I'd planned to stay over; Good Times would be hopping on Saturday night.

"Me, neither," Kevin said, and that was the first time I had confirmed what I'd begun to suspect, that he really wasn't from Houston after all. He didn't quite have a Texas accent. His was a bit softer, more rounded, I thought. Maybe Louisiana?

He waited until a family with two little girls walked by us and into the restaurant, and then he said, "Listen, tell me if you're not interested but… I thought I'd do the tourist bit today. I've never actually seen much of the city. Would you want to join me?" He jammed his left hand into a pocket. "It's not much fun being alone."

I could vouch for that: not much fun.

I hovered on the edge of saying no, but I didn't. Maybe because I was tired of my own silences. I had nothing special planned for the day. I would probably just grade some papers and then surf the net from the La Quinta until dinner and going back to the bar.

Kevin noticed my indecision. "I thought I'd go down to the San Jacinto monument, read about the independence of Texas and all that. Maybe keep going south to Galveston and get some good seafood for lunch."

I'd taught the Texas History course to sophomores, and I knew the story well. But I'd only visited San Jacinto once, when I was twelve.

"If that doesn't float your boat," Kevin went on, "there's the Menil Collection of art that's open this afternoon…"

I'd always heard of the Menil, though I've never managed to get there.

"…and I've finally decided now's the time I'm going to Brennan's for dinner. You want to come with me there?"

He'd finally hit on something that wouldn't commit me. Commit too much of my time or my attention. I'd already given more than I wanted to, than I ever had before during one of my weekends, but…. Much as I'd resisted, I liked Kevin. This I could give him, and it was with a sort of relief that I said, "Brennan's, sure. I haven't been there in forever."

"And I've never been there. I already have reservations for two."

"For two? You were expecting to meet…." I left the question hanging.

Kevin answered me with a quick frown. "I wasn't expecting to see you again, if that's what's got you bothered. Come on, Tom, lighten up. I'm not going to turn you over to the loose-dick patrol. I'm like you, remember?"

"Then why—"

"You are a suspicious guy. I was hoping to meet somebody to go out with, okay? Nobody specific, only…. I get tired of the club, how it's hard to have a decent conversation there, how you never meet anybody real, how artificial it is. Don't you get tired of it too?"

He was talking in a low, intense voice. Even so, I looked around to see if there was anybody around to hear him.

He made a pointed, exasperated sound. "If you're not interested, fine. Forget it. I can—"

"No," I said. "I mean, yes. Yes, I do get tired of the club." It was a permanent feature of my existence, but I was sick of the way I had forced myself into living, how I never connected on any deep level with anybody. Living where I did, I couldn't keep my job and my safety and change that, but that didn't mean there weren't moments when I regretted it all, everything. When I let myself think for a little while about living a normal life.

And here was Kevin offering me a small slice of time when things could be different. He wasn't running off into the dark, four a.m. night, or into the cloudy morning either. He wanted to spend more time with me.

I looked away, tempted beyond belief. "I guess I…." I shoved my hand into my pocket too, my right hand since it's easier for me than my left, and there we stood, two gay men who were mirror images of each other, trying to find a way to connect within our comfort levels.

There wasn't much comfort in any of my levels.

Kevin went off to see the Houston area on his own, but with my promise to meet him at Brennan's at seven-thirty for drinks before dinner.

I spent the day alone, as I'd planned all along, plowing through the seniors' papers on the complex causes of World War I and occasionally thinking about where Kevin was and what he was doing. There was a stretch of minutes when I drove out for lunch during which I regretted not being with him, and I wondered what he must think of me and my decisions. But I lived the way I thought best, the same as he did, and that was that. I pushed those thoughts away and later concentrated on how the silence of my room was good after the riotous chaos of a high school and the pulsing music of the night before. I took a mid-afternoon nap and ironed my suit jacket. A jacket was required, I thought, for the elegance of an evening out at one of the best restaurants in Houston. I budgeted carefully all the time, but I would allow myself what was sure to be an expensive meal; my credit card company's computers would be shocked to see me actually spending money like this on myself.

What I tried not to do was be conscious that I'd handed over some form of control to this Kevin Bannerman by saying yes. I told myself instead that we were far from where I lived and worked, and I'd go back to my regular way of living as soon as I drove away from this town. But in the meantime…. I looked at myself in the mirror as I adjusted my tie. I could enjoy myself tonight, couldn't I? The problem would be enjoying myself too much. My life couldn't be like this all the time, but for now, this one night, couldn't I stop looking over my shoulder? Couldn't I forget what always seemed to lurk half a turn away from my thoughts?

When I carefully walked up to the entrance of the restaurant, he was standing outside waiting for me, and I got two distinct impressions: that he was relieved I'd actually shown up, and that he had to restrain the impulse to kiss me. I knew his kisses now, at least those few we'd exchanged in the heat of the sexual battle, but not the kind someone might give on a Saturday night at a restaurant.

"Hello, Tom," he said, with a swift smile, not even trying to hide how glad he was to see me. "Glad you could make it."

"Glad I'm here," I said awkwardly to cover up the jolt of attraction that streaked through me. Had he been this good-looking on that first night months ago? Kevin's smile made him even more handsome, made me think in a flash of him looking down on me in bed. I extended my hand to slide smoothly against his and then away.

"Me too," Kevin said.

We lingered over drinks in the bar area, but it was too crowded and noisy for us to talk much over our bourbon and waters, and Kevin kept his eyes down most of the time. The sophisticated, quiet dining room the hostess eventually took us to was different, dark red brick enlivened with candles on each white tablecloth. The room looked out over the little street that had been the restaurant's home even back when I'd visited here with my parents. We settled on a bottle of shiraz, took our time checking out the menu, and then took our time over dinner too, all four courses we indulged in.

When Kevin told me he'd spent his teen years in Little Rock, Arkansas and shared that his mom was an art photographer living in St. Louis now, I was shamed by my instinct toward silence. After the waiter came with our turtle soup and okra gumbo, I found the words I was so accustomed to withholding. I told Kevin I was Texan to the soles of my booted feet, and that my family had deep roots here. He asked what kind of roots, and I searched for something to say that would convey how longhorns and sagebrush ran in our blood without saying too much. I settled on telling him about my brother—not me—who presided over the family-owned ranch out near Amarillo, and then ruined my reticence when I added that I went there for holiday celebrations.

Kevin listened to me talk about this—and everything else I opened my mouth about—with his head tilted a little to the side, so seriously intent. He was showing me a different part of him, not the laughing dancer and not the intent sex partner and not even the man who could coax the devil himself to sit down with the angels, because somehow he'd gotten me here, sitting across from him in the flickering light, when I never, ever did this.

That's the thing about a really good restaurant with a discerning wait staff. If the timing is right, if the company is the best, a good restaurant can make a man feel as if he's in a space out of time. The minutes pass differently than anywhere else, and the rest of the world recedes. That's how I began to feel after a while as Kevin, in his charcoal gray suit and his red silk tie, took in each of my words as if it were a special gift. I wasn't made of ice, despite how I sometimes felt. I was there, I was talking, I was being swept away by a current I'd never expected to be so strong. The wine we'd ordered might have helped too.

Besides, how could I have thought we could spend those strangely intimate hours together and not share some things I'd believed I didn't want to say? I was letting down my guard with every minute that passed.

As we enjoyed trout amandine and shrimp Sardou, Kevin told me he'd attended the University of Arkansas in Fayetteville and that he loved the winters there and the sound of a chill wind roaring through the country hollows of the Ozarks outside of town. The way he said it made me realize he loved the land and probably was the kind of man who enjoyed hiking and camping, maybe fishing and hunting. I could see him in sturdy hiking boots, finding his way through a forest along a faint trail marked by blazes on the trees, next to impossible to follow if a man didn't pay very close attention. I began to see the quiet, understated determination that was a part of every way he expressed himself. It seemed to me that he would never stay lost for long in a forest or anywhere else.

It wasn't so difficult to tell him I had my teaching degree from Texas State in San Marcos and had taken half a master's degree worth of counseling courses from Texas Tech in Lubbock, and that the long, dry, isolated drive into Big Bend National Park was my favorite stretch of road in the state.

It turned out that we shared a love of that amazing park, the least visited in the country, and we agreed that we wanted it to stay that way. He knew Big Bend well, and we spent a long time exchanging reminiscences of times we'd hiked one trail or another, how he'd come face to face with a mountain lion one early morning in a box canyon, and how I'd rafted down the Rio Grande river on a perfect spring day.

A perfect spring day. Or evening. I remembered a few, but it had been a long time since I'd added one to the list. Kevin picked up his wine glass and held it for a moment in front of him, a small toast. I did the same, and we both drank.

It was a good dinner.

The night had taken firm hold of the city when we finally left Brennan's close to ten o'clock. A breeze had come up that whipped our pants against our legs. We'd each parked our cars in the small lot with a crumbling concrete surface at the end of the block, so we walked down there together, where our cars were side by side, though facing opposite ways. We each pulled out our keys and clicked the driver's doors open, the clicks sounding one after the other.

I turned around to face him, not sure what I wanted. I was a little drunk and a lot confused. I wasn't even supposed to be here, and none of this should be happening: not the night out or the good company, not the smiles that had been sent across the table or the warm feeling he'd created in my belly, not this had-to-have that sprang up in me as I watched him watching me.

I wanted to kiss Kevin, the way he hadn't kissed me when we'd met for the evening, and he'd so stripped me of myself that I actually stepped up to him and did it. He kissed me back, his breath catching audibly, and I discovered how his lips moved when we weren't having sex and how dessert tasted in his mouth. It was damn good. And dangerous.

I pulled away, already asking myself why I'd done that, especially out in the open where anyone could have seen us. Shit! I didn't want to get involved, never would let that happen, and now that we were out of the clutches of the restaurant, I should have known better. "Good night," I said roughly, and I jerked the car door open and climbed inside.

But Kevin wouldn't let me escape; he held the door open and leaned in to where I was stubbornly staring out the windshield.

"Where are you going?" he asked.

"Good Times," I said. "A few laughs, a few beers, dance a little, find somebody who—"

"You never laugh, Tom," Kevin said. "I don't think you'll do it there."

"Yeah, well, you never know." I fiddled with my key without putting it in the ignition.

"If you go, then I'll go."

"You don't have to."

"Sure I do. I want to get laid tonight too. I'll play the game just like you will."

"Fine."

"But we don't have to."

Of course we didn't. The man I wanted to have sex with was right there talking to me. Was I out of my mind to be thinking of driving away from him? I thought maybe I was.

Kevin came even closer. "Come back to my room with me," he said quietly. "Spend the night with me. Please."

I turned to look up at him. "I don't… I don't do guys over again."

"Sure you do," he whispered.

I had, hadn't I?

Kevin kissed me then, his lips warm and lush against mine, and I didn't stop him. I took what he gave me, and it seemed that the kiss, this connection between us, lasted for a very long time. Lasted through my hand coming up to rest on his shoulder and his palm coming down to cup my cheek, and lasted through the time he drew back to say *Follow me,* and lasted through the Miata starting and finding its way along the streets of Houston all the way back to that Marriott Courtyard, and lasted through the two of us silently walking through the lobby up to his room.

The door closed behind us and we were kissing again, or still kissing, and Kevin breathed against my lips, "Do you do it? Do you? I want to fuck you so bad. I've got stuff for it. Will you let me do you?"

I almost lost it right there; my knees gave way for an instant and I sagged against the entranceway wall. It'd been years, but that didn't mean I didn't want to be fucked, that I didn't fantasize about it and sometimes even dream about it, waking up convinced I was spurting with my legs over a man's shoulders, his cock commanding me. I was used to denying myself the things I wanted, but here he was in the flesh, tempting me. I shouldn't, I shouldn't.

God help me, I was going to let him fuck me.

I launched myself at him and pushed him against the full-length mirror, where we heaved against each other as if we wanted to exchange skins right through our clothes. Then I grabbed his shoulders, spun him around, and propelled him across the room to the bed, where he fell backward, startled and laughing. He wasn't down long but bounced back up to me. I swayed when he hit against me but caught him. My hands went up to his necktie. "Get this damn thing off," I growled, and I started to yank the silk from its knot.

Booze helped me have sex the way I had to have it, and it was part of my ritual at the club: get hammered and get lucky. But I hadn't gone to the club. I'd shared a few drinks and two bottles of red wine with this man who'd wanted to spend the day with me. I'd denied him then, but now he wanted what I'd always wanted and hardly ever trusted anyone to give me.

His hands were on my belt. "Let's get naked," he muttered, his hoarse voice sending shivers through me. "Show me your cock, come on. Show me everything."

We wrestled each other out of our clothes, our fingers everywhere, and a few seconds later, we were naked on the bed. I sucked his tongue like I wasn't going to let it go, making hungry sounds that a faraway part of me was embarrassed by, was alarmed at, but I didn't pay attention. I so wanted Kevin to lay me.

I wrapped my fingers around his cock. It was thick but not too thick, what I'd seen and felt and tasted before. Now, with new purpose, his cock was different, better. He was gripping my waist hard as we kissed, and he gasped as I milked him. One second we were on our sides, and the next he flipped me over onto my belly and then pulled me up onto my hands and knees.

Now was the time I should have protested, should have said that I didn't do this. But the carefully constructed person who lived in west Texas and was 2007 Teacher of the Year had been set aside somehow. I hadn't done it; Kevin had. Besides, he was distracting me with wet kisses on the small of my back, staying there and breathing against my skin, making me tingle and shake and driving a line of sensation from his lips to my cock, lifting it. It jerked and stretched and throbbed, and when I swiped at it—only once, I couldn't stand more than that or I'd come too soon, way too soon—my palm came away sticky wet with my weeping.

It'd been so long. How had I let it go so long between fuckings? It was as if the lid I kept so tightly capped on my desires had been blown off by some dark-haired guy talking football in the candlelight. Kevin wanting me and me wanting him back.

Nothing better than his hands all over my ass, rubbing, scratching, taking the shape of me. He reached between my legs and pushed, trying to spread me more, and I shifted on the bed, aiming to rest most of my weight on my right hand and knee, but I did it, gave him what he wanted. Up against my balls he went, not gently but so right. I hissed when he palmed me from behind.

He rubbed the side of his face against my back as he hefted my balls, and I would have screamed at him to move up to my cock and *touch me!*, except all I could do was heave in air, not talk.

"Okay?" he whispered, and he kissed my back again, both his hands moving to lightly rest on my hips. I froze, feeling as if they were holding me in place, and I did not want to move.

"Okay," I breathed.

I ached, deep down inside where nobody had ever touched me. God, did I ache.

I held my head low as he reached toward his kit on the nightstand. The sound of a rubber being opened and rolled over his erection made me tremble, and then the wet daub of the lube rubbed around my hole made me moan.

I knew what was to come next, and sucked in breath and held it. Taking in a cock was never easy for me. It was the universe thumbing its nose at me, a dramatic irony that it hurt way more than I knew it should have. Kevin put his cock right *there* and held it just outside, where I could feel its lubricated mass threatening. He shifted, seeking the right angle, and then he shoved inside.

His cock pushed all the air out of my lungs, almost like cause and effect: there was too much of me to admit him and so I had to let something go. I stretched my spine to try to escape the immediate cramping, even though I knew I couldn't, and I dug my fingers into the mattress, forcing myself to wait, wait, wait…. If I waited long enough, it would get better….

Behind me, Kevin muttered, "Damn," and then held still, not moving when I knew he must have wanted to. He might have speared me without any thought, could have started fucking right away instead of letting me adjust. One hand went up to my shoulder, and I felt his fingers spread and contract, spread and contract, attempting to ease my discomfort.

Sweat prickled my forehead, and I panted like a woman in labor. Then, finally, the pain began to fade.

Kevin didn't have to ask if it was time to move. I swayed with relief and demanded, "Go, go!" and he did. With my eyes closed and all my attention focused on my ass, I felt that first thrust of his completely, the controlled, smooth pull-back, and then the abrupt, ravenous shove of his braced legs as he drove inside me.

I sucked in air through my teeth and hissed "yesssss" down to the sheet, half out of my mind with the first thrust. I jerked back, desperate to meet the second one.

"Yes!" Kevin exulted. "God, you're tight. So good."

Oh, Christ. It felt so good, after so many times imagining it, to finally have this again. I loved getting fucked, loved cock up my ass. Anything else I could do as a gay man didn't come close to what I got from that strong warmth joined with me, the movement and the sounds of two bodies pistoning together, the slickness and the slapping, the press and the pull, the weight behind me and the hands on me. I gave myself up to the incredible feeling of being ridden, of being filled.

"Oh, yeah. Yeah. Yeah." Kevin chanted with every thrust in, and I matched myself to his rhythm. It was easy to do, automatic, because we were after the same thing. Me and this chance-met man from the bar. Kevin, who was real, who tasted like a man, and who was now proving he moved like a man with the sharp snap of his hips that sent my left hand blindly seeking my own cock.

One pull in time with Kevin's entering, two when he dragged out, and already it was starting, my balls so tight they'd practically disappeared when I ran the tips of my fingers over them. Not long, I wasn't going to last long, three more maybe. One and my mouth opened suddenly. Two and my lips pulled back. I let go of my cock but I was too far gone. Three and I shook all over, gushing regret that it was over so soon, that I hadn't even tried to make it last, and that I couldn't have this all the time.

To have this all the time. The sex, the man, the conversation, the life.

My head spinning from the force of my coming, I pressed my forehead down to the pillow and offered up my ass for however long it would take Kevin to finish, but he wasn't far behind me. One long groan and then that hitch that I expected now, and I could feel him shuddering as he shot his wad into the condom.

I collapsed straight down onto the small lake of my spunk, and he came right with me, keeping us together. The wet spot soaked into the sheet as he pressed me into it, and it coated my belly and then spread up higher. I tried to live intensely in the moment, him in me, his cock in me—fuel for my fantasies, the midnight hour of my wants—but it only took a few seconds and he was gone.

The sounds of him tying off the rubber came to me. Then he was snugged tight against my back again, pulling us both over to lay on our right sides. I let myself be moved as if I had no will of my own, as if I'd passed it all over to him just because I'd let him do me. Where was the fortitude that Kevin seemed to have forced out of me, the resolve that had shaped my years?

There were his lips, brushing against the curve of my shoulder. "Thanks," he said, and his arm slipped around my waist as if we were dancing again. The familiarity of his action shocked me out of my lethargy, and I blinked.

I knew Kevin. Almost by accident and surely against my will, but I knew him: his athletic walk, the way he savored wine, his informed enthusiasm about the outdoors, the betraying clench of his fingers when he asked for something he knew he wasn't likely to get. His innate kindness.

He wasn't a casual fuck. And what I'd allowed myself—this night—had now come to an end.

Unaccountably, sadness swamped me. I touched his fingers, closed my eyes, and abandoned myself to dreams.

I came back to myself slowly, still curled on my side and under the sheet, feeling lighter somehow despite the ache in my ass. I remembered where I was and what we'd done as if I hadn't slept at all, as if there'd been no time at all from Kevin breathing in my ear and this moment where I could see sunlight through my eyelids.

This was how it used to be when I'd been with Sean, when I'd slept over at his dorm and we'd fooled around, two not-quite-men with nothing to lose. In that last semester before we graduated, we'd decided we wanted to, yeah, see what fucking was all about, and not only cocksucking. I'd wake up wedged between him, snoring, and the wall, with the smell of old pizza and dirty clothes thrown all over the room. I'd breathe in the rank smell of our coming together, and there hadn't been anything that made me happier.

"Good morning," came the sound of Kevin's voice.

I didn't want to answer. Answering meant crossing the line between my bittersweet morning-memories of Sean and me and my necessary reality. There was a world of difference between what I wanted and what I could have. Reluctantly, I opened my eyes.

On a chair that was drawn up close to the bed, Kevin was sitting hunched forward with his elbows on his knees, intently regarding me as if I were a prize sculpture in a museum. Kevin. The past two nights with him didn't feel real. Weren't they some movie I'd watched? He was a gay man's dream that I couldn't dream, naked and with his spread legs giving me a prize view of his cock and relaxed balls resting on the seat.

"Hey, Tom Smith," he said with the smallest of smiles. He reached out and flicked his thumb against my cheek. His voice sounded a little more hoarse than usual.

"Hey, yourself," I said.

"You all right?" Kevin nodded in the general direction of my ass.

"I'm good," I said cautiously. The Teacher of the Year was back in full force.

His gaze flicked toward the bathroom, then back to me. "That was really good last night. The way you moved, the way you looked."

"Yeah, it was good," I said, shifting my eyes to look at his feet. He had long toes.

"No, I mean it. You're a pretty uptight guy, you know that? But you let loose a little last night."

"Well, yeah, I guess."

He shifted forward and reached out as if he wanted to take my hand. But my right arm was tucked under me, and it wouldn't have been easy to produce the range of motion to extend and hold out my left arm. "That was fine, to see you like that," Kevin said. "You know, it's okay to let go."

My eyes abandoned the carpet as I consciously allowed a flare of genuine annoyance to spike in me. He didn't really know me, and I didn't need preaching to. "Okay for you, maybe."

"Geez, you're as prickly as a cactus. Worse than my ex-wife."

Right. Sure. I should have known. This guy who came across so sincere, Christ-come-down-from-the-cross, he was just like the rest of us, putting on disguises. Sometimes I thought that half the gay men had taken vows with an unsuspecting woman, and the other half lived with me in the closet.

"Listen, Tom," Kevin said, oblivious, "I wasn't blowing smoke when I said yesterday I was tired of the club scene. What do you say we meet up again? I can usually get away—"

"No," I said definitely. I pushed the sheet aside and sat up in bed.

Kevin sat up straight too. "I know you're a cautious kind of guy. But every few months, we could meet at the bar, have a few drinks, and then… leave with each other. Get to know each other. Maybe… maybe we can make something more of this."

"I said no." My clothes were bunched on the floor, testament to how last night I hadn't cared about anything but my dick. Well, this morning I was sober and I cared about other things. I got up and grabbed for my shirt, shook it out, and didn't look at Kevin.

He stubbornly plowed on. "We're good with each other, don't you think?"

The shirt sleeves were inside out. I remembered Kevin pulling them off me and jerking at the stubborn cuffs that had lingered on my wrists. He'd laughed.

"Tom? Did you hear me?" Finally, Mister Patient stood up. "You can't deny it, we've had great sex."

I finally got the shirt to cooperate and started to pull it on. "That doesn't mean we have to—"

Kevin took a step closer. "I'm not saying we should move in together, for God's sake. Why not think about—"

"Are you that hard up?" I rounded on him, my open shirt flapping around me, and snarled. "There are a hundred guys who'll show up next weekend at the bar that you can pick up. Just leave me alone." Leave me be to put on my clothes, to resume the order of my days.

"What the hell is wrong with you?" He ran fingers across his hair. "Last night was great, the whole thing, the dinner and—"

"I never implied that we—"

"You barely gave me your real name, if that really is your name, but I thought that we—"

"Forget it," I said, intending by the snap of my words for that to be my final say on the matter. I snagged my briefs and hauled them on, then picked up my good dress pants. They were wrinkled so that it was going to be embarrassing wearing them out to my car, but I sure wasn't going to borrow Kevin's iron so that I didn't have that spent-the-night-and-just-been-screwed look as I left.

The pants went on one leg at a time like they always did. Nothing had changed. Kevin was silent as I dressed in haste.

Button up the shirt, tuck into the pants. Zip up and engage the catch, then button the shirt cuffs. Look for the socks, one under the bed, and the tie, over by the mirror where I'd shoved Kevin and tried to crawl inside his skin. It was a good thing the mirror wasn't shattered. That would have been a great way to start some of the best sex I'd ever had, confronting shards of reflecting glass, him and me over and over again in tiny pieces.

I put the tie on and even made a decent knot for it, and by the time I was finished slipping on my boots, I had myself under control.

"Why won't you give this a chance?" Kevin asked like a kid would, plaintively, as if he couldn't understand the workings of an unreachable mind. He was over by the window now, looking out on the parking lot through the sheers. "I'm not asking for much."

My anger, which I was well aware I was using as a shield, drained away, and I was left vulnerable and sad. But I had at least some courtesy remaining, some sense of dignity. I went over to him, came up behind him, but didn't touch him.

"Look, it isn't you. It's…." I stopped myself from saying it was me, because that sounded too much like I was laying blame on myself. "I told you before, didn't I? That first time. That I like to keep things in their place."

"Compartmentalize," Kevin said. "That's what you said."

"Right."

"It's not that you've got somebody at home, a partner or a boyfriend?"

I sighed, and the weariness that lately had become as much a part of me as the necessity to do lesson-planning returned in full force. I felt like I could sleep for a week. "No, I don't have anybody at home."

Kevin turned around to face me. "I don't either. But I'm tired of living like this, and I'm going to make some changes. I need somebody in my life."

"Good for you, then, but that's not for me."

He searched my face. "I think you're making a mistake. If you reconsider, I could give you my cell—"

I actually backed away from him, as if the very idea of having his number could destroy me. "That's not going to happen. Whether you understand me or not, I've got good reason for what I do."

"I guess you think you do. Wish I had the chance to change your mind."

How could he pursue this idea so doggedly after only a few nights spent together? What, did he want to make one good fuck the basis of a relationship? Life wasn't like that, and personal risks seldom paid off. Like I'd said, there were plenty of men who'd be happy to take Kevin up on whatever he offered; he just happened to have picked the one guy who wasn't interested. He wouldn't be alone for long.

He stuck out his hand, and I felt that the least I could do was shake it, though it felt eerie for me to have all my clothes on and to have him standing there bared and exposed.

"So long, Tom," he said. "Good luck to you. Try to let loose once in a while. It'll do you good."

Sure. I'd done that last night, and look at what it'd gotten me. "Goodbye, Kevin."

I walked to the door, my footsteps almost soundless on the carpet, and I felt like… like the smallest leaf from a tree, fallen and caught in rushing water, inexorably drawn downstream. I paused with my hand on the doorknob.

"Don't think this is easy," I said without turning around, my voice low.

My heart pounded in my ear a few times before Kevin said, "No, I don't imagine it is. But it's not necessary, Tom. Think about that."

I left, and I knew there wouldn't be another time Kevin and I would have sex.

CHAPTER 2
GUNNING, TEXAS

THE fire ants were taking over the backyard. There was a telltale black mound sticking up out of the grass over by my abandoned vegetable garden, another one in the corner under the tallest crape myrtle, and a third one peeking out of some leaves that had been blown against the back part of the fence. If I left those mounds there, I wouldn't be able to walk around in bare feet without the tiny red critters swarming up onto my ankles and biting. I'd already endured a rash of stinging bites earlier in the summer, and I absolutely was not going to tolerate any more.

I stomped over to the door that led from the patio into the garage and into the dark, oil-slicked recesses where my Miata lived. My garage was a mess, but I knew where the container of Amdro should be, off in a far corner on top of a stack of boxes. I dumped some newspapers onto the floor, uncovered the ant-killer, and clomped outside again. The poison should control the ants.

Back in Houston I'd regained control just long enough to say "No" to the best opportunity that was likely to come my way. By the time I was headed out of town that control had flown the coop and hadn't been seen again. I was thirty-eight years old—as a matter of fact, I was thirty-eight years old this day, exactly, because July twenty-sixth was my birthday—and I'd had the better part of the past four months to regret what I'd told Kevin that stupid, stupid Sunday morning.

Making my way carelessly in my flip-flops, I took the poison over to the dark lumps of dirt and surrounded them with the flecks of feed that would kill the ants in a few days. I upended the canister and thumped it until the last flakes fell out. Then I tossed it up to the patio and watched it skitter across the concrete until it banged against the sliding glass door that led to my tiny house. Who needed more than tiny? I was the only one living there, and it seemed to me that I'd shrunk down to child-size. My yard was a big corner lot, though. It was surrounded by a high, wooden fence that was outlined with swaying, pink-blossomed crape myrtles on one side, glowing red-leaved bushes on the other, and honeysuckle vines in back. I pivoted on my heel and surveyed it all with a jaundiced air. My home and my refuge and my fortress. I could spend as many hours out here drinking as I wanted to, and no one would be the wiser. So what if Mr. Smith, teacher extraordinaire, was finishing off a six-pack a little more often than usual this summer? Nobody knew it was because he'd finally cracked, because one good dinner, one good conversation, one good fuck, and one good man had revealed his careful deceptions and his ordered life for the empty facades they were.

How was I supposed to go back to pretending this life was good enough? My brief burst of energy suddenly drained away; I could actually feel my reserves headed straight for my toes. I slumped where I was standing and ran a hand over the bristles of my early five o'clock shadow. This summer, I'd pulled myself in like a hedgehog rolling into a ball. I'd been brooding, alternately depressed and angry. Kevin had stolen my equanimity back in that hotel room, and I didn't know how to get it back.

A seen-better-days red oak towered over the patio. Slowly, I walked to it and looked up, as I had most days that summer. I went over the well-worn thought that it might not last another year. The leaves were sparse and small, some of them misshapen. I didn't know how long the red oak had been standing there, but I guessed it'd been a sapling way back when the town of Gunning had been mostly open prairie.

I didn't know much about trees, and I kept thinking I should consult the nursery over in Kenneton about it. Maybe it only needed to be sprayed. But I hadn't been able to stir myself to take a sample of the tree and bring it in for advice. Kenneton was a good twenty-five miles away, and I hadn't done much traveling lately, except in my head. Sometimes I went back to Houston, saw Kevin at Good Times, pulled my fist back, and decked him with a right jab. Other times… well, other times were hazy. How did men like us make something of what had started with a midnight hookup? I couldn't wrap my head around any change to the stark realities of my life. I didn't want to change. I couldn't. For one thing, there were no gay men in Gunning, Texas. No visible gay men, anyway. Here they didn't exist, because the community wouldn't allow them to. That part of me couldn't be.

A fly buzzed nearby, and I followed its flight until it disappeared over the steamy asphalt roof of the garage. Inside the house, propped on top of my TV, were three birthday cards: one from my brother and his family, one from the sister who lived in London, and one from my mom. Probably my mother would try to call this evening, and she'd leave her rendition of "Happy Birthday" on my answering machine. For sure Grant would call.

They cared enough to remember me on this sultry summer day, but none of them had ever asked me why I wasn't married, never dated, and had never to their knowledge had a relationship with anyone. Did they think I was sexless? By God, I wasn't.

Sweat prickled under the back of my shirt as I stood there in the sun. At dawn the temperature had already hovered at eighty-one degrees, and the Weather Channel was forecasting that the mercury would hit one hundred and two by the end of the day. Summer in Texas, just great.

I retreated to the lawn chair next to the gas grill, fished a beer out of the six-pack cooler I had there, sat down, and took a long swallow that made the heat tolerable. Nothing else had made this summer better as I questioned myself *ad nauseam* over what I'd done in Houston. Why couldn't I get Kevin out of my head? I'd bedded plenty of men—I didn't want to think of how many over the years—but none of the others had done this to me.

It felt like he'd forced all the reasonable, mature thoughts of a well-adjusted teacher out of the neat slots in my brain and replaced them with indecision, the emotional ramblings of a teenager, and the bitter recriminations of a disappointed, frustrated gay man who never got enough sex and didn't have anybody to talk to.

I didn't want to think of him. What good did it do to think of him? But I remembered what Kevin looked like down to the pores on his nose. I remembered how it had felt to be touched by him that one night when I'd really known who I was in bed with. The sure way he walked. The way he talked. The way he'd tried to give me his telephone number in case I changed my mind.

You see, Kevin, I'm a fool.

The way he'd invited me to join him on that day's tour, when instead of my precious peace and quiet I could have had a companion, a friend, maybe someone next to me in the place that was always empty.

The way he'd fucked me.

Yeah, I remembered that well. I'd been plastered, and I'd surrendered pretty much completely, had thrown my tough-guy, strong-guy disguise out the window and let everything hidden inside me out. He'd forced his way into me, literally and figuratively, and I still felt the echoes of him there inside. He'd run his hands over my ass and taken the whole shape of me, because he sure had gotten under my skin.

I shifted in the lawn chair, and it rocked back and forth on the uneven surface. My cock was getting hard. That wasn't any surprise, because lately that was always happening. I pressed the Miller Lite can down on it, just enough to feel it, then put the can down on the concrete, on a crack that ran diagonally from one corner across the square and then under the house. Maybe I had foundation problems.

I closed my eyes and lifted my face to the unrelenting sun. The leaves of the red oak, which used to provide a thick coating of shade, only served to filter out the light now and then, so that it flickered behind my eyelids. I flinched but stubbornly kept my eyelids exposed to the sun, then finally gave in and shaded my closed eyes with my hand. I remembered reading an interview with a Catholic priest celebrating his fiftieth year in the priesthood. He'd been asked if celibacy had been difficult for him, and he'd replied that it had gotten easier as the years went on. The less you got, he'd said, the less you needed it.

It didn't work that way for me. I carried a deep craving inside me, usually banked through sheer force of will or maybe my own foolhardiness, and it felt as if Kevin had blasted through to the core and set it loose. This summer's blistering nights had seen me hornier than I'd been since I was a twenty-year-old. Whether I wanted to or not, I ached for that pickup from the bar with the eyes that spoke to me. Or I ached for what he thought he could give me, what we could have made. I wasn't sure which it was. Probably both.

Kevin had related to me as a person, not a cock, when to my shame I'd done my best to relate to him the opposite way. Ever since I'd driven away from that Courtyard parking lot, I'd been longing for that honest give-and-take—the normal company of other people—even as I denied it to myself.

Such a simple thing, such a complex thing. I could call up a number of people—mainly fellow teachers—and suggest we go out for a movie and a beer, but that wouldn't provide what I needed. I wasn't out. Not to anybody. Wasn't that the crux of it? No one I knew from over the long stretch of years I'd spent teaching really knew me; then Kevin had come along and asked me my last name.

I laughed sourly. Kevin. I'd practically slammed the door in his face as I stalked away from him. He probably had been more than happy to consign me to the dustbin of his mind.

Damn.

Damn, damn.

I stayed out in the heat as long as I could, rationing the six-pack, and then I went back into the house and took a shower. After that, I lay down on my bed and retrieved my jack-off towel from the bottom shelf of the nightstand. I tried to take my time, but my coming burst out of me in a heated, angry confusion that didn't do much to relieve my aching. And afterward, the familiar lassitude overcame me. I was so tired of being my own fortress.

I turned my head away from the sunlight filtering through the white curtains. Everything would be better when school started again.

I WAS horrified. "You're kidding, aren't you?"

George shook his head in that deliberate way he had. "Nope, the play's been approved."

It was September at Gunning High School, and George and I were walking down a hallway during change of class. The usual frenzy of kids rushed by us, and as usual it sounded like they were all talking at once at the top of their lungs, which wasn't too far from the truth.

I banged my bag filled with senior files against my leg. "But there's no way that *Rent* is appropriate for high school students." My head was buzzing with ways I could convince him of that. Maybe he hadn't made final plans yet.

"This is the school version. We talked about this, Tom, remember?"

I guess I did. George had corralled me the past April, right after I'd returned from the disastrous trip during which I'd met my personal demon and fueler-of-fantasies. I hadn't been in the state of mind to analyze anything too deeply then, not when I'd jumped down immediately into a funk.

A few years before, George had staged a production of *Bye Bye Birdie*, and he'd asked me for help as assistant director. I'd demurred since I had no experience with the theater, but he'd roped me in anyway. I hadn't actually done much except act as his gofer and organize the supremely talented parent volunteers. The extra pay from the school had been good, but after that I stuck to my history classroom and supported George by applauding from the audience. But in April he'd caught me in my moments of weakness and got me to agree to help out again.

I remember thinking that there was no way the school district committee would approve a play like *Rent*, which was at the top of his list, and we'd do one of the other plays instead. Gunning was west-Texas-small-town-conservative, even if George wasn't. *Rent*, which I'd seen in a gritty production in Dallas a few years before, was filled with curse words, sexual relationships outside of marriage, and drug use. And same-sex couples, HIV, and AIDS. Not exactly *The Sound of Music*. I'd told George *fine, fine, give it a try*, and then I'd dismissed it from my thoughts.

The committee filled with God-fearing churchgoers had approved *Rent* for a cast of sixteen- and seventeen-year-olds? It boggled my mind. *Rent* had onstage kissing between women, between men, and a whole lot more implied. According to the values of the town where I'd lived and taught for the past fifteen years, it was obscene, decadent, and immoral, just like every homosexual man or woman was. None of them, of course, lived anywhere near Gunning.

Dread dropped over me as we walked past the student attendance office. I could not be associated with this play. It might somehow draw attention to me, arouse suspicion. I wasn't prepared to…. If this play outed me, my life would be destroyed.

I stopped right where I was, and George stopped too. We confronted each other like rocks in the river of adolescents streaming by us.

Better to do this right away. I shook my head and then looked up at him. George towered over me, and I'm not short. "I can't help out this year, George. I'm sorry."

He looked a little panicked. "You've got to."

"I've got a full schedule this year, and I was thinking of picking up an adult education course over at the community—"

"If you're not part of it, I'll have to go back to the committee."

"What?"

He sidestepped a charging senior. "Their approval is based on your counseling experience. I said you'd be there for the cast, to help them through any problems they experienced during the play."

My heart sank. "But I don't have my degree, and I only helped out the counselors those two years when they were shorthanded."

"Come on, Tom, I've got the rights and the scripts, the auditions are set up for next week, and this is a great play for the kids. We'll have packed houses every night. And I promise you won't have much to do."

I already knew George wouldn't keep that last promise. He always meant the very best but often blundered into problems. And this was a big one, as big as he was. George Keating was an overweight giraffe, with spindly legs, a beer belly, and puppy-dog eyes. He was a man only his wife could love—and every kid who'd ever acted under his direction in the theater department or sang in his choir. He'd been putting on musicals for the past ten years, but I'd never known him to go off the deep end like this.

I rubbed my hand over my chin and frowned.

“You told me this past spring you’d do it,” he said.

“I said I’d help out as your assistant, but it never occurred to me they’d say yes to *Rent*. I thought we’d be doing something else.”

“Hi, Mr. Smith!” Brenda Salterman hollered at me as she raced by.

“I’ll be right there,” I called after her. I had a freshman World Cultures class that was due to start in three minutes. “Look, George….”

“You can’t back out on me,” he said.

I sure wanted to. “Even if I could clear my schedule, I don’t know that I feel comfortable doing *Rent* with the kids. It’s all about—”

“It’s about life,” George said flatly. “Have you seen it? Do you know what it’s—”

“Of course I’ve seen it.” I hitched my shoulder in annoyance. “I do get to the big city now and then, you know.” The driving beat of dance music from Good Times came to me, and the body-memory of being tapped on the back, and me turning…. George would have a heart attack if he ever knew what I did, what I was, how Kevin and I had danced the evening away, his arms around me, and how my body had needed that. George thought I was good ol’ dependable Tom, as reliable and dull as the west Texas plains, and about as sexual.

Which was the problem, I suddenly realized. If I said no, he’d wonder why. It would be out of character for me, because go-along, get-along Tom would be the one who’d prevented the play from going on. People would gossip about that. I wanted to groan out loud. Talk about being caught between a rock and a hard place.

“*Rent* might place certain issues in an urban context that some of our kids will never experience, but that doesn’t make it any less relevant,” George said with the fervor of the true believer. “At the very least they’ve got to understand the lives of others, but the truth is that the play presents life as they’ll have to deal with it on their own in a few years and what plenty of them are involved with right now. To think differently is to bury our heads in the sand. You think there aren’t drugs all over this school?”

I snorted. The students in the back row of my homeroom knew more about drugs than a vice cop.

"You think there aren't gay kids here?" George went on. I tried not to change my expression at all. "Of course there are, and we both know it."

"You can't be seriously thinking of putting on some of those… some of those scenes. I mean—"

"It's been sanitized for our age group. The language has been cleaned up, a whole song has been cut, several verses are in the trashcan, and—"

"Mr. Keating, can I talk to you about the homework assignment?" A timid youngster I didn't know, probably a freshman, was standing ten feet away, as if he were afraid to intrude into our heated conversation. He was right to be wary; I felt like a mountain lion trapped in a corner.

"Sure, Jared, meet me after school in the Little Theater," George said easily, and he flipped his hand, dismissing the kid. He went away looking disappointed that he hadn't gotten his answer instantly.

The change bell rang as it did eight times a day, but I didn't move. "No matter what cuts have been made," I said, "the play is still about… well, what it's about."

"Right," George bobbed his mostly bald head enthusiastically. "And that's the beauty of it. The message is still there. You know, acceptance. Support. Love."

I'd felt it too, in the theater in Dallas, though I'd tried to put the feeling down as I walked out alone in the crowd.

"But what happened to *Annie Get Your Gun*?" I said weakly. "I thought you were planning on—"

George clapped me on the shoulder and steered me in the direction of both our classrooms. "This is so much better. The students will learn from this. I'll put you on the e-mail list. You're officially listed as assistant director, and auditions are next Tuesday. I'll need you there. Okay?"

There wasn't anybody else in the hallway now except the two of us. I stopped and grabbed his elbow. "As your assistant director officially associated with the production of *Rent,* I've got to tell you that I have serious misgivings about the play. I don't think it's the right choice for this town. Folks here aren't going to understand. Plus you're going to be casting three students as homosexuals. Have you thought about what that really means? In this town—"

"Four," he said. "Angel, Tom Collins, Joanne, and Maureen. Although technically Maureen is bi."

I could see it in his blithe, enthusiastic face. He had no idea what that meant. Not for those of us living the life. Resentment crawled up my spine at the thought that George and some unknown teenagers were going to give a stab at approximating it.

"It's going to be all right," George said, as seriously as could be. "You'll see."

IT GOT worse during the casting call.

Gunning wasn't isolated out on the western prairie. Kenneton was a thirty-five-minute trip away on State Highway 382, and it was twice our size, with an enclosed mall and a multiplex. In the opposite direction, it took under two hours to drive to Abilene. But for day-to-day amusement and to keep the young people out of trouble, our town looked to local church and school activities, like the Wednesday night services and the Thursday night Bible studies, the Friday night football games in the fall, and the twice-yearly theater productions put on by the high school.

Normally an audition for a play pulled in about seventy, eighty kids. For *Rent*, the auditorium overflowed with more than twice that number, but George and I quickly found out that most of them weren't there to try out for the play; they were curious onlookers eager to see how much of the play would be re-enacted in the try-out scenes. Would we ask our girls to prove they knew how to shoot up heroin? Would Mimi re-enact a pole dance? Would we ask the boys to kiss, to prove they had the guts to do it?

"See?" I muttered to George as I walked by him, escorting two of the more raucous seniors out into the corridor.

"But I want to play a drug dealer," one of them piped up.

George made everybody sign in, indicating what role they wanted to audition for. That got rid of the dilettantes, leaving the core of serious theater students and a few determined newcomers in the suddenly quiet seats in front of the stage. Theater directors, I'd learned, had a good idea of who they wanted to cast in a play weeks before the auditions, but George had told me he was going in this time with an open mind.

Right, I'd cynically thought. At the end of a grueling four-hour session—I was already sick of hearing *five hundred twenty-five thousand six hundred minutes* sung by eager young voices—George presented me with a cast list I'd both expected and feared.

"You can't do this," I said flatly, and I dropped the yellow legal pad he'd handed me onto his desk. We were in the glass-enclosed office he kept in the back of the Little Theater, which was what everybody called his classroom, since it mimicked the real thing.

"Sure I can. What's wrong with it? The only problem is that there's just one black kid in the cast, playing Benny, and it would have been better if he'd had the pipes to sing as Collins. But it's probably just as well. Even I know this town can't take an interracial gay couple."

"Thank God you do."

"I think Johnny's right to play Mark, and Sam will do fine with Roger."

"And you've cast Robbie as Angel, the pivotal role of the drag queen." I pushed out air. I was positive that George had never seen a drag queen in person. I'd danced with one the year before and ended up in bed with her.

George looked off to the side, down to the stack of class papers piled on the floor. "Robbie's perfect for the role."

"And that's the point, isn't it?" I tried to rein in my temper. The big institutional clock on the wall showed seven-thirty-eight, and I was tired. The red beans and rice meal I'd nuked for dinner in the teacher's lounge wasn't sitting well.

"George…." I prompted when it was clear he wasn't going to say anything. I pulled up the rickety folding chair and sat down.

"Okay, okay. Tell me what you think."

"I don't think Robbie should be Angel. Mark or Roger, that would be all right, or a smaller role, but—"

"Robbie has the talent to pull Angel off."

"Why?"

"Because he's got a great voice and the boy can dance. And he's got the experience. He did fine in *Bye Bye Birdie*, and—"

"And he's gay."

George's head came up. "Not every boy involved in theater is homosexual. Don't succumb to stereotypes."

"George," I said wearily. "If Robbie isn't gay, I'll eat my teacher's certificate. Come on, you know it. This is typecasting."

"Well, okay. So he's gay. So what?"

"You think so, and I think so, but has Robbie figured it out yet?"

George stared at me like I'd grown a set of antlers. "Has the boy looked at himself in the mirror lately? Or listened to himself talk?"

"Sometimes it takes time for these things to come to a person. I think it would be cruel to cast him in a role that we know he'll take some flak for anyway, when it will expose him to—"

"Tom, you're borrowing trouble. Besides, Robbie's strong."

"What?"

"Have you ever had him in a class?"

"Just in homeroom."

"The kid has it all together. I think you're wrong that he isn't aware of his sexuality. Isn't there some sort of statistic that says when those boys figure it out? Isn't it really young?"

I'd been ten.

"Besides, this is why you're here, to help him out if he needs the help. This might be exactly the right experience for him, don't you think? Now, what do you think of Channing Carlton for Maureen?"

I backed down for the moment. "She's okay. She's got the voice and the long hair you were looking for. She moves well."

"She's beautiful. But she's playing a bisexual bitch. Any concerns about her? Or how about Sandy for Joanne?"

Truthfully, I could hardly imagine any problems the girls might have playing lesbians. Bitterly, I acknowledged to myself that women with alternate sexualities were treated differently by our society than gay men were. The dykes versus the fags, but every straight man in the U.S. who watched porn wanted to see two women getting off together. Lesbians held a unique place in the intolerant American psyche; it was the men who lay with men who challenged the words of the Holy Bible. It seemed to me that the women got a sort of peculiar pass.

"I'm not worried about the girls," I said.

"But how about Steven for Tom Collins? He's okay?"

Steven was the pitcher who'd led the Gunning baseball team to the state semifinals the previous spring. It was rumored that the Chicago White Sox were scouting him already, and in the fantastical world of adolescents, a lot of the students believed that. The entire school would give Steven a pass if he danced naked on the front steps while jerking off. "Are you kidding? He's fine."

"So it's only Robbie you're really concerned about."

"I'm not going to be able to convince you, am I?"

George folded his hands on the desk. "I really don't have anybody else who can do Angel. Did you see anybody else out there who could?"

Any other boy who could jump on top of a desk while wearing a miniskirt and a wig? And dance? No, our town didn't seem big enough to hold two of those kinds of people, and I wearily said so.

"You're going to have to up your energy quotient," George told me. "Even though we've started early, we've got just ten weeks to pull this off. Play season is tough." He rummaged around in his top drawer and plunked a small bottle on the desk blotter. "Have some vitamins."

ONE thing I'd insisted on and that George agreed with, claiming that he'd thought the same thing, was that all the parents of the kids chosen for the play had to attend a meeting. We'd ask them to give their written, informed consent for their child to play an addict, a fag, or one of several irreligious, neglectful children who never returned their parents' phone calls. It wasn't hard to imagine the complaints, and it would be best to deal with them early.

We called the meeting for Saturday morning at ten, a time we thought we'd get the best parental participation, and I promised George I'd give him most of the day for whatever needed to be done. I got to the Little Theater at nine and spent the time arranging the chairs in informal clumps, not rows, though with all of them facing more or less toward where George and I would be sitting. No desks, no tables, nothing between us and the moms and dads who deserved to have all the information.

Once I was finished with the room layout, I retreated to the back office and started going through the parent volunteer forms that had already been returned to us. This was mainly a new group of kids, different from the one I'd worked with four years before, though one family was the same, the Robertsons. I was relieved to see it. They had a supremely talented daughter who'd played the lead in *Bye Bye Birdie*, and now their son Johnny was playing Mark, Maureen's ex-boyfriend who shared a drafty loft with Roger.

Johnny's father's hobby was woodworking, his mother was an artist, and they were the perfect theater parents, not too pushy but involved. They were willing to spend real time and talent on the sometimes-backbreaking backstage work that was essential to every production. With some relief, I put them down on the list I was starting. It was a good thing the creative department for *Rent* wouldn't be relying on the assistant director to paint backdrops, because I had no talent at all for anything except dissembling about my sexuality and stupidly warding off men I wished I'd been able to get to know a whole lot better.

I wasn't even halfway through the forms when the room filled with the adults and a few of the students. I put the papers aside and came out of George's office to quietly sit a little behind where he was standing, bracing myself for what I expected to be a contentious, difficult meeting. I saw the Robertsons, and they waved at me. I waved back. Behind them was Robbie, our problematic Angel, rock-star thin with a shock of black hair and pale skin. Sitting still, he didn't look gay and wasn't dressed all that flamboyantly, but I'd seen him move. He was one of those unfortunate kids who betrayed their sexuality with every flat-footed step, every over-the-top gesture. I guessed he was with his parents: a plump, petite woman who looked like she might feel most comfortable wearing an apron and a tight-lipped, iron-jawed man sitting with his arms folded already. That wasn't reassuring.

My gaze roamed over the rest of the crowd. I knew a few of the adults, but not well. That didn't matter. This was George's show, not mine, and I was glad of it. If it'd been up to me, I would never have wanted to direct this play. Even if I hadn't been gay, *Rent* had too many challenges for the school environment, especially in red-state Texas.

George started talking at ten on the dot, beginning by welcoming everybody and asking if they each had a copy of the script, because he'd sent them home with the kids and asked the parents to bring them. Of course half of them hadn't, so he asked me to give out our extras to anyone who needed them. While I got up to do that, he went on with a basic description of what the play was about and the changes that had been made for the high-school version.

I took the stack wc still had and began moving around the room, handing out the scripts that had come from Musical Theater International, the licensing firm in New York. "Take care of these," I heard George say behind me. "We're contractually obligated to return all the scripts when we're done with them." A few more parents came in while I was doing that. I stood at the door and offered a pamphlet as each came in, one at a time, and I got a "no," and a "yes, thanks," and a "no," and then…. "Tom?"

My name came in a whisper from a voice that I'd remembered too often the past months, and my gaze flew up to see who…. It was Kevin.

Panic ripped through me, and I barely managed to prevent my jaw from dropping. For a wild moment I wondered if I were mistaken and here was only a man who resembled him, if I'd conjured him up from my well of discontent and thwarted desire. But it really was Kevin, with black-black hair cut skull-short and pure blue eyes—though he had facial hair now, more than scruff, less than a beard. Standing there in a striped Izod shirt and navy blue Dockers, he was as devilishly attractive as the day I'd met him.

We stood looking at each other, equally thunderstruck, while George went on about how much of the profanity had been removed from the lyrics. Kevin recovered faster than I did. I watched while he swallowed and seemed to gather his resolution.

"Hi," he said, no longer whispering, though his voice was rich with irony. He stuck out his hand. "I'm Kevin Bannerman."

I did not believe in improbable fables come true, or happily-ever-after, or pots of gold at the end of the rainbow. I'd metaphorically kicked myself many times since Houston, but even so, I didn't feel adequately punished for my prime asshole performance there. And I wasn't a religious man. I did not pray.

And yet standing here in front of me was the second chance I hadn't even thought to ask for—and wasn't sure I was courageous enough to take.

For what felt like a multitude of heartbeats, I didn't move. I probably thought more in those few seconds than I'd obsessed under my red oak tree with my beers, with every scenario possible racing through my mind, including Kevin-flat-on-his-back-with-his nose-bleeding-and-a-vengeful-Tom-standing-over-him, as well as Kevin-flat-on-his-back-naked-holding-the-base-of-his-cock-waiting-for-Tom-to-lower-himself-onto-it. Nobody, it seemed, confused me like Kevin did.

Of course I shook his hand. We were in the middle of a room full of people, and even if nobody seemed to be looking our way, I couldn't take the chance that they weren't. It would look odd if I turned away from him. So, once again motivated by fear and hating the fact that I was, with nothing else but that clear in my own mind, I reached forward.

His fingers were warm and dry, nothing different from anybody else I'd ever greeted this way, though everything was different.

"Hello," I said, and I was pleased that my voice was calm, even. Better than his had been. I could control this situation. I didn't have to do anything I didn't want to do, and Kevin certainly wasn't going to be the one to betray my secrets. "I'm Tom Smith, history teacher and assistant director."

"Oh," he said. "Smith. Really?" I couldn't take my eyes off his rising eyebrow. "Right. I'm Channing Carlton's father."

Channing. Our Maureen, the attractive, contentious bitch whom Joanne and Mark both loved. Of course. Channing didn't have her father's air of quiet confidence, which I'd found so attractive I'd thrown all my cautions out the window, but now that I knew the relationship, I realized she did have his nose and mouth.

I shot a look over my shoulder. "She's over there with… I guess that's her mother."

Kevin grimaced. "Right, my ex. I'd better get…. Nice to meet you, Mr. Smith."

And as quickly as that he left, striding up to where there was an empty seat next to Channing, undoubtedly saved for him. A woman came in right behind him, and she took my last script. Anybody else who needed one would have to share. Kevin, who hadn't taken one, would have to share with his daughter and ex-wife.

I went back to the front the long way, edging my way around the group, and sat down behind George, who was now expounding on the musical virtues of the play. This was the worst thing I could imagine happening: that a man I'd slept with would show up in my professional life. I'd have to be very careful without letting it appear that I was being careful. But… here was the man I'd thought about—for no reason that I could really understand—since April. My summer of regret had changed me. I'd made an exception for Kevin back in the spring, and I'd slept with him again. Could I…. It was hard to even think of it. Could I make another exception here in Gunning? I'd told myself I couldn't, ever, but….

"If you'll turn to page twenty-seven of the script," George droned on, "you'll see that…."

I glanced in Kevin's direction and immediately looked away when I saw he was looking at me. Was he interested? Was I? I hadn't been back to Good Times since the spring. I'd tentatively thought of heading over there next weekend, but Hurricane Ike had hit Houston a few days ago, so that trip was definitely out while the city recovered. Kevin was here.

"My assistant director, Mr. Smith, will be—Tom, stand up so everybody can see you."

I stood up and nodded. I allowed myself to pan my sight from one side of the room to the other, as I think I would have done normally. Kevin was looking at me again with a serious expression, but I couldn't interpret it.

"Among other things, Mr. Smith will be working with the parent volunteers on the behind-the-scenes preparation, which I hope you all know is critical. I couldn't direct this play without his unfailing assistance and dedication. If you haven't filled out a volunteer sheet yet, please see him at the end of this meeting. We can use all the help we can get. If anybody can make a run to Home Depot today for basic materials and has a pickup, that would be excellent. Now, does anyone have…."

I stayed standing next to and slightly behind George in subtle support as he opened the meeting to questions. He hadn't wanted to cede control by doing that, but I'd told him it was necessary. First there were the expected queries about scheduling and rehearsals and car pools. George announced that there wouldn't be weekend rehearsals, and everybody seemed to approve of that. Then the baseball player's mom, Steven-who-was-playing-Tom-Collins, stood up and asked that we please not advertise the play with a photo of her son in any, uh, "uncomfortable" position. The other adults in the audience all seemed to shift in their seats or let out a collective exhalation. Mrs. McDavid meant she didn't want him shown touching his play-lover, Angel, or kissing him, God forbid, though she hadn't said that. Next to her, her son Steven put his hand over his face.

George quickly outlined the photo publicity plans, and she seemed satisfied.

Then one of the fathers got up. I thought his son was playing an extra. "How are you going to handle the drug scenes?" he wanted to know. I wasn't sure what he meant by that, whether he wondered if we were going to have real heroin on the stage or what, but George reassured him.

Two more parents asked questions that weren't hard to answer, and I was beginning to think that we'd get off easy, when Mrs. Porter, the mother of Sandy, who was going to play Joanne, shot her hand into the air.

"Yes, ma'am?" George said easily.

She stood up and I saw right away she was an impressive woman. The kind of tall woman who didn't hesitate to wear heels, the kind of educated woman who didn't mind showing she had a fine mind.

"Let me get this straight," she said. She was also the kind of woman who believed in getting right to the point. It wasn't difficult to tell that she was going to be trouble. She fairly trembled with disapproval. "This play is about eight friends."

George nodded. "Seven friends and one who used to be a friend but who is now outside the group. He married rich and abandoned the bohemian ideals the others live by." He ticked the names off on his fingers. "There's Mark, Roger, Tom Collins, Angel, Mimi, Maureen, and Joanne. And Benny, he's the married one."

Her upper lip positively curled. "One married person in the play."

"Of the principals, right. But it's an ensemble production, really. All eight will get star billing."

"And among these people, they're all friends. The ones who aren't homosexual are easy friends with the ones who are. Forgive me if I'm not getting this correct, Mr. Keating, the play is confusing. It sometimes seemed to me that all the friends are homosexual, as they are exceptionally friendly. Is this a play about the radical left gay agenda?"

Someone in the audience laughed, then caught herself and changed it into a cough. Otherwise, it was dead silent.

"If you'll read the play front to back," George started off, speaking gently, "I think you'll find that it's not. The play is about acceptance, and—"

"Pardon me, I did indeed read this play."

George smiled at her. "Then you will have noticed that there are four major characters who aren't gay. Mark and Roger, who share a loft, and Mimi and Benny. Mimi is attracted to Roger."

"I understand that this is the case in the literal sense. But I had expected them to…. If they are truly friends with the others, then surely they would attempt to get their friends to change such destructive lifestyles. Why doesn't Mark, for instance, try to get his friends to live a more God-fearing life? He seems the most sensible one in the group. Certainly the most normal."

George had the patience of a saint. "That would indeed make for an interesting theatrical experience, and perhaps other plays have been written with that theme. But *Rent*—"

"By the end of the play, one of the homosexuals dies. The one who dresses up as a woman. And the woman who is addicted to heroin also dies, or at least appears to. So the play must be a cautionary tale about the dangers of such lifestyles. Am I not correct?"

"I suppose if a person wanted to view it that way, those conclusions could be drawn." George wasn't smiling any more, and my own blood was boiling. What was Mrs. Porter trying to do? "Was there a specific question you wanted to ask?"

"Of course. I want your reassurance that you will stage the play in such a way that it's clear the actions of the characters are to be condemned."

"Mrs. Porter, I don't know what—"

"I also have an objection to the scenes where the characters refuse to answer the phone when their parents call. The play does a thorough job of ignoring family values, but these scenes are an outright assault on them. I request that they be cut in their entirety."

George took a deep breath. "I'm afraid I can't do that. *Rent* is about totally different lifestyles than what we are accustomed to in Gunning, but that doesn't mean—"

"One last question. Were you planning on enacting a kiss between the two lesbians on the stage?"

"Yes, I was."

"If you are going to allow such a disgusting display, then I'm sorry to say that I will not give permission for my daughter to appear."

A young girl's voice from the audience rang out. "Oh, no!" It was Channing, Kevin's daughter, who would have played opposite Sandy Porter. When I looked her way, she had her hand up to her mouth. Her mother put an arm over Channing's shoulder. Kevin was sitting with a stone face; I wondered if I looked the same way. I hoped so. I could never allow myself to react to any gay slur, any assault on what I truly was.

George turned around to his seat, where he had a clipboard. He picked it up, took out the pen that was clipped on top, and held it poised over the page. “Sandy won’t be joining us, then?”

“No, she won’t. I’ve already told her that, and her father is in agreement.”

George very elaborately crossed off something on the sheet, presumably Sandy’s name. “I’m very sorry to hear that, Mrs. Porter. She’s very talented. We’ll regret not having her in the cast.”

For the first time, Mrs. Porter’s voice trembled. I imagined she’d had quite a scene at home, telling her daughter she couldn’t be the star of stage and screen. “Yes, well, I regret that you haven’t chosen a more suitable vehicle to showcase the talents of our high school students.”

She turned on her heel and walked out with her head held high, and I imagined she’d planned her exit for days. Everybody in the room swiveled their heads to watch her leave. Even though I wasn’t really in favor of *Rent*, either, it wasn’t because of the content so much as I’d been concerned about reactions from people exactly like her. The door closed behind Mrs. Porter and everybody returned to looking at George and me. Mostly George, I hoped. I waited for the next shoe to drop.

“Well,” George said with his hands on his hips. “Is there anybody else who feels like Mrs. Porter does? Now’s the time to say it if you do.” He surveyed everybody in the room. “No? I’m not going to pretend that this play will be like every other musical we’ve done in the past or that you might have already seen. *Rent* was groundbreaking when it opened off-Broadway in 1995, and it’s still topical today. Mrs. Porter asked if I was going to stage the play to emphasize destructive lifestyle choices. The answer to that is no. I will stage it to emphasize what I believe are the core values that *Rent* teaches: acceptance, love, and support. Yes, these values will be presented within the context of drug abuse, homosexual relationships, and people who are dying of AIDS. But that’s the story as the playwright gave it to us, and that’s the play that your children will work with me on staging.

“I believe that the actors we’ve chosen have the maturity level to deal with this material. But if you disagree with me, or if anybody is uncomfortable with your child being in this play, please, talk to me now. Or call me or e-mail me. All the information to get in touch with me is on the school's website."

He stopped there to take a breath. A sheen of sweat was showing on top of his head and his forehead, and he carefully pulled out a handkerchief and patted himself dry.

"Now," he said, "you've all met Mr. Smith. He hasn't worked with the counseling department for a while, but he has experience in that field. He'll be available if you or your children want to talk to him about anything. His contact information is also on the school website, plus we've sent all that pertinent information home with your children." He smiled slightly. "I know that doesn't always get into your hands, though, which is what the website is for."

A ripple of laughter swept through the room, way out of proportion to George's small joke, but people were uncomfortable and looking for ways to relieve the tension left in the wake of Mrs. Porter's accusations.

"So," George continued, "anybody have anything more to say? To me, to Mr. Smith?"

But nobody did, and I was surprised by that. Robbie's parents, who I really had expected to object, remained quiet, even though his father projected a stern, Marine-sergeant-tough attitude simply sitting next to his son. It was hard to believe that all these adults were comfortable enough with the content of the play that they weren't walking out *en masse*. With a church steeple jutting up into the air in just about every direction a person could look in Gunning, it would be hard to overestimate the influence of the churches in the town. But maybe the parents here had allowed Mrs. Porter to speak for them and were content with that? Or, even more cynically, I thought about stage mothers and stage fathers, or how kids could make life at home a living hell if parents opposed something the child really wanted to do.

George dismissed the crowd by reminding them that after-school rehearsals would start the coming Tuesday. He asked for volunteers again. A few adults came up to me saying they'd help, and I added them to my lists. The temporary crisis of defending the play slipped away, and I became hyperconscious of Kevin again. He was standing in the aisle near where he'd sat, talking with his ex-wife and daughter. I wondered if he'd leave right away. My life would be much less complicated if he did leave. But if he stayed.... Under any other set of circumstances that could possibly have played out, except what had actually already happened, I would not have seriously considered talking to him about spending any time with him at all. But I wasn't about to repeat the mistake that I'd already made when I'd walked out on him in April.

Eventually Channing went home with her mom, leaving only Kevin and a few other stragglers. I talked with Mrs. McDavid about her son the baseball player, and assured her that we would do everything we could to protect his dignity, whatever that meant. She seemed oddly reticent to go, and I began to wonder if there was something else she wasn't saying: that she was considering withdrawing her son from the play too. But she never said that, just looked over my shoulder a lot as I talked with her, and eventually she said goodbye and went away.

That left George, Kevin, and me. Kevin had stayed. He stood with one hand in his pocket, diffident, uncertain. I looked at him and he looked at me, and it was as if he had been waiting for that from me, a signal of a sort. The smile he produced then transformed him in a way I remembered. I nodded back to him, trying to subdue my reaction. My body remembered him so well.

"Hi," Kevin said to George, transferring the smile from me to him. "You said you needed a pickup to go shopping today? I'm free, and I've got the truck outside. What did you need? Oh, by the way, I'm Channing's father."

They shook hands while I watched, and George said all the expected things about his talented daughter. Then he pulled out a typed list from his back pants pocket. "We need paint, brushes, plywood.... Well, everything I've put down here."

Kevin scanned the items and nodded. "Okay. How do I pay for it?"

"We've got an account set up with a debit card. Tom will go with you and use that. Okay, Tom?"

I'd promised George I was his for the day, hadn't I? There wouldn't be anything unusual about what I was about to do. This was my job.

“Sure,” I managed to say, though I felt as if maybe it was somebody else saying that, somebody braver than me. I’d never even imagined this scene that was taking place. In my wildest dreams, I ran across Kevin again in Houston, and we had hot monkey sex all weekend long… and then parted. Add a few months and repeat. Then repeat again. My uncertain imagination and inexperienced heart had never been able to go beyond that and had surely never contemplated Kevin-in-Gunning.

Kevin flicked a glance at me, then away, then toward me again. “Are you ready to go now?” he asked carefully. “Or do you want to wait? We can do this later.”

Groundhog Day, I guessed. Let’s give this another try. “No, let’s go now.”

Outside, the parking lot held scattered trucks and cars owned by teachers who were in for a few hours over the weekend, like George and I were. As I walked across the striped blacktop with my hands jammed in both my jeans pockets, Kevin strode next to me with equal concentration. Teaching was so much more than a full-time job. It was an avocation, a dedication to a certain life of service and giving, and one that I loved. I’d thrown myself into it, the life, the demanding rhythms of the weeks. There had been no way to merge my sexuality with teaching; I’d accepted that. I’d welcomed it. But maybe that’d been an excuse for hiding.

Kevin was driving a late model blue 2500HD Silverado with an extended cab. I thought of asking what had become of the Camry, but I wasn’t sure that was the way to start our conversation, by reminding both of us of that weekend. As he climbed in on the driver’s side, I hauled myself up into the cab and smoothed my hands flat on my thighs, carefully not resting my left arm along the console because pressure on it like that would always make it ache. We were silent as he turned the ignition, drove to the exit of the school parking lot, and then out onto Gillette Street.

“Do you—”

“How—”

He let out a chuckle after we’d talked over each other. “Me first. I don’t know this town too well. Which way to the Home Depot?”

"Turn left at the corner. You… don't you live here?" Disappointment settled in my stomach.

"I'm leasing a house over in Kenneton, but I just moved there a couple of months ago. July."

"Oh."

He threw me a glance as he turned the truck onto the main drag of Gunning, which cut through town. As I'd noticed before, his actions were neat, economical, giving the impression that he was in complete control of his body, as I wanted to be in control of my life. "I didn't come here with the intention of stalking you," Kevin said.

"No?"

"I moved to be closer to Channing. Julianne has been having trouble with her lately, and I wasn't too crazy about my job in Baton Rouge anyway. First National of Kenneton had an opening, so I took it."

"I'd wondered if you had Louisiana roots."

"You did?"

"Yes." I looked out the side window at a Kentucky Fried Chicken, propping my right elbow against the door. "The way you talk. Your accent's a mixture. I tried to sort it out."

"I was born in Marathon, but I've lived for long stretches in Arkansas and Louisiana too. But Marathon's home."

That little town was one of the most isolated in the state of Texas, far to the south. "That explains why you know Big Bend Park so well." Marathon was known as the gateway to the park.

"Right." The light turned red and he braked until we stopped. The truck was a big one, powerful, with a V-8 turbo-diesel engine. Vibration subtly shook my body. I was very aware of how close Kevin and I were, how we existed in this enclosed space, and that we'd had sex. I wasn't hard, far from it, but conscious of my cock in a way I normally was not. Kevin had sucked it….

Kevin kept his eyesight trained out the windshield, straight ahead. "This is quite a coincidence."

"That's for sure."

“I didn’t think I’d ever see you again.”

“Me either. So… how have things been with you?”

He flashed a grateful smile, and I was glad that I’d given him that opening. “All right. The move was easy, but fitting into work hasn’t been. There’s lots of politics in that bank. Now we’ve got the economic downturn, and even though I’m the most recent hire, I’m pretty high up on the totem pole. There’s some resentment of me going on.”

“I’m sorry to hear that.”

“How about you? How was your summer?”

Filled with thoughts of you. I bet you find that hard to believe of me. I hope you find it hard to believe, that instead I come across to you as a reasonable, mature man. But that’s how my summer was. Is it reasonable to have thought of you, as if I knew we would meet again?

I cleared my throat. “Boring. My summer was boring.”

He looked at me out of the corner of his eye. “I haven’t been back to the club. Have you?”

“No. I haven’t.”

“I don’t go there all that often, anyway. Actually, I don’t want to go back at all.” The light turned green, and he pressed on the accelerator.

“Right. You sort of implied that. Before.” I held onto the strap overhead as he accelerated through the intersection.

“I’ve got to admit, I was surprised— Am I going the right way? Keep going along here?”

“Right, it’s about three or four more miles straight north. You won’t be able to miss it. It’s in the middle of our only major shopping center, on the outskirts of town.”

“Okay. I was shocked when I saw you today, but even more so because you’re involved in this play. *Rent*. It seems that it’s all about us, in a way. I imagine half the rednecks who live around here will think that the Angel character represents all gay men. I’ve never put on a dress in my life.”

“Or Tom Collins,” I said seriously. “I’m a law-abiding citizen. I haven’t hacked into an ATM recently.”

"Does he do that in the play? Sorry, I haven't read it or seen it."

"Yeah, at the end. His lover is Angel, the drag queen, and after he dies, Tom hot-wires an ATM and sets it up to spew out money with 'Angel' as the password."

Kevin chuckled. The rich sound of it filled the cab; it rounded over me and settled on my skin. I found myself relaxing in the same way I'd relaxed with him during that long, wonderful night at Brennan's. Just two guys enjoying each other's company.

"Extra cash like that would sure come in handy," he said.

More for me than for him, I thought, because it looked like he was doing pretty well for himself. The truck was top of the line and must have cost $40,000 with all the extras it had on it. My little Miata I'd bought used four years ago for $15,995, and I was still paying it off.

"Anyway," he went on, "knowing how closeted you are, I would have thought you'd be too careful to be involved with *Rent*."

I scratched the back of my neck, acting the way we wanted the students to act for the play, trying to look casual. "Normally you'd be right. It's sort of complicated, though."

"And I'm surprised you're with me right now. Talking to me. You made it clear that you didn't want to have anything more to do with me."

I took in a breath. Here was the cautious question he was asking of me. "That… isn't really true."

"It's not?"

"No."

"'No' as in you don't mind working with me if I volunteer for the play, or 'no' as in you wouldn't mind getting to know me better?"

I turned a little in the seat to see him, though I still clutched the hanging strap. "You said in Houston you wanted to…. Haven't you met anybody around here yet?"

He gave a short laugh and steered around the beginnings of a pothole. "There isn't exactly a gay scene in west Texas. At least not one I've found."

"Abilene's not far," I pointed out. "There's a bar there."

"Let me guess. A bar that you've never been to because it's too close and there's too much chance of being seen by someone you know."

He had me figured, but then it wasn't that difficult to do. It wasn't like I had enjoyed the hours-long trips to Good Times. The Texas landscape was flat and uninteresting, and there were only so many times a man could listen to his favorite CDs or the endless drivel of talk radio. But those were trips I'd needed to take.

"I'm not interested in Abilene," Kevin said with a quick shake of his head. "I'm interested in… life. Living normally, with someone I care about. Not being so hard up for sex all the time that I'll go off with just about anybody."

"You can't live like that here," I said. "You can't be out; it would be suicide. Professional suicide and social suicide. Your daughter would suffer for it, and everyone else you're close to would too."

"I know I can't be out here. It doesn't change what I want, though."

The shopping center appeared, up on a hill to our right. Kevin sent the Silverado toward it and turned the truck into the parking lot. He found a spot in the middle of the crowd of other vehicles already there, pulled in, pulled the parking brake on with a loud crank, and then turned the key in the ignition. The engine quieted right away, and the vibration of its power left too.

Kevin stayed where he was, and so did I. We couldn't continue this conversation in aisles stocked with two-by-fours and hammers.

Kevin went back to gripping the steering wheel and steadily kept his gaze on me. "You haven't answered my question."

I looked down at my fingers and then back at him. "I know."

"I'd really like to get to know you better."

At that point, I felt as if I didn't even know myself, whether I was the person who could answer Kevin the way he wanted to be answered or not. Until I said the words. "I don't really know how to do this." That was true enough. "This relationship thing." I'd never let it happen to me. "I'm not sure it's possible in this town. We'd have to be so careful."

Outside I could hear someone shouting, "Wait up!" and the sounds of a Home Depot trundle cart passing behind the truck. A whole world was moving on outside this tiny space that encapsulated us, but I didn't look away from Kevin's blue eyes, didn't allow myself to be diverted from what I was trying to say. "Do you understand?" I said, conscious of a catch in my voice but unable to stop it. "If I'm outed at school, I'm destroyed. I won't let that happen."

Kevin nodded. It looked like he tried to smile, but his lips only quivered. "Okay," he whispered. He reached across the seat and grazed the back of his hand against my thigh.

If life had been fair, or a freely flowing river from thought to feeling to body and back again, right then and there I would have leaned across the center console and taken his mouth, doing what this community that surrounded us considered unspeakable. I could never kiss another man here in public, even in thankfulness, even in a rush of sexless affection because I'd been extended understanding I hadn't ever expected to receive.

Kevin pulled his hand back. "So, how do we do this?"

I looked out the window for a long while as he waited patiently for me to sort through my thoughts. I wasn't ashamed of the way I lived, because I did think my decisions showed my own form of strength. I wasn't a coward, even though there was a form of terror—sharp-edged, new, and throat-clogging—growing in me at the thought of what I was willing to do in order to be with this man. The only gay man living nearby that I knew, not counting Robbie from the play.

A form of strength, a form of terror.

Finally I stirred. "I don't know. I don't know what I'm comfortable with. The situation here is impossible."

"Maybe things aren't as bad as you paint them to be."

"You haven't lived here," I said. "Don't get me wrong, the people here are good folks. If your tire blows on the road, you'll have half a dozen stop to offer to help. But they're narrow-minded. They're afraid of change, and they're afraid of us. Fear turns into persecution and hate. Matthew Shepard could have happened here."

Kevin spread his hands. "Okay, I defer to your experience. Mrs. Porter wasn't encouraging. But…."

"Let's take it slow."

He nodded, as serious as I was. "That sounds good. Let's do that. But I want you to know, I'm not in this for a casual fuck. I'm past that."

"I hear you."

"So. What's next?"

"Find some way to…. But I don't know how to—"

"What do you do?" he interrupted. "Besides teach school, that is."

"That's pretty much it," I admitted. "That and helping with the play, which is going to take up a lot of my time. It's just going to get worse as we get closer to the performances."

He didn't look happy with that, and suddenly I wasn't either. I was committed to *Rent* now and couldn't get out of it, but maybe I could wish that I had the free time it was going to fill. Maybe.

"Do you have any hobbies?" Kevin was asking.

I used to play on an intramural baseball team. I had attended poetry readings in the days before poetry slams got started. I'd been an avid supporter of the local rugby team. I'd gone out and gotten drunk with my friends and thought everything was hilarious.

Years before, in college. Since I'd launched my adult life, far from where anybody knew my younger self, I stayed home and read—my house was filled with bookshelves—or brooded. Occasionally, I went out to a decorous dinner.

"I don't think—"

"Do you golf, by any chance?" Kevin snapped his fingers like he was abruptly remembering something.

My brother was an avid golfer and dragged me out onto his local course every time I visited. "A little."

"Even, uh, even with your arm?"

I hitched up my shoulder. My good shoulder. "Yeah, I'm okay for golf." The therapists had told me it would be excellent exercise for my arm, improve my range of motion, and the first few years afterward I'd dutifully played, and it had helped more than a little. But when I occasionally played with Grant, my arm always ached afterward, and on the course my disability was painfully obvious. Did I want to….

“Then how about joining me tomorrow? If you’re going to have obligations with *Rent*, we should— Is tomorrow too soon?”

Yes, tomorrow was too soon, but next week or next month or next year would be too. Postponing the day wouldn’t erase my uneasiness. I wasn’t being paranoid about this situation. Being out and open worked in big cities, maybe, sometimes, but would surely never work here. Would never work with me.

Golf. Nobody would blink to see men together on a course; it actually worked the opposite, that men playing with women would be unusual.

“I have a lousy swing,” I said, stating the obvious.

“I haven’t played since I left Louisiana,” Kevin returned.

“Aren’t we going to burn up the course.”

“Maybe we will,” Kevin said. “Maybe we will. Then we’ve got a date? At the Gunning municipal course. Ten o’clock? Before the churchgoers get out.”

A date. “Sure. Ten o’clock.”

“Okay then, Tom Smith. Thomas Smith.” A wistful smile appeared then on Kevin’s lips. “Want my cell phone number now?”

Late that afternoon Kevin finally left the school, and half an hour later I found that my car was the last one in the parking lot. We’d spent the day sedately working together with George on scenery and costume planning, and Kevin was now an established part of the team. George accepted his help with pleasure, without hesitation, and without questions.

I unlocked the Miata, got in, and pulled on my seat belt, experiencing an emotion totally unlike anything that had ever accompanied me when I’d started one of my weekend journeys to Houston. Kevin was in town.

I drove down Gillette Street. Thomas Smith: equal parts terror and exhilaration.

CHAPTER 3
ACT ONE

I LIKED what I saw of Kevin on the golf course. Not only the clothes he wore—simple black pants and white golf shirt—or the par he shot on the first hole, but the way he firmly shook my hand when we greeted each other on the practice tee, not holding my eye or my hand too long. And I liked the way he conducted himself as we were paired with two other men by the starter to make a foursome. Especially on the first few holes, I was very, very careful not to look at him too often, not to let my gaze linger on his neat, athletic body as his club swung back over his shoulder and then drove down on the ball, as he finished up high in a way that would have made Tiger Woods proud, the whole stretched line of his body revealed. Kevin Bannerman might not have been the best golfer in the world, but he looked like a million dollars to me.

Of course we had a golf cart together. That was expected, just like Matt Rivers and his brother Jim, playing with us, also shared a golf cart. The brothers were beefy men who produced monster drives, and they sat squished next to one another. Kevin and I sat apart, making sure our knees and elbows did not touch and, as we drove away from the first tee, we said nothing to each other but the murmured, "Good shot."

I'd sweated bullets before I even got to the course, convinced this was a very bad, embarrassing idea that would unavoidably highlight my physical deficiencies, even though I was wearing my typical long-sleeved shirt. It was an even worse idea for a gay man determined to stay closeted, but somehow I'd forced myself to show up anyway. As I'd sat in the open door of the car and laced up my golf shoes, and then as I got my not-new golf clubs from the trunk, it had seemed that a finger from heaven was pointing down at me: *Look, queer on the course! Going to meet another queer!* A shade off-balance, I'd lifted my golf bag, staggered, and then righted myself, telling myself I had as much right to play the ancient game of the Scots as anyone else.

Matt and Jim wanted to bet after the second hole, and I couldn't blame them, considering the way I'd just inelegantly double-bogeyed. "The two of you," Jim said, his fingers flicking back and forth between Kevin and me, carefully avoiding pointing to my arm, "against us." No man would pass up the challenge, pride wouldn't allow it, and so of course Kevin and I said yes. Betting was common on the course, and I'd prepared myself by slipping an extra twenty into my wallet from my savings jar. They wanted to play a dollar a hole with an accumulated score.

"You mean stroke play?" I asked.

"Sure. We do it all the time."

That was one of the more unusual ways to bet on the links that I knew of, but Kevin didn't protest, so I didn't either.

"You know we're going to lose," I said to him as I drove the cart down the third fairway, letting the other two go on ahead of us. Kevin hadn't contested my desire to drive. I felt a lot more comfortable having something to do with my hands, something to hold on to.

He stuck his hand out from under the cart's canopy so that his palm was bathed in sunlight. "Great exercise, great weather, great company. I don't give a damn if we lose. It looks like you might be a good putter. You didn't miss that last one by much."

After only two holes, he'd noticed the best part of my game. Well, the only good part, considering I'd always have a parody of a swing. "You know how to get the ball into the air in your drive."

"Put us together and we'd have a scratch player. We could go on the tour," he said casually.

Putting us together was what this game we were playing was all about. I focused on my hands gripping the steering wheel and wondered what Kevin thought of them, if he remembered my fingers wrapping around his cock.

The next hole, Kevin was the only one of the four of us on the green in regulation. He stood over his thirty-foot putt and shook his head. "Tom?" he called.

I'd been not-looking at his ass, very carefully not. I was strung up tight as a senior convinced he was going to flunk his final exams. "Yes?"

"Come help me line this up, would you? Since we're on the same side and all."

Like hell he didn't give a damn if we won or lost. I stood rooted to the ground while scenarios danced in my head, and I wondered whether I dared do it. But then I realized the sense of it. It would be normal, right? I glanced toward Matt and Jim, down at the neck of the fairway. "Okay with you two?"

Matt waved his hand at us, the picture of unconcern. "Sure, go ahead," he called.

So I did it, tentatively, acting like the caddies did on the pro tour as I paced off the distance and noted the breaks in the surface, and then bending over right behind Kevin as he squatted to try to read the undulations in the green. If I'd wanted to, I could have said anything into his ear and not been overheard, like *last night I thought about the way you fucked me* or *I don't think I can do this* or *how come a man like you wants to date a man like me?* Of course I didn't, I didn't even consider it, though it was strangely, subtly arousing to be leaning over him in public like this, knowing what the two of us were and what we wanted from each other, when no one else did.

And I was going to make sure nobody else knew, that was for sure. "It breaks about three feet to the right for the first twenty feet," I said, "and then it should go left a foot."

He turned his head and looked up at me from over his shoulder. "You're kidding, right? You read the greens that precisely?"

I shrugged and remembered that I needed not to fall into him. I straightened. "My brother really is the scratch golfer the two of us together might be. He's taught me a lot, only I never take the time to practice."

I backed off and watched Kevin come within five inches of holing his ball. The rest of us double-bogeyed, so that was one stroke up for our side.

During the rest of the round I read the greens for both of us, though I started to carefully measure the distance between us and never got as close to Kevin as I had the first time. Twice I asked him to hold the flagstick for me, and he asked the same of me. We helped each other track our shots in flight, because in the glare of the Texas sun it was easy to lose a two-inch spinning ball against the bleached-out sky. After my ball went wildly right during my drive on the seventh hole, Kevin asked as we took the cart after it, "Do you mind if I give you a tip for when you have the driver in your hand?"

His suggestion—or suggestions, as he had plenty of them—would never be able to cure what ailed me, but he'd noticed a problem with my feet placement, so what he said did help. After that, at least I started hitting them straight again. Ninety minutes later, as we approached the sixteenth hole, we were only two down.

All four of us were on the green, with me being furthest out, at least fifty feet away. I lined up, stood over the putt, and hit the ball, then watched while it traveled up, down, over, and around, and finally into the cup.

"Fantastic!" Kevin exulted. He hauled ass crossing the green to get to me, his hand already raised in congratulations. I stepped back and then forced myself not to look toward the other two. I met his high five with one of my own. Our hands connected solidly, the slapping sound echoing across the grass, and the world did not end because we were touching, our fingers wrapping around one another for a few more seconds. The finger pointing from heaven must have curled in on itself.

As the four of us approached the seventeenth tee, Matt was obviously not happy that he and his brother were only one up on us. He stepped up to address his ball with determination oozing from every pore, a person could see it. He reared back with his Big Bertha club and then drove down with a grunt and all the might in his two-hundred-fifty pound frame. It worked. He hit a big league drive—straight to the right and out of bounds.

Immediately he pulled a second ball from his bag and bent to place it on the tee. "Mulligan," he muttered.

Kevin and I looked at one another. Throughout the round we hadn't mentioned mulligans—basically a do-over shot that amateurs often played with—and nobody had taken one before. But there was nothing that said he couldn't take one.

Kevin shoved his hand in his pocket, looking like a photo from *Gentlemen's Quarterly*. "Sure," he said, but I noticed his eyes were narrowed.

Matt's second drive split the fairway and went a country mile. He had an easy chip shot to the green and beamed when he drained a birdie, boosting him and Jim to two up. Basically, right there, the game was over.

Kevin and I shook hands with each of them right after the last ball fell into the eighteenth cup. They weren't bad fellows. Determined, yes, and glad they'd won our little bet, especially when Kevin and I dug into our wallets and handed over the money. I could afford to be generous in my thoughts because this round was over, and I'd survived. Neither of the brothers, I was sure, had a clue they'd just spent four hours and forty-five minutes in the company of two homosexual men.

"Assholes," Kevin muttered as we hefted our bags and walked around the clubhouse to the parking lot. On the asphalt, our spiked shoes made a *crunch-crunch* sound.

I allowed myself an amused smile, my first of the day, but it was so much safer now, off the course. "I'm sure they've each got one."

"I hate that kind of gamesmanship."

"What? The mulligan?"

"No, the key rattling, mainly."

"What?"

We got to his pickup and he put down his golf bag by the tailgate, and I did the same. He wiped sweat off his forehead, leaving glistening streaks of perspiration. September in Texas was hot. "Didn't you hear that? When you were putting on the last three holes, Jim was rattling his keys in his pocket each time you were over the ball."

That was considered the worst kind of gamesmanship by my brother Grant. "You're kidding. No, I didn't hear anything."

Kevin seemed to check whether I was serious, and he must have decided I was because he gave a little laugh. "You really have powers of concentration, you know that? I should have guessed."

He heaved his bag into the bed of the truck without much care and then said, "We did okay, didn't we?"

I shook my head. “One hundred and eight for me, ninety-six for you. We didn’t exactly set the world on fire.”

“Lucky for us neither one of them knew how to chip the ball or we’d be hanging our heads in shame. But I didn’t mean okay on the golf game. You’re not outed yet, are you?”

I couldn’t help myself, I checked around to make sure nobody had heard him speaking in what seemed to be a football-arena-announcer voice.

“Sorry,” he said quietly. “You’re right, I shouldn’t have. Sorry.”

The Miata was a few spots down from his truck, under a Bradford pear tree with gorgeous, lush foliage. I clomped down there and clicked the tiny trunk open, where there was barely enough room for my Taylor Made irons and woods. Kevin followed me in silence, and then trailed around to the side when I sat down once again in the driver’s seat and began to take off my golf shoes.

“I’ll be more careful,” he said. “Okay?”

“All right.”

“I’m not used to this dating thing, either, you know,” he said as quietly as I could have asked him to speak. “I’ve only ever dated women before.”

I looked at him, blinking as sunlight escaped between leaves overhead to dazzle my eyes and obscure my view of him. I knew so little of him, really.

“Your wife?”

“And one beard or another. I needed them for the job after the divorce.”

That was disappointing to hear. At least I’d never done that to a woman, made her think she was in a real relationship. I’d retreated rather than do that, and I didn’t think I’d be very good at dissembling anyway. I pulled off my right shoe and picked up the Reeboks I’d left in the well of the front seat.

“I noticed you didn’t play any of the games those two did,” Kevin said.

“I guess not. It’s never seemed reasonable to count your strokes, except for the worst ones.” I finished tying the one sneaker and tackled the laces of the remaining golf shoe. “I noticed you didn’t call for a mulligan for yourself on the twelfth hole. You could have. How come you didn’t? It’s common enough.”

He tilted his head to the side and got this look on his face like he was a ten-year-old caught in the act of doing something nice for his little sister. “Ahhhhh…. Because you’re a good influence?”

“Right.”

The shoes were on, the game was completed, the afternoon was more than half over, and it was time for me to go home and do some work. I needed to plan as far out into the semester as I could, since so much of my time would be taken up with the after-hours work of the play.

Kevin stepped back, and I pulled the door closed, but then he motioned for me to roll the window down. I didn’t want to. That would look odd, wouldn’t it? I checked again for innocent or devious eavesdroppers, turned on the ignition, and pressed the button that brought down the glass separating us.

He leaned in toward the window, both his hands on his knees.

“Don’t,” I said.

He pulled back a little, but not nearly as much as I thought he should have. “Can I call you?”

“Sure.”

“In the best of all possible worlds, you know, this wouldn’t be the end of our day together.”

Silent, and tensed to cut him off if I saw the flicker of another person anywhere near us, I simply looked at him.

“In the best of all possible worlds, we’d…. ” His voice had turned low, sultry, sexy, and instant heat streaked through me. “We’d go have a beer with those guys.”

I ferociously grimaced at him and growled, “Now who’s the asshole?”

He backed up, chuckling and holding his palms up. “Hey, I was just saying. Doesn’t that sound good? A cold Bud. Wait a minute, you’re a Miller man, aren’t you?”

“Every day of the week.”

“Will you be wanting any help with the rehearsals this week? I could come out and lend a hand.”

I nodded. “Sure. We start on Tuesday this week, though the rest of the time it’ll be Monday through Thursday, beginning at three o’clock.”

“Okay, I’ll try to make it out a time or two this week, maybe combine the trip with some customer visits.”

He’d have to drive over from his bank to help, so I wasn’t going to count on it. Still, hearing that my lousy play on the golf course hadn’t turned him off was reassuring. “That’d be fine,” I said. “If you can do it. I’ve got to go.”

Kevin straightened and slapped his open hand on the side of the car as if to send me off, but then he was back down in my face one last time. “Do you like Australian?” he asked, his voice a whisper I could barely hear. “I’d like to do that to you someday.”

Shit! I gunned the engine and got out of there, not sure what to think about the man who’d said he’d be careful. He was pushing me too far with that. It was a relief to get away, but also a triumph that the day was finished. I’d done it.

That night, I fell into bed after the TV news, but sleep was off somewhere at the North Pole, not in my bedroom. Finally I gave in to my wildly twisting thoughts and got up without turning on the light to activate my laptop. The wireless connection took me to a GLBT website, where in thirty seconds I found out what Australian sex was. The words glowed in the dark as if imprinting themselves on my chest and belly, and then plunged, sizzling, directly to my cock.

I closed my eyes against my arousal, and swallowed. To be touched….

I didn’t get to sleep until past midnight, helpless before my imagination even after I’d jerked off: Kevin was licking his way very, very slowly, over and over again, down my spine.

"TODAY'S test has three essay questions about the nineteen-twenties. We've covered all of this in class, so pick two and do your best."

My announcement in my first history class of the day was met with a chorus of boos and groans—*crap, I forgot to study!* and *why can't it be multiple choice?* and *I hate Tuesdays, he always gives tests on Tuesdays*—but I was used to that. Those groans didn't have the sharp edge of despair. Over the years I'd learned to tell the difference between those and this lingering discomfort, when the kids were being pushed by the hard-ass teacher to study and learn more than they wanted to. It was good for them to be stretched.

"No cell phones," I said right before I gave out the test, and then I stood in front of the blackboard to watch them fidget, chew on the ends of their pens, and stare up at the clock. A few of them went right to work, though. When five minutes had ticked away, I sat down at my desk and looked at the requests for college recommendations that had already come my way. Those were always challenging, because I wanted to give the students the best chance they had to get into a good college, but I tried to be as truthful as possible too. It was an odd source of pride for me that I always had more recommendations to fill out than I wanted to do. I thought the kids trusted me. I hoped so.

Going back to school after my weekend, making my way through the tunnel of students to my classroom, seeing them pour in for the first class of the day and then calling the roll: it had been like returning home. When I'd left the classroom on Friday, my life had been one way. Now it was turned on its head, and it seemed to me that I was a different person. But the school, and particularly my classroom, was still an oasis of sanity and security. I'd feared the back of my neck would prickle with self-conscious guilt and wondered if everybody would *know*. I truly did feel more than a little shell-shocked that I was willing to move out of my much-treasured, hard-fought-for safety zone. But as far as I'd been able to tell over the past two days, nobody had noticed any difference. I was plain Mr. Smith. Anyway, to the kids I existed only in the school. It wasn't hard to remember when I'd been a teenager and been astonished to run across one of my teachers at the community pool or at the grocery store.

In the teacher's lounge during my free period, George reminded me that Danielle Robertson was coming in to start work on the scenery that afternoon. Over my roast beef sandwich I considered, chewed, swallowed, and then, in as commonplace a tone as I could muster, I reminded him in turn that Kevin might show up too. It seemed a good idea to link his presence with Danielle's. They were equally non-threatening, weren't they?

I stayed in my classroom for half an hour after the last bell released the students for the day, as I often did, to give the students the chance to talk to me in private. Over the years I'd counseled them on all sorts of academic problems, talked sternly to a few on the verge of flunking out, and tutored some who wanted extra help. And like most other teachers who tried to make themselves accessible, there'd been a time or two that had broken my heart, when kids had come to me with troubles that weren't easily fixed. My classroom had seen confessions of anger and despair, but not that day. I spent the thirty minutes grading the tests and then packed up and headed for the auditorium in the arts wing of the school.

I loved our high school auditorium. It wasn't youthful anymore, showing its age through the stains on the acoustical panel walls, and the broken chairs here and there with orange plastic taped across the seats, and the linoleum floor with missing tiles the kids loved to jump across. For the next three months we'd be using every nook and cranny of the auditorium—the seats for storage, the aisles for work sessions, the wings and stage for rehearsals, and the backstage for, well, staging—as we put all the different parts of *Rent* together.

There'd been talk of a bond package to present to the voters next year in order to upgrade the place. Secretly I'd been glad when the economic downturn the nation seemed to be entering scotched the idea. I liked the comfort of things the way they were; the lumbering, kid-friendly auditorium was a known quantity that worked fine for study hall and band concerts and play presentations, and of course play preparation. Known quantities were good for a man who needed the safety of the rut and the preconceived notion.

Almost three hours later, the sound of "Seasons of Love," the opening song for *Rent*, came from the stage behind me as I strode up the center aisle. Because George was choir director as well as the theater teacher, he was acting as musical director and stage director for the play, and that represented an enormous burden even for his energetic talents. Most of the play was sung, not spoken. It was, after all, loosely based on and certainly inspired by the opera *La Bohème.*

Five hundred twenty-five thousand six hundred minutes, the actors sang. They sounded good already.

Danielle Robertson looked up at me as I approached her own personal domain in the very back section of the auditorium. She had huge rolls of paper spread across the floor behind the last row of seats, and already I could see the outlines of New York City as it would appear on the stage in early December. Tiffany Davis, our art teacher, had already sketched a lot, and it seemed Danielle was adding to that.

"Doing okay?" I asked, focusing only on her and doing my best to act completely natural. I'd made up my mind and had come to see her for a reason. And then, craning my neck to admire the art at my feet, I added, "You've done a lot of work already."

She pushed a strand of honey hair behind her ear. Danielle was squat like a fireplug, matter-of-fact, and had more talent in her little finger than I had in my whole body. No wonder her kids got leading roles.

"We need to work fast," she said. "Kevin's helped. If we could get more hours out of him, that would be good."

"Sorry that I have to work for a living," Kevin said. He straightened from where he'd been coloring in what looked like a tree in a park scene, and I squelched any reaction to the sight of him, the fine sight of him. Reactions were for other places and other times, definitely not for school.

Kevin had arrived forty-five minutes earlier, around five o'clock, which meant he must have left the bank in Kenneton no later than four-thirty. He'd shown up wearing the same suit that had rested so well on his slender body at Brennan's. Now he stood with his white shirt sleeves rolled up to his elbows, his collar unbuttoned, and his weight distributed evenly on both feet, as if he were ready to spring into action for any emergency.

Danielle was saying, with one hand out to him, "No, of course I didn't mean you should quit your job. I'm grateful for whatever time you can give us."

Kevin bent again to place the paintbrush he was holding on a metal splash plate. “I don’t know how often I can be here, but I like to help. Plus it gives me a chance to show Channing I care about what she does.”

“Oh, that’s right,” Danielle said, “I forgot which one was yours. She’s a lovely girl, if a little on the wild side.”

“Meaning you wouldn’t want your son Johnny dating her,” Kevin said with a wry twist of his lips.

“I’m sure if he wanted to we’d have no objection. But he’s really busy with his church youth group. Besides, I thought Channing already had a boyfriend.” She snapped her fingers as she tried to remember. “Uh….” Snap. “Uh….” Snap.

“JJ,” I supplied. “JJ Russell. First period history, he comes in hungover on Mondays.”

“He does?” Kevin asked, and his frown was deep.

“It’s better than not showing up at all,” I said philosophically. “And he’s a good kid at heart. Listen, George doesn’t want us working past six. So roll up for the evening, okay? And thanks for coming, we really appreciate the help.”

Danielle would be getting a credit in the program as the show’s assistant art director, even if it was unpaid, and she’d be showing up almost every day to help the art teacher. It still didn’t hurt to express our gratitude. I planned to do it as often as I could. Parents like Danielle and her husband John were the backbone of the schools. They were solid, good-hearted people.

“So,” Kevin said, “are you done for the day too?”

Kevin and I hadn’t exchanged a private word since he’d arrived. “No,” I said, “George and I are having a strategy dinner at Little Bit’s down on Fifteenth. Would the two of you like to join us? Sometimes it helps to have a third and fourth point of view.”

As I had counted on her doing, Danielle shook her head. “Thanks, but no thanks. I’ve got a family to feed, assuming the slow cooker hasn’t failed. Kevin, why don’t you go? You’ve seen what I’ve started here. You can represent the art department.”

He tilted his head, measuring me. "Sure that'd be okay with George?" *With you?*

"I'm sure."

He nodded decisively. "Okay, then, I will. I'm driving Channing home, so I'll meet you two there."

Little Bit's restaurant was a neighborhood/school/town meeting place out on highway 382, about ten minutes from the high school. We didn't have any chain restaurants in Gunning besides the Dairy Queen on the east side and the Kentucky Fried Chicken on the north side. The owner of Little Bit's had put four kids through the school system and never failed to have some sort of supportive message on the board outside. When I drove up, close to seven o'clock, it said, "Go Mustangs! Beat the Panthers!" Football would continue to be king until the last drop of oil was extracted from the folds of land under the prairie and probably after that. George never scheduled rehearsal on Friday afternoon; if he had, all the cast members would have skipped to attend the pep rally for the football team.

When I stepped into the rustically paneled, low-ceilinged dining room, Ellie, the manager, was there to meet me, the soul of efficient, down-home charm in a grandmotherly package. She'd make sure her customers enjoyed themselves at her place even if they didn't want to. She didn't know me by name, but she did by sight, and she greeted me warmly. "Meetin' somebody?" Her voice always sounded hoarse, a little like Kevin's did, as if she'd spent all day shouting at the waitresses.

A small voice that I hadn't heard in years sounded in my head: *Wouldn't you like to know?* My mouth opened and then closed as I was stunned into momentary silence. Where had that rebellious thought come from? No, she absolutely would not want to know. Nobody in town wanted to acknowledge behavior outside the norm that would challenge their understanding of reality. Everybody was like everybody else here.

"I'll need a table for three, please," I said pleasantly, once I'd made a show of covering up by scanning what I could see of the diners already there. George had said he'd be a little late because the principal had wanted to talk with him, probably about the budget for the play.

And Kevin wasn't in sight. "Better yet, is the booth in the back available?"

She led me to the last booth along the side of the main dining room, which on a Tuesday evening was less than half full. I picked the side of the booth where I could see the front door and be seen by those coming in, ordered a sweetened iced tea she said the waitress would bring, and then I pulled the game set over in front of me. The set was why I'd suggested to George that we meet at Little Bit's instead of at the Red Top Barbecue or at Fran's Home Cooking. Years ago, plastic Eight-Games-In-One sets had appeared at every red-and-white swathed table in the restaurant. Chess, checkers, Parcheesi, backgammon, and more were available for every harried mother to shove at her kids to keep them quiet.

There was seldom a complete set of pieces at any one table. At the back booth, the white king and the black queen were missing, along with a pawn from each side, and so I went in search of them, going table-hopping until I got what I needed.

I returned to my own booth as the tea was being delivered. The twenty-something waitress I didn't know plunked it down and held out a menu. "Want me to bring drinks for your friend?"

"No, I don't know what they'd like. Two others will be joining me."

"Okay." She put two more menus on the table and wandered off. Then she came back to ask me if I wanted any onion rings for an appetizer.

The sound of the door opening made me look up from positioning the white pawns on their squares. Kevin walked in, holding his suit jacket slung over his shoulder with one extended finger. He checked through the tables and saw me, lifted his other hand in half a wave, and started toward me.

I made a conscious decision to look away, to not allow myself to feel anything at the sight of a good-looking man, as I'd done so many times over the years that it'd become automatic. But this good-looking man was coming to join me. I knew him. The whole point of maneuvering things so he could join us for dinner was to acknowledge him for what he was: a past and potential sex partner, someone I could spend time with as my real self. A man I had decided I could allow myself to be interested in.

I looked up and tried to release the manacles I'd placed on my body, but it wasn't easy. Kevin was a sinful temptation coming closer, a promise of pleasure, of arching up in the body's mindless explosion, and he was a man whose eyes were focused exclusively on me. He stopped at the table with his hip cocked to one side and smiled artlessly down at me.

Devil, I thought, though I didn't think he knew the picture he painted. "Sit down, for God's sake."

He gave me a quizzical look and then tucked himself into the seat opposite me while giving the restaurant a good going-over. "I feel right at home," he said with a smirk. "There's a place like this in Marathon." He nodded toward the sign that said *Sometimes I wake up grumpy, and sometimes I let him sleep.* Little Bit's walls were covered with sayings like that, and they were changed out every few months too. That kept the customers guessing and happy.

"Doesn't every Texas restaurant have a possum sheriff?" I asked. A stuffed possum with a tiny six-shooter in one paw and a one-quarter gallon hat on its head hovered over our table.

"If it doesn't," Kevin said totally seriously, "it's got a jackalope."

"There's one of those here too, behind you."

Kevin twisted around to chuckle at the sight of the jackrabbit with the antlers of an antelope. "That's great." He turned back to me. "Louisiana has its idiosyncrasies, and I enjoyed the music, but there's no place like home."

"No place like Texas," I agreed. "Good people here. Good senses of humor."

"Yep. So." He nodded at the board set up between us. "Do you play?"

I picked up a white and a black pawn and held them out in front of me, one hidden in each fist. He tapped my left hand, and I opened to show white.

He picked it from my palm. "Offense."

I placed the black piece where it belonged and turned the board so black was on my side. "Defense."

Golf might have been his game, but I knew a little something about chess. Years before, my mother had given me one of those Radio Shack computerized chess sets so I could play against the machine, and during more than one evening I'd wanted to throw the thing against the wall for presenting yet another way to pin me in a corner.

Except for Kevin saying, "I'm going to assume your sense of humor—which I presume you've got—doesn't involve hiding a Chess Grand Master's certification," we played in silence for the first few moves, each of us concentrating. I watched while Kevin hovered over a piece for only a few seconds and then decisively pushed it forward with two fingers. I took a while thinking before advancing even my pawns, but he didn't wait even thirty seconds before moving. White gave a decided advantage to anyone who knew what they were doing, but after five minutes, it didn't seem that Kevin was especially skilled. He played with bravura, but with a simple, direct strategy that was more suited to the boxing ring than the grand game of kings.

"So what's good to eat here?" he asked as I was reaching for my bishop.

"Try the catfish platter," I said. "It comes with green tomato relish."

"Okay." He wasted no time bringing his knight out into play. "Channing tells me she has you for class."

"That's right."

"How's she doing?"

"All right. She's a solid B student. She probably would do better if she didn't goof off."

"She told me you were a good teacher."

"I try."

"I bet you really are. Dedicated. So how did you get into education?"

"I don't know. Seemed like a good idea at the time." I raised my eyes from examining the board to look at him. "How did you get into banking?"

His eyes actually sparkled. How did he do that? I couldn't imagine looking as alive as he did right then, just sitting in a restaurant playing chess with me. "I'm not sure," he said. "How does anybody find a profession? It seemed like a good idea at the time."

"Humph," I said, because I didn't want to react to what he said, though I suspect my lips twitched.

We exchanged a few more moves. I was already closing in for the kill, since I was better at the boardplay by about the same degree that he was better than I was at golf. I moved my rook up, preparing to maneuver him into an indefensible position, and he knew right away he was in trouble. He said something low and probably slanderous.

"What was that?" I asked, leaning forward to rub it in. "I didn't quite catch that."

He didn't say anything, instead pointed to something behind me. I turned and there was one of Little Bit's signs that said *Yes, I admit it. I got a thinkin' problem.* It was either that or the one that proclaimed *No Sushi.*

"You're a goner," I told him.

"Probably."

He rubbed his neck as he concentrated. I asked, "Are you sore from our game?" I'd had to resort to my prescription painkiller.

"Yeah, I had to take two Advil before I got to sleep. I'm not in the good shape I used to be, that's for sure."

"You look like you might work out."

That brought his gaze flashing up to me. "Mainly I jog. Nothing like before."

"Before?"

"I was on the university football team. Years ago. Another life. How about you, any aftereffects from the golf? Your…." He nodded to where my arm rested against my side, like it usually did. "Your… everything okay?"

"Sure," I said roughly, and I looked away across the room. What was, was, and nothing I could ever do would change it. I was lucky to have the use of my arm as much as I did. In most settings I could conceal the limited range of motion, and I didn't wear short sleeves outside even in the summer, so the scars weren't visible. It was only because Kevin and I had grappled naked in hotel rooms in Houston that he'd seen them.

He was overtly surveying the board when I looked back at him. "I think you've got me trapped."

"Checkmate in a few moves."

"Do I give up now?" He suddenly smiled. "Or should I fight on?"

But we didn't have the chance to play through because George was there, looming over the table. "Sorry to interrupt your game, gents, but here I am."

"You aren't interrupting, you're preventing a massacre," Kevin said.

"Then I came at the right time. Move over, Tom." While I shuffled over toward the wall, he called out to the waitress for a Coke. Once he was settled, he extended his hand to shake Kevin's over the table. "Hello, there. I heard you were helping Danielle. We sure do appreciate it."

"My pleasure."

"So, what did Hiram have to say?" I asked.

"It sure wasn't about the budget. You're not going to believe this, but Mrs. Patricia Porter wasn't satisfied with what she had to say on Saturday. She came to officially complain to him about the play this afternoon."

"You're kidding," Kevin said. "Is that serious? A problem?"

I took the long spoon and vigorously stirred my tea, trying to mask my unease. The ice cubes made a clinking sound. "There's always one in every group," I said. "You can't be a teacher for long without running into the self-important parent."

"Especially in theater," George said, rolling his eyes. "Spare me from the theater mom. But Hiram said she threatened to take her complaint to the school board."

"I guess she doesn't have anything better to do with her time."

"It won't come to anything," George said. "You know that."

"I thought the board had already approved the play," Kevin put in.

"No, that was the committee the superintendent set up," I said.

Kevin shrugged. "Same thing. Anyway, she pulled her daughter out of the play. What right does she have to complain?"

George unrolled his silverware and put the paper napkin on his lap, tucking it into his belt. "She thinks it's unsuitable for the community, a bad influence, presents the worst kind of morals, you know the drill."

"What did Hiram want you to do?" I asked.

"Nothing, really."

"Nothing at all?"

"He wanted to make me aware of what she'd said. He did say to make sure all the parents were on board with us, and I told him they were."

"Mrs. Porter has a point, you know," I said quietly as I moved the chess set, with the pieces still in play, over next to the bottles of ketchup and Tabasco sauce. I knew Kevin's eyes were on me. "This might be a good time for you to step back and re-evaluate some decisions. I told you this might not be the best play to stage. I'm surprised he didn't ask you to cut the kissing scenes. Remember, those are optional in the script, and—"

"No, he didn't, and he didn't ask me to downplay the drugs either." George spread his hands flat on the table. "What would be the sense in staging *Rent* if those scenes weren't in it? Angel's death has to mean something, has to stir the audience emotionally, and it won't do that if we don't clearly establish his relationship with Tom Collins. The best way to do that is with a nice, chaste, ordinary kiss between them. And if we don't show the heroin use for Mimi, then—"

"Ordinary?" I interrupted him. "George, take your blinders off. No kiss between men could possibly be considered ordinary. And you're asking high school boys to perform it on stage."

I couldn't interpret the look he gave me then. "Do you really think we should cut the kissing from the play?"

I sat against the booth's cushioned back. "From what we've been given to understand from Musical Theater International, that's the intention, and the way other schools have gone. You don't have to include either kiss, George, and you know it."

"No," he said emphatically. "I'm not going to do half-measures. If we do this play, then we do it the way it was meant to be performed and with its complete message intact. Don't let Mrs. Porter spook you, Tom. So, Kevin, how's life in the art department?"

The waitress came then with George's Coke, we ordered dinner, and we didn't mention Mrs. Porter again. By the end of the meal it was pushing eight-thirty. George excused himself to go to the men's room as we left, so Kevin and I walked out to the parking lot without him. Kevin shook my hand when we got to his truck. "Thanks for the invite. This sure beat a cold sandwich alone in my house."

"You're welcome."

He lowered his voice considerably as he released my hand. "Are we doing all right? You're still comfortable?"

Comfortable wasn't exactly the word I would have used. His palm had been warm against mine, and his voice soothed and aroused me in equal measures. I thought of what he'd said on Sunday, that in the best of all possible worlds the day would not have ended with us parting. Kevin was making an extraordinary effort that I could never have imagined anyone would ever make… for me. How was that possible? For me.

"Sure," I told him. "We're good."

"That," he said, "depends on how patient a man is. It's been a long time since you and I got together at Good Times, Tom. Months. Don't you want to—"

He broke off as a Mercury Cougar drove up and parked one spot away.

Once again he offered his hand, and I took it, though this time he squeezed my fingers tightly, even if briefly, and I found myself squeezing back, meeting his intent gaze.

"Later, okay?" he said.

"Later," I agreed.

ON THURSDAY evening, I was watching the opening of a new episode of *Supernatural* when my phone rang. I put the TV on mute, picked up my glass of Dr Pepper, and ambled over to the wall phone in the kitchen.

"Hello?"

"Hello, Mr. Chess Grand Master. It's me."

I sat down abruptly in the chair. "Kevin?"

"In the flesh, buddy-boy."

I snorted over my gratification that he'd called. "Not hardly. You sound like you've had a drink or two."

"Or three or five. Just enough, I'd say. Sorry I couldn't make it over the past two days."

"That's okay."

"No, no, I really want to help. I was hoping to see your pearly whites today, but a client came in at the last minute I couldn't ignore."

"Pearly whites? You've got to be kidding."

"I'm dating you for your teeth."

"Right." I turned my back on the two *Supernatural* brothers, who couldn't really be brothers with the way they flirted. More like poster boys for out and proud. It was amazing what the TV networks could get away with these days. "Danielle asked about you today."

"Good for her. Have you found out what Australian is yet?"

"Bastard," I said with feeling. If I hadn't had the self-discipline of a saint, I would have been thinking of that kind of sex with Kevin all day. Any kind of sex was beginning to sound really good to me. Any sex with Kevin. "Sneaky bastard," I added, because he'd wound me up on purpose. "Yes, I have. A couple websites had it. I bet you were the one who put the definition up there."

"I like licking. You have any objection to that?" There was the faintest slur to his words, and a freedom, a sort of recklessness that I hadn't heard from him before. Had he needed the liquid courage to call me?

"No objections so far. We'll have to see."

There was the sound of a drink sloshing and then Kevin swallowing. Then, "Yes, we will, won't we? But not this weekend."

I was surprised at how disappointed I was to hear that and how relieved that I'd been provided more time to adjust to the basic idea of what was going on. It'd been less than a week since the parents' meeting over *Rent*. My emotional experience of a sexual partner had been abruptly put on hold my last week of college, so I tried to forgive myself for the rush of conflicting impulses that wrenched me back and forth: couldn't wait to have sex with Kevin, wished he'd never shown up, couldn't wait to have sex with Kevin, wished he'd never shown up.

"Not this weekend?"

"I'm flying up to St. Louis to see the mama. Command performance that I totally forgot about, sorry. Her birthday."

"Sure, I understand. You can't ignore her birthday."

"Ain't that the truth. So tell me, Mr. Smith, are you really against putting on this play you've got my daughter in? The play, I'd like to point out, that will have her kissing another girl on stage. Maybe fondling her ass too. I don't know what wild idea George is going to have about the way lesbians behave."

It was the experience of talking to him without seeing him, and his own openness, that unstopped my tongue. In the safety of my own home, who else could hear me? "One of the props," I told him, "is a strap-on."

"O-ho! That's the way to get men into the theater."

"Armed with pitchforks, probably."

"Don't joke, that's my daughter we're talking about."

"You with a daughter. How did that come about, anyway?"

He gave a short laugh. "The usual way, with a twist. Every time I fucked Julianne, which was just barely enough to make Channing and no more, I closed my eyes and pretended she was Paul Newman. I'm queer all right, but I was able to fake being a husband for a whole year."

"You can't blame me for wondering. She has a different last name than you do."

"Julianne remarried ten years ago, but he died."

"That's a shame."

"Yeah. Channing's a good kid when she's not running around with the wrong crowd. And, no, she has no idea that her daddy is hot for her history teacher."

I looked at the phone, not willing to accept Kevin saying that. "No, you're not hot for me."

"What? You think this is a marriage of convenience?"

"Come on, we're the only two gay men in Gunning. Or Kenneton. Who know about each other, anyway. Who else are we going to—"

"If I had been able to find out where you were living," he said, and now he sounded really drunk, like he'd lurched to his feet and was holding himself upright with one hand against the wall, "I would have moved from Louisiana and camped on your doorstep."

"Now tell me something I believe."

"You don't believe me?" He was aggrieved, like a child wrongfully accused. "I'll show you. Someday. You haven't answered my question."

"Which one? I've lost track."

"Are you really against the play? What are you doing as assistant director if you are?"

"I'm not against it. It's just not ideal for this community. We're lucky it's only been Mrs. Porter complaining. I'm concerned about the actors and how they'll be treated for playing gay characters."

"So you're worried about them being harassed in school."

"That." I thought of Robbie and the question of his sexuality. "And other things."

"Channing hasn't mentioned any problems so far. She's enjoying rehearsals."

"Just wait until we're days from tech week and she still doesn't have her lines memorized," I predicted. "So, are you still going to be dating women?"

I blinked in surprise. Where had that come from? I hadn't intended for that submerged question to escape from my unruly lips. I wasn't the one who'd had one too many beers.

Kevin didn't seem to be fazed by the abrupt invasion of his privacy, though. "Nah. I told you, I'm through with that. I want to get cozy with some fine man who'll give me good loving for about forty years or so."

"You'd be, ah, seventy-seven?"

"And the man scores a touchdown." More sounds of swallowing, so I took a swig of my drink too. It still had plenty of fizz left. "But I won't be scoring touchdowns at that age."

"Right, you said you'd played football. Arkansas is a big-time program. You've got to be really good to get on that squad."

"Not good enough. I was a back-up free safety, and I played exactly seventeen downs the entire four years I was there. In games, that is."

"That had to be frustrating."

"Ball-busting, brother, you have no idea. Especially when I was doing my damndest to get into one of the offensive linemen's pants. Do you know how hard it is to hide the fact that you're gay on a football team?"

I tugged at the curtain right next to the table, straightening it out. I could imagine Kevin fifteen years younger, flat-out gorgeous, full of life and running onto the football field with so much energy he was jumping out of his skin, set and determined that he'd contribute to the team that day. That overlaid the Kevin I was getting to know, the serious man, the resolute and steady one. Somehow, it wasn't hard to see the one morph into the other.

"You really want to settle down." I didn't ask it as a question.

"I do," he said more soberly than anything else that had come out of his mouth so far. "I hate living alone. Don't you?"

I paused on the verge of saying no, I was used to it. “I don’t know.”

“Open your eyes, Tomboy.”

To what? I didn’t even have a cat for company, and I didn’t want to talk about it. “How did you go from football to working at a bank?”

“Executive vice president of small business loans, I thank you very much.”

“Sure, that.”

“Finance and statistics major.”

“And….”

“Worked a summer in D.C. on an internship with the Federal Reserve.”

“You’re kidding.”

“Nope. Slid from that into a training program in St. Louis with the biggest bank in the city, though it’s all gone now. None of the regional banks have survived. But from there it was up, up, and away for yours truly.”

“You don’t like what you’re doing, do you?”

“Hate it,” he said cheerfully. “Why do you think I’m trying to sneak out to help with the play? Gives me a reason to wake up in the morning.”

“I thought you were coming to see Channing.”

“And you. Don’t forget you. Wish you were here right now. Bet you could teach me a thing or two, professor.”

“Or maybe you’d teach me.”

“How’d you learn that?”

“What?”

“How’d you get into teaching?”

“I never wanted to do anything else. I was an education major from the day I took my first class.”

“What about the counseling thing?”

Even drunk off his ass, Kevin remembered that. “I never completed that degree. I guess if you’re born to stand in front of a classroom, nothing else will do.”

“Soooo.” He drew it out for seconds.

“What?”

“So I’m going to guess that you like what you’re doing.”

“Yeah. I do.”

“How much?”

“Enough.”

“I get it. You’re pretending to be one of those strong, silent types who won’t ever admit how he feels. That’s for straights, Tom. You don’t need to put up the front with me.”

“Shut your mouth,” I said congenially.

“I can’t lick you until you’re screaming if I shut my mouth.”

Until I was screaming? A ripple of arousal danced across my shoulders and then down my back, where Kevin said he wanted his tongue. I closed my eyes. “You can’t lick me over the phone either.”

“That’s true. What do you say you get into your sexy little car, and I get into my big truck, and we meet halfway out on the highway. We can have hot, wild sex out on the range.”

Outside my window, I heard tires on the street, some vehicle passing by. “Sounds prickly to me.”

“I’ll bottom, I promise.”

I took a breath. “What if I don’t want you to?” I didn’t. I remembered that night, the long, slow slide of him into me.

He didn’t even pause. “Then we’ve got a match made in heaven, I’d say. I don’t suppose I could talk you into having phone sex.”

When I opened my eyes, it was just the table in front of me, and my everyday kitchen. “I think you know the answer to that one.” Though I didn’t know why. If my home was my castle, if no one could hear me, why not?

“Pretend I don’t know. Tell me.”

"Have you ever heard the old joke about the Texan who died and went to hell?"

"Don't think so. What does this have to do with having phone sex?"

"He died and when he got to hell it was frozen solid, with icicles hanging from the ceiling and everybody shivering. He took one look, threw his arms up into the air, and ran around whooping, 'The Texas Rangers have won the World Series!'"

It took a few seconds of stunned silence, but then Kevin chuckled out loud. "Oh, that's a good one. So, when hell freezes over?"

"You've got that right."

"My cautious professor. Scholarly, brilliant teacher by day, wild gay man who stalks men on the dance floor by night."

"I don't stalk."

"True. If anything, I stalked you that first night. What's in your garage?"

"What?"

"I said, what's in your garage? By their garages will you know them."

"You're crazy."

"Nope, a little bit drunk. And crazy, yeah, that too. I'm in the mood to be crazy and there's nobody else around to be crazy with except you. So, you tell me what's in your garage, and I'll tell you what's in mine."

My garage was a disaster. I hadn't tossed anything out of it since I'd moved to Gunning. "My Miata."

"Vehicles don't count."

"My old camping stuff."

"Me too. I got a Camelbak from Channing this past birthday, but I haven't used it yet. What else?"

"Lots of boxes."

"What's in them?"

"Junk. Stuff."

"Come on, play the game."

On the TV, the brothers were running away from somebody. Or maybe they were running toward something, I couldn't tell, since I hadn't been watching until now. "Old bills. Bank statements. Papers. You know the drill."

"Old love letters?"

Love letters. Even if men like us ever felt that way, there weren't any of those in my life and there never would be. "Listen, Kevin, I've got to go."

"So soon? I'm barely started."

"Nope, no more now."

"Who am I going to talk to if you hang up?"

"Get a dog, Kevin."

"Okay, I see where we're at. I'll see you next week, okay?"

"All right. Have a good trip."

"I don't think I will. You're driving me nuts, you know that?"

I stopped halfway to hanging up and then slowly pulled the receiver back to my ear. "No, I'm not."

"Would you stop that? If I say you are, then you are. You're always assuming that you're not…. Just stop it."

"But I couldn't be—"

"You don't have any idea of how I feel. This isn't so easy, you know?"

I grabbed the telephone cord. "It isn't exactly easy for me either. I've never done this."

"And you're nothing like the women I've dated, so we're in the same boat. Don't look at me like I'm the expert."

"Okay, I won't."

"Look, you want to go. Don't let me keep you."

"All right."

"I'm going to go jerk off. My cock's as stiff as a baseball bat. You go have a nice night, do whatever it is teachers like you do. Good night, Tom."

I reached behind me to hang up the phone, but the dial tone was already buzzing.

I ACTUALLY liked most of *Rent*. There was something about its willingness to face up to the way things really were that appealed to me. What I had a hard time accepting was the ending, with most of the cast still standing, singing, even though several of the characters would likely die soon. The truly effective AIDS drugs hadn't hit the market until the mid-nineties. *Rent* took place in the late eighties. The play's grittiness was leavened by more than a sprinkling of an odd sort of hope in the face of the worst adversity that Roger and Mimi and Tom Collins would all face. That Angel, by the end of the play, had already faced.

It was four o'clock on Tuesday afternoon, and I had been helping George block out the scene where Tom Collins staggers on stage after being mugged and meets Angel for the first time. Now I sat in the audience to watch Robbie and Steven try it. The tireless piano player was working with some of the others in the Little Theater, so the boys were going without accompaniment here in the auditorium.

Angel sang, *It's Christmas Eve. I'm Angel.*

And then Collins replied in his deep voice, *Angel, indeed. An angel of the first degree. Friends call me Collins, Tom Collins. Nice tree.*

"Wait a minute," George called from where he was standing downstage. "Turn more toward him, Steven. A step closer. Closer." Striding quickly, George went up to the two boys and literally pushed Steven toward Robbie with a hand on the small of his back. "Come on now, he's not going to hurt you. You've got an instinctive trust of Angel, you know? Haven't you ever felt that way when you meet somebody, that you just know you're comfortable with them?"

Steven threw a quick glance toward Robbie. "Uh, yeah, I guess so."

"Then imagine it happening here, and act that way." George stepped back. "Again." He blew into the pitch pipe for the right note.

When Angel sang, *Let's get a band-aid for your knee, I'll change, there's a Life Support meeting at nine-thirty, Yes—this body provides a comfortable home For the Acquired Immune Deficiency Syndrome,* I made a note on my pad that he wasn't enunciating as well as he might have.

Half an hour later the boys still weren't comfortable with the scene. Steven was awkward as Collins; watching him stand so stiffly on the stage, a person would never guess he was a gifted athlete. Maybe he'd had second thoughts about the role. I hoped not. Having to recast the role that Sandy Porter had given up as Joanne had been difficult enough. The new girl, Marie, didn't look nearly sophisticated enough for the part, but as George had said, beggars couldn't be choosers, and if we had to cast sophomores like her, than that's what we'd do. If Steven backed out on us as Collins, the quality of the show would suffer. He was perfect for the role, if only he could figure out how to be himself on stage: jaunty but sensitive, a facing-forward kind of man.

George dismissed the two of them for the day and left for the Little Theater to work with the boys playing Mark and Roger. Steven jumped directly down from the stage without using the side steps and landed with a huge thump that echoed all through the auditorium. "See you tomorrow!" he yelled back toward Robbie, and Robbie hollered, "Sure!" in return. Steven raced past me with a panted "Bye, Mr. Smith," moving as quickly as if he were diving for a pop fly on the baseball diamond. I watched him run up the aisle, but then something made me turn around.

Robbie was still up on stage where their last scene had left him, and he was staring after Steven. I watched while he watched, until I heard the swinging doors leading out to the lobby open and then close behind me.

Now I got it, why the two boys weren't meshing on stage together. Steven must have caught on somehow that Robbie liked him. Should I say anything? I surely didn't want to, but this was part of my job description, wasn't it?

"Robbie?" I called.

Startled, he looked down at me. "Yes, Mr. Smith?"

"Come on down here for a minute."

He bobbed his head and took the same route Steven had, jumping straight down into what served as our orchestra pit, though not nearly as gracefully.

"If you break your ankle doing that," I said mildly as he came up to me, "you'll be sorry."

His look of utter incredulity reminded me that I was, surely, a hundred years old, and that nothing bad ever happened to exuberant seventeen-year-olds with four times my energy. They were immortal too, weren't they? I'd thought that once.

"Did I do okay?" he asked right away. He didn't lisp. "I know it's early, but I think I know how to do this role, you know?"

"You're doing fine."

"I hit the wrong note in that 'band-aid' line. But my mom's helping me with rehearsing at night. She plays the piano. I'll get it."

"I'm sure you will. Robbie, is everything going all right?"

"All right?" He pushed the hair out of his eyes. George had told him not to cut it, so he could look more feminine as a drag queen. It wouldn't take much to complete that illusion. "What, you mean with the play?"

"That and everything else. I mean...." I struggled to say the right thing. "You know I'm here to talk to if you've got anything you want to discuss."

"Oh, I get it." He looked around as if searching for someone, but there wasn't anybody left in the auditorium except for Danielle far to the back, working on her scrims. "You mean if I'm freaked out because I get harassed all the time 'cause of me playing this role. Angel the drag queen."

"Yes, that's what I mean. Have there been problems?"

"No. Nothing that bad." His gaze slid off to the side, and I didn't believe him.

"What do you mean?"

He shrugged in a way that said a thousand words: Yes, it was that bad and, no, he wasn't going to let it get to him and, yes, it was hard to cope with it but, no, he didn't know what else to do. And then he compressed his lips, as if he'd pledged to keep a secret.

"Are the other students giving you a hard time?"

"They always do," he said simply. "I'm used to it."

"We don't allow bullying in this school."

"Easy to say. Listen, I can cope. It's no big deal. I really want to do this play, Mr. Smith, and nothing's gonna stop me, especially not some dumb jocks."

"It's the athletes who've gotten on your case? Because you're acting with Steven?"

"I don't know. Maybe. Not really, not just them. The past couple of weeks, I've been prayed over a lot, you know?"

"Prayed over?" I asked sharply.

"Like this morning. Before class some of the kids stopped at my locker with their Bibles, and they held a little prayer session over me, hoping that I'd return to God and all that. They want me to give up the role, renounce the play and all its evils, stop being gay, that sort of thing."

Stupidly, I said nothing, though I was shocked. George had been right. Robbie was aware of his sexuality. And the other.... That sort of thing could go on in the hallways of my school, and no adult knew about it? There hadn't been a whisper of these prayer sessions in the teacher's lounge, and I surely hadn't noticed anything like them happening. But we were a big school with lots of hallways, like the streets and alleys of a small city. Like the alleyway where Collins had been mugged.

"You've got to think of it as a compliment," Robbie said, though he sounded uncertain. "That they care that much about me. At least, that's what my mom says."

The press of responsibility that had abruptly landed on my shoulders eased; if Robbie was talking to his mother, then I had less to worry about, surely.

"I know we're asking you and Steven to do a lot," I hazarded. "Playing men who fall in love with each other. It's got to be difficult to pretend when it isn't part of your experience, and it's not really happening to you."

He tried to shove his hand in his pocket, but his jeans were so tight that he could only get his fingertips in, and his elbow jutted out from his body awkwardly. "Yeah, I know."

"Being on stage requires acting on your part," I said carefully.

"Mr. Keating says it takes imagination. That we have to imagine how that feels, to fall in love."

"And still know the difference between reality and script, right?"

He frowned at me. "If you say so, Mr. Smith. Listen, I promised my mom I'd meet her outside for my ride at four-thirty, and it's past that now. Can I go?"

"Sure. If those, uh, prayer sessions get to be too much, you can always—"

"I'm okay."

He took off in an enthusiastic, lumbering gallop, a boy not grown into his own body yet, though in a few years he would be a beautiful gay man. Not like me, not in any way, because if I'd been Robbie this morning with those kids and their Bibles….

My hands literally trembled to think of it, a combination of rage and fear as much for myself as for him: How dare they condemn me? How dare they know my truth? My fingers curled into fists.

It was a foregone conclusion that Robbie's classmates assumed he was gay, even if he hadn't come out, even if he wasn't holding hands with another boy as he sashayed through the hallways. They thought he was rubbing their noses in that fact because of the role he was playing, and so they responded by praying.

Aggressive praying. Prayer aimed not so much at healing or helping, but used as part of a teenager's deadly arsenal to humiliate and exclude. The kids were hiding behind their religion to shield them from any accusations of doing something wrong. Oh, yes, I could imagine what that early-morning prayer session had been like. If I'd been Robbie, I'd have erupted with a volatile mixture of rage and fear, and I would have wanted nothing more than to lash out at someone, anyone. He seemed strangely serene. Certainly not distressed. I was the one who felt that way. I never would have heard about this if I hadn't asked, because Robbie hadn't thought enough of it to come to me, or to anyone, and complain.

Slowly I walked through the auditorium's side doors and headed for the Little Theater at the back of the arts wing. There wasn't anything I could do, I didn't think. Objecting to a prayer session before school would be a very dicey proposition in this highly religious community, and I couldn't afford to call that kind of attention to myself. I'd try to keep my eye on Robbie, though. Maybe I could find out where his locker was and strategically pass by it at some appropriate times.

I was working with the piano player, a member of the school's orchestra, making some recordings for the kids to take home with them and practice from when my cell phone vibrated in my back pants pocket. I pulled it out to check who was calling with no intention of actually answering, when I saw I had a text message from Kevin.

My throat constricted. I hadn't heard from Kevin or seen him since that out-of-sorts phone call. Now I stared down at the phone in my hand with an odd resentment. That call, so unique for me, had lodged under my skin, irritating and caressing me simultaneously, and I wasn't used to that. I wasn't used to anyone occupying my thoughts and driving me nuts. Kevin had said I was doing that to him.

I wanted to ignore this message, and I would have during school hours.

"Just a minute," I told Marianne, and I stepped to the side of the room and scrolled to see what he had to say.

Come 2 back door now dont bring kids important.

I frowned, and then managed to smooth my expression. "Can you play 'One Song Glory' for Sam, please? I'll be back in a few minutes."

The back door was the way almost everybody came and went for work in the theater department. The main entry to the arts wing, on the opposite side, led to the band hall, the orchestra hall, the small soundproofed rooms for practicing, and the choir room. The corridors and classrooms where we were doing our *Rent* work after hours were closest to the auditorium and a step away from a small side lot where my car and most everybody else's cars or trucks were parked. Robbie's mom undoubtedly had picked him up on that side of the building.

I hurried through a sun-filled hallway with windows that admitted the light of the late afternoon Texas autumn, my footsteps clacking against the old linoleum. The sounds of the band practicing for the football game drifted to my ears. If Kevin was pulling a joke, a Texas-Rangers-have-won-the-World-Series joke, I wasn't going to laugh.

The double doors were heavy, painted a dark blue that had chipped with age. They squeaked when I pushed them open and kept them open, as if I were granting Kevin only a minute from my busy schedule. Kevin stood a few feet away on the striped asphalt, next to a red Mustang, in another one of his banker-correct suits.

"What's going on?" I asked, and not pleasantly either.

"Watch out," he cautioned, and he pointed down to the ground.

A broken egg was at my feet, splattered all over the sidewalk. There were more shattered shells and yellow yolk and strings of thick egg white, still glistening and wet, in an arc around where I stood.

"Turn around," Kevin said. "Close the doors first."

On the outside of the doors, somebody had thrown what must have been a full dozen eggs against the metal. The tracks glistened moistly where they had dripped down to the ground. A full, intact yolk, looking ready for frying, quivered smack in front of the center pole.

"What the hell?" I said out loud.

"Is this the sort of thing that happens around here all the time?" Kevin asked, stepping up next to me.

"Never. There's been some vandalism associated with the homecoming game against North Central High, but that's it."

"Is it homecoming time now?"

I shook my head. "Not even close. I guess you saw this when you drove up?"

"Right. Not five minutes ago. It must have just happened. Do you think there's any chance this isn't directed against the play?"

I ran my fingers through my hair. "I suppose there's a reasonable possibility, but I doubt it. What do you think?"

"You're the teacher who knows. I wanted you to see this before I went in search of a bucket of water to clean it up."

"We've got to show this to the principal first. You stay here and I'll go see if Hiram is still in his office, all right?"

"Sure, I'm here to serve."

I turned to go and was stopped when he tugged on my sleeve. "Hey," he said, "this isn't any big deal. You know kids, letting off steam. They probably drove in, lobbed their weapons, and didn't even get out of their truck."

"Sure," I said evenly. "Sort of like shooting your new twenty-two at a stop sign to see if you can hit it. I'll be right back."

Hiram wasn't hard to track down, since he was standing in the school lobby talking to a man in an expensive dark suit. I ducked into the counselors' office and waited a few minutes until Hiram clapped the fellow on the back, shook his hand, and escorted him out the front doors. He came back looking like a man ready to go home to his supper, but I stepped out and told him what had happened. I didn't want to. Mrs. Porter, Robbie, now this. Waiting, I'd made up my mind not to tell him about the prayer sessions going on in his school.

Hiram Watts was an old-school educator, deeply entrenched in the community, a social man who nevertheless ran the school efficiently. I had a mild liking for him and had never had occasion to cross swords with him, but I had no idea what his views on homosexuality were. Maybe he'd think praying over the gay students in his school was a good thing. Maybe he'd join the kids the next morning. Just because he'd given George the go-ahead for the play didn't mean he was ready to endorse gay marriage in Texas or even understand the difficult path kids like Robbie were forced to tread.

Of course I was forced to introduce Kevin to Hiram, though I didn't want to. The "parent volunteer" was also a professional man, a banker who was concerned and responsible as he relayed what little he'd seen. Kevin knew how to conduct himself—except maybe, sometimes, with me.

Hiram took the egging in stride and didn't make a big deal of it. I was grateful for that, as I didn't want to make a big deal of it either. Kids would be kids, the three of us agreed, each of us deliberately being casual about it. Hiram said there wasn't any need to make a report to the police, then said he'd go look for Randy the custodian and ask him to take care of the clean-up job. He thanked us, made some remark about theater people keeping longer hours than the principal, and took himself off.

"Well," Kevin said, and he massaged the back of his neck. "This school is a barrel of laughs, isn't it?"

"Every day. How was your trip to see your mother?"

He eyed me carefully. "If I said it was maddening because I'm hornier than hell and I didn't want to be there, would that be going over the line?"

I looked away. "Yeah. Saying that here is over the line."

"Damn, this is frustrating."

"Welcome to my world."

"Your world, where the kids are probably wondering where Mr. Wonderful Smith is."

"Right. Let's get going."

I was so tempted to stomp on the broken eggshells as we went up the few steps and opened the doors, but I didn't, because teachers didn't give in to their frustrations that way. Kevin and I walked back to the auditorium, where he took off his jacket and draped it over a chair in the back row before joining Danielle down on her knees, painting what I thought was a detailed portrait of a skyscraper. I left him there with her and went back to George and the kids and the piano player, telling myself that no part of what had happened this day was a big deal.

AT NINE o'clock Wednesday night, I grabbed the cordless phone from the handset in the living room and kept lugging my load of dirty clothes toward my laundry room. After tucking the phone under my chin, I said, "Hello?"

"So now I'm telling you that my visit to my mother was frustrating because I'm hornier than hell and I didn't want to be there. Okay?"

I heaved the laundry basket up on top of the dryer, leaned my good elbow on the pile of clothes, and said, "Okay, okay, I can't really disagree with you."

"No, you can't. I'm the one who knows how I feel."

I'd thought a lot over the weekend and come up with no real answers. "Kevin, why are you and I—"

"Why aren't we going immediately to bed and screwing like minks in heat?"

"No, why are you interested in me?"

"You were the one who said it, right?" His voice reverberated with rich irony. "We're the only two gay men who know one another in a queer's wasteland. That's got to be it."

"Come on."

"Can't I be attracted to you? Can't I like you?"

"Kevin, I'm just an ordinary—"

"Let's go out to dinner together."

I didn't even stop to think. "I can't."

"You didn't let me finish. Let's go out to dinner in Abilene. Can you do that? Two businessmen consulting over steaks on Saturday night? It's more than a hundred miles away, and nobody you know will see us."

"Businessmen?"

"I don't know that I have the patience to keep dancing around you like this. It'll take a hundred years for us to get to know one another when I can only exchange two words with you at school, and when I can only get away on Tuesdays."

"You were the one who said you weren't in this for a casual fuck," I said.

"Right now a casual fuck sounds great, doesn't it? Like we had back in Houston? Remember them?"

I pushed away from the laundry basket. “You’re good in bed.” I could feel his ghost-hands on my ass.

“Give me the chance to remind you of that.”

“I thought you said you wanted to go out to dinner.”

“And something afterward. Only if we feel like it. A motel. A city like Abilene has hundreds of them.”

I rubbed my arm across my face, my bare arm, because in the privacy of my own home I had put on one of my few short-sleeved shirts. Who was I trying to fool? There was no way I was going to pass this up; I was hard simply talking to him.

“Yes,” I said. “Why should we stop fucking just because you’ve got some weird idea of dating each other? It’s not natural. Let’s do it.”

“You like having sex in a different city, don’t you? You get off on it.”

“Yes,” I said again. And then, “No.” This really was scary, chill-up-my-spine, cock-stiffening scary. What was I agreeing to? Abilene was right up the road, where the mothers of my students went to shop for Christmas.

“Saturday. I bet you don’t want me to pick you up.”

“Let me drive you in the Miata.”

“You do love that car, don’t you? With the top down.”

Could a thirty-eight-year-old man feel giddy? “With the top down. I’ll come get you at your house.”

“I’ll make reservations someplace nice. Come at five o’clock? Saturday?”

“I’ll come,” I growled, wildly emboldened, “every chance I get.”

Kevin groaned. “If you don’t want phone sex, you’d better hang up right now. I’m busting out of my shorts.”

“Goodbye, Kevin,” I said wickedly.

“Bitch. See you soon. All of you.”

I spent the rest of the evening wondering what it was about him that so pulled me out of myself that I’d agreed to a date in the city that was the home of Abilene Christian University, one of the most conservative schools in the state. Around ten-thirty my cell buzzed with a text message from him.

Forgot address 237 darwin. Can't wait.

Ten minutes later another one came through.

No mulligans No beards.

Fifteen minutes after that came another.

Forget top down. Know you won't want that. Good night sleep tight.

CHAPTER 4
RIDING SHOTGUN

IN APRIL of our junior year, Sean and I drove to New Orleans. We'd only been more or less together a few months, everything casual, nothing any-big-deal, but he had a car and got us fake IDs, I had some money my folks had sent me, and New Orleans was only eight hours away. That was nothing for us. We were young and dumb and full of come, and the whole world was before us. Even though we were faggots, back then we still thought the world was before us. Or at least I did.

We left San Marcos at mid-afternoon on Thursday and pointed the car toward Bourbon Street. I'll never forget that ride, the high point of my time before manhood, though I'd been convinced at the age of twenty that I already was a man. We rolled the windows down, all four of them, and the air swept through Sean's clunky old Oldsmobile like some magic carpet that was transporting us to heaven. Heaven. Three days of drinking, finding the gay bars, and sex. Nirvana.

Sean laughed at everything, the dumb billboards and the corny music on a country music radio station and how we were skipping class, and he pulled me right along with him until everything seemed funny and I couldn't help but laugh with him. We made our way across Texas and then across Louisiana as the sun set behind us, rocketing like maniacs across the long stretch of elevated highway that was Interstate 10, not inching our way over the posted speed limit but blasting through it. When we stopped to take a piss at a McDonald's outside Lake Charles, we tossed the empty six-pack of Bud. We didn't stay to eat because we were only two hundred miles from the fabled city on the bayou.

Before we got to Lafayette, Sean grabbed me around my neck, pulled me close, and kissed me while we were going eighty-five. His lips were hard against mine, first and only man so far for me. "I love doing this," he told me straight into my face, not even seeming to care about the road or being seen. Who cared? "Let's keep driving forever."

The road went on and on, and I could not imagine any other way, any other time, any other me.

As we left the outskirts of Baton Rouge, I stuck my head out the window and howled at the moon like a dog. The car behind us suddenly decelerated; I watched its headlights retreat. Sean said, "That's my man."

We rolled into New Orleans at eleven-thirty, got to only a few bars before closing time, and staggered down the streets of the French Quarter until past four. The ships trolling the Mississippi let loose their foghorns as if we were actors in an old Basil Rathbone Sherlock Holmes movie. Sean and I liked to watch those late at night with our hands down each other's pants as we lounged on his bed.

On Friday night we found the bars that were filled with men like us. I got blown by some dude wearing leather in a back room. Sean dared me into it—Go ahead, it's why we're here, you know you want to—and the fear and the strange lips on my dick and the sounds of the other guys doing the same thing as we were in the nearby shadows gave me my most intense shooting ever. Then a cop pushed aside the curtain that pretended to shield us from the outside world, growling, "Everybody back up front, let's keep this place legal." My instant fear and then relief erupted in a small hysterical hiccup of a laugh; the cop shoved me on the back as I walked past him.

Back where he was leaning on the bar, Sean wanted to know what it'd been like, and half an hour later he disappeared, returning with a smirk and a case of the clap we both had to get treated for two weeks later.

But we didn't know that then. I changed that weekend from virgin-except-with-Sean to experienced-gay-man, a rite of passage we both had felt we needed. When we drove across the river to our motel, swimming in booze up to our eyeballs, we sang "YMCA" at the top of our lungs, convinced nobody else knew what it really meant—really, really meant—except us.

On Sunday we slept until almost noon and were awakened by the housekeeper banging on the door, shouting, "Get out in thirty minutes or we charge you for another day" in an accent so thick we could barely understand her. We untangled ourselves from each other and then rolled back to the center, me toward Sean, him toward me, each of us suddenly on fire. He climbed on top of me and we humped until I was almost rubbed raw, but seeing him when he came was worth it.

We drove back with everything casual, still nothing-any-big-deal, with the sun shining down on us and everything right with the world.

THE palms of my hands were slippery against the leather-clad steering wheel as I turned onto Darwin Lane in Kenneton just past five o'clock. It was a soggy, humid day in west Texas, but I couldn't blame my nerves on the sun and the shimmering air. It seemed since the day I'd met Kevin—at least since the second time I'd met him—he'd been edging me away from my comfort zone, where I lived hugging the wall. I was aware of it and was, inconceivably, letting it happen. Not for a second had I considered not meeting him, not driving with him to Abilene, not having dinner with him, or not falling into bed with him later that night, but I had wished I didn't own the only Miata I'd ever seen in the area. At least it was alpine green, a nice sedate color that didn't demand attention. I hoped.

Kenneton was a more prosperous town than Gunning, bigger, with the malls and chain stores we lacked. While Gunning had an old-time, traditional Texas flavor—local fiddlers played on the town square every Saturday night—Kenneton could probably have been picked up by a giant hand and put down as a Houston suburb, and it wouldn't have been out of place. While Gunning citizens gathered at Little Bit's in the mornings for coffee and home fries, Kenneton boasted the elegance of the Mourning Dove Country Club. The differences between the two towns had grown because of the proximity to the interstate. Gunning was far enough away to have escaped modernization, and it moved at a different pace with a different mindset, more than those who lived in Washington, DC, or San Francisco or even the state capital of Austin could know. You couldn't get much more middle-American, though some might say backward-American instead.

Driving over to Kenneton always did feel like stepping from one world to another. Kevin's street was in an upscale subdivision—

Gunning had no subdivisions, only the right side of the railroad tracks and the wrong side—with crape myrtles still in bloom along the houses and sharply edged, vigorous green lawns. It was the kind of neighborhood where the only trucks parked in front were the ones owned by the lawn mowing services.

I pulled up in front of Kevin's house, killed the engine, and without letting myself think, hauled myself out of the low-slung seat of the Miata. My feet took me up the walkway with my judgment in suspended animation, though my heart was beating wildly as I wiped my sweaty palms on my pants. It occurred to me that we could skip the dinner and the driving and go directly to his bed. My body had been turned on since that phone call, simmering on the edge of a constant arousal like the dick-ready, trigger-happy boy I'd once been. But Kevin wanted it this dinner-date way, even though we both knew how the evening would end. Besides, could I envision sauntering over here for sex with no cover, no disguise, no reason other than that he was here and I wanted him?

Not anybody else: him.

A few weeks ago, I'd known the answer to that question. Now, maybe not. I was doing something I would never have contemplated six months before, that I'd considered much too risky. Somehow Kevin had forced me into rearranging what was important. How had he done that?

My thumb pressed the doorbell, the door opened, and part of my answer was standing right there. Sex-on-a-stick. Kevin looked like he'd just come in from running a mile in the Texas heat, in a black T-shirt and white gym shorts and his scruff of a beard, a far cry from the put-together elegance I'd met in Houston. I couldn't believe that here was the man I'd spend the rest of the weekend with, this attractive, personable man. Not staring at him wasn't an option.

He mopped the sweat off his face with the hem of his shirt, exposing his flat belly and his navel and the hair that ran straight down. He had to be doing it on purpose, didn't he? "Sorry I'm running late," he said. *I bet.* "Come on in."

He stepped back from the open door, holding it wide for me. I walked into his foyer that was all chrome and glass and high chandelier and creamy tiles underfoot, and he closed the door behind me. Through the archway I could see newspapers strewn on the carpeted floor and a coffee cup turned on its side next to the sofa. I managed to dredge up, “This is a nice house you’ve got.”

“Thanks. Tom?”

I turned to find he’d come close enough to kiss. He had bluish-grayish eyes with dilated pupils.

I suppose if we’d been younger, it would have been different. Or if we’d been in Houston where the rules of nonengagement while having sex were clearly spelled out, and desperation was the name of the game. I might have shoved him up against the wall, or he might have dragged me down onto his living room couch. That’s what I wanted to have happen; that’s what I was familiar with and knew. But instead Kevin tilted his head and closed his eyes. Awkwardly, I tilted my head and closed my eyes too, and I moved forward, blindly seeking, until our mouths rested against each other.

That was it for a long span of seconds: no movement, no sound… the smallest kind of kiss, the kiss of children who didn’t know how to do it, or of lovers who’d done everything and could encompass the universe with a mere touch. Then Kevin made a noise at the back of his throat, slid his hand to the back of my neck, and slowly traced the shape of my upper lip with the tip of his tongue.

Unfamiliar. Uncomfortable. Sexy as could be. This was a kind of kiss I couldn’t remember exchanging with anyone. It took all my resolve to stand there, take it, and let him do it to me. My tingling lip, his wet tongue, the stroke of his thumb against my neck, my deep, accelerating breathing. It was… a kiss I could associate with no one at all except Kevin.

I needed something to hold onto, because bits of me seemed to be flying off into space. My hands moved to his hips, the folds of his clinging shorts against my fingertips, and then around to his hard ass. I remembered it, small and muscled, the athlete he’d been. My palms gripped, flexed, gripped again, aiming for an elusive anchor I couldn’t quite find, would never be able to find merely in the body. I pulled him full against me instead, releasing myself to the purely physical kick of him wearing so little that revealed so much, while I was dressed in the armor of going out for dinner. I forced him to abandon the delicate, painter-like dabbing against my lip and plunged into a full, open-mouthed kiss. His tongue against mine still tasted sweet, the way it had before.

I tore my mouth away from his before I wouldn't have the will left to do it. "You slut," I growled. "You dressed like this deliberately. Did you think you needed the extra to turn me on?"

He kissed the base of my neck, above the collar of my green button-up shirt. "I remember from before, Tom. You don't need anything extra."

"You're right," I said, and I humped into him.

His eyelids dropped and then fluttered in arousal. "Do you want to…."

Just asking that was enough for him to regain control. He straightened, and only then did I realize he'd sagged against me, that I'd been taking on a lot of his weight with my hands on his ass.

"No," he answered his own question. "I promised you dinner, didn't I?"

"Dinner, yes, prime rib. And after dinner, this too." I released him completely only to palm his basket in front, his half-hard cock and the swell of soft nuts. The yielding cloth of his athletic shorts revealed everything to my fingers.

"Bastard," he said with real appreciation. "I am so going to bang your brains out tonight."

If I'd been turned on before, that was nothing compared to the wave of lust that swamped me then. I could imagine it: the sounds we would make, his weight on me, the smell of sex filling whatever motel room we'd find, reaching, reaching to shoot off with every thrust of him in me.

I let go of my hold on his bulge and stepped back, resisting the urge to say *Promise?* "We're not going anywhere," I said, "with you dressed like that."

He held up both hands. "Okay, okay, watch me fly. I'll go take a shower and we can get on the road."

He went past me in a rush and was halfway through his living room when he abruptly turned back. "Listen," Kevin said. "I've been thinking. Would you mind if we took my truck?"

Seconds passed while I processed his words. I was busy taking him in and simultaneously trying to subdue my reaction to taking him in. "What?"

"I said, how about if we take my truck tonight?"

At that moment it occurred to me that I hadn't needed to come to his house at all, that we could have simply met in Abilene, away from prying eyes. Why hadn't I thought of that before?

I shook my head. "I don't really want my car sitting out in front of your house overnight."

"You can put it in my garage out back. What do you say?"

It wasn't a good feeling, knowing I was retreating from my bold enthusiasm of a few nights before—*let me drive us with the top down*—to this cautious assessment of realities—*let's hide my car where it can't be seen.* It was hard to picture being comfortable riding in the shotgun seat of his Silverado, not being in charge, but I told myself that with Kevin I didn't need to be in charge in order to protect myself.

"All right."

"Good. There's only one side cleared out to park in, so you switch them out while I shower. The keys to the truck are on the dining room table, and the garage is out back. The code is 4747. Give me ten minutes and I'll be right with you."

I did all that and then waited in his living room, listening to the sounds of the shower going, of him toweling off and then dressing. I stared down at my hands a lot, wanting to go in to him: Kevin naked, his skin sleek with water. My throat was dry thinking of the two of us together after a six-month drought, and when he came in fully-dressed, ready to go, I swallowed heavily to see him. Tonight....

THE drive along the two-lane blacktop from Kenneton to Abilene was beautiful if a person favored flat prairieland, lots of cattle, the occasional windmill turbine twirling along the top of a mesa, and the decorative addition of rocking horse pumps pulling oil from the ground. The sun tracked us to the left, dodging streaks of clouds as it headed for the horizon. Kevin twisted his visor over to shield him from the light, and I noted that his pale eyes must be sensitive.

Sitting next to him as we drove through Kenneton was especially uncomfortable. I fought it, because I didn't want to act like Ennis Del Mar from *Brokeback Mountain*, convinced everybody was looking at him and knew his secret. But even so, it was a lot easier once we left the last strip shopping center behind and the highway stretched before us. I put my elbow up on the window rest, reminding myself that a man could keep his own secrets, and be cautious, and still be a man with pride in himself and his decisions.

"So," Kevin said, breaking our silence. He looked at me sideways and smiled, and it was easy to offer a small smile back.

"So," I said.

"You're looking good today."

Kevin was handsome in a black short-sleeved shirt and gray slacks that were perfect for his coloring. I hadn't seen him yet not looking good, including without his clothes. I wanted to reach over and rub my hand over his half-a-beard, to know the rub of bristles against my palm, but I wasn't ever going to succumb to doing anything in public that could expose me, not even on the highway with the nearest vehicle seventy feet away.

"You too. How has your week been? Busy at the bank?"

We talked about his work for the next fifteen miles, and it seemed that with every mile further away from Gunning, I was able to breathe just a little easier. I couldn't release my perfectly reasonable fears, but it was possible to smooth them down to a manageable level. Maybe it was an automatic reflex, tied to my infrequent trips for weekend sex. Distance equaled safety in my mind. Or maybe it was the company I was keeping.

This was the first time, really, that I'd heard much about what Kevin did every day. The quality of his bank's portfolio rested on his shoulders, as he was in the process of establishing new lending standards, given the mess the economy was in. Plus the bank examiners were coming within the next few weeks, which was why he'd been putting in extra hours and couldn't get over to help out with *Rent*. When Kevin talked about his work, he got serious, his voice a bit deeper. Surely depositors and borrowers alike were impressed with him, and I could understand why he'd been hired. He knew the banking business, he was smart, he expressed himself well, and he was good-looking. They would have been missing out on a sure bet if they hadn't taken him on.

Most important of all, what I knew and the bank didn't, he liked men. He liked me. I was still having trouble wrapping my mind around that.

I asked him what kind of office he had and he told me, "A glass cage. Set off from the teller's row but where everybody can see me. I can't pick my nose except in the men's room. Thank goodness I can get out and make sales calls."

"Better you than me. I can't imagine walking into some company and asking for their business."

"And I can't imagine standing in front of a bunch of sixteen-year-olds and trying to keep their attention for an hour, much less teach them anything."

"It's not hard. I like it."

He clicked on his turn signal, got out into the outer lane, and accelerated past an oil tanker. "How's the play going? Any more problems? Any more eggs?"

I hadn't talked to anybody about Robbie, though I had found his locker and had made a point of walking by Friday morning. But nothing had been going on. He'd seen me, frowned, and turned away as if he didn't want me there.

"What?" Kevin asked. "If there's something going on that might affect Channing, I want to know about it."

"No, nothing like that. There hasn't been any more vandalism. I did find out that Robbie's been having some trouble at school with kids getting on his case. But I think it's more about him being, well, the way he is than the play."

"Kids can be vicious to each other."

"A reflection of the human race as a whole."

"How's Robbie taking it?"

That had been on my mind a lot lately. Robbie did seem to be fine. As fine as he could be, being a widely assumed gay senior in a conservative town's high school, playing a gay character on stage. It boggled my mind that he was handling it. Boggled my mind that he'd auditioned for the role, accepted the role, and told me he was determined nothing would stop him from playing Angel on stage.

How did he do that?

"Tom? Is it confidential or something?"

"No," I said slowly. "It's not that. I'm… thinking about it. He's okay, I think." Though I didn't know how or why he was okay. Was there a secret to it that I didn't know about? "Anyway, there's nothing going on with the play to worry about. Channing's doing fine. She's good onstage."

"That's good to hear. Maybe being in the play will steady her. And, by the way, she was pretty happy with the mark she got on your latest test."

"Do you talk to her much?"

"Yeah, a couple times a week. And she comes over to the house every now and then. You gave her a B plus."

"She deserved it. She wasn't one of those who cheated. You can pretty much tell which ones do."

"Is that a big problem?"

"You wouldn't believe. Lately the kids have been taking pictures of the test with their cell phones. They sell the questions or text them to a friend sitting in the school commons with the book open to find the answers."

"You're kidding."

"Nope, I'm not. If there's a way to cheat, they find it. I do what I can to stop it, but I know they get around me. It's not like I was some angel when I was in high school, but they take it far past the corners I tried to cut."

"There's a lot of pressure on some of these kids to get into good colleges, you know."

"That's always the excuse, but it doesn't hold for most of them. They're lazy. They don't care."

"Not like you. You give a damn. You really care about the subject."

"Learning, yes. History, yes. We're doomed to repeat mistakes if we don't learn from history. But mainly I care about...." Abruptly, I shut up.

"What?"

"You don't want to hear this."

"Sure I do."

Who else did I have to say things like this to? Had I ever said any of it to anybody? Maybe Grant, my long-suffering older brother, who kept me company one night of every visit I made to the ranch, staying up late with me while we drank our way through bottles of wine. I'd talked like this to him.

I caught Kevin glancing at me. His expression was open, inquiring. He really did want to hear what I had to say.

"Okay, you asked for it. Coming up: stupid mini-lecture on ethics from Thomas Ibsen Smith, nerd asshole supreme."

Kevin flashed what I was coming to recognize as his Kevin-smile. "Hold that thought. Let me say something."

"All right."

"You have a very sexy asshole. Not nerdy in the least. Okay now, return to what you were saying. A lecture on ethics, remember?"

"Devil," I said, meaning it. My hole seemed to contract all on its own. I wasn't sure I liked being teased. But the teasing had been going on for days, hadn't it?

"Cat got your tongue?" he asked.

"What I wanted to say," I said deliberately, "is that I care about trying. That's it. I hate half-assed effort, and half-assed people don't appeal to me either."

Kevin was nodding. "That makes sense. No mulligans."

"That's it. No do-overs in life, so live it all the way. Even if that means staying up late, studying for a test. At least try. I know people have different life challenges, and some of my students work thirty hours a week in convenience stores helping their families make ends meet. I don't mean them. We all make compromises, and the older we get the more compromises we make, and I understand the contradictions between what I'm saying and the way I live, so don't give me shit about that." I ran out of breath and paused.

"I won't. I was thinking it, but I won't say it."

"Good. The main thing is I hate to see these kids starting with a 'whatever' attitude. And don't even get me started on the drug use." I pulled the seatbelt forward to loosen it and then let it slide tight again. I could feel his eyes on me. "What?"

"You are so fucking sexy when you get wound up. It's a shame it's not ten o'clock at night already."

"Oh, yeah?"

"Then it would be dark."

"So?'

He pointed as we drove by a pull-over for a historical marker, "I could stop right there, and we could screw right here in the truck."

Right away, two things happened. My cock throbbed and lifted, that little bit that said given half a chance it would get hard in a hurry, and I glanced over at the side mirror. Compulsively, I looked as if to check whether the people in the vehicles close behind could hear us, or could read my mind and know how next-to-impossible it was for me to sit next to Kevin and not want to duck down to his zipper, slide it down, and suck on his dick. A burst of saliva coated my tongue, equal parts anticipation—I would do that soon, in a few hours—and what I had to admit was irrational paranoia.

I tore my gaze from the mirror and told myself how ridiculous I was being to worry. We were safe, miles away from Gunning. No one was going to see me and recognize me, or even know why I was with Kevin. And… and didn't I deserve this evening? I did. I did. All over the world, people would be with their lovers tonight. Or… or their sex partners. Whatever Kevin was to me.

I searched for the thread of our conversation again and came up with, "Oh? Is screwing in the backseat of a truck your idea of a hot date? Is that what you did with those women you took out in Louisiana?"

He tapped with his index finger on the steering wheel cover. "Listen, Tomboy, those women thought I was the ultimate gentleman because I never tried to get into their Victoria's Secret undies."

"Or maybe they thought you were still pining after your wife."

"After a year of marriage and umpteen years of divorce, I doubt it."

"You think you really fooled them?"

He licked his lips. "Me using them for a cover really bothers you, doesn't it?"

"I don't know. I don't have any right to judge you."

"Maybe not. But like you said about the way you live, you've been carrying on your own deception, haven't you?"

"I know. That's just the way it is. I can't imagine…." I looked out the window at the world traveling past us. That was the way to think of it, wasn't it? We were separate from the limitless landscape of Texas, the cars and trucks around us, and the people who judged us. They were moving, but Kevin and I were unchanging. My trips to Houston, they'd been propelled by a need that no amount of resolve had been able to destroy. The need was real.

I swallowed. "Can you imagine what it would be like if we could be honest?"

He took a breath that I could hear over the road noise. "I think the activists can. They must be able to see it somehow, and that's what drives them. Thank God for them. I don't have their strength. Or maybe the men who live in a gayborhood can see it, who can walk down the street holding their boyfriend's hand and nobody cares. Have you ever done that, ever visited a place like that where we can be free?"

I turned to look at him. "Kevin. I've never had anybody I wanted to hold hands with, much less had the chance to visit the Castro or the Village."

The arch of his eyebrows showed his surprise. "Nobody? You've never, you know, had a boyfriend?"

I couldn't talk about Sean, not even to myself. Besides, he didn't count. "No." I resettled myself in the plush leather bucket seat. "No, not like that."

"You could. Somebody like you shouldn't have any trouble finding whoever you're looking for."

"Oh, yeah, right, I'm Mr. Universe over here."

"There you go again, putting yourself down."

"There you go again, talking nonsense."

He gave me a sidelong look and then an impish grin that made me think of leprechauns. "You found me, didn't you?"

"Through the most unbelievable set of coincidences."

"That's true, Mr. Universe. But I don't mind. Otherwise, I wouldn't be looking at spending the night away from that big house of mine and—"

"That big, beautiful house," I interrupted.

"That big, beautiful, lonely house. I'd much rather be here on the road. With you. Looking forward to the evening."

"Beggars," I said solemnly, "can't be choosers," and it was good when he laughed.

Our conversation flowed naturally, the way it had when we'd gone to Brennan's, that dinner-out-of-time that stood clearly in my memory. When, years before, I'd accepted the offer of a job from the Gunning School District in the aftermath of everything that had happened after college graduation, I'd gone underground even to myself. The pickups who gave me sex didn't give me conversation or company or any way out of the hole I'd dug to bury myself in, but Kevin did. As more than an hour passed, our talk was alternately serious and lighthearted, and under it flowed a long, steady wave of my gratitude. Kevin was an extraordinary man. I was with someone generous-hearted and quick to forgive. I didn't have to pretend in front of him. He thought I had a sexy asshole, for God's sake. I really hoped he was going to have a closer acquaintance with it in a few hours.

I looked over at the sharp, defined profile of this very masculine man, and need unfurled in my stomach. Then a little more. And more again. As difficult as it had been to force myself to drive to Kenneton and begin this evening, as much effort as I was expending to put aside my worries that I was making a terrible mistake, still this time was delicious, both the moments now and the anticipation of sex soon. My first evening like it, first date with a man I liked, whom I wanted to spend time with in and out of bed. That one person turned right then to face me, his expression telling me without doubt he was thinking of our bodies together, our hands on each other, and that he was pleased with my company too.

Fifteen minutes later Kevin asked, "How about a few drinks before dinner?"

The opening was too good to ignore. "A few drinks? Are you trying to get me lubricated?"

He groaned as we drove by a sign that said *Abilene: 37 miles.* And under it *Springrose: Next Exit.* "Oh, that's awful. And the man has a sense of humor after all. I knew it. Yes, I'm trying to get you lubricated, in more ways than one, honey."

We exited, and it became clear that Springrose was a tiny place, probably boasting no more than a thousand souls, the kind of west Texas town where the wind was strong and belief in the literal meaning of the Bible was even stronger. We pulled up in front of the Heritage House Tavern, a two-story, gabled Victorian house.

Kevin turned the key in the ignition and then stepped on the parking brake. "Is this okay? Are you comfortable stopping here?"

Of course he'd noticed my discomfort. Kevin was one perceptive guy. But I really didn't want to be a Nervous Nellie, tiptoeing through the evening, especially when compared to him. Or compared to Robbie. Lord, couldn't I have the balls of a teenager? "Sure," I said, trying to tuck my unease in an imaginary back pocket. It's not like we had *We're out on a date together* tattooed on our foreheads. "No problem."

We got out of the Silverado and stood together on the graveled lot. The building was on its way to being transformed into a bed and breakfast, but with scaffolding all around there wouldn't be any sleeping customers for a few months at least. A sign promised five sleeping suites within easy driving distance to Abilene, *Coming*

Summer 2008, which meant there'd been a small delay in their plans. Maybe the noisy gas station with a few roaring diesels going next door had something to do with it.

"No way you just happened to stumble across this," I challenged. "Admit it."

The smile he tried to capture made him look like a five-year-old stealing from the cookie jar. "I might have noticed a refinancing package submitted the other day."

"I thought so."

"Credit's dried up from the larger banks," he said, trying to defend himself. "It's only small banks like mine that will take a chance on this kind of project. I might have thought it was a good idea to check it out."

There were three other pickups in the lot, all dusty vehicles used every day for work. We had to walk up a set of wooden steps to a large porch to get inside. Half the house was painted in gleaming white with green trim, but the other half, like the steps themselves, probably hadn't seen a paintbrush in several decades.

The bar spanned one side of the house in two rooms, with creaking wood floors and oddly brilliant white paneled walls. Big windows would have let in the harsh glare of the setting sun but for shades that muted the light. It was about as different from the kind of bar I expected in a small town as it was possible to be, except for the three good ol' boys in place, hunched over their drinks in a row along the counter, and the relic of a jukebox that was currently playing Emmylou Harris.

Three genuine cowboy hats were tipped to us as we found our places on stools up by the bar, and the bartender asked, "What'll it be?"

"I think I'll live dangerously tonight," Kevin said, folding his hands in front of him. "Do you make a decent Manhattan?"

"Sure do," the barkeep said. He had a military man's bearing and the buzz cut too. "On the rocks or straight up?"

"I really prefer it with the rocks."

Kevin certainly didn't look at me, but I knew that had been said for my benefit. Rocks, family jewels, testicles.

"And you, sir?"

There was no way I was going to play the same game, so I didn't get what I really wanted. "Bourbon straight up, please." That was almost as bad.

"Jack okay?"

I couldn't expect much else here. "That's fine."

We appreciated the alcohol, watched a little of the college football game on the TV, and listened to the locals talk about how low the country had fallen, because the Democrats might get into office if that Obama fellow won the election. I sipped the bourbon better than the way it deserved and settled in to a radically different version of Good Times, finding I could do it even with Kevin next to me. Or maybe because Kevin was next to me.

Two of our fellow drinkers left and three more came to replace them, and then two couples sat down at a table behind us, and after them came a family with two kids who couldn't even be kindergarten age. I was aware of them all. The family made a beeline for the table in the bow window up front, and the kids pulled out crayons and coloring books like they were veterans of the place. Our bartender, who we now knew was named Ernie, didn't say anything about kids not being allowed but brought over peanuts and chips with dip as their parents ordered beers.

Everybody knew everybody else, and soon enough they knew us as well, that we were from south of there, and that the two of us—co-workers and friends—were headed for Abilene for a banking conference that would start on Monday. That was the story Kevin glibly told. Being known in a place like Springrose was unavoidable, and familiar, and a big reason why I had always been so careful—so very, very careful—in conducting my high-school-teacher life.

"No different from Gunning," I said quietly when Kevin turned back to his drink and me. "Everybody's in everybody else's business."

"Or Marathon," he said, "though I never lived there as an adult. There's nothing like a small town, is there?"

I drank from my second Jack. "Not for me there isn't. The good, the bad, and the ugly. You ready to be going soon? Dinner awaits, right?"

"That's right. But first, a little something I wanted you to hear. You'll like this."

He slid off the stool and wandered over to the jukebox to punch in a selection. A man started singing a song I wasn't familiar with. But when Kevin came back he said, "Rufus Wainwright," and I nearly choked on my swallow. Wainwright had to be the only gay singer listed, though of course nobody in Springrose would know that.

The music hadn't come to an end yet when the door opened behind us and I heard, "Who owns that fancy blue Silverado outside?"

Any comfort I'd managed to feel dropped to the floor. Kevin and I exchanged quick looks, and then he swiveled on the stool and slid to his feet. I did the same thing right after him.

"That's mine," Kevin said. "What's wrong, you want me to move it?"

"Your windshield's busted," the stranger said. He was somebody's grandfather, with a bushy white moustache and a gray suit jacket on over jeans. He gestured over his shoulder. "Just saw it happen. Some eighteen-wheeler cut through the lot from the gas station, and a rock came flyin' out from under his tires. Hit your truck square on."

"Damn," Kevin swore. "I guess he's long gone?"

"Not sure he knew it'd happened."

"Thanks for telling me."

I was already putting money on the bar for our drinks. I drained the glass and said, "Come on, let's go see the damage. Maybe it isn't that bad."

"It is," the grandfather said as we passed him going out.

He was right. Maybe there'd been a weakness in the windshield already, because there was incredible damage from the golf-ball-sized rock that was sitting in the driver's seat along with a small cascade of loose glass. A neat but definite three-inch hole gaped in front of the driver, cracks ran crazily everywhere else, and small cubes of safety-glass were strewn here and there from the impact. The truck just wasn't drivable for anything but the shortest distance, and for sure not on the highway.

Kevin actually kicked the driver's side front tire. "Fuck! Hell and damnation! Who would've thought?"

I stood there, wanting to do the same, feeling like a frustrated kid who'd been told Christmas wasn't coming tomorrow—tonight—after all. I didn't care about the condition of the truck except as it was supposed to bring me my one night out. In the past sixteen years, only one night out with a man I knew and liked and lusted after, and I couldn't have it? My long-enforced habits of control and caution bent and then broke: I picked up a silvery cube of glass from where it rested on the hood, turned on my heel, and threw it straight at a bedraggled tree. Seeing it hit and then bounce down to the ground gave me no satisfaction at all. "Hell," I said, and I meant it.

"I can't believe this. Can you believe this bad luck? How could this happen?"

"Chance. Coincidence."

"Fuck coincidence. I never should have stopped here."

"You couldn't know this would happen."

"We're caught between Abilene and home, aren't we? It's not like we can rent a car in a place like this and keep going."

"There won't be anything like that here."

Kevin banged his fist on the top of the truck. "Shit!" he shouted. And then, a lot lower, looking over at me across the hood, he said, "I had plans. You and me…."

"Nothing compared to my plans."

"If we don't get to—"

"Shut up," I said roughly. "Don't make it worse."

We peered into the cab from either side. Kevin keyed open the doors. He started to brush some of the glass off onto the ground, but a voice calling behind us stopped him.

"Wait a second! Don't do that."

It was Ernie, still wearing a white towel around his waist. "What a mess," he said, coming up and surveying the damage. "You two won't be going anywhere tonight. It's a good thing your conference don't start 'til Monday."

"Oh, yeah, we're lucky," I said.

He gave me an odd look and then said, "Even so, it's a bad thing. You don't often see the glass shatter that much. How you gonna get this fixed?"

Kevin ran his fingertips through the sparse growth of hair on his head. "I guess I'll call up my insurance and—"

"What insurance you have? Might be I could help you out."

"State Farm, why?"

He nodded, looking pleased. "My brother-in-law does work for them, fixing windshields and a bunch of other stuff. I'd appreciate it if you could give him the business. Him and my sister are hard up."

"Could he get it done soon? I'm not sure what the insurance will be asking for, but—I'd pay him extra to get it done soon."

"Let's give him a call and see what Avery says, but I don't know that he could get to it tonight. Maybe tomorrow, though. We got a motel here, so you folks'll have a place to stay. We won't let you sleep out here on the ground. Only thing is, it's Indians who own it. That okay with you?"

"We don't mind," Kevin said quickly.

"I bet we can rustle up a ride to get you over there. It's on the other side of town."

I kicked at a rock on the ground to hide my thoughts. If Ernie had known we were men who loved men—Tom Smith whose body cried out to lay with Kevin Bannerman—he would have spit on us, turned his back on us, and probably would have lobbed a rock at the truck himself. Small-town values led to pinched hearts where sexual differences were involved. But Ernie didn't know about us, and so his essential humanity emerged. It was like I'd told Kevin about the people who lived in Gunning: if your car had a flat tire, or if your kid got sick, or if your house burned down, there'd be plenty of folks stopping by with offers to help. Small town values led to big hearts too.

"That's real nice of you," Kevin told Ernie. Then he looked over toward me. "Okay with you?"

We didn't have any other choice, and at least there was a glimmer of recovering something. A motel, Ernie had said. I nodded. "Okay."

We went back inside, and I got the chance to see Kevin argue with the insurance people over his cell phone, nicely, insistently, stating his case with clarity. We took our same seats at the bar, and while Kevin talked I was asked three times in succession what had happened, and then I was commiserated with all around. The manager of the local Purina Feed Store told me he was a member of the town council and would take up the issue of the trucks cutting through the lot. I thanked him, though I doubted we'd ever be back in Springrose. That I'd ever be back. Kevin's eyes smiled when I turned to him, and then he explained to the third person at State Farm that it wasn't a small crack in his windshield, no, not at all.

I asked Ernie for another round for both of us without checking with Kevin if he wanted a drink. I knew I'd appreciate one, so I guessed he would too. He took his with a grateful nod and stayed on the line.

"Ain't modern life a bitch," Jack the feed-store manager told me.

I was developing a real appreciation for Jack Daniels. The rest of the fellows at the bar were too. "It sure is."

"Your friend there will prob'ly have to fill out a hundred forms."

"I bet his insurance rates go up," one of the other men put in, "just cause of this bitty thing that wasn't his fault at all."

"And look at how your friend's bein' transferred from one dumb person to another," Jack said. "Everybody givin' him a hard time. It's a shame."

I looked at the friend in question, who was contemplating the bar counter. The corner of Kevin's mouth quirked up; he was listening to us, I guessed, while he was on hold. He did look good and was undoubtedly up to the task of negotiating with the insurance people. Hopefully he was up to every task he'd be called on to perform this evening, because we weren't going to be stuck here all night. There would be an ending to this bizarre sojourn at the Heritage House Tavern, and then we'd find that motel. My gaze got stuck on Kevin's arm, on the way he held his cell to his ear, and at the hair on his forearm. I liked hair on my sex partners. Not too much, not bears, but men like Kevin. I sort of got off on that, on the unmistakable evidence of masculinity on chests, arms, and legs. Quickly, I took a breath and turned back to Jack the Purina man. I had to be careful not to look at

Kevin too long, or with too much more than friendly interest. But Jack didn't notice anything unusual. He started a long story about the last time he'd been rear-ended, and I had to carefully hide my amused reaction.

After State Farm gave their okay, Ernie provided Avery's phone number. Kevin made the case to Ernie's sister for a weekend repair by her husband, who was out with his dogs in the field and couldn't immediately be reached. So we had to wait longer, because Avery would be back any minute, Beth said. Ernie asked if we wanted another drink.

"I think this one will do me," I said. I had plans for later on. For once I didn't think I'd need the booze to let go, and I sure didn't want it to impede what would happen. I wanted to be hot and hard for Kevin.

"No, no more for me, either," Kevin chimed in. "Hey, the music's stopped. Tom, what do you want to listen to?"

I had the good sense to go for a George Strait album, which seemed to please the guys drinking with us so much that when the four pizzas they'd ordered from the place down the road arrived, they insisted that we join them in finishing them off.

Finally Avery got back to us, and we got the truck repair scheduled. He would replace the windshield, with the insurance company's blessing, the next morning before eleven, he guaranteed.

"Eleven," Kevin said into the phone, but his eyes were on me. "That's perfect. It'll give me the chance to sleep in."

The entire population of the Heritage House Tavern listened to his every word until the last detail was finally arranged. A satisfied, self-congratulatory stir went through the bar when Kevin flipped his phone closed and said, "I guess we're set."

Grandfather Ray, who'd announced our bad news, was going in the direction of the only motel in town, the Motel 6, and offered to drive us there. Kevin put money on the bar for our drinks, and I got to my feet, feeling the effects of the booze only a little and mildly shocked that Kevin and I were escaping with good wishes, no suspicions, and the most important part of our evening still beckoning. I nodded my thanks to everybody there, and then I followed Ray outside.

The western sky showed the faintest hints of pink and violet left over from the sun that had set a while ago. A single tall lamppost stood guard over the bar's parking lot. The glass that was still scattered on the Silverado glittered in the artificial light. Ray's truck was off to the side, a battered GMC that used to be red and now glowed a strange pink. I didn't mention it; the fellow was doing us a big favor. He got in on his side, shoved a pile of papers onto the floor, and leaned further over to open the passenger side door from inside. "Hop in."

"You sit in the middle," I told Kevin.

"I'll flip you for it," he said, and he pulled a quarter from his pocket.

"No way, I've got longer legs than you do. Come on, get in."

Ray leaned over again toward us and said, "I don't bite and I ain't queer, so you don't gotta worry 'bout sitting next to me."

Kevin climbed aboard, but before I could follow, he said, "Wait a minute. We're going to need our stuff for tonight."

"Stuff?"

"You know," he said urgently, "our stuff. In our bags from the truck for overnight."

Oh, right. Lube and rubbers that I knew I had packed and he probably had too. "I'll go get them," I said, not feeling like the sharpest pencil in the box at the moment.

Kevin handed over the keys and I retrieved a gym bag for each of us, mine blue and Kevin's red, picking off a stray piece of glass first. I transferred them to the GMC, climbed into the still-open door, and said, "Let's go." I watched the Heritage House Tavern retreat in the side mirror, not sorry to see it go but knowing we'd been lucky to receive the support we'd gotten there. We'd played the roles of friends—well, we really were friends, weren't we?—and were escaping with a genuinely nice good old boy guiding us to a safe haven for the night, where I fully planned to perform unspeakable acts with Kevin that would have made poor Ray's eyes bug out if he'd known. Probably give him a heart attack.

I glanced down at how close Kevin's thigh was to mine. Not touching. But close. Then up to his face, to find him looking at me with

I dare you amusement dancing in his eyes. He shifted, and I felt the press of his knee against mine, there without any doubt.

"Sorry," he said out loud, and then he shifted away again. I could have killed him for taking the chance, but the danger did nothing to subdue the prickling in my cock.

It didn't take five minutes to cut through town. Ray talked some, and Kevin answered, and I concentrated on keeping my body away from Kevin's, when if I'd moved an inch to my left he would have warmed my perpetually cold arm. Highway 382 looped around Springrose like it was taking the town in its loving embrace, the way preachers told people Jesus embraced them, so the Motel 6 was on the north side of town but still on the road to Abilene. We saw its neon sign blocks away; there wasn't much else lighting up the deserted streets. When we pulled up, there was a white banner hanging from the side of the second story that said *Free Breakfast Free Wireless Internet.*

"Here we go," Ray said as he shifted into park. "The only game in town."

"It'll be fine," I said. I leaned across Kevin with my arm extended, offering my hand sincerely. Small town folks: I'd learned to appreciate them over the years, so long as you didn't let them know the truth. "Thanks for the ride."

"No problem. You take care now. Maybe you'll find something good on HBO tonight."

"Maybe," Kevin said, taking his turn with a handshake. "Thanks. Good night."

We got out in front of the office doors as the rumble of the ancient engine faded down the street. There were only a few vehicles in the lot, but the place didn't look like a dive. There were even chrysanthemums in pots by the entrance, and the small spots of grass were neatly mowed. In the sudden silence I could hear a bird chirping a nighttime song.

Kevin scratched over his ear. "Well. This hasn't turned out the way I thought it would."

"That's for sure."

He cocked an eye at me. "Are you still game?"

"You've got to be kidding." I answered fervently.

His slow smile was laden with promises, his voice huskier than usual. "Let's go salvage the evening."

When we opened the door to the front office, the unmistakable odor of onions cooking stopped me in my tracks. And the sound of a baby crying. And a TV blaring. And young voices shouting. Behind me, Kevin said, "What the…."

Ernie had said the motel was owned by Indians. A little boy chased a little girl down the long hallway of sleeping rooms to our right, each of them in bare feet and screaming at the top of their lungs. I realized Ernie'd meant Indians as from India, and that his caution might not have been the prejudice I'd instantly assumed, but maybe came from the fact that the family seemed to live in the motel and certainly cooked there. I craned my neck as we got up to the desk to see the room directly behind it, door wide open, and there was a family sitting around a kitchen table, eating a late dinner. A mother, a father, a baby in a high chair, two older children, an old man, and an old woman, all of them ignoring us.

"You're kidding," Kevin murmured.

It wasn't off-putting; it was funny. Could the day get any more ridiculous? Even I had to see the humor in it. I'd been cautiously surfing through the hours as the day took a sharp left turn, then a right, then a left, keeping fierce hold of the possibility that maybe, just maybe Kevin and I could have sex after all. In anger and frustration, I might have slapped my hand on the bell innocently sitting on the desk, but there were rooms with beds within sight, and even the aroma of frying onions and green peppers wasn't going to stop us from closing ourselves inside one of them. Besides, Kevin was doing enough chuckling for both of us.

"Shhh."

He pressed all ten fingertips to his forehead, looking down to hide his face. "Oh, this is too much."

"Don't make a spectacle of yourself."

The younger man got up from the table and came up to us, asking "Can I help you?" in impeccable English as he wiped his mouth with a napkin.

We registered for two rooms, both of them on the second floor, numbers 202 and 204. The kids who were playing tag zoomed through the lobby at the finely calculated right time and the boy asked, "Take your suitcase upstairs?"

"Of course," Kevin said, and he handed over the accoutrements for our sex acts to a seven-year-old. I gave mine to the little girl, who was probably no older than four, but it was too heavy for her, so we compromised by each taking a handle and walking up the steps side-by-side.

I gave her a dollar when we got to Room 202. Kevin and I watched the two of them race down the hallway, their footsteps pounding *boom boom boom* and actually making the floor vibrate. The noise was surely enough to annoy whoever had rented the rooms below them on the first floor. Then the kids disappeared as they turned into the stairwell, and Kevin and I were left alone, holding the keycards.

"Your place or mine?" Kevin asked quietly.

"Mine," I said. It was further away from the front.

He tossed his case forward and it hit my door with a soft thud. He took a step closer so that his chest almost grazed my right arm, and I couldn't tear my eyes from his face. His eyes were glittering, desire in them that matched what was sizzling in my belly. Suddenly nothing was funny anymore. This was it, sex at last, Kevin and me together at last. A shiver traveled down to my fingers.

"What are we waiting for?" he whispered.

"Nothing," I said out loud, and I shoved the card in the slot. I grabbed his elbow with one hand, turned the door handle with the other, and pushed both our bags forward with my feet.

The inside of a motel room was familiar territory, safe territory. As I dragged him into the room, the peculiar smell of carpets and bedding cleaned and cleaned again but never truly fresh was overlaid now with the remembered smells of sex: a man's hot load and the musky, deep odor that wafted from behind his balls. The room was dark, silent but for the sudden clang as the door shut, but then behind me Kevin must have reached around and flipped on the bathroom light. A muted glow filled the room beyond where I saw the expanse of a bed, inviting.

I turned to him deliberately. I could touch. There wasn't any reason to delay, to dissemble, to pretend to do something else like unpack or channel surf. Months of forcing myself to wait in my little house, with no Good Times, with lots of self-control, months of not having but needing were finally gone.

I took his face in my hands, the shock of *first touch* racing through me, along with the shock of touching him only there when my whole body yearned to be stretched out against him, our hips together, our cocks side by side, our legs tangled, our chests pressed close, our mouths pressed close. Need rose like a desperate animal. Here was another man with me, cock and balls and ass for me, and he hadn't been desperately picked up, and he wasn't unknown. He was here because he wanted to be with me. What I used to fear, now I abruptly valued.

His dark slash of eyebrows, the strong nose, the high forehead: I saw more clearly as I adjusted to the low level of light. I felt the bristle of his beard against my palms and moved my hands up, down, up, rubbing to know it better.

"Hi," I said, needing to say something, not knowing what else to say. My voice sounded flat, as if it didn't travel far. But it didn't need to.

"Hi there, Thomas Ibsen Smith," he said, his words enriched by a slow Kevin-smile, what I had barely seen the ghost of in Houston.

He'd heard me say my middle name and remembered it. What cosmic circumstances had shifted so that I'd met Kevin? He was so much more than a random mouth picked to suck my dick.

"You like to kiss," I said. *Let me give that to you.*

Delicately, the way we'd done hours before in his house, with our lower bodies not even touching, our lips met in the quiet dark, though the sound of our mouths sliding together sent a lustful chill through me immediately. I opened my mouth and sucked in his tongue, and every thought in my head went whirling away at the wet, solid connection. He moaned and slammed against me, his arms wrapping around my back with fingers spread to keep us tight together. His tongue danced inside my mouth, touching here, there. My erection lengthened; I could feel it as if I held it in my hand, inevitable response to Kevin-here, sex-soon, this change in me so right that it swept away everything else.

Kevin pulled back to breathe and then came to me again, mouth seeking. His hardness, too, was seeking, up against me.

"I like to kiss," he said quietly, licking his lips and then opening them along the line of my jaw. "But I like to screw more. I've been waiting all day for you."

I closed my eyes as something inside me shuddered and abruptly realigned. I'd been waiting… longer. Much longer.

"For God's sake," Kevin said, "let's go to bed."

Separation seemed impossible. I was so thirsty for the press of him, the touch even through clothes, but the promise of naked skin against my own naked skin was inducement to push him away. I stumbled over one of the bags at our feet and went staggering across the room, catching myself by leaning with both hands on the mattress at the foot of the bed.

Immediately, Kevin was behind me, grabbing my hips and pushing his cock against my willing ass. He rubbed along the line of my crack. Even through the layers of cloth, his cock was blissful iron against me.

I collapsed down onto my elbows, adjusted right away so most of my weight was tilted to the right, bent my knees to maximize our contact, and squeezed my eyes shut. Yes. Yes. My cock throbbed, and I squirmed against him, trying to feel more, more.

Air whistled in and out of his open mouth as he humped me. "I want to ride you, Tom. I've barely thought of anything else."

My head lolled low, my forehead brushed against the bedspread, and every molecule of me wished we were doing it right then, right there.

"Will you let me? Even though I know it wasn't easy for you before, you liked it by the end, didn't you? Let me. I was gonna wait, ask you later, but I can't, I can't, I—"

I twisted so I fell onto the bed on my back, my fingers hastily unbuckling and unzipping, trying to kick off my shoes with my toes at the same time. He made a sound—exultation, a sudden cry of gladness—and raced back toward his overnighter, dragging it clumsily to the bed as he tried to unbutton himself at the same time.

I pulled off my briefs seconds before he was done, exposing myself completely, with my cock looming up tall and starving. I tried to push up on my elbows, but right away I collapsed back down. "Damn it!" I said, and then instead I wriggled higher up on the mattress. Then I reached down to grab myself and pulled.

"You are so hot," Kevin panted. "And you don't even know it. Do that again."

Kevin stood at the foot of the bed and threw his balled-up shirt across the room to the curtained window. I heaved in breath to see him bare at last, first new-sight of the sturdy cock that had ruled me so thoroughly months before, stretched me with its insistent thickness. I thought of all the regrets I'd poured down with my beers this summer and the fantasies I'd had of him. The memories I'd had of him. He'd never appeared before me like this, though, with his dick at full mast and his hips cocked forward. I stroked my cock again, not because he'd told me to do it, but because I couldn't help but touch myself.

"You do it!" I said.

In a blink he was pumping himself furiously, jacking himself as if he were right on the edge, but then he abruptly let himself go and spread his arms wide.

His chest heaved. "Now you. Do it!"

My hand was jerking before he finished saying it, and my hips rose with the first stroke, the second, the third—

"Don't you dare bust your nuts yet," Kevin said, and he grabbed hold of my right foot. "Wait for me."

If he hadn't stopped me, it would have been so easy to keep going and unload everything. But I forced myself to grab my thigh instead of my prick and stared down at him. Kevin waited until he had my attention, and then he leaned over and sucked my big toe into his mouth.

My head dropped back to the pillow. "Oh, Christ," I groaned, and I threw my hand across my eyes and fought for air. His tongue swirled around the nail, the tip, and then down and up. I'd never had anybody.... What an incredible sensation, where I'd never even thought....

"Do you like this?"

"Hell, yes. You pervert," I forced out.

He grinned at me up the length of my stretched-out, at-his-mercy body. "Every chance I get."

He licked again, and then the cool air drifted over my unbearably sensitized toe, and he crouched over my ankle, suck-kissing it as if it were something he really wanted to do. From the sounds he made, he did. His thumb rubbed along the sole of my foot, just this side of tickling, just firmly enough not to send me jackknifing forward, but more than enough to send air rushing jaggedly through my mouth.

"K… K… Kevin!"

I could have tackled him. I could have rolled him over and gone after his dick, filled my mouth with it. I could have shoved him down to the bed and jumped on top of him so we could hump our way to completion. But I didn't do any of those things, things I was accustomed to doing when I controlled the pace and mood and intensity of my sexual encounters with nameless men.

I'd decided to ride shotgun with Kevin, hadn't I? Not drive.

"Watch." Kevin pushed my legs together and said, "Like a mummy." Then he got onto the bed and licked a long wet line up from my ankle to my left knee, with his hands and legs planted on either side of me. And then he went to work on my knees, licking his way in circles around each one.

His mouth busy, he mumbled, "You taste fantastic."

I was jelly. I couldn't stay still. Within the limits of not knocking him over, within the space he'd defined for me, I thrashed on the bed. If he didn't grab me where it counted soon, if he didn't give me what I needed, I began to think I was going to shoot right then and there without even being touched.

"Kevin," I gasped. "Come here, come here."

"No," he said, but he moved a supporting arm up next to my side and leaned his weight on it. His other hand reached for his own cock. "This. Hold yourself up like this. Let's…."

The tip of his cock touched mine when I held myself steady, like his was kissing mine. It was the most maddening sexual experience I'd ever had because everything in me was screaming for pressure, for more contact, for the hot encasement of a hand, a mouth, between his thighs, his ass, anything, but what I got instead was this slow-motion touch guaranteed to drive any gay man insane. Kevin was torturing me.

And pleasuring me and himself. I pounded the mattress with my free hand and heaved up, running the side of my cock against his, trying to jab myself into his pubes.

"I'm not kidding," I gritted out between clenched teeth. "Fuck me right now or—"

Air rushed out of my lungs as he abruptly dropped his entire sweat-tacky length down on me. "Right now," he promised, and then he was up and off the bed, battling the zipper of his overnight case, pulling out the lube and a strip of rubbers.

Finally released, I sat up and grabbed the Trojans from him. "Come here. I'll take care of this."

Holding the base of his cock, he turned to stand in front of me as I sat on the side of the bed. I tore one packet off and tossed the rest to the floor, and in a second I had that one out and in my hand. I looked up at him, at his needy face. I'd thought Kevin was a handsome man the first night I'd seen him dancing in Houston, but Kevin in a civilized setting was nothing compared to Kevin stripped, with a hard-on, his nostrils flaring, his chest rising and falling noticeably, presenting his weeping cock to me.

I'd been thinking about sucking him since he'd opened his door to me, and I couldn't resist now. He cried out when my lips went over the head of his dick, over the yielding crown that stretched my mouth, over the jutting ridge, and then below, to where he should be sensitive, where Kevin should love having me suck. I could taste him, salty and hot already, and then his fingers were in my hair, holding me where I was. But I wanted to be there. I pushed against his hip, and he stepped back while I slid forward onto my knees. We did not separate. I did not allow my teeth to nick him or my tongue to stop moving against him, but I stuffed my mouth with him and took him all in.

Had I sucked him when we were in Houston? There was no body-memory of his dick in my mouth because that had been a different, resistant Tom who'd had sex with this different, known Kevin. As if from another world, the thumping beat of music came to me: not the dance-floor tunes that had engulfed me, shaken me, whirled me around, and then deposited me in front of Kevin Bannerman, but some unfamiliar, persistent song that the Indian family must be playing on the floor below.

One of his hands slid down to my ear, but the other came to my lips and slipped a finger inside as I went down on him again, so I held his cock and his finger in my mouth together. It broke my suction and my concentration, and I pulled back reluctantly, gulping air, feeling the stretch at the corners of my mouth.

With hands under my arms, he urged me to stand in front of him. Moments of awkwardness passed as we did not touch, though our naked bodies were scant inches from each other. As I swayed toward him, he brought a finger up to trace a line down the side of my face. I turned and caught it with my teeth, nipped at him, kissed his knuckle.

He lifted his face to the dark ceiling and offered a long sigh. It was as if his spirit were spreading upward, filling the room, imposing stillness and an odd kind of calm I hadn't lived with for a long time. And then he looked back to me.

"Put the glove on me, Tom."

I'd never rolled a Trojan on anybody but myself, and so I looked down while I did it. My own dick jerked as if I were touching it. I couldn't help but wrap my fingers around him once I had him sheathed; the hot pulsing of blood in his prick, trapped and defined by the latex, made my blood pulse too.

His fingertips landed gently on the back of my hand, keeping me there. "Wait," he whispered. "I need…."

He raised his face to mine and sought my lips, and I offered them to him, everything between us reduced down to this, our mouths connecting and our fingers joined on his cock.

I discovered that I needed this simple union too, just as much as the wild, fulfilling sex I knew we were about to share. I ached for it, reached for it, and then….

What I had been looking for back at his house, the elusive anchor not of the body. Suddenly it was there, flicking through my awareness in rich, startling seconds of Kevin and Tom, banker and teacher, the seeker and the cautious one, and, yes, the top and the bottom too. We exchanged ourselves back and forth, and I was breathless. So much in just a kiss. I took him in through his breath brushing against my skin, through his unmistakable taste, through the rasp of his hand on the back of my neck.

We parted slowly, our lips clinging through our mingled spit, our gazes locked as we expanded this moment another second, and another.

He didn't resist when I moved my hand to the base of his cock. His hand moved with mine, and then I stroked the circle of my fingers from the base of him to the tip. I watched the pleasure bloom in his eyes as we did that, us together.

"You," he said. "Right now. You."

Kevin forced me back until I was up against the bed, and down I went, with Kevin over me, pushing me this way and that until my head was on a pillow.

"Up," he said, reaching under my knees and pulling, and only as I bent my knees to my chest did I realize he had the lube.

Before, he'd simply rubbed the lube around my hole and shoved inside, the way the very few men I'd done this with had. Including Sean, in his heated, careless need. With Kevin in Houston, I'd suffered through the sharp stabbing pain that always accompanied the first minutes any cock was in me, my body's revenge for craving it so much. I was ready for that now, to give us both what we wanted. But this time was different. I felt his finger outside, daubing the slickness around my traitorous ring of muscle… and he didn't immediately move away. He lingered, massaging, playing there, and I shifted against the bed. A new and subtle form of heat, one I hadn't felt before, unfolded from where his fingertip was moving. It spread. It felt….

I lifted my head, an effort while holding my knees up. "What're you doing? That feels—"

"Shhhh," he said, and his other hand rested on my ankle. "It wasn't easy for you last time. I thought if I took my time getting you ready, it would help. Is it helping?"

I didn't know what to say. "It doesn't hurt."

He pressed a fervent kiss on my asscheek. "Lay back and enjoy. Feel good."

I let my head fall back against the pillow and closed my eyes. The seconds ticked away. Kevin tongued all over my ass but his finger never left my hole as he skimmed it, stretched it, slipped barely inside, withdrew, applied more lube, as I lay there and listened to his heavy breathing, as I allowed the sure touch of him on me. I felt the difference not only where his finger was, in my discovery of how that could tingle, could shoot to my cock and make it harder, but in the quality of the night: Kevin taking his time.

Or trying to. "Damn," he whispered on the hitch of quick breath. "I don't know if I can…. Time to move on."

His finger found my center. Pushed in. Went all the way in with its load of slick gel, and I pushed my head back against the pillow. It felt… excruciating. Violating. Wonderful. In my sexual encounters, so carefully managed—*just so much and not more, unless it's you, Kevin Bannerman*—I'd never had a man's finger up my back alley. The few times I'd let myself be fucked, I'd never trusted enough to ask for it, and so I'd never received.

"Okay?"

His wide eyes stared down at me. This was what having sex with someone you knew led to: his finger reaching ever higher into me. I didn't know how to stop that. I didn't want to stop that. Then there were two fingers stretching me, or maybe more—I didn't know in this delirium of exposure. I arched back against the pillow, loving it.

"That's it," he whispered. "I want you to feel good." Kevin's husky voice fell over me like a blanket, covering both of us and separating us from the whole rest of the world. "You are so…. You look so good. Is this okay?"

I felt drugged, like the two of us'd had a toke, or maybe that my asshole had. "Okay?" I half-laughed. "Oh, God, yes."

Kevin pulled his fingers out, wiped them on the bedspread, and then knee-walked until he was between my spread legs. I lifted them higher and straightened them so the inside of my calves rested against the outside points of his shoulders. They seemed to fit naturally in that position. He leaned forward, planting his palms flat on the bed so his arms rested within the crooks of my knees, and that exerted pressure on my legs, helping to hold them up. My pelvis inched up as he rocked forward, and suddenly there it was, his cock pressing against where it belonged.

"Ohhh." He breathed out a long exhale. "I'll go slow. At least I'll try. Relax, relax. Push out, that might help."

Before I could do anything he nudged inside, and then he froze.

I gasped, and for a few agonizing seconds I felt as if I'd been truly stabbed by a knife, straight into my guts. Not that long of a knife, but one that was wide and commanding. And then, just as quickly, the pain receded like the swift retreat of a wave.

Kevin was gasping too, and his arms, pressed against my legs, were trembling. "Okay? Okay?"

It wasn't painless. I still throbbed, but as my ass folded itself around the tentative advance of Kevin's shaft, it was nothing like I'd expected and had been resigned to endure. "Good, it's good. Try more. Come on."

He pulled back, not completely out, and then pushed in more and held himself there.

With every second that passed the cramping faded. "Come on. A little more. Move, you can move."

His hips flexed. Out and then back in he went, and then out and back in, and out and back in, tiny taps that brought him deeper each time, smooth pull-outs that never completely separated us. I could feel his wider cockhead stretch me as it threatened to leave through my sphincter muscle, which had miraculously slackened for him.

His expression was intent as he hovered over me, his eyes wide, his mouth half-open. The play of his muscles as he moved in the dim light caught me; the push against my legs when he thrust in captured me. It was so good to see his face. Already I could feel I was opening up, and his passage in was smooth, welcoming. I pushed back using the minimal leverage I had and heaved into him, meeting his thrusts.

"Oh, yeah!" he said. I remembered the sounds he made from before, the grunt with every push in. "Yeah, do that. Come on, honey, do it."

I did, shoving myself toward him as he drove into me, then over and over and over we rocked together. The feeling he was giving me:

good, indescribable, because it wasn't only that my cock was pulsing where it was trapped between us. There was something more that moved in me, that was spreading from the pit of my stomach, that tightened my chest as well as my balls, that was unknown and yet strangely familiar. My arms had been bent on the pillow, curled around my head, but now I stretched them to either side, straight out, and stared up at him. I didn't know what this was. I'd never understood why I was a gay man who wanted to be filled like this, but Kevin was giving it to me just right, just right.

"Oh," he moaned. "I've gotta, gotta, can't help it." He speared me with a fierce snap of his hips, and I met him. Everything narrowed to his swift slide that finally filled me completely, his cock forcing me open, on and on and on in decades-long split seconds until finally he grunted and stopped.

We stayed like that for a hovering moment, two, three….

"Up," he insisted. "Up."

A buzz sounded in my ears when I realized what he wanted—closer, higher, impossibly deeper—and a tickling thrill danced straight down my spine to my prick. His hands went under my butt, forcing me up, lifting me and settling me even more firmly onto him. I went willingly until my legs were hopelessly hoisted up and over his shoulders, my only point of contact with the bed the braced line of my outstretched arms fingertip to fingertip. It seemed the only thing holding me to this world at all was Kevin thrust up inside my ass.

Hated it. Didn't I? Hated it, me who'd always been so certain to be in charge. Kevin had me where he wanted me. I could barely move, as curled up on myself as I was, caught and held. My cock, now freed from where it had been pressed between us, wept with grief, with excitement, and my pre-cum literally dripped down into my pubic hair. I wanted to jerk myself off but couldn't because my one good arm wouldn't support me. I was hard like a man who hadn't had any sex at all in nearly half a year, who'd spent the summer wanting exactly what he'd gotten here, now. How I wanted this.

"Let's go," I growled, and I pushed onto him as best I could.

"Yes!" Kevin exulted. "I'm close already. Take it. Take it!"

I couldn't keep his face in focus. We moved too fast, the time was too intense. My need to come rose even higher when I knew I wouldn't come until he was finished and could touch me. Even so, perversely, I wanted him to last a lot longer, to let me grab these memories and store them: Kevin pounding into me, his grunts and ragged inhalations, his fingers digging into where he was holding onto my legs, the stiffening of his thighs, his unmistakable, quickening thrusts.

I looked up into the raw slashing of his eyes. "Now!" I urged him. "Come on, come on, now!"

He shoved in and stayed in, his cheeks stiffened, his mouth rounded, and I followed everything, felt it as if in my own body, felt the tightening of balls and the supercharged flaring of the cockhead. And then he jerked and howled. His gravelly voice filled the room, and the heat of his jism flooded the rubber. My cock shuddered, wanting desperately to explode.

"Uhn. Uhn." Four times he thrust as he came, as I held myself open for him.

When he was finished, his head sagged, but then he looked down at me, out of air, with a sheen of sweat on his forehead. Victory sparkled in his eyes. "Oh, yeah."

"My turn," I demanded.

Kevin grabbed my knees more tightly and grinned. "You sure?"

"Bastard!"

He lowered my legs and pulled out at the same time, his cock making a wet, sucking sound as it left me, and then right away he leaned down to take my cock in his mouth.

Two good sucks, that's all he managed to give me before I clamped my hands in his hair and erupted, two, three, four, and one final fifth time.

Right away, post-sex exhaustion swept over me, and I couldn't keep my eyes open. Kevin had taken everything I had to give. I slept.

I OPENED my eyes to the kind of stillness that drifts over the skin and tells you it's the middle of the night. I lay there for minutes, half-awake, half-asleep, drifting in and out of awareness, not entirely sure what was real but still knowing that all was right with the world. Cool air drifted across my face. Overhead a jet sliced through the sky far over Texas.

A sheet covered me. Languidly, I turned my head toward the clock on the nightstand. It glowed three oh two in green numerals. I was in bed in the town of Springrose. My left leg was pressed against something warm and yielding, and with a thump of my heart I realized that it was Kevin's leg. He was the one next to me; his soft breathing was a reward for living.

Sunday. A new day and week that I was starting with Kevin. The world had been remade.

I thought of retrieving Kevin's truck from Avery-the-windshield-man. We'd do that together, just two guys who needed a ride to Abilene when we were so much more than just two guys. I thought of paying for two rooms in this motel when we were only using one, and how that didn't make a lot of sense. I thought of Robbie and the life he might lead, and then of the life he was leading right now. Was he reluctant to go to class? Had anyone ever shoved him to the ground or threatened him? Did he dream of going to a place where he could be honest and live free? Would he ever awaken in the middle of the night the way I just had and know the goodness and rightness of who he was because the man next to him had shown it to him?

I thought of Kevin and how he'd made penetration easy for me, and I was filled with a sense of wonder. I didn't know how to respond to such a gift, or how to act with a man who was that considerate, who cared for my comfort and showed it in the most tangible way possible. What he'd done had really helped. Why hadn't I insisted my sex partners always do that, so I could have been having the kind of sex I'd been wanting all along? But that would have meant finding somebody I trusted the way I trusted Kevin, and I couldn't imagine that happening. Kevin had muscled his way into my life and almost forced me into that trust, but it was real in me right now.

I turned over to see him. The light that had illuminated us when we'd had sex was still on, so my dark-adjusted eyes could make him out clearly.

He was on his back, one arm across his stomach. I couldn't see where the other one was. His legs were spread, his right one crooked at the knee to touch my own. The sheet had slipped down to his waist, so I could appreciate the slow inhalations and exhalations that raised and lowered his chest. What an amazing man. How had he done this to me? Turned me to mush, for sure, with my mask of a strong, defiant, self-protective man who managed his life precisely stripped away.

Kevin was so easy on my eyes, and I let my eyes range down his body, linger on the sheet-covered package between his legs, and then settle on his face again. I could imagine him, years younger, on the football field—not better-looking, just younger, maybe even thinner—or better yet, stripped and taking a communal shower with the rest of the team, maybe stealing glances at and lusting after that offensive lineman he'd said he liked. Kevin stripped, yes. Despite how we'd already made love that night, my cock stirred at the thought, and I wanted him again.

It was harder to imagine him in that first and only year of marriage to his wife Julianne, doing his best in the conjugal bed but without heart, without passion. That's how it must have been, because I knew how he was with a man, with me, and the essential rightness that we each had brought to this bed and to each other. Kevin had been born to make love to a man, the same way I had.

I could imagine him waking up every morning with somebody he cared about, yawning and stretching, then turning over with a smile and kissing that someone awake—that lucky someone. Kevin wouldn't hold back on the smiles, the laughter, the quick concern, the easily given confidence, the love. Kevin was an emotional man, a caring man, and I knew he was looking for somebody to share his life with.

Against the warm cotton of my pillow, my fingers curled. I wanted to touch him so badly, but I didn't let myself. At least I had that much control. I needed to let him sleep.

For all that the sex between us this night had been so different for me—out-of-my-head exciting, but different in a host of other ways too—still it had seemed so natural. Comfortable and valued. Maybe that was always how it was for men with friends who would willingly scratch their itch, but I didn't think so, and Kevin wasn't that kind of friend. Plus he had a knack for making our times together seem extraordinary but easy at the same time.

I hadn't been easy in my mind or my body in years, not since Sean and that one night that had changed everything. My life had been a struggle between my commitment to my profession and the raw needs of my body that I couldn't ignore. What I had needed beyond that—waking up every morning with someone I cared about—I had shoved aside as a failing I could not afford to indulge. I had convinced myself I would never have it and that only weak men wanted it. Not men who lived in the real world, who felt the real, brutal consequences of being gay, and who had been forced into black-and-white choices.

And now… I wasn't so convinced. Was there any middle ground?

Kevin—good, interesting, compelling, wildly attractive—already had a strong hold on me, on my thoughts, on my body, and in the way I was changing because he quietly demanded that I change. What we'd done hadn't just been screwing; it had been different from any night or afternoon I'd spent with a pickup, different even than those times in Houston I'd spent with him. More of me had been present with Kevin from the very beginning, and it seemed that he was coaxing the rest of me to appear: with kisses at his front door and maybe just by being himself.

I couldn't possibly be the one he was looking for. Could I be?

I shivered, though I didn't know whether from fear or excitement or the ground shifting out from under me. Maybe I could. Maybe I wanted to be. In the best of all possible worlds…. But life in Gunning, Texas was far from that best world. How could there be a Kevin and me together?

I forced myself to roll away and stare up at the ceiling instead of at him, trying to empty myself of thought, of feeling, the way it had always been safest for me, tried and true for the long span of my teaching career. But even when I could control my thoughts and deny my feelings, I'd learned the body couldn't be shut out. As I tried to simply lie there, a subtle ache in my ass insisted on calling to me. I ached just enough to know that I'd been fucked—body-knowledge that I'd been stretched and taken there—and it was the best feeling I'd had in a long time. Kevin had done me good. Six months since we'd done it first, and now this time… and when next?

When next?

Rebellion that I had not allowed for sixteen long years blasted past my defenses and rose in me, hard and strong. I wanted the ache, the sex, nights like this, and contented mornings all the time. I thought… I thought I wanted Kevin. I did. Why could some men have this when I couldn't? Why could the straights have the intimacy, the comfort, the easy companionship that Kevin offered me when I had to turn away from it? Why did they reach for love and find it, when I'd walked down a long, difficult road feeling myself forced to deny it?

"Why can't I have it?" I whispered.

After a while my full bladder forced me up and into the bathroom. I could tell from the wet washcloth and the tied-off condom in the wastebasket that Kevin had been there before me, cleaning himself from the realities of our kind of lovemaking, and yet the light had been left on. After I pissed and cleaned myself, my hand hovered over the light switch. It was the middle of the night and we should be sleeping. But maybe Kevin had kept it on for the same reason I did; I wanted to be able to see him.

When I got back to the bed, Kevin had turned onto his side. I tried not to jostle the mattress as I got in beside him again. The bed wasn't overly large for two men and the use we had made of it. I settled in under the sheet and turned my head toward him, letting the sight of him fill me up across the few inches that separated us. I didn't care about sleep. I wanted to take this all in because I feared this night, this feeling, this man might go sliding away, sucked into that other world I usually lived in. Here, now, everything was different. Hope lived here, and Kevin, sleeping, was beautiful.

The sight of him soothed me, and though I blinked to keep myself awake, eventually I couldn't keep my eyes open. I feel asleep to the sound of him breathing and the knowledge that, regardless of what else happened in my life, this night was real. My dreams were good.

I didn't know how long I'd slept, but it felt like a long time when I woke up again. It was still night, though. The bed dipped and the sheet lifted behind me as Kevin stirred. I'd rolled away from him during the hours, onto my right side. A moment later his arm was around my waist and his knee pushed within the bend of mine. The point of his chin brushed my back. “Hey,” he said, and then he cleared his throat and said it again, louder, with his voice not as husky. “Hey, do you mind this?”

To prove I didn’t, I rested my left arm over his and squeezed. Then I settled with my fingers spread over his tendons, his knuckles, the strength of his hand that matched my own. He took in a small, just-heard breath and let it out slowly, and the sound of the effect I had on him about did me in: my own private swell of good feeling crashed over me, and there where he couldn’t see me, I smiled. He edged forward until the rest of him was pressed against me, I wriggled back to help, and it was perfect. I relaxed on my side against the pillow and let him hold me.

“You must be feeling okay after what we just did,” he said. “You’re not hurting, are you?”

Not unless hurting meant everything was better.

His flaccid cock pushed against my ass. We’d never touched like this without both of us wanting sex. As close as we’d been during sex, the way we were now seemed… more. Closer. We were pressed against one another without the driving urgency, just because we wanted to be. Yes, I wanted this too.

Don’t think about how impossible it will be to continue this, and how the wide world waits. Just feel.

“Did you think I’d break?” I asked lightly, drumming my fingers once against his knuckles.

“No. That’s one of the things I like about being with a man.”

I gripped his hand hard, then settled my fingers between his. “Me too.”

We were quiet for a while. I felt myself sinking not into sleep again but into the pillow, the mattress, the silence, and him, into the wonder of being with him like this. I wanted to turn over and see him again, to touch his face and let him touch mine, but this was good too, good enough to keep me where I was.

But eventually he moved. Kevin untangled his hand from under mine and rested it instead on the point of my left shoulder. I couldn’t help but tense. Kevin traced the length of my damaged arm, his fingers dancing against my scars, ending by resting lightly on my wrist.

“Does your arm hurt all the time?” he asked softly.

Nobody else asked me questions about it, but I should have known that Kevin would. I hid my arm, and I compensated for it, and I tried to forget it. For a long time it had made me feel like less of a man.

I swallowed against my instinct to dissemble. He deserved an answer. “No. Well, sometimes.”

“You don’t have much strength in this arm. Or mobility.”

“I have enough. I manage okay.”

“Yes, you do. Most folks wouldn’t even notice. I didn’t, for a while. It’s amazing you can play golf with it.”

He didn’t say anything more, for once not tapping against my ineffectual boundaries. As if to prove that there was some strength in me and that arm, I turned my hand over to grasp his and roughly pulled him back to where the two of us been before, with him embracing me from behind.

“You know how I wasn’t ready when you came over?” he asked right away. “I wasn’t leading you on, being dressed like that.”

I was happy to talk about something else. “No?” Kevin knew how he’d looked.

He laughed softly. “Well, not much. But I had a good excuse. I was just getting ready to do some yard work when Channing and her boyfriend drove up and surprised me. She wanted to introduce me to JJ, because I think she’s getting serious. Isn’t that ridiculous, at her age? But I sat and had a daddy-talk with them, and then when they left, I hopped outside and took care of the yard.”

I’d walked up to Kevin’s front door a lifetime ago. Even so, my stomach clenched just a little at the timing. If they’d been later, if I’d been earlier…. “Kids. They don’t think their parents have any lives of their own.”

“Or teachers too, right?”

“Or teachers. You should tell her to call before she drops in.”

"I should, yeah. But I'm rebuilding a relationship with her, and I don't want to put any barriers between us. She can drop in on me any time, that's what I've told her. It's nice that she wants to see her old man."

"Old man? Were you forty when you fathered her?"

"I was twenty. And desperately trying to pretend I was straight."

I bumped back against him. "You're not."

"Thank heaven for that. I finally figured I had to succumb to the inevitable."

The air conditioner clicked on, sounding like the ocean's roar. There were a million questions hiding under the waves, so much I wanted to know about him.

"Your voice," I said. "Did something…." I stopped. I couldn't ask him what I wouldn't answer myself. Wanting to know about him didn't extend to telling him everything about me.

"I sound like I've swallowed a frog, don't I?" he said lightly.

"Not all the time. Sometimes you sound like a cicada." Even so, his words were easy to listen to.

"That's a new one. Nobody's ever called me an insect before, at least not to my face."

"Still not to your face," I said, tugging at his arm.

"Turn around and say it, then."

I did, and our hands found each other again in the space between us. Kevin and his capable hands. "Cicada," I teased.

"Professor," he shot right back.

"I don't mind that." I liked that, but not as much as I liked Kevin.

"I was tackled during practice with an arm across my throat. I thought I'd never breathe again. When I finally was able to talk a week later, this is what I sounded like."

"It's not bad," I told him. "It's distinctive."

"At least I can talk at all. It could have been a lot worse. A gay man without a voice, that would have been a disaster. In case you haven't noticed, in the right circumstances I can talk a lot."

"Not me."

"You listen a lot, don't you? But when you have something to say, people listen to you. They know what you have to say is worth saying."

"Maybe."

"No, it's true, I've seen it. You've earned a lot of respect at the school."

"You don't have much of a data pool."

"If Channing says it, then it's so. And Danielle. You've got a fan club."

"You're hallucinating."

He squeezed my hand. "I've never been so lucid in my life."

I didn't know what to say to that, and so I said nothing at all. I lay there and looked at him, and I felt his eyes on me too. Despite the dark, he saw me.

"Already I'm thinking about next weekend," he said softly. "Do you want to do this again?"

Yes, I really did. "Okay."

He gave a little laugh. "That's great. Come over to my house, spend the weekend with me? A little music, a little wine, my nice king-sized bed, way bigger than this thing."

"You already know the answer to that one."

"You can't blame a man for trying. So, somewhere else?"

The answer popped up as if I'd been planning it for weeks. "Fredericksburg. Maybe three hours, three and a half hours from your place. It's a tourist town."

"I know it."

"I bet we could find some cabins outside town in the hill country. They might be private enough."

"I know you need your privacy." He touched my wrist with his fingertips. "Should I find us something then? Or do you want to do it?"

The balance of our relationship teetered on the edge of realigning—Kevin was the one who called, who drove, who pushed, who topped. *Either do it or walk away,* I thought, *the way you already did once in Houston.* Walk away? Pass up the best thing, the best person that'd ever happened to me? "All right," I said. "I'll make the reservations."

Next weekend again with Kevin, great sex, a chance to get away from school… getting to know him better. I smiled.

"Hey," Kevin said, "that's really great."

"What?"

Kevin's fingers traced my lips, tickling with a light touch. "Right here…." He poked my mouth at the left corner. "And right here…." He poked me at the right corner too. "Oh, the rarest vintage, Tom Smith smiling at me. I think I want to bottle your smile and take it home with me."

"Imbecile," I said most sincerely, but I was chuckling as I said it.

"And he's got a fine vocabulary too." Kevin was smiling twice as widely as I was.

"Moron." I felt about twelve years old, but it was such a good feeling. Light.

"I love it when you call me names."

"I don't think I've ever called you names, but I've got plenty. I'm a college graduate, you know." I grabbed him around his waist.

"Amazing. Give me some more." He bucked against the sheet and inched closer. His skin against my fingers made the base of my spine tingle.

"Nincompoop. Idiot. Uh…."

"Jerk?"

"Not quite the same. Fool," I said, maybe a little fondly.

"Tomfool?" His amusement ground to a sudden stop. "Oh, yes," he whispered, and then he breathed against my lips. "I'm a Tomfool. I'm a fool for Tom, absolutely."

He kissed me, a quiet, full pressing of his mouth against mine. I could hardly let myself believe it was really happening, but it was.

I pulled away before we were finished because suddenly, maybe irrationally, I had to know. “What’s your middle name?”

“Nothing interesting like yours. Mine’s boring. Robert.”

Boring? Anything but. Kevin Robert Bannerman.

FREDERICKSBURG was a Saturday morning hike up Enchanted Rock after a long, difficult week, with both of us triumphant when we reached the top, grinning at each other like loons. Fredericksburg was good German food for lunch in town, and our easy conversation about books we’d read and shows we’d seen, and what we really thought of Obama’s chances in the upcoming election. It was a simple, effortless afternoon out on the deck with our feet up and beers in our hands, watching the birds in the sky and a solitary deer that came to greet us as I felt my stress and worry over the play recede because I was there with Kevin. It was the Jacuzzi inside the cabin filled with hot water and both of us laughing as we slid against each other, the incredible feeling of Kevin slick in my arms, the warm taste of him, reaching for him and finding him reaching for me.

Fredericksburg was steaks on the grill with sweet, sweet corn. It was the look on Kevin’s face when I pulled out my laptop after dinner inside, set a CD to playing, and stood there with my arms extended. “Dance with me?” I’d racked my brain trying to find a way to say thank you for the special care he’d given me the weekend before, and this was the best I’d been able to come up with.

What I’d guessed from the nights in Houston was right: Kevin loved to dance. What I’d remembered from Houston was confirmed: We danced together pretty well. We slow-danced through the album, laughing together when the music turned up-tempo and we refused to part in order to do it justice, but then I’d carefully picked moody, evocative ballads when I’d put the music together.

“This was the best idea,” Kevin whispered in my ear.

We finally fell onto the bed to the sound of k.d. lang singing “Crying” in a duet with Roy Orbison, but we’d already made love four times that day—after waking in the morning, right before lunch, twice in the Jacuzzi—and so contented ourselves with touching and kissing until the baseball game came on. I was almost sorry when it did.

"Wait a minute," Kevin said, and he slid out of bed to pad over to a backpack he'd brought into the cabin the night before. He pulled out two brand-new baseball caps and tossed the Boston Red Sox one to me before he got back on the mattress. "This one's for you," he said as he settled a Dodgers cap on his head. "I thought we should do honor to the game. You're a Boston fan, right?"

I put it on and adjusted the back to fit, pleased past what I should have been that he'd thought to do this. "How'd you know?"

"You were talking about it at the bar in Springrose, remember?"

I did remember, but it'd been when he was on the phone with State Farm. He must have been listening to me talk with the other men there.

We watched the sixth game of the playoff series between the Red Sox and the Tampa Bay Rays propped up, eating popcorn, and with Kevin's arm around my shoulders.

As we left on Sunday afternoon, I leaned back against the headrest in Kevin's Silverado, and I remembered what he'd said the night before. After the fifth time we made love.

"Let's do this again," Kevin whispered as we lay in bed facing one another, forehead to forehead. "Again and again. Every weekend."

Oh, God, yes. If I could just keep this time with him set off from everything else and stop myself from dwelling on the impossibility of it being anything other than what it was, then again and again, all the time. The days in the week when I was Mr. Smith, teacher, had nothing to do with who I could be—who I was—with Kevin.

"Come over to my house?" he asked as he turned onto the highway. We were three hours from home. "Wine, music, no women, a big bed? Probably more baseball we can watch together."

I grabbed the overhead strap as alarm shot through me to think of the two paths of my life intersecting. Even if the picture Kevin painted of how it would be at his house—just like this past weekend in the luxury cabin—was tempting beyond belief, I still had to say no. I could go just so far… and no further.

So instead, the next Saturday we finally made it to Abilene. We put the *Privacy* sign on the door of one of the rooms we'd paid for, called for room service when we were hungry, and stayed in bed to use as many condoms as we could. Kevin licked me from head to toe and back again, and I quivered for hours. We squeezed the lube flat and started on a second tube. I couldn't get enough of him.

When we drove away that time, again in Kevin's truck, I looked over at him. His eyes were intent on the road. I thought: my lover. My weekend lover. He was.

Everything had changed except the voice that told me none of this could happen in the real world.

CHAPTER 5
THOSE WHO WANDER

THE night before Kevin left for a conference in Phoenix, we talked for almost an hour on the phone. After three weekends in a row out together—getting to know that he was a fan of John Barrowman in *Torchwood* but didn't think much of *Doctor Who*, that he had a passable singing voice, that he'd tried to learn French and couldn't, that he took his coffee black, and hundreds of other things that made him distinctively who he was—we wouldn't be seeing each other for a while. He'd be in Arizona visiting his cousin this coming weekend before attending a genuine bankers' conference the next week. I'd miss him, though I didn't tell him that. Kevin and I didn't say things like that to each other. At the same time, it was almost a relief to have some time off. I hardly felt familiar to myself anymore, and I needed the time to take a breath and think.

Even though it was late once we said good night, past Leno and time for sleep, I couldn't be still. I walked around the house looking for something to release the nervous energy Kevin had roused in me and ended up spending an hour going through some of the junk overflowing my garage. I managed to go through just three of the boxes filled with old paperwork from years before; I dumped all of it in my big trashcan. After that I was able to sleep, and I woke up the next morning to the sound of Kevin's voice—his hoarse, damaged, sincere voice—ringing in my ear. I didn't know what he'd been saying in my dreams, but he'd been there for sure.

As I drove to school that Thursday morning, the day before Halloween, I felt strangely bereft. *A few fucks and Tom's an easy mark,* I thought to myself. I was a pushover for a little attention. I was so lonely I'd be happy with just about anybody. I was emotionally stunted.

There were kernels of truth in all those thoughts, but I pushed them aside. Besides, Kevin wasn't just anybody.

Like I did a few times a week, I made sure to walk by Robbie's locker that morning before first bell. Steven was there, as he was sometimes, wearing not his Gunning High School maroon baseball cap but the flat cloth hat that distinguished Tom Collins on stage. He and Robbie seemed to be deep in a serious conversation. Despite what seemed to me to be Robbie's obvious crush on Steven, they'd developed a friendship that I was pleased to see. There was no sign of kids gathered to pray over the misbegotten faggot, and I didn't think the boys noticed me. I walked on to let them be, but a voice called, "Mr. Smith! Wait up."

I turned to find that Steven had come up behind me. Like most star athletes, he was physically mature beyond his years, almost as tall as I was at over six feet and with the walk and shoulder set of a grown man. It would be a few years before he filled out, though. But he was a good-looking kid with brown hair that he was wearing short for the play, to serve as a contrast to Angel.

"Have you seen the paper, sir?" he asked anxiously. "Rob has a copy. Come on back to his locker, please."

There was time before classes started, but more importantly I felt Steven's urgency as he literally pulled me back the way I'd already come by tugging on my sleeve. I saw the glint of withheld tears in Robbie's eyes as we got close.

"What's the matter?"

Steven took the newspaper that had been clenched in Robbie's hands and handed it over. "Here. It's awful."

The *Gunning Gazette's* Thursday edition was turned to page seven, where the editorials and the letters to the editor were usually printed. There were two letters that day, and as I scanned the headings, my mouth twisted in distaste. I looked back up at the boys. "They're against the play?"

"Go ahead," Robbie said, though he put his fist up to his mouth. I didn't know if it was to cover up fear or anger or what. He looked even paler than usual. "Read them. We'll wait."

"WHERE ARE THE VALUES IN PLAY AT GHS?" was the headline for the first letter.

Dear Editor,

Its been years since one of my kids was up at the High School but I'm worryed that the School will be putting on Rent in December. Who got such a bee in their bonnet? Rent might be good for the Crowd that goes to New York and sees the latest nonsense on Broadway but there's no Place for it here in Gunning. We don't want Drugs here we don't want the Homosexuals here & we want to raise kids with good respect for their parents. Its hard enough in this day and age to raise Boys that will be a credit to their Fathers without High Schools pointing out all the wrong things & turning them into sissys. Why can't we put on a different play that will uplift our Spirits? Whose the idiot on the School Board who thought a play about homos in high heels and dresses was all right for Gunning? They sure won't get my vote next time if thats the sorts of things they do at the Board Meetings. Nobody has any sense of shame any more. When I was a student the School stood for decency & I was proud to graduate. Now I'm shamed of that School. What's happened to the folks up there? What are they thinking?

Yours,

Lynda Whitman

If that had been it, I could have dismissed the letter. One opinion from an older woman, probably set in her ways, who maybe hadn't learned as much from her English teachers when she'd been at school as she should have. But I couldn't ignore the second letter.

"BOYCOTT PLAY AT GUNNING HIGH SCHOOL" it started.

> Dear Editor:
>
> As an elder of the First Baptist Church of Gunning, I feel it necessary to alert the citizens of Gunning to the forthcoming production of Rent at the Gunning High School. Anyone familiar with the play knows it is totally unsuitable for a high school presentation, as it focuses on the glorification of the drug culture. Even worse, a play that makes no moral judgment on the evils of homosexuality is not suitable for impressionable teenage minds. At a time when it is ever more imperative to convey biblical teachings to our youngsters, the choice of Rent is more than unfortunate, it is counter to everything that our community stands for.
>
> If Hiram Watts, principal of GHS, and George Keating, director of the show, don't withdraw the production, then I sadly but boldly call for all citizens to withdraw their support from the play. Show your Christian values and boycott Rent at Gunning High School.
>
> Yours most sincerely,
>
> William Tate,
>
> Elder, First Baptist Church of Gunning

My three-weekend bubble burst almost audibly in my head. To my shame, I didn't think of the kids or the good the play might do or George's probable distress: I thought of myself.

I didn't want the spotlight like Robbie and Steven did. I was content to labor backstage in anonymity. I had wrapped anonymity around me for years, and even my name helped me blend into the background: Mr. Nothing-Special Tom Smith. But letters like these two turned harsh, exposing lights on everybody involved in the play, and I couldn't afford that. I had a lot more to protect now than I'd had at the start of the school term. I had Kevin now. Would George's bulk be big enough for the two of us to hide behind? If people began looking at me, would they find Kevin? My stomach clenched into the granddaddy of all sickening knots.

Kevin and I had planned to go hiking at San Angelo State Park the next weekend, so there were nine more days until I saw him again. I deserved to see him, damnit. Because I wanted to go hiking for a day, because a man deserved a weekend off after working sixty hours a week on school and the play, because I wanted to spend time with my friend. Because Kevin had reawakened something in me that had been slumbering, and I needed to make love with him. Or maybe this startling need I had for him was brand new, and he'd created it all himself.

Christ. Why had I ever told George I'd help him out? Without *Rent* going on, I wouldn't have to be worrying about anything except where Kevin and I would meet next. Now…

I bit my lip and then released it immediately; the kids needed to see that the adults leading them were resolute. Besides, I was jumping the gun. If we were luckier than we deserved to be, Elder Tate would be called out of town on important church business and forget all about us. There might be no reason for my fears, and so I set about doing my job. All the years of hiding had given me plenty of experience in feeling one way and pretending that I felt another. I was probably the best actor in the school.

"Do you know either of these people?" I asked, lifting the paper into the space between the three of us.

"Nope," Steven said, and Robbie shook his head.

"I don't either. Gunning has a lot of people in it, doesn't it? Five, six thousand, something like that."

I watched as what I was implying sank in. The boys were standing side by side, close together, as if giving each other support. Steven had on jeans and a Dallas Cowboys T-shirt, but Robbie stood out by what he was wearing, as he did in so many other ways. He had on brown pants with thin black stripes, and a black muscle shirt that barely conformed to the school's dress regulations.

"Here are just two opinions," I said. "I think it's important that we not make more of this than it really is."

"But he's calling for a boycott, Mr. Smith," Steven ventured.

"That's right," I said as I folded the paper and tucked it under my bad arm. "Did you really think that a play like *Rent* wouldn't get some sort of attention in our town?"

Robbie had been looking truly distressed, but now he pushed his black hair away from his eyes and frowned. "But it won the Tony Award."

"That doesn't mean anything in Gunning," I said gently. "Broadway might be something you follow, but to most people here it's far away, and maybe an example of how they don't want to live. You've got to understand how others are thinking."

Steven snorted and swept his hat off his head. "Oh, yeah, sure, I understand. I understand that they live with their heads in the sand, and they don't want to give anything new and different a chance. Trying new stuff is what life's all about. They're just a couple of homophobic bigots!"

"Name-calling never solved a single problem in this world," I said as mildly as I could.

I'd been through my own period of wanting to call names, during the time when my family had turned their backs on me just when I had needed them most. If my brother Grant hadn't helped the way he had—though we'd never talked about what was most important—I had sometimes thought I would have put a gun to my head. But what would it have gained me to scream at the people who were afraid of the differences I represented? I had pushed the angry words down so deeply that they'd never, ever emerged, not once in all these years. They were still there though, captured.

"The people who might agree with these letter-writers are your neighbors," I said, "your friends, and the people you live with every day in Gunning."

"Not my family," Robbie said.

They sure had been mine. It'd been years before my father had talked to me again. For half a second, I wondered about Kevin's family. "Maybe not, but—"

Steven interrupted me. "What should we do?"

"What do you want to do?"

He scowled and scuffed a shoe against the institutional tile on the floor. "I want to shove the paper down their throats."

"Now tell me something realistic, because I don't think you really want to choke a little old lady, do you? Besides the fact that you'd be arrested and go to jail for it."

"I want to—"

"Mr. Smith," Robbie butted in as if Steven weren't talking, "you don't think that Mr. Keating will cancel the play because of this, do you?" His voice was distressed-high, but it seemed even higher because of the contrast to Steven's determined rumble.

"Only Mr. Keating can speak for himself, but I certainly don't think you need to worry about that. Just for a couple of letters? So tell me, how do you realistically want to respond to this?"

"Keep going," Robbie said right away.

Steven gave him a disgusted look. "Well, yeah, Rob, sure. He means something else."

"I want to hear whatever you want to tell me."

"I want to write back," Steven said. "I could tell them to go to hell."

Robbie shoved him in the chest. Steven didn't even blink as he was forced back a step. "That wouldn't help, numb nuts. Didn't you hear what Mr. Smith said?"

"Okay, okay. So I get sincere and tell them we're, like, working hard, and it's a play with a good message, that sort of thing. Just because somebody's gay or a druggie or spreads her legs too easy doesn't mean there can't be a play about them, you know?"

"Admirable sentiments, Steven," I said. "Though maybe it would be wise to wait until next week and see if there's any response to these letters, don't you think? And consult with Mr. Keating. Remember, just two in the whole town."

While we'd been talking the hallway had cleared out, and now the first bell rang. The boys grabbed their backpacks, and Robbie slammed his locker shut, but I told them, "Come with me to my classroom so I can write you excuse slips for being tardy."

As they trailed along behind me, I heard Steven say quietly, "Don't listen to that old lady. You aren't a sissy."

ON THE night before I was supposed to meet Kevin in the parking lot of the San Angelo State Park, I sat in my kitchen with my cell phone in front of me on the table. I needed to pick up that phone, dial him, and tell him I couldn't make it. The past three issues of the bi-weekly *Gazette* had each printed letters against the play, with only one solitary supporter. The cast and crew were understandably upset and restless. A reporter from the paper had left a message at the school that she wanted to interview George, but George hadn't answered her yet.

Principal Watts hadn't said a word to us; I suspected he was waiting to see if the school board stepped in. Teachers stopped me in the hall, wanting to talk about the play and asking whether I thought it should be staged. Even a former student who was working at Safeway had asked me about it the night before in the produce section. He'd specifically wanted to know if there was going to be same-sex kissing onstage. At least he'd had the courage to put the question into words. Everybody else wanted to ask the same thing but had gone at it sideways, and I'd been able to slip away from answering.

I was trying to look at the situation rationally, not go overboard, and trying to take the advice that I was giving to the kids. But I'd developed a lot of knee-jerk, self-protective habits since that Saturday night long ago—*my face raised to the night sky, the sound of an engine revving, "Faggot!"*—and they told me to make this call to Kenneton and cancel.

I hadn't seen Kevin in two solid weeks, since we had kissed goodbye in his garage after coming back from our sex-drenched weekend in Abilene. I'd thought I wouldn't be able to get it up for days after that, but the next night in my own bed all I'd had to do was think of him licking wetly at my ear, re-imagine the slippery sounds of our bodies moving against each other, remember the force and salty taste of his come flooding my mouth, and I'd reached for my aching cock.

I half-groaned, half-laughed right there in the company of my microwave and my toaster. How had I ever managed to go without sex for months at a time? I couldn't imagine going back to that self-imposed celibacy.

I'd been shocked at how much I'd missed Kevin the past weekend. Maybe I didn't have the body of a twenty-year-old anymore, but I wanted Kevin as much as I had wanted Sean back in college: night after night, quickies between classes, during study sessions, and even after wild college parties when we'd been drunk out of our minds.

What was I going to do? I was flat-out spooked by the letters to the editor and all the talk they'd stirred up, and the safest thing to do was to go back to my simple, hidden life. The only problem was that I didn't want to.

Sitting staring at my phone wouldn't solve anything. I got up and wandered through the living room, ending up over by the sliding glass door to the patio. I pushed the curtain aside and looked out into the night, but I couldn't see much. It was drizzling and overcast, and the lights behind me reflected against the glass so that it was my own image that stared back at me. Sandy hair growing a little too long, prominent, narrow nose that only a mother could love, thin lips that didn't smile enough. Eyes that I knew didn't look straight at people the way they used to.

Somehow I'd gone from my solitary life to wanting Kevin all the time. He'd found my "ON" switch, flipped it with just a touch, a kiss, a few words—"Spend the night with me, please"—and kept it turned on now for weeks. I'd jerked off like a teenager the weekend before when Kevin had been out of town, feeling as if I were being deprived of something that was my right. But even more than the sex, I'd missed the sudden, vivid color he'd brought to my days.

I reached out and touched the glass with my fingertips, drifting them across my lips. It made no sense, my feelings about Kevin. I didn't love him. How could I love him? Gay men like me didn't traffic in the softer feelings.

But I could love him. I could.

"You really like this, don't you?" George asked as we went out to the parking lot late one Wednesday night.

"What do you mean?"

"Directing, working with the kids for the play." He shrugged as he pulled open his car door and threw his briefcase on the front seat. "Lately you've been a lot... a lot happier. I can really see a difference in you. You should do this with me every year."

The image of a man in the glass shook his head. No, George, it isn't my delight in working on your misguided, dangerous pet project. You see, I'm different—happier? definitely happier—because of this guy I picked up in a gay bar, who has this way about him of listening to what I say, who understands my life, who's got this gravelly voice that I still want to listen to all the time, whose touch makes me hungry-crazy for more, who's handsome and intelligent and is the best company I've ever had. Ever. He's brave, too, trying to make changes in his life that I can only dream about—am I dreaming about those changes? And he wants me.

"Wants me," I whispered against the window. Out of all that was most improbable in the world, he did. This thing between us: it was a two-way street.

But I wasn't just happier. I was scared now too. I was worried about the controversy over *Rent*. Where would it lead? Straight to the assistant director, who had more knowledge of what the play was about than anybody supposed?

I stood mired in my indecision for a long time, long enough for the drizzle to end and then start again, and for the moon to peep out from behind the clouds and then disappear. I was in the middle of an impossible situation, propelled there by my own wants, my own decisions, and I couldn't blame anybody else. Thinking for years that I'd had myself under control: what a joke. All it took was the first man to come along and really test me, and my control disappeared.

Well, maybe not the first man. I'd danced with plenty of others, had sex with them. But that first breakfast with Kevin at the IHOP in Houston, that had done me in good. I remembered how he'd looked eating pancakes and sipping coffee as clearly as if it had happened yesterday, and as if every second of that meal were somehow meaningful.

How did I expect this to end? Happy ever after wasn't in the cards. Happy for a year wasn't in the cards. I knew that. *Hard reality, Tom Smith, face it.*

Hard reality was wanting to see Kevin this weekend even when I knew I shouldn't.

I'd told the kids to have faith. I had to try to have the same.

HIKING in west Texas wasn't anything like walking through a lush, green, picture-postcard park. San Angelo was on the edge of the arid, almost-desert Trans-Pecos region where rain was a stranger, the dirt was a hard-packed yellow-brown that resembled puke, and the flat land could fall into a cutting, dangerous gully at any time. What vegetation managed to live under the haughty sun didn't dare lift its head very high; the trees and timid bushes pulled in on themselves. Green wasn't the green of golf courses or rose gardens here. It was an almost-green, an off-color green with lots of brown and even a hint of blue to it that reflected the cloudless skies. And it was still hot here. Even in early November, hiking out into the backcountry of the park brought out sweat on my forehead and across my shoulders.

Kevin and I walked along the Horny Toad Trail to start because he'd insisted. I'd protested that it was out of our way, he'd asked me where was my sense of adventure and fun, I'd told him he was acting like one of my students, and he'd raised his eyebrows and said that no student had better think about me the way he thought about me or he'd knock them down with his good left hook. Or right jab. Or maybe a two-by-four.

"Oh, shut up," I'd said, but I was smiling.

We'd met at the park at nine that morning, and it had felt awkward and just not-right to shake hands instead of embrace. I suddenly and deeply resented the fact that I couldn't act naturally with Kevin. I wanted to kiss him, and from the look on his face, he wanted to kiss me. Maybe in Massachusetts I could have, or in the gay neighborhoods of some big cities, but for sure not in west Texas. It would be a cold day in hell before Texas joined any other states in tolerating the public expression of affection between men, and it'd be the end of the universe as I knew it before I'd ever be able to marry….

I shut that thought down and released Kevin's hand.

After putting on hiking boots and suntan lotion—even with the long sleeves I was wearing, I needed it with my fair skin—we set out at an easy pace. One of the park's simple cabins was reserved for us for the night, and we had nothing to do and nothing to prove between now and then. We'd walk as far as we wanted to and then turn around and go back, and that was it. My worries about the Sunday edition of the *Gazette* that would be waiting for me when I got home faded with every step. This was the alternate version of the real world, at least on Saturday it was, my time-with-Kevin that stood apart from everything else. I'd been insane to consider canceling. What had I been thinking? Here, with Kevin, I could drop the act and just be myself.

We encountered more than a few people the first hour on the Horny Toad trail, but when we took the turnoff by the sign that said *Desert Loop Trail, Primitive Camping, No Fires,* we left the other hikers behind. For a solid hour we passed no one and no one passed us, and that was fine with me. The farther away from the world and the sudden complications of my life in it, the better.

"Hey," Kevin called from behind me, "wait up."

I stopped by a prickly pear cactus, and he came up with long strides. There was a line of sweat down one side of his face, but that didn't suppress the little jump my body gave at the sight of him. He looked good enough to eat in his lace-up boots, shorts, and gray T-shirt that said *Not All Those Who Wander Are Lost*. "I thought you said you weren't in good shape," he protested.

"I'm not. Sorry, I guess I was thinking about getting away, and—"

"And off you went racing, leaving me in the dust. Come on, let's walk together."

Most of our hike so far had been single-file because of the trail, but here it wandered across a wide, flat expanse that was mainly sagebrush and cactus, and side-by-side was possible. I took a swig from my Ozarka water bottle, Kevin sipped from his Camelbak, and off we went.

"So, professor," Kevin said, "you've been quiet. What's on your mind?"

I tucked the bottle back in my pocket. "Oh, the play. I'm worried about this boycott."

"If all the proposed boycotts actually happened, the whole world would have come to a screaming halt years ago. Don't let it get you down."

"It's not me. I don't care. I never wanted this play to begin with. It's the kids."

He looked at me almost quizzically, as if he were trying to figure me out. But he knew me, didn't he? "It's always about the kids with you, isn't it?"

"What? No, it isn't."

"I think it is. All kids and no Tom."

"They deserve some consideration, don't you think? This last round of letters, some of the kids were really upset and crying."

"Was Channing?"

I was sorry that I'd mentioned it, but I wouldn't lie to him about his daughter. "Yeah, she was. Sorry."

Kevin hitched up the straps of his Camelbak, settling it higher on his shoulders. "She'll get over it. Time for her to grow up and face the real world. Not everybody will like what she wants to do or what she believes in."

"That's a hard approach to take, coming from her father."

"I want her to be tough. The world hasn't exactly been easy on you and me, has it? Channing's almost old enough to be on her own. It's about time she learned nothing's going to be handed to her, and that the good guys don't finish first."

"That's for sure. If they did…." I kicked a rock out of my way and watched it roll through the sandy dirt. "If they did, you'd be president of some big, multinational bank somewhere."

He laughed softly. "Definitely, that's me. I've been waiting for the call, considering how I like banking so much. But if life were fair, not only would I be some bigwig interviewed by CNN, you'd be president of Harvard."

I snorted out a laugh despite myself. "Idiot."

"You sure do like to call me names. I'm smart enough to know a man who'd be perfect as a university president when I meet him."

"A few advanced degrees might help. Experience, knowledge, knowing the right people."

"I bet you wouldn't like all the schmoozing that a job like that involves, would you? Back-clapping and all that stuff."

I shuddered, exaggerating it. "Especially since I'm such a social person and love crowds."

"So, no university presidenting for you."

"Presidenting? That's not even a word."

"So give me an F. Maybe you'd be a best-selling author of history biographies, like that guy who wrote the book about John Adams. What's his name?"

"David McCullough, and you're nuts."

"Tsk, tsk, tsk. Sticks and stones may break my bones. I bet you've read that book."

"I have, but I bet you have too."

"Guilty as charged. But tell me what you think. If the good guys finished first, what would you be doing? Assuming of course that you consider yourself a good guy."

I stopped to wipe more sweat from my face with my arm. Global warming was alive and well in Texas. If the weather kept up like this, the public pools would be open for swimming at Thanksgiving. "You ask annoying questions, has anybody ever told you that?" I said when we started walking again.

"Everybody. Constantly. But I usually get my answer, and questions are a great way to get to know somebody. So, tell me. What would you be doing?"

I took my time and thought about it, enjoying the fact that Kevin had asked. "I think I wouldn't change," I said finally. "I'd be doing exactly what I'm doing now."

"You do love teaching. But you'd change one thing, right? You'd be able to be honest about yourself."

Sure, while we were talking fantasy, why not? "And what would you be doing?"

He answered right away. "That's easy. I'd be asking you to please come over to my house this weekend."

"Kevin…."

"I can promise you my nice king-sized bed, where I'm way too lonely, and the best possible company. At least, I'm assuming you think I'm the best—"

Not one but three lizards went skittering across the path and paused right in front of us, going into the defensive *if I don't move you won't be able to see me* freeze that made no sense unless you were a dumb animal. I grabbed Kevin's arm to stop him and he pulled up short, skipping a little to keep his balance and finishing up pressed against me, surely not by accident.

He stayed there, looking into my eyes as I looked into his.

"What do you say?" Kevin whispered.

I swallowed against the dry air. I'd told him about the letters to the editor over the phone the past week. Surely he understood what that meant for the two of us. "I…."

"Dear professor, please come to my house."

"I… I don't think so."

Despite the disappointment that appeared instantly in those eyes that matched the sky, Kevin erased the distance between us and pressed his lips to mine. I closed my eyes and gave him that kiss, because even though I was desperately grateful for what we had—these meager hours together away from it all—in the best of all possible worlds I'd be knocking on his door every day. Did he understand that? I tried to tell him so without words.

He pulled away slowly so that our mouths clung to each other for a second or two, and when we parted, I daringly kissed him again. Quickly, but I wanted him to know that I liked his kisses too.

Kevin flicked his thumb against my cheek and went on as if we hadn't done anything to interrupt our conversation. "I'd cook you breakfast on Sunday morning. Scrambled eggs with cheese, bacon, cinnamon buns from Sara Lee…."

The lizards were long gone. I resettled my Red Sox baseball cap and started walking again. "What do you want to do, smother me with cholesterol?"

He caught up with me easily. "I'll serve it to you in bed. And afterward, we can make slow, sweet love. Or hot, quick love, whichever fires your jets. I'll treat you good."

I knew he would. "Kevin…. You know I can't."

"No, I don't. I know you won't. There's a difference."

A desert willow bush, big by the standards of the park, had grown in the middle of the hardly-there path we were following. I turned to go around the left side of it, but Kevin roughly grabbed my wrist and pulled me to the other side with him instead.

Annoyed, I yanked away from him. "Damn it—"

Wordlessly, he turned and pointed. On the side of the path where I'd wanted to walk was a coiled rattlesnake, just raising up in warning, and now rattling in a way nobody ever forgot. Even though I'd killed my share of rattlers when I'd been growing up on the ranch, I'd just as soon avoid them when I could.

"Uh, thanks," I said.

"Sure."

We didn't talk after that for a while. I was embarrassed, and maybe Kevin was pissed at me, I didn't know. I sure couldn't blame him if he was. After five minutes of silence I dropped back to where he was walking behind me. "This wouldn't be the best day if that rattler had buried his fangs in my leg."

Kevin cocked an eye at me. "The best day, huh?"

"Yeah." What could compete with the time I spent with Kevin? Drinking beer in my yard? Finishing a book and not having anyone to talk to about it? Planning another desperate trip to Houston?

"Me too," he said.

"Right. Beats old *Star Trek* reruns."

"I like *Star Trek.* What's your favorite episode?"

And as simply as that we were back together again.

The rest of the morning was great, a lot like the relaxing, natural weekend we'd spent in Fredericksburg. The sun got as high in the sky as it was going to get, and then it began its long slide down to the horizon before we stopped for lunch. I spread an old, lightweight blanket I'd packed under a lone, stunted mesquite tree. It'd grown on the edge of one of the slashes in the land, which must have been filled with rushing water in the spring. The tree was on its last legs, about as bad as the one in my backyard, but it was clinging to life, and there were clumps of leaves overhead that provided deep shade. I checked for snakes first and then made sure the blanket took in as much of that shade as possible. I knelt down on it and opened up my backpack to pull out lunch. That included a corkscrew and a bottle of pinot grigio in an insulating wrap. I looked up at Kevin, who was sitting across from me next to his own backpack with an odd expression on his face.

"I thought we might have some wine with lunch," I said, aiming to sound off-handed. "You, ah, you like this, don't you? White wine?"

"We're going to regret drinking this much," Kevin said, and he unwrapped a bottle of chardonnay, sweating in the hot air just like my bottle was. "Great minds think alike?"

We decided to drink the grigio and keep the chardonnay for dinner. I uncorked and poured it into red plastic glasses that Kevin held out. Kevin held up his glass for a toast. He waited until my cup met his, stared at me meaningfully, and then broke into a grin. "Cheers," he said.

"*Salud*."

Kevin drank, and then he rested his arm on his bent knee and held his cup in the air again. "May we get what we want," he intoned, "may we get what we need, but may we never get what we deserve." He took another sip, more slowly this time. "This isn't bad wine. Okay, now it's your turn."

A pebble under my ass forced me to shift on the blanket while I thought. Clever toasts hadn't ever been my specialty, but I'd heard a few, and I strained to remember one. "May you live to be a hundred years, with one extra year to repent." Belatedly, I touched my wine to his, and we both drank.

"That's a good one," he said. "How about 'Here's to us. May we never drink worse.'"

“Six on a scale of ten. Maybe five. Yep, five.”

“You really are a hard marker. Don’t the kids ever complain?”

“Constantly.”

“I can see why. Okay, do you have another one?”

“Uh….” I made a show of scratching my head, loving this little game that had sprung up between us. “May we both be alive this time next year.”

Kevin made an elaborate face. “Yuck. Negative fifty-seven for that one.”

“Hey! You do better.”

“Thanks, don’t mind if I do.” Kevin got nimbly to his feet, though he looked down as he spilled some of the wine in the process. “I hate feeding the ants. Okay, here’s a good one I learned in college. My second week in Fayetteville, as a matter of fact.” He cleared his throat—not that it would have any effect. “Here’s to you and here’s to me, may we never disagree. But if we do, then fuck you, and here’s to me.” He chuckled and looked down at me. “It’s the ‘fucking you’ part I always liked, though I never let the other guys know it.” He flopped back down next to me and sat cross-legged, though carefully safeguarding the wine this time. “Score?”

“Any toast that has fucking in it has got to earn big numbers. Eighty-six.”

“Not sixty-nine?”

I choked on my wine. “You have the mind of an adolescent sometimes.”

“And the truth comes out. Will you still date me, you old graybeard?”

“Date?” I asked lightly. “Is that what we’re doing?”

“That’s right.” He tapped me on my knee. “You know what they say, don’t you?”

“No, what?”

“Here’s to those who wish us well, and those that don’t may go to hell.” Kevin pushed his legs out straight. “That’s an old toast. At least in my family it is. My father used to give it every New Year's dinner. So, are you ready to eat?"

The wine had been my small attempt at offering something to him, and I thought that he'd done the same for me. We ate sandwiches—he'd brought leftover chicken, I had deli ham—and apples and chips, food made special by the company. Afterward we lay back, side-by-side in the small patch of shade, and watched some birds spiral up higher and higher into the sky. I reached over and took his hand in mine, but what I really wanted to do was roll on top of him and look into his eyes. Maybe find in them what I was looking for, or maybe just… look. For the pleasure of it. For the freedom of it.

We clutched at each other's fingers while the birds climbed so high that even the black specks they'd become disappeared. How long and how high would they go?

"There's been something I've been wondering about," I said.

Kevin's voice was low and drowsy-sounding, as if he were on the verge of a nap. "What's that?"

"Nothing. Later."

He struggled up onto his elbow and twisted around to see me, shaking his head as he did. "No, tell me. Or ask me. What?"

The hand he'd been holding made a good pillow for my head as I stared up at the insubstantial wisps of a cloud. "How is your family about you being gay? I mean, you say you want to live out, eventually, but have you even told them? Does your mother know?"

"Yeah, they do. Even my favorite grandmother did before she died."

"And they're okay with it?"

He gave me one of his quick grins. "I didn't say that now, did I? My mom's your liberal's liberal, and she's always acted like she's delighted to have a gay son." His expression turned contemplative. "But she's brittle, you know? I've never believed her. She's too forced, too jolly. But it's better than being cut out of the will."

"And everybody else?"

"My dad died a month after I married Julianne, so he never knew. My sister, she's great. The year I divorced Julianne and told everybody why, that whole year afterward Bridget would call and have long conversations with me, asking all sorts of impertinent questions." Kevin snorted. "I guess that part runs in the family. But she asked, and I answered, and by the end she knew more about me than I did, I think. She gets it. So, yeah, Bridget and her husband are great." He sat up. "She's always said that she wants to meet my partner. Except, of course, I don't have one. And before you ask, yes, Julianne knows too."

"That must have been difficult, telling her."

Kevin rubbed the back of his neck. "It wasn't easy. The hardest thing I ever did, I think. Except, you've got to know, the marriage was a mistake for all different reasons. Even if I'd been straight, it wouldn't have lasted." He looked down at me. "And how about you? I don't suppose you're out to your family."

How to explain when I didn't want to talk about this at all? But then why had I brought up the subject if I wanted to avoid explanations? But not with Kevin. Somewhere in the back of my mind, the thought had been there for a while, that I could tell him, at least some part of it.

"I am and I'm not."

There was compassion in his voice, his face. "Tell me."

Just a little bit. I could get that out. I never talked about this; who would I talk to? But for years all the parts of it had crashed through my mind like boulders tumbling down an endless mountain. *Young men always think they're invincible, the surgeon said. You're not. You should have known this would happen.* As if it had been my fault. As if he would only begrudgingly operate on my arm. Faggot, after all. I focused on a tree branch overhead.

"I know they know. Something…." I took a breath. "Something happened a while ago. A long time ago, so that there's no way they couldn't understand what I… the truth. They've got to. But since then, they've always just looked the other way and not talked about it. I mean, my father barely said two words to me for years after that, had barely started talking to me again before he died. My mother… fussed. She's always fussing and nervous around me, but never asking me anything about my personal life. It's like I don't have a personal life, just… school."

Kevin's hand settled on my knee. I still didn't look over to him, but the contact felt good and maybe gave me the little something I needed to keep going.

"My older sister is just like my mother. Her husband slaps me on the back too hard and talks about sports every second I'm around him, like it's a defense against what I am. I give their kids gifts every birthday, but they don't know me. My other sister doesn't count. She lives in London and I hardly ever see her. She comes over every three or four years to join us for holidays at the ranch, and I'm a sexless bachelor uncle for her and her kids."

The light was too bright, the sun too high. I pulled my hand out from under my head and shaded my eyes instead, shaded them really well, covering them completely and plunging me into darkness. "It… it would be one thing if they didn't know. If they were just guessing. But they *know*. How could they pretend?"

In my head, I heard Kevin's voice, what he didn't say but surely must be thinking. *And aren't you pretending too? Have you ever forced them to get to know you the way you are?*

He was rubbing my thigh with the flat of his hand, around and around against the stiff fabric of my jeans. "I don't know, Tom," he said, his voice low and thick. "It's wrong."

Nobody had ever comforted me like this, and I felt the deep rush of emotion threatening to come forward, clogging my throat. But I wasn't going to break down in front of him. I had a little dignity left, didn't I? "Not my brother," I managed to get out. "He… well, at least sort of."

"Grant, right? Who golfs with you."

Without looking, I lifted my left arm. "Even with this. Yes."

"Hey. You do all right with that arm."

"Grant wouldn't let me slack off. He made sure I did rehab, he pushed me when I didn't want to be pushed." And invited me to the ranch when the rest of them didn't want me there, when my father turned away from me. Let me get to know his kids from the days they were born.

"He sounds like a good guy. I'd… I'd like to meet him someday."

And that was the crux of the matter, wasn't it? What was I going to do about Kevin? Where did he fit in my life? Abruptly I sat up and put my arms around my knees. "I don't know—"

"You don't know that you can do it, I know."

"You must be tired of hearing that."

"Frankly, yes. But I keep telling myself that—"

"That it's early days with us, and that I'll change."

Kevin scooted closer to me so that our thighs touched and he could grasp my shoulder. "Come to my house next weekend," he said, not so softly this time. "We can't keep meeting everywhere except where we live. What's next, San Antonio? Going back to Houston? Flying to the moon?"

I quirked a sad, discouraged smile. "There aren't any beds on the moon."

"But there is one at my house."

"Kevin, I want to. I really do. But my job, and now the play…."

He released me, not cruelly and not impatiently. "Think about it, okay? Don't say no just yet."

"All right. All right, I'll think about it."

"We can be careful for you. I've permanently cleaned out the second spot in my garage so you can park there right alongside my truck, and I won't have to put that outside. Nobody needs to know you're there. I want you there."

He was really pushing now, in a way I suddenly realized that he hadn't pushed when I'd been telling him about my family. He hadn't asked about what I wouldn't talk about, but the issue of spending time at Kevin's house, maybe even staying overnight there, was a huge stumbling block between us, and it really mattered to him. If I couldn't say yes….

"I've been wondering if you'd like to spend Thanksgiving together," I said quickly, the words tumbling out of my mouth. "At Big Bend. You like that, don't you? We could hike and maybe camp out. It should be warm enough. It'd be a long drive, but we could get there by midnight if we left right after work. All day Thursday and Friday and Saturday at the park, and then drive home on Sunday."

He didn't answer right away. Instead he looked out to the horizon, where a low escarpment showed that some long-ago earthquake had transformed the land. He squinted, and my heart sank.

"Thanksgiving," Kevin said slowly. "I thought you always went to the ranch, to Grant's."

My mouth was dry, so I grabbed the water bottle and drank from it. "I usually do, but I don't have to this time."

Kevin looked at me directly, steadily, and very seriously. "It won't make up for the other, you know. Are we going to be fuck buddies on these weekend trips, or are we going to make more of what we've got? I want more with you, Tom. And I need more. If you can't do this…."

What? If I couldn't, would he just say goodbye, so long, it's been nice knowing you but I've got a life to live, so off I go? "I said I'd think about it, okay? I will. I… maybe I can…. Give me a few days."

"Okay." Suddenly he was shaking his head, and a small, wry smile appeared. "God, you drive me crazy, you know that?"

I was beginning to drive myself crazy. "I guess it's a specialty I never knew I had."

"Big Bend for Thanksgiving. Yeah, I want to do that with you. That would be fantastic."

Relief made me weak, but I didn't let him see. "You mean fabulous, don't you? Any gay man worth his salt would say fabulous. Haven't you ever watched *Queer Eye?*"

THAT night in the cabin, we pushed the two single beds together and made love. Then we lay pressed against each other in the solid darkness. The temperature had fallen and it was cold. We were warmer together, with our arms around each other and with his breath gusting in my face.

I was drifting toward sleep when Kevin said, his voice low, "If you come over next weekend, I promise you a massage you won't forget."

Next weekend. I was trying not to think about that when I'd promised I would. I didn't need this, him pressing, and the play too. I kept my reply light, disguising my turmoil. "I thought you liked licking."

"I do. And touching. And all sorts of other things. What do you like, Tom?"

The answer was so clear in my mind that I didn't even try to stop it from coming out.

"You," I said roughly.

He moved within my arms, restlessly, as if some charge went through him so that he couldn't stay still. Then he stopped and whispered, "Perfect. Because I like you too."

THE cast and crew seemed determined to bring in each edition of the paper, cut out the letters, and tack them on the Little Theater bulletin board with a nervous, brittle defiance. Kids. One of them had brought in electrical tape and made a black-bordered box around the letters. All in all, they were doing pretty well, handling their anger and worry in healthy ways, I thought, but then it was still three and a half weeks to opening night. We hadn't heard from the members of the school board yet, which was a small miracle, and I didn't think they'd stay silent for much longer.

That afternoon my last class was out on a field trip with the biology teacher to count the number of saplings in a local nature preserve, so I got to the Little Theater for rehearsal work early. The room was deserted. George was teaching voice lessons in the choir room, which gave me time that I needed to work on schedules. He and I had worked up a comprehensive listing of what needed to be accomplished when. I agreed with him that it was the only way we could keep track of whether we were on top of getting the play ready for audiences by the first weekend of December.

I settled myself at George's desk, powered up my Dell, and started going through the list. *Costumes*, check. Every single one was already hanging in the back wardrobe room. *Buy stage makeup*, no check. But we had it on order and it should arrive soon. *Choreograph*

"La Vie Boheme," three-quarters of a check. That was the middle-of-the-show blockbuster song-and-dance scene that ended act one. We were close, but it was a work-in-progress.

I chewed on a hangnail and stared at the screen, seeing what wasn't there. *Decide if you're willing to just be fuck buddies with Kevin or if you have the courage to reach for something more.* Definitely not a check.

If I turned away from him, I was a fool. I knew that. Somebody—a wonderful man—was offering me the kind of intimacy I had always craved and always denied myself, and I desperately wanted that with him. Not anybody else. Him. But if I said *yes,* then I was begging for the destruction of the small, secure life I'd built so carefully; I couldn't see how we could keep our relationship a secret. I knew Kevin didn't want that anyway, him with his invitations to his house.

Here we were, our lives intersecting during an unexpected and magical few months, when my eyes had been opened and my heart touched. But he was aimed right and I was aimed left. While I admired what he was determined to do, and even deep down wanted it for myself, I didn't have the courage to reach for that golden ring.

I hadn't slept well the past few days, as I asked myself if I could try with Kevin when my only other attempt at a serious relationship had ended in more pain than I ever wanted to endure again. I had no answer, so alone in bed, I'd let the anger out: Didn't Kevin get it? What right did he have to demand this of me? I'd already given him more than I had ever imagined I'd give. Forget it. I didn't need him. If he didn't understand what I was risking, then it wasn't worth being with him.

My anger was always short-lived. Kevin had turned my life upside down. Like a dumb teenager struck by an infatuation that he's convinced is love, I wanted to be with him all the time, wanted to hear his voice on the phone, and I couldn't imagine saying goodbye. I hurt even considering it and could barely touch the thought. Except I wasn't a teenager. I was a grown man, and shouldn't I be past all this emotional rigmarole?

How had I gotten myself into this situation?

The phone on the desk rang. I glared at it, but it kept on ringing, reminding me that I was George's assistant and I'd promised to help, and that even if this was the paper calling, I could at least take a message. I grabbed the phone and caught myself before I growled into it. "Hello?" I said as moderately as three nights of interrupted sleep and an insolvable problem allowed.

"I want to talk to George Keating." A man with a deep voice was talking. Middle-aged, solidly middle class.

"I'm sorry, Mr. Keating is not available. May I take a message?" I opened the desk drawer and pulled out a pen.

"Are you involved in the play too?"

I frowned and pushed the drawer closed by rolling the chair forward and shoving it with my belly. "I'm the assistant director, Thomas Smith. Are you one of our parent volunteers?"

"I wouldn't be caught dead volunteering for that play."

I looked at my laptop and bit my lip. "Is that the message you want me to write down?"

"No, I…. Listen, I'm sorry for saying that. It's just… this play has me all riled up." I imagined him running his hand through his hair. He sounded genuinely upset. "This play is all about drug addicts and faggots, right? The scum of the earth. Why would there be a play about them?"

I'd constructed my life so that nobody would ever call me a faggot to my face again. But he wasn't calling me that. This man on the phone had no idea he was talking to one of the scum, just like nobody in the school knew it.

"There is drug use in *Rent*, yes," I said firmly, putting on my teacher voice to cover up my anger and a sense of injustice that was suddenly brimming over. And a little bit of fear. I didn't think I'd ever get rid of that; it was buried in me, along with the metal rod in my arm. "Though of course the drug use is simulated on stage. And there are homosexual relationships among the characters. But that's not what *Rent* is about."

"How could it be about anything else?" he challenged.

"It's about how these young people have learned to make their own community. They live with each other, they fight with each other, they make bad choices, but ultimately they learn to support each other."

"That's not what Pastor Hunnicutt said."

We had three Baptist churches in town, and Hunnicutt led the flock of the most conservative member of the Southern Baptist Convention. "Has he seen the play?"

"I guess. Sure, he must have."

"Then I guess we're involved in a disagreement in interpreting the play, and that's certainly possible."

"Not when there are Biblical principles involved."

There was absolutely nothing I could say in direct response to that. I'd left the Presbyterian church my parents had raised me in the first week of college, and I'd never wanted to go back where I wasn't accepted and didn't belong.

"The way the school is presenting *Rent* is that the characters are all ugly ducklings in one way or the other," I said, "rejected by society, in part on the outskirts because of some of the choices they've made. But they haven't lost a vision of something better that they're trying to construct themselves. Do you know what the ending lyrics are for one of the biggest songs? It says 'Measure your life in love.' That's the ultimate message of the show."

"Love, huh?"

"That's right."

He snorted. "Love's all well and good for storybooks, but I've got to deal with the here and now. Look, I've got a daughter in this school, and she's all worked up because we've told her she can't go see the play with her friends. She's a freshman, just fourteen. Her mother had to sit down and explain to her why homosexuals are perverted. What, you know, what they do. No mother should have to describe those godforsaken acts."

I could hear the disgust in his every word. Men kissing. Sucking each other off. Ass fucking. What I did with Kevin, what I was driven to do and what I loved doing with him, part of what had made these past weeks so great and what had caused George to notice that I was happy. Any and all of that was so horrible that this man could barely bring himself to talk about it.

He was still talking. "Irene wouldn't have had to explain all that filth to Janey without this play."

I couldn't sit and just take this. I jumped to my feet, pushing the chair back on its rollers, though once standing I had no idea what else to do and simply stood there facing the wall. But I knew what I had to say. Every closeted gay man, I suspected, knew how to dissemble. Or to lie outright, denying what was essential to himself.

"I can understand how speaking about homosexuality with your daughter might be uncomfortable, Mister…."

"I'm Ed Walker."

"Mr. Walker, you certainly have the right to—"

"But it's the school's fault, see? Oh, forget it. I'm talking to the wrong person. You don't have any say in this, do you?"

"I do support the production of *Rent*," I said carefully. Carefully, but not entirely truthfully. Another half-truth.

"I bet you do. Pastor Hunnicutt said you'll be having boys kissing boys on stage. That's disgusting. That's sick. It's everything a good Christian should be against."

I wasn't going to debate theology with this man. "I really can't comment on the specific directorial choices that will be made about staging the play, Mr. Walker."

"Which means you're going to do it. You'll be run out of town."

My heart was thumping, and I hated myself for the fight or flight response this well-meaning bigot was drawing from me. I had to change George's mind about the onstage kissing. A peck on the cheek would do as well, right? With the opposition to the play rising, surely he would see the reasonableness of it.

"I'll be putting in a call to the principal about all this," Walker all but snarled, his earlier politeness having dissolved in his frustration. "Keating doesn't have to call me back because I'm going straight to the top. Goodbye."

I slammed the phone down. "Damn it!" Self-righteous, arrogant, narrow-minded, poorly informed—

"Tom?"

"Jesus!" I said as I whirled around, startled out of my wits. A large, looming figure stood not ten feet behind me in the doorway, both arms raised as if ready to strike. For a breathtaking moment I thought

I'd have to defend myself, that the strength of my own arms would be put to the test and inevitably be found wanting, that once again I'd find myself down on the ground….

But it was just George, all six foot six inches of him. He'd hooked his fingers onto the edge of the overhead doorjamb and was sort of hovering there, an astonished look on his homely face.

"Sorry," he said right away, swaying, and then he finally pulled his arms down and stuffed his hands into the pockets of his lumpy brown sports coat. "I didn't mean to…. I thought you knew I was here all the time."

"I didn't," I snapped, and felt ashamed of myself for it. I heaved in a breath and calmed myself. This was embarrassing.

"Another phone call from a concerned citizen?" George asked. "Threatening to talk to Hiram?"

"You've had others? You haven't told me about that."

He shrugged. "What would be the use? Only two others, though."

"George—"

He held up a hand to stop me. "It's just the way it is. There are people who disagree with what we're trying to do here."

"What we're trying…. George, what are you trying to do? I thought you were putting on a school play. Is there more? Is this some crusade you're on?"

Before answering me, he moved over to the desk, saying "pardon me" as he passed. He picked up a book and then bent over to stuff it into his briefcase on the floor. I stepped back to where he'd been in the doorway.

"Well?"

He straightened and faced me. "Tom. Come on. I think it's obvious."

"No, it's not, at least not to me."

"People are just people. Folks are folks. Right?"

What was he talking about? Suddenly I wanted to punch him. "What?"

George spread his hands. "I want our students to understand that. To know that we're all here together, and we're not all the same. Not everybody lives in Gunning and thinks like the people here. I've gotten really tired of the students who come through here not understanding that there's a world of options and differences out there."

"We aren't here to teach—"

He talked right over me. "And I'm sick to death of directing inoffensive, out-dated Rogers and Hammerstein when there are so many other musicals we could be putting on that are challenging and thought-provoking. I've been wanting to do something new and innovative for a couple of years now. For myself, for the kids, for the community. For you too, because I wanted to work with you again as assistant director. When I saw that *Rent* was available in a school version, I figured for sure you'd want to be involved with that, so I jumped at the chance." He shrugged. "I thought we might as well go for broke. Once the community sees *Rent,* anything else won't even make them blink.

"So, that's what I'm after, a double agenda. Better plays for me to direct and teaching what you of all people should know the truth of, that people are just people."

I was blinking. And terrified. Was George saying.... What was he implying about me? I had to know what I was dealing with. I could barely get it out, but I asked, "What do you mean, me of all people?"

He looked at me hard, as if parsing exactly what I'd said, and a few endless seconds passed during which I could imagine him saying the worst. He finally answered, slowly, drawing it out. "Well.... I guess I mean how well-read you are. How I've sort of figured out you have an open mind. You've got to be a liberal. Aren't you?""

Then he didn't know... of course he didn't know I was gay. I'd been careful. I was safe. Wasn't I?

But he'd somehow guessed my politics, and I didn't know how that had happened. I'd never discussed what I thought of the political scene with anybody in Gunning. The town was a hotbed of conservatism, both politically and socially. There'd been *McCain for President* signs everywhere. Keeping my political views to myself—except when I got to talk about them with Kevin—was common sense and part of the role I'd been playing. So how did George know I was one of the few in town who'd quietly celebrated when Obama had been elected the week before?

"Yeah," I said slowly. "But that doesn't mean anything one way or the other when we've got to deal with the protest against the show. What are we going to do?"

"Keep on keeping on," George said, reminding me of what Robbie had said. "Unless the school board closes us down, and I don't think that will happen."

I wasn't so sure, and I couldn't imagine the kids' reactions if it did. But oh, how it would simplify my life.

George opened up the desk drawer, pulled out the whistle he used to keep rehearsals in order, and draped it around his neck. I turned around and preceded him into the Little Theater, which in a few minutes would fill up with cast and crewmembers. "So you picked a play about AIDS, heroin, and homosexuality just so you could crash through the barrier and put on… what next year?"

"*Sweeney Todd: The Demon Barber of Fleet Street*," he said promptly.

I stopped in my tracks. "You're kidding. Gunning High School, cannibalism, and slitting throats for fun and jollies? It'll never happen."

He clapped his hand on my shoulder, thankfully not too vigorously. "And you never thought the committee would approve *Rent.* The world is changing, Tom."

We couldn't talk anymore because the kids started pouring in, chattering about their day, complaining about homework assignments, dumping their books and backpacks in the corner of the room we'd designated for that. A few of them started drawing on the chalkboard. So long as it wasn't obscene, I usually let them do that, and right now I wasn't up to playing disciplinarian. I needed to get my head back together after that phone call, and most especially after the scare that George had given me. I went over to the piano we always had there and sorted through sheets of music, but I barely saw what passed through my hands. Slowly, I calmed down. If I started jumping at every little innocent remark made by a fellow teacher…. I had to get hold of my fears. It was bad enough to have them threaten my time with Kevin. I couldn't let them expand to fill the school hours too.

After five minutes or so most of the kids were there, so George blew his whistle to get their attention and started reading from the schedule I'd drawn up that morning and e-mailed to him before first class started.

Some of the crew always did the same thing—scenery or props work—and some rotated, especially the core of eight actors playing the Bohemian friends and their one outcast, Benny. George dismissed everybody but those eight and turned to me, saying, "Would you stay here for this? I want to talk to them about Roger."

There'd been some problem the last few days over a few scenes with Roger and his roommate Mark, or maybe it was Roger and his heroin-addict, HIV-positive girlfriend Mimi, I wasn't quite sure which. When the room emptied, George looked the remaining kids over—Robbie and Steven, who played the gay couple Angel and Tom Collins, Johnny Robertson and Sam who were Mark and Roger, Channing and the sophomore Marie, who were going to scandalize the audience as Maureen and Joanne with their same-sex affections onstage, Sarah, who knew how to play the sincere but nevertheless sleazy Mimi, and finally Preston, who had the smallest role of the group as Benny.

"We're just three and a half weeks from opening night," George began. He was immediately interrupted when Johnny starting groaning, and once one started, the others all had to join in. He let them get it out of their systems and then kept going. "No, no, don't worry, we're doing fine. Mr. Smith has a detailed schedule of everything that needs to get done before then, and we're right on the button." He turned around to me and lifted an eyebrow. "Right, Mr. Smith?"

I stepped up next to him and nodded. "Better than that. We're ahead on most things, a little behind on just a few others, but nothing significant. Overall, it's very good. It's excellent. You should all be very proud of yourselves for what you've accomplished so far."

The kids took that in with a grain of salt, I could tell. Everybody there knew that they'd be working long, grueling hours to become as perfect as possible before opening night. Steven clapped his hand on his forehead theatrically and falsetto-sang, "Good for us!" sounding like a chipmunk. The others laughed at him except for Channing, who was looking a bit pensive. She barely reacted at all.

"Before we start for today," George went on, "I wanted to address.... Wait a minute. Let's sit down and get comfortable." The kids sat right where they were, on the cleared, carpeted floor. George and I pulled up some orange plastic chairs, the same ones that I'd put out for the parents' meeting what seemed like an eternity ago. Most of them we kept stacked along the edges of the room, but there were always a few left out.

"Okay, that's better. I wanted to talk about understanding and believing your parts. I know we've concentrated on singing, but don't forget that you're acting up on stage too. If you don't believe in what's going on, then we can't expect the audience to. They won't be moved by this story unless you present it convincingly.

"Now, Sam, I'm going to use you as an example, but all of you should do this and examine your character's motivations. Really get to understand why they're doing what they're doing. Sam, in the beginning of the play, why do you think Roger hasn't left his apartment for six months?"

Sam was a gangly redhead with a voice from the heavenly choir. His rendition of "Your Eyes" at the end of the show, when Roger believes Mimi is dying, would bring down the house. If there was anybody in the house to start with, anyway. He'd been struggling, though, with convincingly portraying Roger outside of the specifically staged songs.

Sam shrugged in the classic seventeen-year-old-boy-almost-a-man fashion. "Uh, because he's depressed?"

"Yes, that's right. Depression can paralyze a person, sometimes closing them down so they can't make decisions. But there's more. What's going on in his life?"

"Nothing much. He's sad 'cause he's lost his girlfriend."

"And...."

"Uh, she killed herself because she had AIDS."

"Right. We don't know from the script for sure, but it would be interesting to think that he might have actually seen her do this. Or, more likely, maybe found her body."

"Oh, gross," Marie said.

"That's a traumatic, upsetting thing to happen. Unexpected violence leaves its mark on people."

I could certainly testify to that, though I never, ever wanted to. I resisted the urge to shift in my chair, because no movement could get me away from my memories. Booze didn't help either, not really, no matter how I'd tried.

"Don't forget that since the girlfriend had AIDS," Steven put in, "Roger has it too. She gave it to him. Sam, that's part of it."

"And AIDS back then was a death sentence, to a slow and awful death not far in the future," George said. "That's something that the four of you who are portraying the HIV-positive characters need to remember. That kind of death is what Roger is inevitably facing. But here's the thing. Is *Rent* a real downer of a show? Are these characters moaning about their fate? Are they half-living? Or are they going about really living?"

Sam raised his hand at the same time that I raised my head and gave George a hard look. He'd always given good pep talks, and I thought he was a good director, but all of a sudden I was seeing more of the man and the way he looked at life. He knew I was liberal? He wanted to direct *Sweeney Todd*? What else was in this genial hulk of a man?

"Well," Sam said, "until he goes outside, Roger's sort of moaning. You can't really live stuck in an apartment."

"And now we get to the heart of the matter. Roger is frightened, isn't he? Can you imagine being that scared and that sad that you pull in and don't even go anywhere?"

"It's like being closeted," Channing said, finally looking more like herself and speaking up.

"What?" asked Preston, who was a little clueless. "Closeted?"

"You know," Channing said, tossing a lock of her dark hair behind her shoulder, hair the same color as her father's. "Like the gays. Hiding. Cutting yourself off from society."

"Pretending you're somebody you're not," Johnny added.

"Oh, that," Preston said. "Because they're scared of the gay-bashing, sure. But wait a minute, Roger's not gay. He's got HIV from, you know, regular, uh, regular fooling around. Not from being with a guy."

Steven hunched forward and planted his palms flat on the carpet. "But it's the same thing," he said intensely. "It doesn't matter if you're gay or straight, it still doesn't make any sense to shut yourself off like that."

He looked directly across the group to where Robbie was sitting to one side, and all the other kids did too.

"Hiding in the closet is for cowards," Steven said. "The brave people step out, or never go inside to begin with. I think it's really cool when somebody's brave like that."

Robbie flushed scarlet and turned his head, but there was a smile on his face.

"But Roger does go out after a while," Sam pointed out. "He doesn't stay shut in the closet."

"Yeah, good for him," Channing said.

"It's the only way to do it," Johnny said. "Just get out there and deal with it, whatever it is."

Marie chimed in. "Yeah, whether it's being gay or having some bad disease or, or, or…."

"Or freaking out 'cause his girlfriend killed herself and he saw all the blood," Preston said with a certain relish.

"Right," Marie said. "All of that. You can't let any of that stuff get you down, can you?"

"My dad says *Rent*'s a good play," Channing put in, "because the characters don't run scared from what they are and the things they believe in. Though it's true Roger plays the wimp in the beginning."

"I'd have a hard time playing a character who was that scared," Steven said. "That's one of the reasons I like Tom Collins. He's gay, and he's cool with it."

"I'm glad you like Collins," George said, "but right now let's finish up with Roger, who's a really interesting character because he does indeed change. Sam, you're right, Roger does overcome his fear and his depression. That's courageous, just like Steven says, because whether a person is gay like Angel and Collins or straight like Roger, change is a hard thing to accomplish."

Sam stuck out his tongue in Steven's direction. "Roger's cool too," he said.

"I think they are all fascinating characters," George said firmly. "It takes Roger a while, but eventually he, uh, shows his coolness. I want you to really understand that so you can portray his courage in leaving the apartment and finding Mimi. Despite the inevitability of his death, Roger decides to embrace life, doesn't he? He's brave, and there's joy in him, in all of them, when they break into the song 'La Vie Boheme'. Part of that joy is Roger's victory. Get it?"

Sam nodded vigorously. "Sure."

"Good," George said, and he stood up. "Let's head for the big stage now.

I let them all leave without me; I felt as if I didn't have the strength to get up from my chair. They didn't have a clue what they'd done, none of them did, but they'd cut me open, dissected me, judged me, and thrown me out with the trash.

Is that what they thought about life in the closet? These teenagers who hadn't lived much sure thought it was despicable, my life. It wasn't so easy to leave where it was safe, damnit! They didn't know about Mr. Ed Walker and men like him, and how much my life would change if people like him knew.

George stuck his head back into the classroom, holding on to the doorjamb. "Are you coming, Tom? I could use your help."

Sure, I would help out. I stood up and took that one step forward that I needed to take. I'd call Kevin this evening, and let him know that, yeah, I'd be at his house this Saturday after all.

CHAPTER 6
A MATTER OF TRUST

KEVIN barely gave me a chance to kill the engine of the Miata after driving into his garage before he was hollering from where he stood in the doorway to the house. "Hurry up! Notre Dame and Navy are just starting. Get your butt moving."

He punched the control to bring the garage door down and disappeared. I stayed where I was behind the wheel of the car as the door slowly cut off the November sunlight from outside, until only the bare bulb overhead illuminated the space. That wasn't exactly the reception I'd been expecting, after all the fuss to get me there. This was a big deal to Kevin, I knew, so why…. I shrugged and got out, leaned over to the passenger seat to grab the beer I'd brought, and followed Kevin inside. The laundry room with a strong smell of detergent greeted me first. Next came a bright and airy kitchen with a window at one end that showed the branches of a tree with a few leaves lingering. The weather had suddenly turned chilly. It felt more like mid-November should now, and at last my habitual long sleeves would fit in with what everybody else was wearing.

"Okay if I dump the beer in the fridge?" I called, not really sure where Kevin was in the house.

He was close by. "Sure, go ahead."

The television was going, and I heard the announcer say "kick-off." The refrigerator was a side-by-side model, and the two packs of Michelob fit in with no problem when I hoisted them up. Past the snack bar was a media room where Kevin was seated on a blue leather couch in front of a big-screen TV. He was leaning forward with his hands between his knees, intent on the game, looking a lot like Grant would have in the same situation. Except Grant was gangly like me, and no pair of jeans ever looked as good on him as they did right now on

Kevin, snug straight down the length of his thigh. And Grant, with his fair coloring, would never have been able to wear a green pullover sweater with the same eye-delighting appeal. Kevin looked good and casual, right at home and a little anxious… about the game, I thought, and not about having me here. He was so comfortable with me being there that he wasn't even looking my way.

I was a true idiot to be standing here hesitating. This was going to be as good a weekend as all our others had been, and it was stupid to allow my resentment over what the kids had said to color how I felt about Kevin. He'd been right about this: we could meet at his house safely, at least once in a while. No boogie men had followed and harassed me on the road. Nobody had jumped out at me in the garage, and no one would be coming to the front door. This was going to be all right.

"Hey, there," I said as I went in and sat down next to him "What's the big deal about this game?"

He looked at me sideways as if reluctant to take his eyes off the action for even a few seconds. "Haven't I told you I'm a big Notre Dame fan?"

"You're kidding."

He turned his attention back to football. "I'm from Marathon, professor, home of Saint Mary's church, first communion, and all that jazz, at least until we moved to Little Rock. I didn't get out of the clutches of the Catholic Church until I went off to college. Notre Dame is in my blood."

"I didn't know you were Catholic."

"Recovering Catholic, please. It's a lifelong job, but somebody's got to do it."

"I used to be Presbyterian."

He offered me a high-five without even looking my way.

A big square coffee table with four inset glass panes was perfect for putting feet up on, so to the sounds of the excited crowd I put mine up next to Kevin's, slouched down a bit, and got myself comfortable. I wasn't exactly sure what I'd been expecting once I got here—Kevin had been so insistent, and he'd sounded so happy when I'd told him I'd come—but it hadn't been this casual welcome.

Maybe my body language spoke for me, because Kevin turned to me. "Wait a minute," he said. "This isn't right." He grabbed the remote from the cushion between us and turned down the sound a notch or two. Then he soundly kissed me, ending with a loud smack as we parted. "There, that's better. Hello. I'm so glad you're here. And, sorry, I can get a little wound up in this."

"I'll say. I was getting ready to wave my hand in front of your face."

"Hey, I'm not that bad. See, they're cheering and I'm not even looking." He kept his gaze steadfastly on my face, so I obligingly looked at the screen and told him, "Navy was tackled for a loss."

"Okay!" He grabbed my shoulders with both hands. "Please tell me you don't hate the Fighting Irish. Because if you do, I'll have to toss you out on the sidewalk or bury you in the yard or something."

Kevin was in a very good mood.

And despite my worries driving over, as the game wore on, I was too. Kevin's high spirits were contagious, or maybe it was that I pretty much always felt good when I was with him, and it was only when I was anywhere and everywhere else that the doubts crowded in. I settled into watching the game and didn't have to work hard to start having a good time. The Irish returned a blocked punt for seven points, and after Kevin finished cheering and a commercial came on, I wrapped an arm around his neck and pulled him close. "One kiss for each point, okay?"

Kevin's eyes widened, and he looked about as shocked as I'd ever seen him, maybe because it had been my idea and not his. But he sure didn't fight it. We took our time, starting out closed-mouth, and after the first one we broke apart and Kevin murmured, "One." Then after the second, I licked the tip of his nose and said, "Two."

At three I slid my tongue between his lips and he hummed in approval, and then showed me exactly how much he liked sucking on my tongue. I hitched closer and spread my fingers through his hair, loving the feeling of the short strands against my hand, loving the sound of Kevin's quickened breathing even more. "Three," I said a minute later, and then we went back to it. In the background Nissan was advertising the Altima, and I didn't feel the least bit guilty ignoring the pitch.

We were still going when the commercial ended and the crowd started roaring for the kickoff. Kevin pulled away and then planted his lips along my jaw line, four times, from my chin up to my ear. It sort of tickled. "Five, six, seven, and one for luck," he whispered as the kicker's foot impacted the ball.

I would have been happy to keep playing that game, but through the rest of the first quarter the Irish looked hapless and Navy looked worse, and nobody came close to the end zone so we could celebrate some more. That was, curiously, okay. It gave me an incentive to get into the game and root for the Irish. After all these weeks, I was sure that Kevin wanted to suck my dick as much as I wanted to suck his; it would happen, only not right now. Soon, soon….

After the first quarter I nudged him and said, "Hey, how about lunch? I'm starved." It was almost noon.

"Hold on, just a minute." During the next commercial he dashed to the kitchen and brought out spinach-artichoke dip that he'd made himself, a bowl of chips, and barbecued chicken wings. We munched on those and drank beer for a while and watched while Navy tied the score at seven apiece with a twenty-yard run. Kevin swallowed a chip wrong when that happened, and he choked. I pounded him on the back and said, "Drink some beer." He did, gulping, and finally got his breath back.

"You give good advice."

"No kidding," I said. "I've got half a counseling degree, remember? Everybody thinks counselors know what to do all the time, when they really don't." I was hardly listening to what I was saying. My back-pounding had turned into flat-handed rubbing across his shoulder blades and up and down his spine. Kevin stretched and shivered under my touch.

"Oh, God, that feels good," he pretty much whimpered.

It felt good to me too. I knew he ran in the mornings, but other than that I couldn't imagine how he kept in the shape he was in, so fit it seemed he could step back into his college days and play again. I loved touching him. His skin, his muscles were a delight to my fingers.

He closed his eyes and sighed. "If you wanted to reach under there and do some back scratching, I wouldn't stop you."

"Give me a year to stop?" I chuckled as I pushed his sweater up and went to work with my nails from side to side.

"Harder," he said. "Over a little. No, the other way, left, left. Oh, right there."

"Sensualist," I accused him.

"Darn right I am. I like having my butt scratched too." He suddenly sat up straight. "But not right now. Game's back on."

I tucked that bit of information into memory and did nothing to stop the prickling that went through me to think of my hands all over Kevin's taut, hardbody ass.

The second quarter dragged on with nothing much good happening, so I razzed him unmercifully about being an Irish fan and pointed out that Notre Dame wasn't even close to being one of the top twenty-five teams; he was a real chump to root for them.

"Oh, come on," Kevin said with the fervor of the true believer. "Our quarterback knows how to throw the ball. Look at that spiral."

"No way. Navy's even worse than the Irish are this year. And look at them, the midshipmen are holding their own. Notre Dame must really stink this year for that to happen."

Kevin tore his eyes from the screen, gave me a look fit to kill, and deliberately flicked a tortilla chip my way. "Asshole."

"The good nuns wouldn't be happy to hear you say that."

I sure was having a lot more fun watching Kevin than watching the gridiron. Here was a different side of him, restraint and professionalism totally discarded and a boyish enthusiasm on display. Nobody at the bank had ever seen him this way, I was certain, and I was more than a little awed that I, unmistakably, brought this out in him. Well, me and Notre Dame football. He looked great, too, and he'd finally—

It finally clicked. "Hey, you've shaved." I reached out and rubbed my palm over his smooth cheek.

He threw me a bedroom-eyes look. “Took you long enough to notice. Yeah, I thought you might like a change. What do you think?”

“I think I’ll throw you down onto the floor and have my way with you right now.”

“Sounds good.”

“Maybe a blowjob?”

“After the game,” he grinned.

From the first time we’d had sex back in Houston, Kevin had assumed easy comfort between us, even before it had existed. Way before it had existed, but we’d developed that over the past weeks for real. Now, I thought it was great that he was acting a little goofy and didn’t feel he had to hide that part of himself. For some reason, the old musical *Damn Yankees* popped into my head. Some guy who was nuts about his baseball team had met and married his wife during off-season, so she’d had no idea that he was a true fanatic.

It was on the tip of my tongue to ask Kevin if he had any other secrets he wanted to share with me besides being an ex-Catholic and a Notre Dame nut, but suddenly I realized asking that would imply a certain obligation for me to be as open with him. So I kept my mouth shut. But seeing that Kevin was this rabid of a fan showed me that the weekends we’d gone off together meant even more to him than I’d thought before, because he’d missed those games. He must have really wanted to fuck. Or to get into my mind. Or something else…. I leaned back, smirking at myself. Then again, there was always the DVR.

Right before halftime, the Irish managed a field goal to go ahead by three points, and so all was right with Kevin’s world when we headed for the kitchen to make ourselves some sandwiches. Except…. “Three points,” I pointed out.

Necking for a full five minutes in front of his microwave got me so turned on, as if I expected we would head straight for his bed when I knew there was no way he’d miss the rest of the game. Or maybe because of that: I was beginning to really appreciate the concept of delayed gratification. Before Kevin, I had taken what I could get as quickly and surely as I could, because I never knew if the guy I’d picked up would bolt or provide what I needed. But now…. I got my hands on Kevin’s bare ass—I’d been thinking of it a lot over the past half hour—by loosening his belt, slipping down the back of his jeans, and letting my fingers take over. Spreading them, feeling the elastic give of his butt had my cock taking notice. Kevin too.

He inched his hand between the two of us—not an easy thing to do with how close together we were pressed—and palmed my package. "Hey there."

I scratched and he squeezed until we parted for air. "You," Kevin said as he re-buckled his belt, "aren't getting any until the Papists win."

"If I left, you'd be sorry."

"That's for sure." He opened the refrigerator. "You want ham or beef?"

He'd bought hoagie rolls and avocados and olives and everything to rival the local deli, enough to feed six of us, and I liked thinking of him ranging up and down the grocery store aisles, trying to pick food to please me. We had a good time piling it on.

In the second half Kevin's team racked up seventeen more points, and for the minutes that the score was 24 to 7 we celebrated by pretending we were teenagers, going at each other hard and fast as if our parents were bound to walk in on us at any minute. He pushed up my shirt, shoved me back against the arm of the couch, and played vampire on my nipples. Having him draped half on top of me was more than half of the turn-on. I went back to his ears and feasted on his lobes, which turned fire-engine red, and I could tell he liked my nuzzling, my little licks and tugs.

The announcers going crazy penetrated the sex-fog I was entering, and Kevin and I turned back to the TV at the same time. Kevin sat up abruptly. It was the very end of the game, less than two minutes left, but Navy scored a touchdown. Kevin cursed out loud. I sat up too, tucked my shirt back in my pants, shook my head, and got back into the game. By that time I almost cared as much as he did; he pulled me into his world that definitely.

And then Navy scored again when the Irish mishandled the ball, and Kevin about had a heart attack. "Shit! Can you believe that?"

"Sit down, would you? There's only a minute left."

Kevin stood there with his hands clenched as he counted down the time, and finally Notre Dame won, 27 to 21. He collapsed next to me like he'd given all his energy to his team.

"Whew, that was close."

"That team always makes their fans suffer," I said. The remote was next to me, so I flipped the TV off. The sudden silence in the house was startling. My ears rang a little from the cheering during the wild finish; that big screen TV had a devil of a sound system.

We stayed slouched there together for a minute or two. Then, lazily, Kevin turned his head toward me. "Hey," he said with a small wattage Kevin-smile, more than a little sheepish too. "Maybe I should have warned you what you were getting into?"

I reached out and rubbed all over the bristles of his short-short hair, like he was a dog that needed petting. "Kevin Robert Bannerman, fan extraordinaire."

"Thanks for watching that with me. Thanks for coming over today." Our feet were both up on the coffee table. He moved his right leg closer and tapped my Reeboks with his Nikes. "See, nothing weird happening over here. Everything's okay."

I didn't much like having my hesitation in visiting his house pointed out, but I could move past that. "Depends on what you define as weird."

He waggled his eyebrows at me. "I've got something that might fall into that category, if you're game for it."

"What is it?" I pulled my feet off the table, planted them on the floor, and sat up.

"How about if I show you in a couple minutes. You want another beer?"

We'd each already had two during the game. "Nope, I'm good for a while."

"Anything you need to get from your car?"

"My bag'll keep."

"Okay then, how about I give you a tour?"

I couldn't resist the opening. "Of you or the house?"

He laughed, unfettered, a joyous sound that darted straight to the middle of me. "All in good time, don't you think? We've got all weekend."

Even though he was only leasing, Kevin showed a lot of pride in his house. I might have been constrained by a teacher's salary and no real desire to do much of anything for my little place, but Kevin had apparently had the money and the vision to get good furniture and even a few pieces of art. He showed me the living room, the only room I knew from arriving for our weekend adventures, the generous hall bathroom, and the two spare bedrooms, decorated as if he'd taken a page from *Southern Living.*

"This looks great," I said as we stood in the doorway of a room done in delicate blues and eggshell white. "You really are a gay man, aren't you?"

He looked proud to hear that. "This was meant to be Channing's room. I'm hoping to get her to stay overnight sometime with me, some weekend that you and I aren't busy and I'm not out of town. So far…." He put an arm over my shoulder. "Do you realize that since we met over at the school, we've seen each other every weekend except for when I've been away?"

I turned into him with my fingertips on his hips. "A whirlwind romance," I said lightly, and then I kissed him. Seriously, with intent.

"Oh, boy," he said. Kevin grabbed my hand and pulled me into the hallway. "Come here, I want to show you something."

The master bedroom was neat, if a bit more sparsely furnished than the rest of the house. The famous king-sized bed, which I'd been enticed with for weeks, was covered in a deep wine-colored comforter with gold accents, but that wasn't what got my attention. Kevin hauled me over to the side opposite the closet, pointed across the bed, and said, "See what I've done for us?"

I caught my breath. On the closet door and on the walls to either side of it were mirrors. Four of them, gleaming, at least eight feet wide in all. Reflected in them now were all of the bed, the curtained window behind us, one grinning dark-haired man, and me.

"For us?" I squeaked.

His arm was around my waist. "I wanted to put them up overhead, so we could, you know, see ourselves more easily. But I figured, since I was leasing, that might not be such a good idea. You, uh, you like it? Too much for you? Not enough? Come on, Tom, tell me."

I didn't know what I thought about this…. Oh, yes I did. My body told me I couldn't wait to hop onto the mattress and see…. Oh, God, yes, see Kevin in his naked glory. See myself the same way, and all the things we'd do together.

I literally growled. "Bastard," I said, my voice low and throaty, sounding like he did all the time.

"Is that a good bastard or a bad bastard?"

"It's a bastard bastard," I told him. As quickly as I could, I grabbed him and pushed him down onto the bed, following him and covering him. I looked down into his face, his face that wasn't unfamiliar anymore, a face I saw all the time now in my mind's eye.

"You," I told him, "are full of surprises."

"Tell me you aren't going to be a prude about this."

I sensuously rubbed against him; it wouldn't take much to get me all riled up. "Does this feel like I'm a prude to you?"

I watched the light in his eyes the way I'd wanted to—what, a week ago? In the park. I'd forced myself to wait a whole week for this pleasure, and in this minute I didn't know why I had.

"I can't wait to see you," I said.

He rubbed the back of his hand down my cheek. "See me now," he whispered.

I expected him to roll us over so we could look at our images in the mirrors, but he didn't. Instead he kissed me, long and hard, threading his fingers in my hair and grabbing my head so I couldn't leave, but I didn't want to anyway.

"This isn't it," Kevin finally murmured against my lips.

"What?"

"It's not what I wanted to show you."

I pulled back, panting a little, and let out a small laugh. "Kevin! What else do you have to surprise me with? An ostrich in the backyard?"

"How about…. No, wait."

He pushed and I rolled off him, sitting up with one leg tucked under me and the other one dangling off the side of the bed. The wine-red sea of the comforter rolled around us, with the give of the mattress just right. Kevin sat up too, rubbing at his mouth.

"What do you think of porn?" he asked.

"Porn? You mean…."

"As in X-rated DVDs. Do you have anything against them?"

Over the years I had very quietly and carefully collected a few. They were locked in an old brown leather briefcase in the junk closet of my middle bedroom, and I didn't let myself watch them nearly as often as I wanted. I had them memorized anyway, every move and every come shot. It'd been nearly two years since I'd added one to the case.

I stood up and looked down at him. "Are you telling me you've got some porn you want us to watch together? And that's what's weird?"

"Yeah, because it's good porn." He chuckled. "Unusual, anyway, because most of the time those films aren't any good except to jack off to. But this one's got some genuine—"

I hauled him off the bed and shoved him toward the door, in the direction of that big screen TV. "Lead me to it. Right now."

Kevin looked over his shoulder as we went back down the hallway. "Right now? As in immediately? As in Tom Smith is a porn connoisseur?"

"Shut up. What've you got?"

"You haven't seen *Dangerous Liaisons*, have you?"

"The one with John Malkovich and Glenn Close?"

"No, the one that stars every gay porn hunk who has ever strutted in your dreams. It won some big award a couple years ago."

By then we were back in the media room. He grabbed the DVD from a bookshelf, put a hand on my shoulder, and held the cover in front of me. I touched it but didn't take it from him. It had the expected photos of four stars on the top half, though they were all head shots. It was the bottom half that riveted me. There on a brass bed, on a bare mattress, were two men. One was on his back with his legs splayed, and his arms went around—possessively—the man he was holding on top of him. They were kissing. Really into it from the tilt of their heads and the tension of their arms, from the press of lip to lip. The top's muscled arms erotically extended past the bottom's head to slip through the bars of the headboard.

"Like it?" Kevin asked.

"Sure," I said, and I looked again. Gorgeous men, experienced men, men who knew how to give a pounding and take one, men with ten inch dicks no doubt, but it was how the top was crouched over the man he was kissing and how he was being held that caught me and brought everything else to a standstill. I looked back at Kevin.

"I.… I want to watch this with you," I said roughly, and already I was half-hard, but that was really only half of what I wanted to say. *I want to see us like this. I want to see you holding me this way. In your mirrors, because maybe that would make it real….*

"Yeah," Kevin said. "Let's do it."

It didn't take long for the DVD player to accept the disk and shuffle round to the movie. We sat pressed next to one another from shoulder down to knees. The opening sequence began, but it wasn't any kind of close-up porn shot like most of these movies, only some guy who looked vaguely familiar getting into a limo.

"It starts a little slower than you expect," Kevin said. "But it has production values like you wouldn't believe."

Slow…. "I have an idea. Hold on, pause it."

We reached for the remote at the same time, his hand over mine, and that was enough to produce that deep-down tug in me: sex, sex, and more sex, coupled with that something more that had plagued me all summer when I'd been moping over leaving Kevin in Houston, over giving him up.

He lunged at me and we were at each other, groping to get a better hold than the tight one we had on each other already, and I was kissing his chin, his eyes, across his forehead, and he was muttering, "yeah, good," and took his turn sucking along my jaw. I drifted backward, falling to the cushion and taking him with me, perfect, perfect, and I lifted one leg over him to keep him there. He was hard against me.

"We've got to stop meeting like this," Kevin wheezed, pulling away only enough to talk. "We've been fooling around since you got here. Should we forget the flick? Huh? Just head for the bed?" He raised an eyebrow in that way he had, and I loved it, loved being freed of my fear of being here at last. He was teasing, hot, and I was free to watch porn with another live human being. I hadn't done this in a very long time. Only once, really, Sean and me slipping off to a triple X-rated shop on the interstate, picking one of the three gay tapes they'd had, going to one of their small back rooms.

"No, let's stay here," I tried to say, but I only managed an insubstantial whisper. I pushed him off, wiped my mouth with the back of my hand, sat up and tried again. "Let's watch. But…." There was something about Kevin's house that was doing strange things to me. "Let's see how long we can last without touching each other."

Kevin literally did a double take. "What?"

"If it's too much for you, then—"

"I didn't say that. What, you mean…." He slid over to his left, so that there was space between us. He looked uncertain, disappointed even. "Watch separately? That sort of destroys the whole idea, doesn't it? I've been looking forward to seeing this with you."

The static image on the screen was of a beautiful man, but in front of me was a man who was even better. He'd given me the mirrors in his bedroom; I wanted to do something to return the favor. "How long do you think we'll last if we start this and don't impose some rules?"

He rolled his eyes. "About five minutes."

Sean and I hadn't gone that long. "If we're lucky. So, let's see if we can go… say, fifteen minutes without touching each other."

"And then? Assuming we're still sane."

"And then we can, uh…."

A startled expression crossed Kevin's face. "Touch ourselves," he said slowly. "I'm beginning to see the point. This is hot." He pressed palm-down against his crotch. "Fifteen minutes with no touching, and then another fifteen minutes when we can touch ourselves but not each other."

"And no coming."

"This is going to be incredibly hard."

"I'm incredibly hard already."

"I'll say. And after that, finally, we get to touch each other?"

Already the palms of my hands were itching to touch his bare skin, and my cock strained against the zipper of my jeans—my best pair, new and as tight as I ever wore them. It seemed impossible to watch sex-on-the-screen for half an hour until we could head for his bed, those mirrors, the lube and condom, and Kevin over me, in me.

I almost said *the hell with it*, almost rode the wave up to the top that absolutely required tumbling down immediately with him, but I didn't.

I reached for the remote to start the movie again. He stopped me with a hand on my arm, and then pulled it away as if I'd burned him. "I…." he started, but then he stopped. He looked down at the area carpet, a rich green color, and it was strange to see my confident Kevin looking, for once, bereft.

My confident Kevin. The house was a space warp, taking me somewhere I never thought I'd be. Except he was with me other places too.

He glanced back up. "I am so glad you came today, Tom."

And then he kissed me again, softly, gently, almost a goodbye kiss, as if we were going to leave each other, and my stomach clenched at the thought.

We parted, settled with a good three feet of space between us, and I said, "Ready?"

He nodded tersely. "Go."

The opening scene seemed to take forever. It wasn't sexy but was the set-up for the sex to come, rules of betrayal and revenge that should have repulsed me—or at least fascinated me, the way the old Malkovich film had. Instead it bored me, because all I wanted was for the clothes to come off. Some fashion executive enlisted the aid of a photographer to get at his ex-boyfriend where it would wound the most: by seducing his new lover. It was more than a little convoluted, but at least it was a plot. I could tell right away it was a real movie, with a stab at more than awful acting, but who cared?

Impatient, I looked around and wished the room were darker. So I got up and pulled the blinds down and then went into the kitchen and pulled closed the curtains over the one window. As I went back to him, Kevin reached over and shut off the freestanding light. It wasn't nighttime dark, but it was dim. Shut off from everything else. Neither one of us said anything. Belatedly, I looked at my watch. Three twenty. At least another ten minutes to go.

Finally the movie really started. Sebastian, a gorgeously broad-shouldered man with short cut hair like Kevin's, got a call that he'd been booked for a photo shoot, but his lover Tom warned him that the photographer couldn't be trusted.

"Tom," Kevin said softly. "He's got your name."

"It's not much of a name."

Kevin snorted. "Maybe it's not the name so much as the man who's wearing it."

I kept my eye on the screen because I never knew how to react when Kevin said things like that. Sebastian was letting movie-Tom know he had nothing to worry about, that he'd be faithful no matter what. It was easy to see how that was going to end further down the line, but for now, the hunk sounded like he meant it. Well, they were both hunks. Each of them was taller than me and muscled like nobody's business. Almost too much muscle for me, because I preferred my men strong but understated, like….

I glanced over at Kevin, who turned and gave me an incandescent smile. Right. Like Kevin. One of his arms was pressed on the arm of the couch. His other arm, closest to me, was resting on his thigh, but his fingers were curled as if he wanted to drum them over and over, and his stillness looked mostly like tension. My gaze followed his arm from elbow to wrist to fingers, fingers awfully close to the bulge in his pants, where I really wanted to be. I remembered what his cock looked like, the way he was a left-leaner, the ripe smell of it after he'd come, the taste of his skin stretched taut over the fire inside.

What had I gotten us into? I wanted to see, touch, taste, be on the receiving end of Kevin's cock, which he knew how to handle. Handle with me, anyway, because we hadn't had sex one time that he hadn't given me what I wanted. I took a deep breath that I knew he heard. Ten minutes before Kevin hauled it out....

I turned back to the movie, where the two guys were trying to reassure each other, and I wished I had the reassurance of Kevin nibbling at my neck. I could almost feel it, the phantom touch. I glanced at my watch again. Time seemed to be passing as slowly as on the last day of school.

Back to the movie. Sex was the best reassurance, wasn't it? In this kind of film it was. Movie-Tom's ass was everything I was sure mine was not, and a close-up proved it as finally the clothes came off. Normally at this point in watching a porn movie I'd have myself unzipped with my cock in my hand. But I couldn't.

I heard Kevin give a deep, sexy grunt when Sebastian went straight for movie-Tom's dick, swallowing him whole and then slurping up with a long swipe of his tongue. The shot was a classic porn close-up of cock and tongue and lips, and though I'd seen plenty of those on my DVDs back home, the whole idea of it, the indisputable reality of it happening in front of me never failed to shoot electricity straight through me. And then there was knowing how Kevin and I would end this movie-watching.... One sizzle from my chest went rocketing down to my dick, which lifted so quickly into super-hard that I gasped.

"You and your bright ideas," Kevin said.

"You got something against blow jobs?"

"No, but I sure don't think much of terminal frustration. We've got six minutes."

My watch said seven, but I wasn't going to argue with him.

No wonder *Dangerous Liaisons* had won awards. The guys were studs, beautiful men, with sexy eyes that gobbled each other up every time they looked at each other. That... yeah, that was good. Unusual for a porn flick, and I'd never cared before, but with Kevin right here next to me and the past two months behind us, I knew what that was like now, swallowing the dick of somebody you actually cared about.

Making love with Kevin the past few times had been a combination of lust and familiarity and my growing feelings for him. That's what these movie-men were trying to portray on screen in the middle of one of the best going-down scenes I'd ever watched.

Movie-Tom wasn't content with what he was getting; he grabbed Sebastian with palms over ears and started to fuck his mouth. Sebastian opened wide and took it easily, even though shots of movie-Tom's flexing ass muscles proved he wasn't holding anything back. I could barely stop myself from moving too, and that surprised me. But this was Kevin I was with, after all, and not anybody else, and that was a liberating, wild moment of realization. I wanted to grab myself through my pants, or turn over and hump the cushions, or throw myself on Kevin and push up against him.

"Jesus!" I whispered. The shot was all motion, movie-Tom's dick flying in and out of Sebastian's pursed lips, his licking tongue, with plenty of sex-noise from both of them. New. Fresh. Not related to anything that had come before.

Kevin turned toward me, his head thrown back on the cushion and his hand reaching out into the space between us. "Do you know how much I want to do that to you?" he asked, his voice low and intense. "Fuck your mouth?"

I abandoned the TV screen and draped my gaze all over him. "About as much as I want to let you do it."

"I wouldn't hurt you."

"I know."

"You know how to do it, let me all in."

Nothing turned me on like deep-throating him, and I could take the mouth-fucking and like it, I knew it. God. If Kevin kept looking at me like that.... His eyes were eating me alive. I tore my sight away from him. The scene had changed and they'd switched positions. Sebastian groaned loud and long when movie-Tom went down on him. And then I couldn't help it; I groaned too when he slipped one finger up Sebastian's back chute. My asshole flexed, because I knew how that felt, and I—

"You love it when I do that, don't you?" Kevin whispered. "One minute to go."

I wanted to laugh out loud because of the way Kevin was compressing time, and I loved that he was, that he wanted to, that he and I could play like this even now, but I was too busy panting and feeling his finger move in me….

On the screen the two men were still going at it, another oral scene that would last a good long while, and way before it was over we'd…. Another forty seconds? Sure. I began to count how many times Sebastian was lucky enough to have that generous, possessive, demanding mouth go all the way down on him. Once, twice, three times, four, five. Surely a minute had passed. Six times, seven. Were we using Kevin's watch, for God's sake, or mine? If I couldn't release my cock to the open air I was going to rocket off the couch, and that might happen even if I could, because one touch and I'd—

"Watch me," Kevin whispered.

I whipped my head around to do exactly what he'd commanded. Deliberately he unbuckled, unsnapped, and unzipped. My mouth flooded with saliva as he lifted up and skimmed his pants down to his knees, and then he hooked his thumbs in the waistband of his boxer briefs. There was a huge wet spot staining the front, and the head of his dick pulsed purple-pink against the white fabric.

"Wait," I said. "Let me do it. I won't touch."

I wouldn't touch, no. I'd only go out of my mind.

He moaned, his head lolling back again. "No, no, we agreed. You stay over there, or I'm going to show you how fast I can fuck you into next week. Just watch."

So I did, and a moment later there it was, and a moment after that his fingers were wrapped around his thickness. Kevin sighed loud enough to be heard over the grunting from the movie, which I was hardly aware was still going on. His eyes closed in what looked like bliss as he gave himself a stroke, then two, then three, and then he squeezed himself and stopped. His eyes popped open and stared right at me. When had I jumped to my feet in the small space in front of the coffee table?

His eyes were wide and dark. "Now you."

I pushed the table back without looking at it, and then I wasted no time: I opened my jeans and shoved them and my briefs together down to my ankles. I knew there was no way I could kick off my Reeboks—and I had to have them off, had to be free of clothes and shoes and inhibitions—so I sat back, bare-assed on the table, and tried to pull them off. But the angle was wrong for my arm, so I shifted and tried again. This time I did it, pulled them off with two huge jerks that scraped the back of my feet, but I didn't give a damn. I tossed pants and briefs in the direction of the kitchen, and then somehow Kevin had me standing in Kenneton, in his home, naked from the waist down, showing him my hard-on that was so frustrated I could feel a dribble of pre-come drip down it. I cupped my hand around the underside and lifted it half an inch higher, showing it to him like I was one of those porn stars still going at it behind me, and then I let myself go.

Kevin stared up at me, panting, his mouth open. "You are so fucking hot," he managed to get out, and then he was pulling on his cock again. "Uh, uh, uh."

Behind me in the movie, the men were making the same sounds… *uh, uh, uh*. I didn't know how all of me didn't explode into a million pieces, because the sheer willpower I was exerting not to touch my own naked dick again was matched only by the total unreality of it all. None of this felt real. Not me in Kenneton, in this house where I'd sworn I'd never be, not me with a lover, a real lover, not a fake one like in *Dangerous Liaisons* but my Kevin jerking himself off in front of me, and for sure not me turned on more than I'd ever been before, with Kevin panting and red-faced, with neither one of us willing to break the artificial barrier that I'd placed between us.

I threw myself back next to Kevin and slid down low until I was half-sprawled with my legs spread wide and my cock sticking straight up. Movie-Tom was sitting backward on Sebastian's face. As I watched, he leaned forward and engulfed Sebastian's impressive, porn-movie-sized cock again. Sebastian shivered and jerked, but then he lifted his head and began licking out his partner's ass, where his finger had been the last time I'd looked. My legs straightened as if I had rigor mortis and quivered, and still I knew that if I touched my hardness I might not have anything left for Kevin.

I rolled my head to look at him, at his cock, which was as effective as he was when it came to making me remember what I used to like way back when, when it came to making me recall the dreams I used to have. The head of Kevin's dick was hugely swollen, surely on the edge of exploding. His fingers were wrapped in a fist just below it, motionless, clenched so tightly it looked almost painful to me, and I winced to see it.

"See what you do to me? This isn't much different from when I had to go to Arizona," he said breathlessly. "Or during the week. God, especially on Tuesdays."

I swallowed around my desire. "I do that too."

"What? Tell me what you do. Tell me!"

"Jerk off thinking of you. Especially after I see you on Tuesdays."

"Tuesdays when we can't touch," he groaned. "Just like now. Goddamn it, Tom, you've recreated the worst day of my week right here, when I have to see you and pretend I don't feel anything for you at all. I'm sick of it. No more."

Explosively, he sat up and pulled his Nikes off, shoved his pants off his ankles, and two seconds later was kneeling between my spread legs. I didn't try to stop him. I cried out and lifted my pelvis at the same time that he bent, and his lips opened to take in the head of my cock.

The world narrowed to a pinpoint of sensation. Kevin's mouth on me started from nothing and made everything. Here he was, demanding that I relinquish myself to him even though the second fifteen minutes we'd set ourselves hadn't come close to ending yet. One possessive hand clutched at my thigh, the other held the base of my cock, and that was right, natural, the way it should be, and I knew it. I wanted to give it all to him, I did. From the beginning, it'd been natural for me to follow where he led, hadn't it? Hadn't it?

I don't know how I did it. Pride? Stubbornness? Long years of preventing anything good from happening? Even though my balls were drawn up as tight as marbles, I managed to stop myself from shooting everything into him.

"No, no," I moaned. I slapped my hands against the cushions and then shoved against his shoulders until he pulled off.

It was a relief not to have that sucking mouth on me still; at the same moment it was inconsolable loss.

"You," I said, leaning straight into his bewildered face. "You let me do that to you. Right now. Up, get up, get up."

"But I—"

"Kevin! Do it!"

He sat, I slid to my knees, I turned and positioned myself between his legs the same way he'd been before me, and I slid my lips over him.

Immediately his hands were on my head, pushing me down, but I didn't need any urging to take him in. A spurt of pre-come splashed against my tongue. His cock was steel, on the edge.

"I love this," Kevin panted above me. "I love everything you do to me. Love it, love it, love—Tommy!"

Bitter and hot, his come flooded my mouth, and that was what I'd needed. Without touching myself, my own cock jerked and released. I couldn't help myself, and I sure couldn't stay on Kevin. I wrenched myself back and gave myself over to my orgasm, to crying out with the sharp, indescribable waves of relief and pure body-pleasure that splashed against the front of the couch and dripped down onto the floor.

And then it was over. Drained completely, I twisted down onto my butt and rested my cheek against his leg. Only then did I realize that my chin and neck were wet with his coming that I hadn't been able to hold and swallow.

We sat there together, me at his feet, as we came down to Earth again. His fingers were still in my hair, but slowly his grip on me loosened. Behind me, *Dangerous Liaisons* was still going strong with a sex scene. I waited a minute until more of my strength returned, and then I looked over at it. Sebastian was screwing movie-Tom energetically, grunting with every wild thrust in, grinning as he gyrated his hips to reach every part. I guessed when they were finished the two of them would think they'd reassured each other sufficiently, but by the end of the movie I doubted they'd have the same trust in each other.

"Should I turn that off?" Kevin asked from above me.

"Yeah, why don't you."

I guess he found the remote somewhere because there was a click and the screen went blank. I heard a clatter as he put it down again on the side table. His hands returned to my hair, stroking and petting. It felt good. Better than good. Kevin's touch had fallen into the same category as going out to see Grant or the day I walked out of physical therapy for good. One of my best-things.

Finally I stirred, sat up a bit, and looked up at him as his hand finally fell away.

"Tommy?" I asked, giving a small smile so he'd know I didn't really mind.

He chuckled. "I might have called you that already a few times when you weren't around. You know, like in one of those Tuesday night sessions. Tommy comes trippingly off my tongue as I, er, come. Okay?"

I hadn't been called Tommy since I was twelve years old. Sean hadn't called me that: we had both been way too conscious of our near-adult status.

"Okay," I said.

Kevin leaned over and kissed me. "You're drenched," he observed as a finger under my chin lifted my face to him. He looked at me critically, tilting his head left and right. "Get on up here and give me a chance to lick you clean."

Five minutes after I'd come, there was no chance that I'd be able to get it up again for a while, but still Kevin knew how to send a faint thrill through my depleted balls and cock. I let him pull me up next to him, and I let him lick me clean too. He was like a house cat going over my face, the rasp of his tongue somehow comforting.

"I didn't have the chance to return the favor," he murmured when he finished. He'd been lapping at me for the past five minutes as I halfway drowsed in his arms. His hand drifted down to carefully cup my cock.

"Later," I said. "With the mirrors."

"Oh, honey," he said. "I can't wait for tonight. You are going to be the star of that show."

I chuckled, waking all the way up, and realized that I wasn't in the least put off by that remark. "I can't wait either. But I guess we'd better get cleaned up now. I kind of made a mess on your furniture."

"You're not the first one," he said.

"I didn't think I was. It looks like you've had this couch for a while."

"Uh-huh. In Louisiana, where sometimes a friend would come visit for a weekend.... But you know what?"

"No, what?"

"I haven't been with anybody but you since June. And I like it that way."

"For me too. Nobody but you since...." Since that first time in Houston. "Last November."

Kevin untangled from me and sat up, so I did too. He held his hands folded between his knees, hunched over a bit, and looked at me seriously. "You've been here... what? Five hours?"

"Almost."

"You know I don't want you to leave. Do you understand that? What I'm saying?"

I looked down at the area carpet that covered his hardwood floors. Kevin's house. Kevin. "I know."

"I really like you."

And I really liked him too, even if I didn't know how I'd managed to find my way to his house. I liked him enough that I'd let the kids and their thoughtless comments overcome my objections and propel me here. I liked him enough to understand what he was really saying, what we each were on the verge of saying and what I knew in my heart I was feeling. For all my fears and worries, I knew that feeling.

"You got here," Kevin went on. "I didn't think you would. So now I think you can do anything."

I gave him a small, incredulous smile. He didn't know that it'd been pique and embarrassment that had brought me here, as well as pride. And him. "Anything?"

"Yep. Superman. Come over next Tuesday, why don't you? Just... follow me home. Nobody needs to see or know. Don't make us both suffer through that night alone." He nudged me with his elbow. "Tommy."

I didn't immediately say no. I didn't even turn away from him. Instead I kept his gaze, and thought: this is how it could be. Kevin and me against the world. No more fitting myself into a box too small, no more hopeless trips for sex. Baseball and football games shared, this is how my day went, how was yours, porn DVDs, and it's time to get the oil changed in my Miata, let's take care of your truck too. My Miller Lite in the fridge next to his Michelob, the end of the day on Tuesday not spent alone and frustrated, no more elaborate plans for weekends away, but every day, every night, Kevin and Tom together.

"God, I wish," I murmured.

"Me too. Think about it, okay?"

Another gentle push. I knew where this was going. I knew what he wanted as well as he did: from this weekend here, to a Tuesday night shared, to every Tuesday night and every weekend, and why don't you move in with me? And after that, me never seeing Kevin again because I just couldn't do that.

It wasn't fair, what I was putting him through, or what I was allowing myself to endure. Wanting and having were two different things. A hope resurrected was the strongest of all… and the most painful to kill.

But I didn't have the strength to say no, not right now. It looked like I would be going through hell one way or the other, either now—*So long, Kevin, thanks for the lunch, have a nice life*—or later—*Goodbye, Kevin, thanks for wanting me forever, have a good day*—so why couldn't I revel in this much happiness before then? Why couldn't I have the man I wanted for at least this long? I took the coward's way out. Tuesday. Maybe.

"Okay," I said. "I'll think about it."

He clapped me on the knee. "Great!" He grinned. "Or if that decision is a little delayed, then maybe we can, you know, give each other a call? Do it over the phone?"

I groaned out loud. "Pervert. Besides, that can't come close to the real thing, and you know it."

"That's right," Kevin said with a wink and a nod. "A case in point. Come on, let's get dressed and clean up. And eat, because I'm starved. Beer, queso, and chips?"

That sounded great to me. I stood up and smoothed down my long-sleeved polo shirt; it might be a little wrinkled, but it would do since it was only Kevin and me there. This was going to be a *who gives a shit* weekend, and it had gotten off to the best possible start.

I retrieved the rest of my clothes, put them on, and went back to the garage to get my overnight bag so I could dump it in his room. Finally I got a cloth from the kitchen and spent some time cleaning up the mess I'd made, relieved that the leather didn't stain, because the last thing I wanted was a permanent memento of me coming on Kevin's furniture.

I rinsed out the rag at the kitchen sink, and Kevin turned on the microwave to warm up cheese and picante sauce. "I figured you wouldn't want to go out to dinner tonight," Kevin was saying over the noise as he stood right in front of it. "We could get a—" when I thought I heard a noise. A door opening? Closing? I froze with my hands under the running water.

"Kevin?" I said, uncertain.

But before he could answer, there was the unmistakable sound of feet on the carpet and some person walking through the living room, headed this way.

"What?" Kevin asked as the microwave chimed that it was through.

"Daddy?" called a young woman's trembling voice. "It's Channing. I need to talk to— Oh!"

She came around the corner like she was running a race, a red-faced, frowning, anxious-looking girl… but she stopped abruptly when she saw me, the thirty-eight-year-old man who taught her history during third period.

Channing looked from me to her father and then back to me again. We stood motionless in a three-person stage play, waiting for someone to remember the next line.

She knew. I saw it the second comprehension kicked in, from the shocked look in her eyes to the way her mouth opened in an astonished "O."

My stomach heaved, and for a dizzying span of seconds I fought the very real likelihood that I would throw up in front of her. I managed to catch my bile and force it down, but the guilt that must have shown on my face swept through me. I'd just sucked off her father, for God's sake! My own come had just washed down the drain from the cloth in my hand and—shit!—the DVD case lay in plain sight on the coffee table.

In that moment I hated Kevin. I hated myself.

Channing drew an audible breath. "Daddy! You should have told me you and Mr. Smith had gotten together!" She said it with all the artless earnestness of a seventeen-year-old who thought she understood everything.

I turned away from her and shut off the water. Into the silence Kevin said, "Honey, it's not like you think, we—"

"Don't treat me like a child!" she said with a sudden edge. "Now I know why you wanted to volunteer for the play."

Kevin took a step toward her, his hand out. "Channing, you know that's not the way it is. I wanted to help you out. And Mr. Smith and I are just—"

"It's okay, it's okay," she said with a distinct hiccup. "It doesn't matter, really, and I don't care. I really don't. I don't care about anything!" Tears were but one step away.

Kevin drew even closer, approaching cautiously, as if he were dealing with a wild animal that might bolt at any moment. "What's wrong? We don't mind that you came over, do we, Tom?" He threw a desperate look over his shoulder.

But I didn't get the chance to answer. Channing said, "I don't care that you two are…. I mean, I even wondered if you knew Mr. Smith was gay too, and if you would…. You have a right to…. But it doesn't matter! Nothing matters!"

Finally Kevin was close enough to put a hand on her shoulder. "What's happened?"

She looked up at him with despair in her eyes. "Oh, Daddy, I've got to talk to you. I'm in big trouble." She threw herself into his arms and burst into tears.

Kevin put his arms around her and held her tight, patting her on the back and murmuring, "It'll be okay."

But I stood rooted in one place. She knew her father was gay? And Kevin hadn't told me that? He'd kept that from me, when I'd needed to know. Because she'd said….she'd said…. She'd said *I wondered if you knew Mr. Smith was gay.* The words ran over and over in my head. *If you knew. If you knew. I wondered if you knew Mr. Smith was gay.* As if everybody knew. Channing knew. How had she…. The cast. George. *You of all people should know people are just people.* My students. Because if Channing could say it, then…. Principal Watts. The elders of the First Baptist Church of Gunning.

Who else knew?

One girl crying in a kitchen, and my whole world staggered. I put a hand out onto the kitchen counter for some kind of stability, but nothing would ever be stable again. She *knew?* Channing Carlton, ordinary kid, nothing special except she could sing, and she knew I was gay? Suddenly I was a piece of trash caught up in the whirlwind of a tornado, being tossed around and around.

My eyes focused on Kevin and Channing, and I realized time had passed, though I didn't know how long. I thought of looking down at my watch or over at the clock on the microwave, but I couldn't get my head to move. It was as if there was so much whirling in my brain that the rest of me was forced into stillness.

Kevin was still patting her back and sometimes patting her on the head. As I watched he rested his hand protectively over her high ponytail. His mouth was moving, and I tuned in to hear him say, "Honey, crying isn't going to help. You've got to tell me so I can help you."

Honey. He called me that sometimes. And now Channing. Desperately, I gulped for air.

Kevin turned his head and looked at me, rolling his eyes significantly toward the media room that was open to the kitchen. He had realized about *Dangerous Liaisons* too. He wanted me to go take care of it.

Not an unreasonable request. I could do that. I walked past both of them, over to the coffee table, and picked up the DVD case. Movie-

Tom embraced Sebastian as if he meant it. But they were naked and making love, and Channing couldn't see that kind of monstrous perversion. She'd better stay out of Kevin's bedroom too. What had he been thinking, with all those mirrors? What had he wanted to see with them?

I picked up the case and tucked it into the bookcase where Kevin had gotten it in the first place, and then I put a copy of James Frey's *A Million Little Pieces* in front of it, so there was no way she could see even the DVD's edge.

I turned back to the scene being played out in the kitchen. Channing had stopped crying but was still clutching Kevin's sweater. Kevin said, "Now, will you tell me what this is all about?"

She lifted her head and sounded like a five-year-old when she said, "I will, Daddy, it's just that…."

Time for my exit. I wanted nothing more than to get out of her presence. "I'll leave the two of you alone then." The garage was behind me, but my keys were on the counter.

"No!" Channing turned around within Kevin's hold. "Oh, Mr. Smith, please don't go. I was going to talk to you on Monday anyway. You might be able to help."

Damn kids. Damn her and my counseling experience that had gotten me into all this trouble. And damn that somewhere underneath my shock and my rage I actually cared, and damn that, based on what she knew of me from school—Mr. Smith, always ready to listen to a student who needed to talk—she expected me to stay and help her, when all I wanted was to get out of there and try to pick up the pieces of what I'd thought had been my carefully constructed, carefully closeted life. *Who else knew?*

I glanced at Kevin. He was looking at me with wild eyes; he knew the position she'd put me in and the conflict I was going through. Maybe he wondered if he'd ever see me again. Well, I wondered that too.

"Please, Tom," Kevin said. "If you can."

Of course I could. I'd done every other thing he'd ever asked me to do, so why not this? Why not sit down with father and daughter and help them out of a rough patch, when I cared? Why not?

"Okay," I heard myself say. "Let's... let's go to the living room where the three of us can get comfortable. Channing, do you want some water?"

God, anyone listening would think I was calm and had it all together. *I really should be in the movies,* I thought as I ran water into a glass and followed them away from the incriminating evidence. With every step I tucked the seething, terrified Tom back where I'd always kept him, into the space I'd chiseled into myself sixteen years ago.

A large floral sofa, blues and creams with a touch of apricot, dominated the living room, and that's where Kevin and Channing sat. I gave her the water and took the armchair to the side, sitting forward with my hands clasped, trying not to look like her father's lover.

"Okay now?" Kevin asked.

"No," she said, with the weight of the world on her shoulders. For the first time, I had the presence of mind to actually wonder what her problem was. I could barely gather the interest.

"You've got to promise," Channing said, hitching around and facing her father, "that you won't... that you won't hate me." Tears started again.

"Channing, no matter what you've done, I will always love you."

My father and mother stood over my hospital bed. I was in so much pain I could barely keep them in focus. "Mom?" I said. I wanted to reach out to her, touch her, but I could barely move for all the bandages. "How could you do this to us?" she asked, keeping her hands to herself. My father said, "I thought we knew you. Is this why we sent you to college?" There'd been no love in their voices.

"Mr. Smith? Do you promise that—" She hiccupped again, loudly, and then gulped. "You wouldn't.... I mean—"

"Calm down, Channing," I said.

"No, no! It's not you who.... Promise!"

"Whatever it is," I said steadily, hoping she wasn't going to go off into full-blown hysterics, "I will keep your confidence as long as I am legally and morally capable of doing so." I was beginning to think I knew what Channing's problem was.

Kevin was staring at her as if he knew now too. “Channing? What is it? Don’t tell me you’re—”

“It wasn’t my fault!” she cried, and covered her face with her hands. “I didn’t want to do it! But he said…. He said….”

Kevin gripped her arm. “Who? JJ?”

She looked up at him, her face blotchy red and white, despairing. “Of course JJ! I’ve been going with him forever. Since sophomore year.”

“And he forced you to….”

“It was right after I got the part. You know, Maureen. Some kids at lunch were messing around, calling me dyke, asking me if I liked kissing other girls. And JJ, he got…. I mean, he knows I love him, but… but….”

“But what?” Kevin growled.

The words came tumbling out now, probably what she had rehearsed driving over here, or maybe what she hadn’t been able to get out of her head at night. “He said I had to prove to him that it wasn’t true and that it wasn’t what I really wanted, to be with girls. I told him he was crazy, it was only a play, but then he heard how we’d kiss onstage, and he got all mad and said he’d date somebody else who wouldn’t embarrass their boyfriend, and what choice did I have?” Her voice rose. “Daddy? What choice did I have? If I hadn’t slept with him, he would have dumped me, and everybody would have thought… would have thought… would have thought it was because I was a lesbo.”

And all this time, shortsightedly, I had been focusing on Robbie, looking out for his interests, trying to smooth the way for him, while right under my nose Channing had been teased in the cafeteria and maneuvered into sex when she hadn’t wanted it. Because I hadn’t worried about the girls. I felt like the world’s most incompetent teacher, and for sure I needed to forget any pretense I’d ever had of being a decent counselor.

Kevin asked, “You’re saying you’re pregnant, right?”

She pulled away from the grip he'd been maintaining on her arm and frowned at him. "I didn't come over here to tell you I slept with JJ! Of course I'm pregnant."

"Are you sure?"

She sniffed. "I took the test three times since Thursday morning."

For the first time he reacted. He stood up, fists clenched by his side. "For God's sake, Channing. Don't you have any sense?"

"I do, I do!" she cried, her face upturned to him.

"Not then you didn't."

"But he—"

"Didn't you use any protection?" Kevin asked as harshly as any parent in this position would ask. "Condoms? Surely you know about condoms!"

"Of course I do!" Tears ran unchecked down her cheeks. "I know all that stuff."

"But you didn't use one? Channing, how stupid can you get?"

"I know, I know. I was so dumb."

"And what about an STD? For God's sake, you could get any kind of a disease if you don't use your head when you have sex. You could even get AIDS!"

Her eyes flashed and she jumped to her feet to face him. "Oh, thanks, Dad, that's just what I wanted to hear! That's what I should be saying to you, not the other way around. Ever since I was old enough to understand, I've been afraid of that for you. Bad enough I have a gay daddy, I always thought, but the icing on the cake would be to have you die of AIDS."

As soon as she finished, panic sprang up all over her face. "Oh, God." She closed her eyes and flopped back down, slumping and covering her face again as if she wanted to disappear. "I'm so sorry. I didn't mean to say that. You know that, don't you?"

"I know," Kevin said grimly. "And you don't have to worry, I'm not dumb enough to have sex without protection, and I don't have AIDS."

Channing peeked up at him through glistening eyelashes. "Daddy, I love you."

"And I love you, but that doesn't mean anything compared to what you've done. How could you, Channing? It's… it's brainless."

"I know," she said, subdued.

"I moved here from Baton Rouge for you, and now look at you. I didn't do you any good at all, did I?"

"I like having you here."

"But now you're going to have a baby, and your whole life is going to change. What are you going to do?"

He turned on his heel and stalked away from her, back toward the kitchen, not what I would have wanted or advised him to do, but he was entitled to his own reaction and his own way of dealing with this. Whatever he thought, Channing surely wasn't the first senior from Gunning High School to get knocked up.

That was cynical and I knew it. I rubbed my hand over my face, feeling a hundred years old.

"The next thing to do," I said, speaking up for the first time, "is to tell your mother. You haven't told her yet, have you?"

"No," she admitted. "But I was hoping Daddy would, you know, maybe come with me? Daddy, would you do that? Please, I'm scared to do it myself. She's gonna kill me."

"No, she won't," Kevin and I said at the same time.

We looked at each other as he came back into the room, and Kevin actually offered me a small, uncertain smile, but I was so far away from that I could barely process what he was doing or what he meant by it.

I said, "You're not the first young woman to be pressured into having sex before she was ready for it."

"I guess not," Channing said as she picked at a thread on the cushion.

"You made a very bad decision," Kevin said.

"But it's done," I said, not wanting Kevin to go down the road of lectures and advice that I didn't follow myself, that wasn't relevant for men like Kevin and me. "Now you've got to deal with the consequences of it. The first step is to tell your mother, and then the three of you need to discuss this situation together. You know what the options are. I don't need to spell them out for you. Now, while you aren't very far along, that's the time to decide what to do."

"That woman who ran for vice president, her daughter's keeping her baby," Channing said wistfully.

"And you might do that too, but that's a serious decision that you need to weigh carefully."

"Daddy? Will you come with me back to the house? I really don't want to tell Mom alone."

Kevin sighed. "Sure I will."

That brought Channing up and into Kevin's arms again. "Thanks, Daddy," I heard her whisper against his neck. "You're the best."

He held her off a little and looked into her face. "No, I'm not. Do you feel up to driving back? If you do, I'll follow you."

Channing nodded vigorously. "Yeah, I feel good enough to drive." She stepped back and wiped at her face. "Could we, uh, could we do it right now? I don't want to put it off."

Kevin glanced at me and then quickly back to her. "Sure."

"Thanks. I guess I'll…. Let me use your bathroom first, and then we can go, okay?"

Off she went down the bedroom hall and disappeared with a slam of the bathroom door.

Kevin stood in the middle of the room and shoved both hands along the eighth-of-an-inch growth of his hair. "Fuck!" he said, loud and clear. "Damn it."

He made a move toward the kitchen, then took a half-step to the hall, and finally he stalked over to the living room windows and looked outside with his hands on his hips. He stood there for a while as I watched him. He was still Kevin, attractive, talkative, persuasive Kevin, but now he was something more too.

I looked away, not wanting to admit how angry I was even to myself. I tried to concentrate on Channing's problem—abortion?

Adoption? Keeping the baby to raise as her own?—and on how Kevin must be feeling, how one thoughtless act could change more than one life catastrophically, but I couldn't. How dare he not tell me she knew he was gay?

In the bathroom, I heard water running and maybe a little crying. Yes, definitely she was in there crying again. I didn't care.

"I can't believe it," Kevin finally said. "She was giving Julianne a little trouble last year, but then it seemed like she calmed down. We thought getting her involved with the play would get her away from her old crowd, introduce her to new people…."

He walked away from the view of the street, my clever, athletic, smooth-as-silk Kevin. He didn't make false moves, not on the football field, not on the dance floor, not in the bedroom. From the first time I'd met him, Kevin had exuded a sort of controlled, intense vitality in everything about him.

He went over to the front door where he turned the deadbolt lock. "If I'd had this locked she wouldn't have walked in on us. That was close." And then finally he looked up at me. "Tom?"

"What?"

"You were right about the play, weren't you? You said that it would cause trouble." He ran one hand over his hair again. "Except I never dreamed—"

"Why didn't you tell me?" I asked in a harsh rasp. I gripped the arms of the chair as if I needed the anchor. My nails dug into the fabric.

He knew immediately what I meant. Chagrin was written all over his face. "I didn't think…." he started, but he didn't go on.

"You told me about your parents, your sister, and your ex-wife," I went on, because I couldn't keep quiet about this, no way, "but somehow you never told me that your daughter, who I see in my classroom every other day at school, knew you were gay. What, somehow you thought that wasn't relevant?"

"No, I—"

"You can call Channing stupid all you want, and maybe you want me to call you the same thing, but I know you. You're anything but stupid." Rage that I couldn't contain ripped through me. "You deliberately didn't tell me, right?"

Kevin spread his hands where he was standing, over by the door. We were conducting this conversation in tense, vibrating whispers. "What did you want me to do? Tell you the truth?"

"Yes!"

"That would have scared you away and you know it. We would have had no chance, none whatsoever."

I stood up. "And now you think we do?"

He took two frantic steps toward me. "Tom, come on. You're upset right now, but—"

"Upset doesn't come close to how I'm feeling."

"I know, I know, but give yourself some time. Think about it. Things aren't as bad as you think they are. You can't know if—"

"All I've done since I met you is think about it, and look at where I'm at now!"

"You don't know where you are! So Channing might have suspected, so what? A good-looking teacher who doesn't date, isn't married, lives alone… It makes sense that she might have guessed. But that doesn't mean— Come on, Tom, we were having such a good time. This weekend was going to be special! It already was, because you're special. We're special together, don't you see it?"

Right then, no, I sure didn't. "Fuck you, Kevin."

He bit his lower lip and looked anguished, but he didn't say anything. Behind me there came the sound of the toilet flushing, and then water starting again. Channing would be out any minute.

Kevin knew that too. He erased the distance between us, grabbed my face and kissed me—hard, hard enough to hurt as he ground our lips together. Or tried to, because I pulled myself away and wiped my mouth on the back of my hand.

"You really are stupid," I spit out, "if you think that makes a difference."

The bathroom door opened and I turned away from him and went all the way into the kitchen. I picked up my keys and then stood over the counter, as the hell that I'd thought I'd be able to postpone suddenly elbowed past my anger.

I looked up at the light fixture, blinking. God, why had I even tried?

"Mr. Smith?" Channing called behind me.

I swallowed down… everything. And then I turned and looked at her with what I mightily hoped was a bland face that showed nothing. "Yes?"

"I wanted to say thanks."

"I didn't do anything. Good luck to you, Channing."

"You'll keep my secret?"

I nodded. "It's up to you to decide what you'll say about this and when. If anything at all. I leave this in your parents' capable hands. You haven't consulted me in any official capacity for the school, after all."

"Anyway, thanks."

She started to walk away, and for a few wild, desperate seconds I wanted to beg her to keep my secret the way I had pledged to keep hers. *I can't afford to have this get out at school…. Please keep what you've seen this afternoon to yourself.*

But my pride wouldn't let me talk like that to a student. And wouldn't saying that be admitting there was something going on? Besides, there was no way I could ask her the question burning a hole in my gut: Who else at school thinks Mr. Smith isn't straight?

"Wait out front, and I'll pull around behind you," I heard Kevin tell Channing. "I'll be right there."

The front door opened and closed, the deadbolt turned, and then he was in front of me. I looked down at his shoes, not at his face.

"I'll call you tomorrow."

"Don't."

"Okay, then I'll give you some time, and then I'll call you. All right?"

"Sure, it's always whatever you want," I said.

"Tom, that's not—"

"Go, Channing's waiting for you."

I pulled my car out first and waited in the driveway while he backed out the Silverado and brought the garage door down. Only then did I realize that my overnight stuff was in my bag in his room, but I wasn't going to ask to go back in there. Kevin drove away, undoubtedly around to the front of the house where Channing was. I might have gone, too, and followed them all the way back to Gunning.

But I was through with following Kevin, so I waited.

Ten minutes later, I drove home on my own.

"HELLO?" I said.

"Tom, it's Sean."

I took in a sharp, angry breath. "You've got balls. I didn't think I'd ever hear from you again."

"Well, you have. Here I am."

"I don't give a shit."

"I guess I.... How are you doing?"

"Like you care."

"I wanted an update. Grant called me last month. He's a nice guy."

"There are a few in the world."

"Tom.... I'm sor—"

"No! Don't you dare say it."

"It's why I called."

"Well, you can fuck off."

"I deserve that."

"You do. Remember when I thought I loved you?"

"Tom.... Look, the police never came by. I guess you didn't...."

I laughed as cruelly as I knew how, even though I was shaking all over. "They aren't interested, Sean. Get with it. Who cares? Nobody gives a fuck."

"I do."

"Like hell."

"Yeah, I guess you would think that."

"You son of a bitch."

"You don't understand, that night I couldn't—"

"Don't go there."

"You won't give me any satisfaction, will you?"

"Not if I can help it."

"Then there's no sense in talking, is there?"

"That's right. No way in hell."

"Ah, come on. Don't you remember.... I remember a lot of good things." His tone turned soft and intimate. "Can't we take the good things away with us? Skinny-dipping in the lake? That trip to New Orleans?"

Sweet memories of waking up in his dorm room, wedged between Sean's snoring and the whitewashed wall, when there'd been nothing better in the world than that moment. But my arm throbbed from the therapy I'd been through that morning. Grant was talking about getting me out on the golf course, even when I hollered at him that I was a cripple and would never be able to do anything like that.

The phone in my hand was suddenly too heavy to hold. Everything hurt. "Goodbye, Sean. Have a shitty life."

"Tom, I'm sorry. Hear me? I'm sorry."

"Nope, I don't. Goodbye."

I'D ALWAYS thought that the most difficult thing I'd done had been staying on the phone with Sean that day. Now, on Monday morning, I found that walking into Gunning High School was a very close second.

I'd spent the rest of that weekend wrapping myself with every scrap of defensive armor I could imagine and convincing myself that Channing had a lot more on her mind than outing her history teacher. If she did that, she would out her own father too. It didn't make sense.

But cell-deep fear rooted in violence and pain didn't make a lot of sense either. I had good reason for the way my palms sweated as I walked from the teachers' parking lot and up the steps to the administration wing. From the moment I'd entered Gunning High the first time, the school had been my sanctuary. Nobody had known me, and I'd been able to construct my own persona, as far from the college student at Texas State as it was possible to be. At least, I'd thought I had. Now I wasn't sure; maybe all my sacrifices to construct that image had been useless.

"Good morning, Tom," the assistant principal said, speaking around his habitual morning granola bar.

Farther down the hall two secretaries were walking toward me. "Hi, Tom," Glenda said. "Did you get the message from the printers that I left in your in-box? They wanted to know about the change for the program."

I went past Robbie's locker, where for once nobody was lingering, and then closer to the cafeteria. "Tom, wait up!" George boomed from behind me.

I waited for him, my stomach jumping. His suit jacket was already rumpled, but George himself usually gave the impression of cheerful composure in the midst of bedlam.

"I wanted to make sure you knew all the makeup got here on Saturday," he said. "Could you go through the boxes and check it out this afternoon, make sure it's all that we ordered?"

"Okay. Sure, fine."

He walked ahead of me rapidly and then turned around and walked backward. "Have a good weekend?"

I nodded, a lie. "All right."

"Gotta run, I'm giving an early test." He waved, and then off he zoomed.

Three minutes later and I was in my own classroom, home and refuge, and I felt safer. Here at least I was accustomed to being the man in charge. No students were in yet, so I had a moment to re-secure my composure. So far, so good. I took off my jacket and draped it on the back of my chair, tugging on my sweater vest to make sure it was straight. The cold weather had lingered. Once my laptop was on the desk and running, I sat down to work on *Rent*'s schedule for the day. Carefully, I typed a check mark next to *Makeup.*

"Mr. Smith?" Jake Somerset came barreling into the room. "Hi, I had some trouble with the homework, and I know you said I needed a good mark, so would you take a look at it before I turn it in to you?"

That's how it went the rest of the day. If anybody at school treated me any differently, I couldn't tell. Or if they knew they were harboring a subversive, perverted homosexual in their midst, it was impossible for me to detect that either. Still, I spent the day with my skin crawling, as if everybody's eyes were on me.

Rehearsal that afternoon was a chaotic mess, with kids forgetting lines they'd learned weeks ago and half the songs sung off-key. I had to uncheck the makeup on the schedule because they'd sent the wrong kind. I spent half an hour on the phone trying to get that straightened out, while emphasizing that the play would be opening, yes, very soon indeed, and we needed that makeup for dress rehearsals pronto.

"Don't worry," George said with irritating self-confidence as we walked out to the darkened parking lot at seven-thirty that night. "There are always days like this toward the end. You don't want them to have their best performances when they're practicing. They'll straighten out."

I went home, made myself an omelet, and watched something on TV. The phone rang at eight-thirty on the dot. I stood over it and looked at the caller ID. It said BANNERMAN KEV.

I'd been expecting it. Kevin was, if nothing else, persistent. But I didn't trust myself to talk to him. That was the issue, wasn't it? I'd trusted him, and in hindsight it seemed I'd done so for no reason whatsoever. A dinner in Houston during which I'd felt that we connected, the coincidence of him moving to my town.... That still bothered me. Had he really not known I was Channing's senior year history teacher? But then, what reason did she have to mention Mr.

Smith to her dad living in another state? What reason did he have to connect that Mr. Smith to the Tom Smith he'd met when he hadn't even really believed me when I'd told him my name? And if he had known, if he had moved for me, wasn't that flattering beyond belief? He'd said it: *I really like you.*

The phone gave one last, abortive half-ring and then stopped. He hadn't even waited for the answering machine to roll over. So much for my thought that if he'd known where to find me this past spring, he would have followed me. I walked past my fifteen-year-old, good-enough TV in the living room and across the ancient gold shag carpet into the middle bedroom, the one where I kept the porn in the old briefcase. One tug opened the closet, and there it was.

The phone began to ring again, but I stayed where I was. I'd really let Kevin have it on Saturday, and my anger hadn't gone away. I felt betrayed, had been outright scared this morning, and had spent some time imagining hauling back and punching Kevin hard enough to knock out his teeth. No, I really wasn't going to answer that phone. Let him stew.

This is 432-555-5678. Please leave a message.

"Tom, please pick up. It's Kevin. Are you there? I did what you asked and waited, even though it's been killing me. You've got to be hearing this. Pick up, why don't you?"

I bent over and grabbed the handle of the briefcase, then lifted it. There weren't all that many DVDs inside. I still had an old VCR machine, so I'd kept all the tapes, and that's what made up the bulk of my meager collection. So what if I'd never watched any of them with anybody? This was the life I'd chosen, goddamnit, and I wasn't going to let anybody jeopardize it. Definitely not Kevin Bannerman with his arrogant, know-it-all ways.

"Tom, listen. I'll see you tomorrow at the school. Could we… I'd like to go out with you for dinner afterward so we can talk. Would you do that with me? Please. At the very least, we've got to make some decisions for our trip to Big Bend. Remember?"

I let the case drop to the floor. No, I hadn't remembered, because I'd been nursing my anger awfully close, encouraging it to stave off a sadness just as overwhelming, but I remembered now. Kevin in a bedroll with sleepy eyes. The first time since college that my life had expanded enough that I'd have something else to do on a holiday besides visit the ranch. Kevin must have guessed how much I was looking forward to those days with him. Well, I knew he was too. What had happened at his house sharpened into knife-like reality. No Big Bend for us.

"I need to tell you I'm sorry. You have a right to be angry with me. I screwed up and I know it. I wasn't being fair to you and to what you need, and to your own… your own strengths. I won't do it again. Give me a chance to show you that I won't screw up again."

My own strengths? Who was he kidding? I didn't have any, and wasn't that half of what had enraged me back at his house? The knowledge that he was right: if he had told me Channing knew he was gay, I would have never dated him. Never gotten to know his ready laugh or his steady thoughtfulness or how thoroughly he kissed me.

I closed my eyes and tried to contemplate life without Kevin, but I couldn't. I couldn't go there.

"Tom…. Honey, I'm really sorry. I hope everything went okay at school today. I'll see you tomorrow, all right?"

"Don't call me honey," I said to the air. Then I opened up the suitcase and grabbed the first tape on top. The rest of the night I spent watching other people make love.

GEORGE was right. Tuesday's rehearsal was better than Monday's had been, except that Kevin arrived an hour earlier than his usual late appearance. By four p.m. he was casually waving to me from the back of the auditorium where he was working with paints and brushes. I waved back as if everything were fine. Letting on that something had come between us could lead to disaster. We were just Mr. Smith and Mr. Bannerman, nothing-special friends who'd met through the play. No big deal, even if it was a big deal to see him again. I was still angry, but I wanted him…. It was hard to turn away.

George and I both stayed in the unheated auditorium that afternoon. He wanted me to critique the final form of the two major duets from act one, plus the kids would be using their microphone headsets for only the second time. They needed to get used to volume projection and control. I didn't want to stay; I wanted to be anyplace where Kevin wasn't. I settled into a seat in the tenth row, feeling conspicuous, holding my clipboard and pen with red, cold fingers. Danielle wasn't working today, and neither was the art teacher, so it was only Kevin back there with the long rolls of scenery. I wondered if he was wearing the old ratty T-shirt he usually put on when painting—he looked like James Dean in that shirt—or if he'd brought something warmer today that didn't show off his arms and the flex of his shoulder muscles.

First one up was Mimi and Roger's song, "I Should Tell You." In my opinion the whole show had difficult melodies, especially for high school kids, but this song that Sam and Sarah were tackling was the worst. Even with the piano player clearly providing the tune, Sam kept going off key. Sarah was standing way too stiffly, and I told them that from my place in the audience. So George motioned to the pianist and had them start over again.

I should tell you I'm disaster, Roger sang.

I made a note that Sarah needed to turn more toward Sam during that line, and couldn't help but think how true this song was. Every couple should have some sort of required upfront confession before they started out together.

Tom, you teach my daughter, and she knows I'm gay.

Kevin, I'm disaster. This arm of mine. This heart of mine. You can't be interested in me. You're dangerous, and I don't trust you.

But I wished I did. The porn didn't cut it, not as far as giving me what I needed. My empty house didn't cut it anymore either, or the prospect of barren weekends without him. Needing sex. Missing Kevin. Facing loneliness. It all combined so I couldn't separate out one from the other.

What was I, addicted? Like Mimi in the play, addicted to… more than I'd had before. To Kevin. How could I consider telling him goodbye? It was just one mistake he'd made. We could have more time together before we had to….

I shifted in the hard seat and stared fiercely at one of the broken chairs roped around with plastic orange tape so no one would sit on it. What was the sense of reaching out to Kevin again when I knew it wasn't going to work between us? I already had ample evidence that our relationship was impossible to keep quiet; I was teetering on the edge of being outed by a careless, emotional girl. Why not keep things the way they were right now? I could say: Remember the good times, Kevin. Have a nice life.

Not a shitty life. A nice one where you'll be happy. Where you'll find that person you're looking for.

Bleakly, I knew I wasn't going to be that person.

"No, stop there," George told the kids on stage. "Tom, were they enunciating enough there?"

I had no idea, but I called out, "They could do better."

And so Sam and Sarah started again, and I tried to force my attention back to them. That had to be their seventh time through the song. Actors, I'd learned, had to have a high tolerance for repetition. How did the people who played on Broadway night after night manage without going out of their minds with boredom? Then again, I supposed some plays might engage a person enough, in the same way that some long-married couples never tired of each other's company. Like my mother's sister Christine and her husband. It was a family legend how they'd met on a Tuesday and stood before the preacher the Monday after that, and then gone on for fifty-two fulfilling years. They'd known they were right for each other from the beginning. The rest of us weren't that lucky.

Sam sang, *I'd forgotten how to smile until your candle burned my skin.*

My face burned. Ridiculous, really, to notice that line on the eighth repetition. Kevin had said that about me in Houston, that I never laughed. It wasn't true. He'd made me laugh plenty.

I was supposed to be taking notes and helping, not acutely conscious that Kevin was listening to the same lyrics I was. The space between my shoulders prickled, as if his gaze were on me right then, touching me, caressing me, caring about me the way I knew he really did.

And I cared about him. I loved him.

I drew in a shuddering breath. Now was a bad time to admit that to myself. It didn't change anything, not really, except to explain why I felt flattened by the world.

Here goes, here goes, here goes, here goes.

"Excellent!" George enthused. "Just right that time. You're showing the feeling now, that they're both willing to start trusting each other. They're on the edge and now ready to jump off the deep end. Jump! That's what lovers have to do sometime. All right, off you two go, back to the Little Theater. Send Robbie and Steven down here, would you? Tell them to bring their headsets with them."

A minute later two energetic seventeen-year-olds came bounding down the main aisle, leaping like gazelles and shouting at each other.

"Slow down!"

"Catch me!"

"Not fair!"

"Slowpoke!"

I hollered, "Boys, no running!" But by that time they'd already flashed by me.

Steven jumped up onto the stage directly from the orchestra pit, and the thump from his large-sized sneakers reverberated through the auditorium. Robbie wasn't far behind him. His ascent to the stage wasn't so graceful, but almost as effective: he leaped up backward so he landed on his butt, then scrambled to his feet.

"I won," Steven said smugly.

"No way, Stevie. Not when you take a head start like that."

Long-suffering, George said, "Boys, your attention, please?"

"Sorry, Mr. Keating."

"Sorry."

Within a minute he had them in their places for the love song from *Rent*, "I'll Cover You," which was the setup for the pain of Angel's death later in the show. The love had to be believable, as George had hammered home, or the emotional depth of the show would be stunted. The boys dropped into their roles seemingly without effort. One second they were school-boy foolish, and the next they were facing each other solemnly. Angel started to sing.

Live in my house, I'll be your shelter. Just pay me back with one thousand kisses. Be my lover, and I'll cover you.

Unlike the other two, Robbie and Steven now had this song down pat, and they both offered rich, powerful vocals. George and I had come up with some complex, interesting blocking for them, and they effortlessly danced around each other, came together, fell apart, caught each other's hands, and ended the song perfectly with both of them singing: *Oh, lover, I'll cover you, Yeah, Oh, lover, I'll cover you.*

And after that came the kiss. They'd done it often enough that there wasn't any hesitation between them: it was brief but sweet, lasting long enough to go with the fading notes of the song. And most definitely lip to lip. They parted, but not completely, holding hands and pulling back enough to grin at each other again.

"We nailed that!" Steven exulted.

From behind me, Kevin said, quietly, "My God. I hadn't seen that before. That was beautiful."

A jolt went through me to hear him so close. He must have abandoned his work during the song, when I'd been concentrating on the stage. But I couldn't bring myself to turn and look at him. "Yes, they are."

"They kiss like they mean it."

"Maybe."

From the corner of my eye, I saw him come into view, into my row, until he stopped a few chairs from where I was sitting. No one else could have heard him when he said, "I know what it is to kiss like that. Was I wrong to think that you do too?"

"Kevin! Shut up," I gritted out. Wouldn't he ever learn? Not at school!

"No," Kevin insisted, intensely, but that was all, because George had dismissed the boys and the piano player; he came striding up from in front of the stage toward the two of us. He was an unlikely savior, but I grabbed at anything I could. If I was going to talk to Kevin, it wasn't going to be in the middle of rehearsal.

"That was fine," I called to him when he was still twenty feet away.

George beamed. He had to be proud of the way his show was shaping up, light-years better than when I had helped him on *Bye Bye Birdie.* "Yep, pretty good, don't you think?"

Noticeably, Kevin stayed quiet until George joined us, but then he said, "They're great. And you've done a terrific job staging the song."

"Thanks, but Tom had a hand in on this one too."

"I'm not surprised to hear that," Kevin said, and this time I did look up at him. There wasn't a trace of lightness to him. "Tom's one talented guy."

"Right," George agreed. "I'm glad he's working with me on this."

I tensed, waiting for Kevin to go completely over the line and say something like *I wish he were working on something with me* or something equally incriminating. But he didn't.

George, thankfully, was oblivious to the tension between the two of us. "Tom, would you make a note for me? I don't want Robbie to look too feminine. Anybody who sees him on stage, even when he's in drag, I want them to know that's a man up there."

I expected Kevin to make some smart remark to that, but he didn't. My fingers didn't want to work, but I managed to write on my clipboard: *Robbie shouldn't look like a girl.*

"What's next?" George wanted to know.

I consulted the schedule. "Channing with 'Over the Moon'."

"Okay, I'll go get—"

"Mr. Keating!"

Johnny Robertson sounded urgent and more than a little frantic. Visions of a car wreck or some sort of accident in the lobby immediately came to my mind. I jumped to my feet and watched him come jogging down the main auditorium aisle, waving a yellow piece of paper.

"Here!" Johnny said, and he thrust the flyer into George's hand. "Look at that!"

George held it out, both Kevin and I left the row to stand next to him in the aisle, and I read the big block letters with dread. This wasn't going to end, was it? It would go on and on, only getting worse.

GOD DESTROYED SODOM AND GOMORRAH!
CHRISTIANS, JOIN US FOR A
PRAYER VIGIL
AROUND THE SCHOOL FLAG POLE AT 6 P.M.

PRAY WITH US FOR THE MISGUIDED
SOULS INVOLVED IN THE GUNNING
HIGH SCHOOL PRODUCTION OF RENT
LEARN THE TRUTH OF WHAT THE BIBLE TEACHES
ABOUT HOMOSEXUALITY AND DRUG USE
BRING YOUR BIBLES!

"Mr. Keating?"

George looked more resigned than anything else. "Yes, Johnny?"

If there was anybody down-to-earth in the cast, it was him, but the boy's forehead wrinkled with worry. "I think you'd better know Principal Watts has been watching the rehearsal from the back, sir. He's got somebody with him who's not too happy with us."

"Okay. Listen, let's not sensationalize this, okay?" George lifted the flyer. "We knew we'd run into opposition to the play, so this is just another—"

"Mr. Keating, could I have a moment of your time, please?"

That was Hiram Watts striding down the main aisle toward us, and with him was that "somebody" Johnny had seen, a short, barrel-chested man with gray hair and a pleasant, inoffensive, round face.

"Of course, Hiram," George said right away. "Johnny, why don't you go back with the others? Tell them we'll be there soon to continue rehearsal."

Hiram didn't waste any time. Before Johnny was out of earshot he said, "George, I'd like you to meet Pastor David Hunnicutt from the First Baptist Church in town. Pastor, this is George Keating, our choir and theater teacher here at school, and the director of the school play."

My fight-or-flight response screamed at me to follow Johnny, but I was caught. Assistant directors didn't abandon their directors, and friends didn't abandon their friends, even if every possible problem that I could have imagined when I'd agreed to help George with *Rent* was coming true. What was this minister here for? To pray over us the way the kids had done over Robbie? I could imagine his prayer if he knew he was standing in the presence of two Sodomites. Would he want to talk to the students? I'd fight that tooth and nail, even though Johnny was undoubtedly carrying word of this back to the kids right now.

The two men shook hands, George faking a cordiality I knew he didn't feel. "This is Tom Smith," he said, gesturing to me, "our assistant director. And this is Kevin, ah… "

"Bannerman," Kevin put in.

"Right, sorry. Kevin Bannerman, one of our faithful parent volunteers."

"That's real fine you do that," Hunnicutt said, in an *I'm-a-regular-folksy-Texan* manner. "Parents need to be there for their kids." Then he shook both our hands, with a strong, definite handshake.

There was a noticeable pause. I braced myself.

"George," Hiram said, "Pastor Hunnicutt would like to have a word with you about the, ah, the content of the play."

"We could go someplace where there aren't little ears hanging out, if you want," Hunnicutt offered.

"No," George said. "It's okay. Now's a fine time to talk." Everybody who'd been working around the edges of the auditorium had abandoned what they'd been doing and riveted their attention on us, but nobody was all that close. It wasn't likely they could hear.

"There's no better time for the truth than right now, I agree with you. Now, Mr. Keating. I know you're an educated man or you wouldn't be on the faculty of this school. You know that this play you're putting on here, this *Rent* play, is the subject of some controversy."

"Of course. I read the newspapers like anybody else." George said. He'd dropped the false front he put on for the cast and crew whenever the subject of opposition to the play came up. He was deadly serious now.

"I have racked my brain 'til it's sore," Hunnicutt said, "but I cannot figure why you decided to give us a show that undermines the morals of our young people."

I glanced at Kevin at the exact time that he glanced at me, and for a moment we were in tune again. He looked as worried as I felt.

"*Rent* is topical, award-winning, and speaks to teenagers. We've never had as many students audition compared to when we were doing, say, *South Pacific.* It's good to have interest and enthusiastic participation."

"But what are they enthusiastic about, eh? If you dangle temptation in front of them, Mr. Keating, they'll jump at it."

"Or you can look at it in another way. *Rent* speaks to this young generation with its music and willingness to confront real issues that show up in the headlines every day. It's more pertinent to their real lives."

"Real lives? Not in this town, surely." Hunnicutt ticked off on his fingers. "Drug use, homosexuality, the AIDS disease, children not showing the respect they should to their mothers and fathers. That's what's in this play, exactly what we don't want our young people getting into. None of that is for the greater glory of God."

I wanted to close my eyes. *You can't fight religion, George. The Bible is the last word. Reason falls away in the face of ingrained belief. Ask me. I know.*

"Maybe, maybe not. I tend to look at different issues the playwright addresses more subtly."

Hunnicutt took a step toward George, out of the circle of the five of us into the center. "I'm asking you for the good of the children. For the whole town too, and the school, of course. Do us all a favor and pick another play."

"Reverend, we've been in rehearsal for almost two months. The kids have worked hard."

"And they deserve credit for that, you're right, but they've been… let's say misguided. If they're as talented as the principal here tells me, then I bet they could work over the holidays and give us another, more suitable play in January."

George shook his head. "We've generated a fair amount of publicity with those letters to the editor. I think we're going to have record audiences, probably sell out every night. And I would hate to disappoint the cast and crew."

For the first time, Hunnicutt frowned. "I think you're wrong. Nobody's likely to step foot in this place those nights. I saw what I saw this afternoon, Mr. Keating, and it turned my stomach. To force two boys to… to engage in such… to go against their natures and—"

"To kiss each other, you mean."

The pastor threw George a ferocious look. "Yes, to kiss," he said as if the words burned his tongue. "It's unconscionable to force them into it."

"Believe me," George said, "there was no forcing involved. These students are committed to the play and the message it provides."

"The message is ungodly."

"I disagree, respectfully, but that's a matter of opinion."

For the first time Hiram spoke up. "George, have you considered—"

George rounded on Hiram in an instant. "Do I have the support of this school's administration, or don't I?"

Hiram was definitely caught where it pinched, literally standing between his theater teacher and the pastor of one of the more prominent churches in town. "I support my teachers, yes, but it's clear that—"

"Until I'm instructed otherwise, *Rent* is the play."

Hunnicutt sighed loudly. "I am sorry to tell you that you will be instructed otherwise. I had hoped that you'd see reason somehow, but that's not to be, I guess. I hope the good Lord changes your mind in the meantime."

"What do you mean?" Kevin asked.

"On Thursday the God-fearing people in this town will let the school board members know what we think of all this… this filth and perversion being sponsored by a public school."

George's eyes narrowed. It was clear he hadn't expected that, even if in my worst dreams I had. My worst dreams: the play debated in public. *And here is Mr. Smith, the assistant director, the teacher nobody's ever looked at closely before, stepping into the spotlight.*

"I've seen the agenda for the meeting," George said. "There isn't anything there about—"

"We're the last item on the agenda. We just got it in to the board in time."

How had I been trapped like this? I would need to be there, acting again, pretending to support a play I'd opposed from the beginning even if for my own most personal reasons. If Channing wasn't the only one clued in about Mr. Smith's private thoughts and desires, then I'd be the gay assistant director pushing my own perverted, disgusting lifestyle on the innocent children of west Texas. All because George had been too persuasive back in September and because Kevin had come back into my life. I wanted to howl.

"Pastor Hunnicutt." That was Kevin speaking up. "Have you had the chance to talk to the students in the play? My daughter Channing is in one of the lead roles, and she kisses another girl on stage. She…." He paused. He must have been remembering JJ. "She doesn't have a problem with the character she portrays, and her mother and I support her one hundred percent."

If Channing's pregnancy became known, there were some in the community who would lay the blame for it at our doorstep. And with good reason too. What a nightmare. *Give it up, George!*

"Then all I can say is that I'll offer prayers for the two of you, Mr. Bannerman," Hunnicutt said, "because no God-fearing Christian would ever support this play. Are you a churchgoer, sir?"

"Not recently, no."

"Then maybe your wife and you would like to join us some Sunday morning. We'd be pleased to welcome you."

I could see it flash in Kevin's eyes: the impulse to tell the reverend to kiss his ass, that he'd divorced his wife because he liked men. He even opened his mouth, and I took a tiny step backward.

His gaze flicked to me, and he closed his mouth. If there was a God—not the one that Hunnicutt worshiped, but the one who looked over bitter, wounded, cynical men like me, who wished that everybody in His creation could accept everybody else just the way we were—then that God urged Kevin to say instead, “Thanks for the invitation, but I don’t think so.”

“Our church has stood on Jefferson Street for one hundred and ten years, so if you change your mind, we’ll be there. Mr. Keating, I imagine we’ll see you on Thursday.”

With a hopeless glance at the three of us, Hiram escorted Hunnicutt up the aisle and then out of sight through the back doors. I felt as if I’d been tensed, on the edge of battle, for hours. My arm was on fire.

“Are you going to take that sitting down, George?” Kevin asked.

George’s self-confidence had disappeared. He was pale as he rubbed the back of his neck. “What else do you want me to do?” he snapped. “I’ll show up Thursday and defend the play from narrow-minded people who don’t live in the twenty-first century yet. The rest is up to the board.”

“You said that the board already approved the play, right? Back in the summer?”

“A committee,” George said wearily. “Not everybody. Look, I’ve got a play to get on stage, and time is running out. I’m not going to waste the last hour of rehearsal.”

I stepped in front of him as he moved to go. “Rehearsal?” I said incredulously. “You can’t ask them.... Wait a minute, George, you need to rethink that.”

“What do you mean?”

I gestured toward where Johnny had disappeared. “All the kids know that something’s happened by now. They’re going to be worried. Rehearsing isn’t nearly as important now as calming them down and telling them the truth.”

He seemed to visibly deflate, as if suddenly his clothes were much too large on him. “The truth? I thought we could bluster our way through this.”

"I know. But I don't think we can."

He sighed heavily, then said, "Okay, let's go. We'll talk to the cast. This isn't going to be easy."

"No, wait," Kevin said. "We need to alert more than the kids. What about their parents? What about drumming up some support?"

George looked at me, but I shook my head. I couldn't imagine spending the night phoning parents and begging for support. I couldn't imagine spending tonight any other way than locking my doors, closing my blinds, and getting drunk.

Kevin understood. "Okay, then, let me do it. I've got all the contact information that you handed out at the beginning, plus I bet Channing has more numbers in her cell phone. If we could get a group together to come to the meeting, that would have to help. We can show the board there are two sides to the story."

George waved his hand in the air as he headed for the Little Theater. "Sure, do it, but you're on your own. This is unofficial, and I don't have any part in it."

I followed him up the aisle, but Kevin called, "Tom."

Damn him! "Sorry, I don't have time right now."

He called louder. "Mr. Smith! I need to ask you something about the contact sheet."

There were still plenty of people watching our every move, and I couldn't afford to ignore him so obviously. I stopped where I was and worked not to clench my fists. Then I turned and said, "What?"

My confident Kevin was gone; he looked desperate as he came up close to me and pleaded, "Tom, we've got to talk. Tonight, could we have dinner? Please?"

He really didn't understand, did he? I wanted to tell him that he was out of his mind, and ask him if he'd heard what Hunnicutt was threatening. The play, George, and me, we'd be under the public microscope, and I couldn't afford to be seen with Kevin no matter the truth of how I felt about him.

"No," I said, and I left him.

CHAPTER 7
MEETING OF MINDS

THE school board meeting room was packed. In the tense hours between the end of a subdued rehearsal and the eight o'clock start time, I'd debated whether to sit with George, but that decision had been taken out of my hands. I'd hidden in the Miata for a good five minutes with my fingers clenched on the steering wheel as I wrestled with my out-and-out fear of going inside, but when I finally got myself moving and into the meeting hall, George and his wife Jenny were seated in the fifth row with no spots open near them.

I didn't even try to catch his eye. I was desperate to glide unseen and unknown through the evening, and that meant not calling attention to myself in any way. So I gratefully headed up the steps to the last row, where the overhang from the projection booth threw the seats into shadow. As I climbed, the hair on the back of my neck prickled and rose, and I felt as if that spotlight were on me. I waited for heads to turn or for the whispers to start, but nobody seemed to notice me at all. Except Kevin. Of the two or three hundred people in the place, my eyes riveted on him—staring at me, unblinking, unhappy—but just as quickly I trained my attention somewhere else, anywhere else. I couldn't afford to be seen looking his way. Didn't he understand that? He had to understand that. It felt like everything that had happened between us had disintegrated: the good times, the good words, his support, his hands on me, *Tommy*. I could hardly wrap my head around how wrong everything had gone in less than a week.

I wiped my sweaty hands on my Dockers and edged into the row, past the good citizens of Gunning to the open chair. Once seated, I intended to stay there; others were more than capable of arguing for our cause. I was wedged between an intent woman holding her Bible and a man in a leather jacket and blue jeans with his gray hair pulled back in a ponytail—he looked like a biker, totally out of place in Gunning—who quietly nodded to me.

While everyone waited for the board to start, I scanned the crowd. Whatever Kevin had done over the past two days and nights had worked. There were a lot of familiar faces from the cast and crew along with plenty of other students, some with parents, others clumped together the way teenagers tended to do. Every parent of our eight lead actors was there, including Julianne Carlton and Kevin, sitting with Channing three rows in front of me. They were close enough even in the subdued lighting of the hall for me to see how solemn Kevin looked. He wasn't my weekend friend of the sparkling smile and *joie de vivre* any more. Robbie and his parents were right next to them, Mr. Sutton stern like always and Mrs. Sutton seeming serene. Robbie and Channing were seated side by side, looking scared and whispering to each other. I breathed a sigh of profound relief that Robbie wasn't next to Steven instead. I wasn't sure what was going on there, but the two of them together could only raise eyebrows that wouldn't do us any good.

No eyebrows raised, no suspicions triggered, no vague guesses confirmed: that was my personal goal for the evening. I hadn't been able to swallow any food before I came, and I'd resisted the temptation to down a jigger—or two or three—of whiskey. The echoes of a genuine hangover already sounded through my head from the night before… and the night before that.

The board filed in, and everybody stood for the pledge of allegiance to America and then the pledge of allegiance to Texas and then the invocation, given by none other than Reverend Hunnicutt. Any hope that I'd had of the evening going George's way disappeared right then. I was tempted to walk out. But from the back row? Everybody would see me.

A full ninety minutes passed while the board took up one order of business after another, until finally the last item on the agenda came up. "Agenda item number thirteen," the school board president said from his place in the center of the table facing the audience. "Citizen objections to the performance of *Rent* at Gunning High School."

The president, John Mayfield, announced that the board had decided the best way to approach the subject would be to allow the public to have their say, and he hoped everybody was prepared to stay for a while, because there were many people who'd signed up to talk.

Mayfield was a small man with quick, precise mannerisms. He adjusted his microphone and said, "We'll call five at a time. We mixed them up, so this is a random drawing. We'll start with these." From a stack of index cards in front of him, he picked some from the top and called out five names. "Come on down here in that order," he pointed to an area next to the board's table, "and wait for your turn."

The first person to the citizen's input podium was a middle-aged woman in a Sunday dress. "That's my neighbor," the woman next to me told me.

"That's nice," I murmured.

"I'm Ella Dexter," the woman announced to the board. She glanced behind her anxiously. "Uh, I didn't expect to be the first one to talk, but…."

"It's all right," Mayfield encouraged. "Tell us what you think. But short and sweet," he said with a smile, "would probably be better than long and involved."

"All right. I'm against this play for two reasons. First, I think homosexuality is disgusting. It's against the Bible, and if everybody was homosexual, we wouldn't have families, and no children. There wouldn't be any more people in the world now, would there? Eventually we'd all be dead."

The man next to me stretched out one leg and then pulled it in sharply as titters swept through the audience. I recognized that sound: teenagers amused at the rank stupidity of their elders. Savagely, I wished that I could clap my hands over their mouths to shut them up. This wasn't a laughing matter, and there'd be plenty of well-spoken opponents protesting the play, even if Ella Dexter wasn't one of them.

She heard them; she threw a nasty look up into the crowd, and the amusement died down. She pointed a finger, right where several of the cast and crew were seated together. Steven was in that group, two rows up from the floor, with George three rows behind them. "It's easy to laugh, but not so easy to live an upright life. Using illegal drugs can ruin your life, and it's a sin that heroin is in this play, that it's actually on the stage! That's my second reason. My sister went to New York and died of a heroin overdose, so I know what I'm talking about."

She turned back to the board and blinked back tears. "I'm sorry, I didn't mean…."

"That's all right, take a minute."

"No, no, I'm all right. Listen, I feel very strongly about this. The drugs, the homosexuality, it's all immoral. We expect our kids to attend church on Sunday, but then up at the school, are we going to let them see this… this… this… I don't know what to call it."

"Perversion!" somebody yelled from the crowd.

"Right. If this play goes on, I'm going to be outside the school picketing. My sign will say 'In Donna's memory', because that's my sister's name."

Vigorous applause erupted from the audience, and the woman next to me jumped up and cheered, "I'll be with you, Ella!" Other voices from the crowd joined hers, and dread filled me. Their protesting wasn't casual; it was heartfelt. If the play went on, there might be a real demonstration outside Gunning High School.

Mayfield pounded his gavel. "Calm down, please!" When the audience quieted, he asked, "Anything else?"

Dexter lifted her chin. "Yes. I don't mean to sound negative or anything, but there's a school board election coming up next May, and I will not vote for any member who allows this play to go on. And, past that, I'm glad to be heard, and thank you."

The five men and two women who were seated in the hot spots all nodded, and none of them seemed too frightened at the prospect of not getting her vote. Maybe they'd all been threatened like this before, or maybe they'd already made up their minds about the play and knew they didn't have anything to worry about.

"Thank you, Mrs. Dexter. Okay, next up?"

An old man, limping a little, approached the mike this time. "You remember 1962 in this town?"

"If you would state your name, please," Mayfield said.

"You know well who I am. I'm Curtis Felton. I was born in Gunning in 1932, so I'm seventy-six years old. In 1962 Olin Winchester was arrested for the rape and murder of a little five-year-old boy, out in the cotton field that used to be north of where Jerry's garage is now. That was a sorry, sorry day, and I was glad when that bastard was sent up to the prison for good."

He paused and seemed to be satisfied with what he'd said. Mayfield asked, "Did you have something to add about the play at Gunning High School, Mr. Felton?"

"Sure I do. I thought that was the blackest day Gunning could have, but if you let this play go on, you'll all rot in hell for letting this kind of perversion back into our town. We've got to protect the kids, no matter what these big city sign-wavers say." Felton looked to the floor, as if he wanted to find someplace safe to spit. He didn't, so he swallowed noisily. His gullet-clearing came through over the mike.

"And another thing. I don't understand the folks who let their sons and daughters act in this *Rent* thing. Where'd common sense go these days? If one of my great-grandsons wanted to be in this here play, I'd whip them good. God created Adam, and then he created Eve, and he wants us joined in marriage to one another. It's the way things are, see?"

"I hear you, Mr. Felton. Thank you for coming to the meeting today."

"Humph." Felton didn't want to leave the podium, that was clear, but he didn't say anything more. He didn't bother to return to his seat either. He stumped across in front of the entire board and left the hall. The members of the board all watched him as he left, their heads turning and then swiveling back when he disappeared.

The next one up was a young man, about thirty, wearing a good gray suit with a striped tie. He consulted a sheet of paper as he approached the mike and then placed it on the reading surface of the podium.

"My name is Stanley Littrell," he said in a smooth, well-modulated tone. "I represent not only myself but the members of the Calvary Baptist Church. We thank the board for giving us the opportunity to express our views on the production of *Rent* at Gunning High School."

Here was trouble. Littrell scanned the seven board members, catching each of their eyes, engaging them in what he had to say. Then he picked up the paper and began to read.

"While *Rent* is commonly referred to as 'the AIDS play' because of the number of lead roles who suffer from that disease, it also presents characters who practice homosexuality openly, who are drug addicts, and who engage in criminal activity. The play is filled with profanity. It is made clear that individuals engage in sexual relations outside the bonds of marriage."

He glanced at the board members, pushed his glasses up higher on his nose, and kept reading. "It might be hoped that each of these aberrant activities are condemned within the play and held up as anti-social and anti-Biblical. They are not, even though morality plays have been a time-honored theatrical tradition for hundreds if not thousands of years. Instead, they are glorified in song and dance, and the classic modes of theater are perverted as love songs are exchanged between characters of the same sex, and as religion is mocked in the song 'La Vie Boheme'.

"To make matters worse...." Littrell drew a dramatic breath and paused. "To make matters worse," he continued, "playgoers will be treated to the sight of our young people re-enacting homosexual behavior on stage." He stopped again, gripped the sides of the podium, and addressed the board directly. "Members of the board, I don't know about you, but I would never want to attend a play presented by my local high school, or any play, only to see men embracing men, and women doing the same, and even worse. Imagine if there were children in the audience."

He pulled back, having made his point. "To conclude. The members of the Calvary Baptist Church of Gunning, Texas, find *Rent* to be a play objectionable in content and presentation. A public institution such as a school should not be in the business of putting on a play that is so contrary to the values of the community of which it is a part. We respectfully request that the board suspend the production and perhaps establish another show in its place. Thank you."

He left to enthusiastic applause, although there were noticeable groups of people who were silent. The gray-haired man next to me, who'd sat on his hands when the woman on my other side had clapped vigorously, leaned over and said, "Sweet-talking devil, wasn't he?"

I didn't even nod. Three speakers in a row against the play had me wondering if the deck had been stacked, literally. But the fourth person to speak was Danielle Robertson. Kevin had spent so much time over the weeks working with her. He straightened in his seat as she approached the podium; I couldn't help noticing. I noticed everything about him. He hadn't spoken to Julianne since I'd arrived, though he'd leaned over and said something to Channing and Robbie together.

"Hello," Danielle said as she smiled at the board and reached to pull the mike down, since she wasn't much over five feet tall. "Maybe I need a stool to stand on," she joked, and a breeze of laughter swept through the room. I didn't join in. I was strung tight. But inside I cheered for her, because that light approach was just what was needed, I thought.

"It's really hard to speak after the eloquence of Mister Littrell," Danielle began, "but I'll give it a shot. My name is Danielle Robertson. My husband Gus and I are the proud parents of Johnny Robertson, who is playing the role of Mark in *Rent.* We happily support this play, and request the board to allow the production to move forward.

"Before any decision is made, I would ask that you take into consideration the time and effort that the students have already put into the play. Rehearsals take place four days a week from three until six o'clock, and they've been going on since mid-September. Behind the scenes work often goes on during the weekend too. Costumes are ready, scenery is in place, props have been gathered.... It's a big undertaking.

"Now, let me tell you all a little about my family," she said with a smile that showed who Johnny had inherited his charm from. "We are musical theater devotees. Yes, I know that's unusual, but what can I say? We've probably watched every musical available from Netflix. We've even been known to go to Houston for their Theater Under the Stars to see a show or two.

"So I know musicals. And I can tell you that *Rent* is one of the most profound and moving musicals ever written.

"It is true that the play is shaped around unusual subjects for a musical: heroin addiction, love between people of the same gender, and terminal illness. But the playwright uses those jumping off points to explore universal themes that are good to contemplate. People who go to the play and pay attention will see a lot of beauty. They'll see beauty and a lot about supporting each other in tough times. They'll see that the play preaches that it's good to reach out to one another and to persist in sharing love.

"Our director, George Keating, ably assisted by assistant director Tom Smith—"

I jerked in my seat to hear my name, and biker-man threw me a quizzical look.

"—is not sensationalizing the content of the play and he is not exploiting the cast. He's doing a marvelous job, and I can't wait to see the finished product."

Danielle lifted her shoulders. "I don't know what else to say. Except… please don't cancel this play. It's beautiful, it has a great message, and it speaks directly to the youth of today. In the end, we'll regret it if we miss out on this kind of production that opens our minds and hearts. Thanks for letting me speak."

Danielle didn't go back to her seat right away either. Instead she picked up a shopping bag I hadn't noticed she had with her, and she took it up to the board members. "These are for you," she said with a laugh that I could hear even in the last row without amplification. She handed out what looked like plastic bags of something or other, and a stir went through the audience. I couldn't see exactly what they were, but somebody down front laughed and turned around to say, "Homemade cookies."

I sat back in my chair, suddenly tired. It killed me that she'd said my name, but now I wanted to pump my hand in the air and say, "Go, Danielle!" Except I had to remind myself that I wasn't for this play. Cancellation would only help me, wouldn't it? It would let me go back to the life I'd led before *Rent*. Maybe to a life-before-Kevin too? I'd be safe. Safe and… without Kevin. I stared at the back of his head, wanting even tiny bits of him, because that might be all I'd get.

"Musicals!" the woman next to me harrumphed, and I cut my eyes away to some other man, a man who meant nothing to me.

The next person up was Mrs. Hunnicutt, wife of the reverend. I tuned her out and did allow myself to slump a little. This was going to go on forever, and I couldn't help but think that the board had already made up its mind one way or the other. Wasn't that the way these things worked? This citizen input was for show. The real decisions were made in out-of-sight consultations. Hiram had told us that a decision wasn't likely to come down tonight anyway.

Thirty minutes passed and then an hour and then an hour and a half. People talked without much skill but with a lot of passion. Every part of *Rent* was ripped apart, but the one thing everybody mentioned time after time was the homosexuality.

"Perversion!"

"Disgraceful!"

"I'm a Christian and…."

"Not suitable for teenagers."

"Anti-family."

"Left-leaning ideology!"

The first speaker had started a trend. Almost all of those against the play threatened to vote the school board members out if they let *Rent* go on.

"Not representative of the community as a whole." That was the one I couldn't help but agree with. It's why I lived the way I did, and nothing was going to change that, especially not some high school play. How had George thought he could get away with this?

The kids visibly sagged as the night wore on. "This play pretends that two men love one another!" one of the more emotional speakers raged. At that, Steven twisted round in his seat and looked up where Robbie and Channing were huddled together. The anxious look on his face was heartbreaking. Whatever kind of friendship he and Robbie shared, sexual or not, the feelings he had for the dark-haired boy he kissed in the play were genuine.

I wasn't counting how many pro and con, but Channing was. I heard her when she stage-whispered, "Eighteen against, and only seven for!"

"It's okay, it's okay," Robbie soothed her.

"No, it's not okay!"

I wondered if he knew she was pregnant. That was another friendship that had come as a surprise to me. Was it because Channing was already accustomed to relating to a gay man?

The stack in front of Mayfield wasn't close to disappearing: it looked like at least another hour, maybe two, would pass as the same opinions were expressed over and over again. I wished that the board would call it quits. They'd heard what they needed to hear, surely. A few people here and there had left, but most of the crowd seemed determined to stay.

"Jose Garza, Margarita Podnozky, Jane Gogan, and Kevin Bannerman."

My head snapped up. Kevin?

I couldn't take my eyes from him as he got up from his seat, buttoned his suit jacket, and found his way down to the floor. He was easily the most handsome man in the hall, but then maybe I was seeing him through eyes nobody else had. He looked up into the audience as he stood there, and Channing in front of me lifted her hand to him in acknowledgement. But then his gaze shifted, and it was me he wanted. I'd tried to deny that for weeks because I didn't understand it: how could he want me? But he did.

I wrested my eyes away. It seemed all night that was all I'd been doing: looking and then not looking, at him, at the kids, at everything. Furiously, as I stared at my shoes, I told myself that I should be a blind man, shouldn't I? Maybe that's what I should do, just poke out my eyes, and then maybe I could go out in public again.

I bit the side of my mouth quite deliberately, because I couldn't allow bitter thoughts like that to take over. I was Teacher of the Year and all that. Remember? I had that precious, tiny, Kevin-less life I needed to protect.

"Hey, man, are you okay?"

That was biker-man again. I hadn't realized I was leaning forward with my hands welded together, shaking. Christ! What kind of spectacle was I making of myself?

I sat up straight in a hurry. "Fine. Thanks."

Kevin wasn't looking at me anymore. He was saying something to the woman who would speak before he did. Kevin could afford to make a public statement. No one would question him the way they could question, even crucify me. He'd been married; he was a father; his daughter was in the play. I couldn't do the same, not even to support a play with Tom Collins and Angel in it.

And for the umpteenth time, I reminded myself I didn't want the play to go on.

"That was only four," somebody from down front yelled. Others said the same thing, and Mayfield looked over at the four people waiting their turn to speak.

"Four? Oh, sorry." He picked up one last card. "Robert Sutton."

Robert Sutton? Robbie? What more could happen?

"Don't," Channing said loudly enough for me to hear.

"I've got to," he said. "You know I do. I've got it all planned."

Panicked, I watched them hug, and then he left her to go stand next to her father.

"Now, folks," Mayfield said. "Let me have everybody's attention, please. It's almost eleven already, and it's a workday and a school day for most of us tomorrow. We're pleased to have such hearty attendance at one of our meetings, and your elected school board members are always happy to hear from you. But I'm going to cut off this conversation about the *Rent* play after, uh," he consulted the card, "after Mr. Sutton speaks. He'll be the last one. If anybody else has something more to say that hasn't already been covered, please feel free to e-mail any one of us on this board, and we'll be more than happy to read what you've got to say. All right now? Mr. Garza, please step forward."

I had no idea what the other three said. I'm sure they were well-meaning people, sincere in what they believed, but the night had narrowed down to Kevin and Robbie. I heard no one until Kevin stepped up to speak.

"Good evening, everyone. Members of the board. My name is Kevin Bannerman. I'm a citizen of Kenneton, so I can't vote for or against you, but my daughter Channing has the role of Maureen in the play, and I've been volunteering to help with scenery when I can." He was trying to speak especially clearly, I could tell, so that his voice could still be heard despite his constant hoarse handicap. I heard him fine up in the top row, but then, I'd heard him when he whispered.

"I'm glad I slipped in under the wire and have the chance to let you know what I think about *Rent.* I don't have a lot to say, just two things, really, so I won't keep you long.

"First, I think a lot of people against the play are attempting to shelter children from what they perceive to be bad things. Others see it differently. I can't imagine trying to keep the real world from my daughter. I think that's part of my job as her father: to prepare her for the future. I haven't done as good a job at that as I would have liked to, but I don't think forbidding her from acting in the play would help. It would have the opposite effect. Channing's role is thought-provoking, and the thing is…." He paused and looked down the line at each of the board members. After hearing so many, they were trying hard to pretend they were paying attention. "The thing is that there really are people like Maureen and Joanne and Angel and Collins. We might not know much about them here in west Texas, but they are part of our world."

I was paralyzed. I felt as if any blink, any breath would reveal how moved I was by what he was saying and how proud I was of him. I had no right to own that pride because I didn't have the guts to be with him, but oh how I admired his courage. My Kevin, my pickup from the bar. What a joke. What a sorry, ironic joke the fates had played on Tom Smith.

"So, you can tell I'm for the play continuing. But I have a second reason for supporting this production of *Rent*, and here it is. It's about love and friendship. And in my opinion, love and friendship are what make life on this planet worthwhile."

Kevin looked down at where his hands were grasping the edge of the podium, and somehow I knew what he was going to say. My throat got tight.

"Without those two things, life is hardly worth living. That's what gets us through the hardest times in our lives, times when we don't think we can get through another day, or times when we're asked to do the hardest things, things we can't imagine ourselves doing. But if we've got love backing us up… we can do it."

He looked back up at the board members. "I know you've heard from a lot of people tonight who are against the play, and I'm afraid of what your decision will be. So if you don't mind, I want to take this opportunity to publicly say thank you." Kevin turned to face the audience and raised his voice, since he didn't have the mike anymore. "Thanks to the cast and the crew of *Rent*, who have shown me how high school students can make great art. Thanks especially to Mr. George Keating, the director of the play, and to Mr. Tom Smith, the assistant director, for letting me in, and providing me with an incredible experience that I won't soon forget."

He turned back to the board. "That's it. Please let this play go on."

The crowd had long since stopped clapping for the speakers, but there was a smattering of applause as he went back to his seat. Channing hugged him, and Julianne did too. I sat three rows behind him, mute and motionless.

"And now the last speaker for the night, Robert Sutton."

It flashed through my mind that when this night was over—one of the most nerve-racking, difficult nights of my life—I would be going home to my house alone. The only way I would have to de-stress would be opening the refrigerator and reaching for a beer or finishing the bottle of Jack Daniels I'd cracked open the night before. I had no one to complain to, no one to share my anger with. I didn't even have a dog to howl at the moon with me because of what Robbie had said in some misguided attempt to convince the board to let the play proceed.

I feared what he was going to say, mightily.

"Hi," he said at the podium. "I'm Robert Sutton. I play the role of Angel in *Rent*. Angel's gay, and he's a drag queen too. Pretty weird, huh?"

Robbie jammed one hand in his pocket. His voice was trembling, and he seemed even younger than seventeen.

"Angel has AIDS in the play, and he's the one who dies. He has a great death scene where he goes offstage in a white sheet, off to heaven. At least I like to think it's heaven, though I bet not everybody here thinks so. Some of you probably think he's going to hell. But I don't see that Angel does anything bad, really. He's a good guy. And he loves Tom Collins. They've got a song they sing together, and after it, they kiss."

The hall was so quiet you could have heard the pages of a church choir book being turned. Robbie touched his lips with his fingertips, as if to remember that kiss. With a shock, I recognized the feeling behind that touch. He was afraid the board would close *Rent* down, and so he'd never rehearse with Steven again, and they'd already had their last kiss.

Our last kiss, Kevin's and mine, had been an angry one. I'd told him it didn't make any difference, but I was wrong. Kevin's kisses had changed me… just not enough to make me the man he wanted me to be.

Robbie went on. "A lot of people have talked about how awful it is, that kiss. But I agree that love is what the show's about, and without that kiss, well, it would be, like, faking it. You can't have one without the other, not the way those two characters feel about each other.

"Oh, and one more thing. You heard how Mr. Bannerman said that there really are people like Angel and Collins and Maureen and Joanne? I'm one of them. I'm gay."

The entire room, it seemed, gasped out loud. Dear God, why had Robbie… why had he said that? I dropped my head into my hands. His life was going to be a nightmare until he graduated.

"I'm one of those people the play is written about, only it's 2008 and I live in Texas, and I don't have AIDs or do drugs or anything like that." He spread both arms to either side of him. "But here I am. As real as could be. The way I look at it, this is the way God made me. If you ignore me by trying to ignore the play, then you're dissing on God's creation. And I don't think he'd want you to do that."

His hands dropped to his sides and he stood there, a slender, pale boy who'd just come out in front of hundreds of people, when he already knew for sure many of them would never be able to accept him and many would probably even hate him for it. Because in this town, gay people didn't exist.

"He is one cool cat," the man next to me said quietly. "Bravest thing I've ever seen." Abruptly he stood up. "Hey!" he called down to

Robbie. Everybody turned to look at him. "I'm just visiting here, rode my bike in to see my cousin and heard about all this. I'm gay too. There's plenty of us all over. You find yourself a better place than Gunning some day, and you'll do fine."

A few seconds passed while Robbie smiled shakily up at biker-man, but then all hell broke loose as it seemed every person in the hall had something to say. Some of the roaring was angry, no question. Mayfield grabbed his gavel, rapped it on the table, and hollered, "This session of the Gunning School Board is adjourned." I could barely hear him.

Biker-man turned around and jutted his hand in my face, asking for a shake. "Seems you've been taking this play thing a little hard," he said. "Hope it all works out, but I'm hitting the road tomorrow and can't hang around to find out. Do you know that kid?"

I nodded, because I couldn't find any words.

"You give him this, then." He hauled out his wallet, selected a card, and thrust it into my hand. It said *Phoenix Pride*. "I gotta go."

I sat there for a while, not seeing anything but a blur of people getting up and leaving and not hearing much of anything either. Like the biker had said, what Robbie had done was the bravest thing I'd ever seen too, and the stupidest. But he'd done it, and now it would be up to teachers like me to help protect him… except, of course, I couldn't do it too obviously, or people might talk about me the same way they would undoubtedly be talking about Robbie for months to come.

But maybe his coming out of the closet could be a good thing for me. Maybe it would work the opposite of what I feared. All the attention would be focused on him, and maybe nobody would even notice Mr. Smith standing in the shadows. And Mr. Bannerman, the man who'd spoken at the school board meeting that time back in November? Well, nobody would ever remember him. Hadn't he left town?

Eventually I left with the last of the stragglers. I'd successfully evaded George and anybody else who might have wanted to talk to me. I didn't feel as if I could tolerate the postmortems, the speculations. I didn't have it in me to dissemble that way right now. I'd been stripped naked by life and had no protection anymore. As I pushed the double doors open, the cold night air hit my face and woke me up as if from some sort of sleepwalking episode, and I thought: I made it through. Nobody knows about me. It's November. Thanksgiving's next week. I'll go to the ranch. No Kevin.

A long line of cars with their headlights cutting through the dark was trying to leave the parking lot through the two inadequate exits. The lot itself was dotted with cars and trucks that had their motors running, people sitting inside them, waiting. I started off across the striped surface to where I'd parked.

"Mr. Smith."

I whirled around as if I'd need to defend myself and even had to hold my hand out against the glare shining off the asphalt to see, but it was only Mr. and Mrs. Sutton coming toward me. Looking as grave as ever, Mr. Sutton extended his hand and shook mine.

"Just wanted to say thanks for all you've done for Robbie," he said gruffly. "He's told us how you've been on the lookout for him."

"I'm a counselor for the play," I said, falling back to my fail-safe position. No way I'd be helping him out because I was gay too. "It's my job."

"Still," Mrs. Sutton chimed in, "we appreciate it."

"Look," I said a little desperately, looking at their placid faces, "maybe you don't get it. What Robbie just did, it's.... Well, I wouldn't say it's dangerous, but he's going to have a tough time at school now."

"We know," she said, nodding.

"If they let it go on, you really need to think about pulling him from the play. If he plays Angel, it's going to bring him so much attention, and it won't be the good kind."

"Oh, no," Mrs. Sutton said. "We can't do that. We support Robbie all the way."

I wanted to shake these two. "Don't you understand? He's set himself up for a world of hurt! A world of isolation and depression and… and… and difficulty."

"Of course," she said gently. "But how different is that from any high school student?"

I stared at her. "Don't you want to protect him?"

"Of course we do. He's applying to the most gay-friendly colleges we can find. There's a website online where you can find out about these things."

"But—"

"High school's hard for a lot of kids," Mr. Sutton said. "But Robbie's tough. I'm real proud of him. When he told me last night he was gonna do what he did, I almost tried to talk him out of it."

"Me too," Mrs. Sutton said. She pulled her jacket more closely around her.

"But then I thought I shouldn't," Robbie's dad said. "Everybody's got a different way of showing who they are. Mine was military service over in Desert Storm. 197th Infantry Brigade, Mechanized. But that's not Robbie's way. I'm proud of my son. What he did tonight called for a lot of guts."

"Yes indeed," his mother agreed.

"Yep, I almost forgot that life ain't no picnic, that's for sure, and what Channing's dad said is true, a father can't protect his kid forever. And I can't change him, neither." He laughed briefly, a fierce eruption from his overlarge frame. "That boy of mine is one of the most stubborn kids in your school, didn't you know it? We tried to get him to stop playing with the dollies when he was three, and he went on a hunger strike that almost wasted him away to nothing. Nope, the boy's got to be what the boy is."

"He'll be all right," his mother said. "It'll take some time and care, but Robbie will find his place."

"Anyway, just wanted to stop by and say thanks for the help with him so far. I'm guessing you won't have to worry about the play and him being on stage in that role, cause there ain't no way it'll keep going."

"It's such a shame," she said.

"Yep, but that's the way the cookie crumbles."

I watched them leave and wondered if they realized what they'd said. They'd watched their son come out for no reason at all? Then why had he done it?

THE streets of Gunning were quiet as I drove from the administration building to my house on the west side of town. After the tumult of the meeting, the silence all around should have been soothing, but it wasn't. I was a jumble of thoughts and feelings, as if my brain were moving as quickly as my car, and I wouldn't be able to settle on anything until I was fixed in one place in my home. So I drove too fast. South on Jefferson past Hunnicutt's church and then west on McCarthy for twelve blocks before I could turn into my modest, aging subdivision. Hardly anyone was on the road, though, at almost midnight. Where had all those impassioned people from the meeting gone?

Fifteen years ago, after therapy had made me as good as I was going to get, it'd been turn left onto Suppression Street, then travel along the straight and narrow Hidden Cove Drive and stay there, going on and on and on. I'd traveled ten million miles on that road.

Why was I thinking about that? I'd been letting myself remember Sean and those bad days too much lately. I had enough trouble to deal with without reliving the disaster that was my past.

Turn into English Estates, then left, right, left, and there was my house at the end of the street, and past it my attached garage, and finally home and safety.

Except I didn't get as far as my garage. Parked in front of my house was a familiar Silverado.

With a thump of my heart and a wrench of the steering wheel, I pulled in directly behind it and killed my engine. Nobody was in the cab, but a shadow sat on my doorstep. As I watched, he stood up.

Anger was safe to feed on, so I gulped it down. The car door couldn't let me out of the Miata fast enough. I stormed up the walkway, my shadow reaching him first because of the streetlight behind me. My fists tightened by my sides and I was barely able to stop myself, inches short of Kevin.

"What are you doing here?" I ground out between lips that didn't seem to want to move.

"Returning your stuff." He lifted my overnight bag that he was carrying in one hand.

"Then give it to me and get out of here."

"Tom…."

I got right up into his face, as if we were going to kiss right there on Somerset Drive in front of all my neighbors. I wanted to kiss him. I wanted to throw him back into his pickup and kick his ass. Kiss his ass. Kick it. "You need to leave, now."

"No."

"I said, go."

"I'm not going anywhere."

"Give me that." I reached for the bag, and we fought for control of it, me trying to pull it away from him, him trying to keep it to himself. He punched my right shoulder to shove me away, and I staggered back empty-handed, gasping.

Kevin threw the bag behind him, and it landed against my outside door with a clunk on the metal, so loud on my slumbering street that I winced.

"You don't get it until you let me in."

"Into my house? No."

"We need to talk. Let's go inside."

"We can't. Kevin, just leave."

"If you don't let me in, I swear I'm going to start hollering right here and wake everybody up."

"You wouldn't."

His eyes narrowed. "Oh, yes I will. Try me."

"That won't solve anything."

"The only way to solve anything is to talk. C'mon, let me in before I start shouting."

I hesitated, but there wasn't any question what I would do. My keys were in my pocket and then in my hand, and I brushed past him to unlock the door. Any idea I had about darting inside without him he got rid of by crowding behind me and pushing up against me, the way I loved him to do. I instantly stilled, closed my eyes, and tucked my chin into my chest. He couldn't have gotten any closer. His breath caressed my neck, and his groin warmed my ass. I wanted to say what I'd said before, that what he was doing wouldn't make any difference. But I knew better. The way I felt about Kevin, how I longed for everything to be all right between us, how I wanted to go inside, rip off his clothes, leave bite marks all over his neck, and bruise his hips with my possessive grip: that made everything more difficult.

"Stop it," I managed to get out.

"I don't want to. You don't want me to, either."

The key turned and the door opened. We tumbled inside, and he slammed the door behind him, leaving the bag outside.

I flipped on the lights and whirled around to face him, there in my tiny entryway with the fake Mexican tile, with the plastic overhead lamp glowing yellow and making me blink, with the living room behind me and the front room open to the side. Even in my most irrational, deepest imaginings, I'd never seen him here where I lived: Kevin in the perfectly fitting suit he'd worn to work and the board meeting, stubble on his chin, and determination in his eyes.

I had to get rid of him. Having him here was a representation of the impossible when the impossible was all I wanted. No one could tolerate that, especially not me.

"Kevin, this isn't going to work. Don't make it any harder than it already is."

"Why won't you talk to me? I make one mistake and…. Are you really saying this is it between us?"

"You know we can't be together. We're never going to work out."

"Why? Because of what I didn't tell you about Channing? Tom…." He took a step closer, one hand reaching for me and pleading. "I'm sorry. God, I can't tell you how sorry I am for that. Give me the chance to—"

"No, it's not that. Yes, it…. Shit, it's that and everything else. Don't you see?"

"See what?"

"If we keep seeing each other, there's no way we can keep it quiet. We'll both be outed." I backed up a couple feet away from him. "Just go. You can't stay here."

"Sure I can."

"Are you crazy? This is my house and I don't want you here. Get out!"

"That's bullshit. You want me here and you know it, but you're afraid of your own shadow." Relentlessly, he came up close to me again, I backed off, and he followed me. He'd herded me to the edge of the foyer, almost to the step down to my living room. "Don't be afraid, Tom."

I knew what he wanted, and I put all the scorn I could muster into my words. "So you think I should be inspired by you and by Robbie? Is that right? For God's sakes, Kevin! You want me to follow his lead and throw my life away?"

"No, I want you to reach for the life you deserve."

"I'll be the judge of what I want and what I deserve, not you. I'm fine the way I am."

"You are? You're fine? Finally, the elephant in the room that we were never able to talk about!"

"Yes, I'm fine," I stubbornly insisted.

"You've got to be kidding!"

"Don't you dare to presume anything about me. I make my own choices. What, are you going to out me yourself?"

"This doesn't have anything to do with outing or not. If you were as straight as John Wayne, I'd still say the same things to you. This has to do with living."

I saw red; my throat got so tight I could barely breathe. "How dare you say that to me," I gritted out to him. "Get the fuck out of here."

"I am not going away. Look at yourself. Take a good look at yourself. And then think of how things could be if you stopped being so afraid."

"Go to hell."

"You hide all the time. Constantly. Your every move with me.... Come on, leaving town for weekend dates?"

My face flushed with heat. "Shut up, Kevin. Shut up."

"Being so afraid to come to my house? Freaking out over this play?" He threw his arms wide and gestured wildly, as if taking in the whole of my doll's house. "What kind of life have you been living?"

I lunged for him, clawing at his chest and pushing him back brutally against the door, and I was right there, up against him. "It's my life!" I screamed. "You don't have any right to change it."

He stopped fighting me, collapsed willingly back against the wood, and every part of us was pressed together.

"Sure I have a right," he said calmly. His blue eyes were beautiful. "I love you."

That was as painful as a punch to the stomach. "You can't," I gasped.

"Do you think a person has any control over something like that?" Then his voice turned soft, caressing, and his hand came up between us. The tips of his fingers stroked my face. "Damn it, Tom, I love you. Listen to me, please."

I was numb and not able to move.

Slowly, Kevin straightened against the door. "I'm on the edge of changing everything," he said, as sincere as I'd ever heard him. "In a few months, in the spring, I'm going to be leaving here and starting everything new. Quit the job and go someplace where I can be honest and open about who I am. When I go… I want you to go with me."

Before that night at Good Times when we danced, I would have laughed at him. But since that first time I'd touched him, Kevin had been… not pushing me forward, but pulling me backward. He made me remember the young man I'd been: in love, full of hope, when I'd honestly believed there wasn't anything I wouldn't be able to do. I closed my eyes and remembered that man, honored him, mourned for him, and wished with everything I was that he still existed.

But he didn't. I opened my eyes and sneered at Kevin because he was appealing to someone I wasn't, and because he had the audacity to think otherwise. This small life, this restrictive home was my reality.

"Go with you? Don't you mean you want to take me with you? Put me on your leash so I can be your boy toy you can push this way and that, get me to do anything you want?" I hardly knew where that had come from, but once said, I realized how truly I felt it, and how I'd resented what Kevin had tried to do to me.

"What?" He released me with something like horror in his eyes. "You can't believe I think of you that way."

"Why not? I'm nothing like the man you want me to be, so you keep pushing me…." I reached for the ammunition that I knew would hurt him most. "You like that, being in charge, making me the way you want me."

"Goddamnit, no!" he roared. "You stupid fuck! I can't believe you…. That's what you think?" Suddenly he spun away and stepped down to the front room. He paced the short length of it while he ran both hands through his hair, and then he turned to face me. He didn't speak right away but took a few deep, definite breaths, and I saw the effort he made to calm himself.

"Look. If I've made you think I don't respect you…. Hell, that thing with Channing, what a mistake, but it doesn't mean…. I do respect you, Tom, and I'm not interested in dominating you or changing…. Well, okay, so I do want you to change, but it's for your own…. Shit, this is impossible!"

"Exactly," I said, but my voice was hollow. The entire day rolled in on me in one giant wave, and I'd rarely been so tired. I wanted to sleep forever, to have good dreams, to wake up next to Kevin and have it be an everyday occurrence. "This is impossible. We're impossible. I want… I wish I could do this, but I can't. I'm a coward."

"No, you're not, you're—"

"Yes, I am," I said calmly, and admitting the truth to him was eerily easy. "I used to think the opposite, but not anymore. Do you think I want to send you away? You're the best thing that ever happened to me. You think I don't want a life like everybody else has, with somebody to talk with, somebody to share with, somebody to love? I do. But I can't."

He walked over to me again but stopped before taking that one step up to the foyer that would have put us on equal ground. He looked up to me and asked the one important question.

“Why?”

For a few trembling seconds I let the question hang. Surely I wasn’t going to….

“I already told you,” I grated out.

“That’s labeling, not explaining. Why? Why can’t we be together?”

“Because of….”

“What? What?” Kevin grabbed my arms, and I didn’t resist when he shook me. “Tell me!”

I broke away from him and stumbled down onto the shag carpet I hated, across the room and through the door into the little area where I kept the kitchen table. I leaned on it, exhausted, my head hanging down, and I began to tremble. I’d never told anyone….

“Because of graduation night.”

He’d come up behind me. “What? I didn’t hear. What?”

“I said, because of graduation night. And this.” I turned around and held my left arm out.

He looked at my arm, clothed in the black sports coat I’d worn for the meeting, from my shoulder down to my wrist. He took my hand and held on, his fingers bearing down hard on me. “Tell me,” he said intensely, looking into my eyes.

“I’ve never told the truth. Not even to….”

I collapsed down onto the chair I used to eat dinner and breakfast. Kevin followed me without letting go of my hand, onto the chair that only Grant had ever sat in.

With my arm stretched out on the table between us, I looked over at him. I should have known. I should have known months ago that this man would require everything of me.

“You never told who?” Kevin asked quietly.

"The cops," I said. "Grant." Nausea rolled up in me. I swallowed, but I couldn't force it down. It was an old feeling and an old taste. "It happened…."

"When you graduated from college?"

I nodded, a monumental effort because I was dizzy with the memories. "I had a boyfriend in college. Sean Harrison. I loved him." My mouth twisted. "Or I thought I did."

"You were, what, twenty-one? Twenty-two? We all make—"

"No," I said clearly. "This was more than a breakup. This was…." The night everything broke.

In a moment my queasiness turned into full-blown vomit, heaving up from my stomach. I ran for the kitchen and spewed my guts out into the sink. I'd tried so hard to put that night behind me, to forget, but I hadn't. It was all still there, rotting inside me, poisoning my heart and my brain. The filth burned my mouth. I heaved some more, clutching the edge of the sink, choking and wanting it all out of me, out of me, oh, God, out of me.

Finally there was nothing more that I could spit out, but I didn't move. I couldn't. Hanging on seemed as much as I could do. A minute later Kevin reached past my head to turn on the water. I watched my puke wash down the garbage disposal, only inches away. Kevin rubbed the back of my neck.

"Just breathe," he said. "Breathe."

If he'd said one more thing, I felt as if I would disappear too, swirled around and around and down. But he didn't. After a while I opened my mouth, and words I'd never said out loud were finally said.

"I hate him!" I gasped. "God, I hate him."

"Tom…." I felt Kevin embrace my shoulders, and a moment later lips brushed the back of my head. "It's okay, it's—"

I shrugged him away. "No, it's not! Don't patronize me." I got myself up onto my good elbow, leaned on the counter, and wiped at my eyes with my other hand, but they were dry. "I hate him for being a coward, and I've become the exact same thing, haven't I?" I turned just my head and looked through blurry eyes at Kevin. "Look at what you've done to me."

"Tom, I'm—"

"Shut up," I snapped at him, and then I stood up. "You want to know what happened? I'll tell you, and then you'll know why I'm not the man you need." I reached for a glass I kept on the counter, ran water, and rinsed out my mouth. I dumped out what I hadn't used and deliberately set it back where it'd been, delaying yet another second or two. I suddenly saw that I'd been doing more than keeping Kevin at arm's length with my constant demands to conduct our relationship anywhere it couldn't be real. Somehow I'd seen this moment of confession creeping up on me, and I'd been pushing it away and away…. Well, I couldn't do that anymore.

I turned and faced him. In the fluorescent light from overhead, his face was drawn as if he'd been kept awake for days.

"They ran over my arm," I said bluntly. Maybe I wanted him to be so horrified he'd leave me alone, or not want to hear any more. I watched while he drew in a quick breath, as the look in his eyes changed. "With a pickup truck. I was lucky with the way I was laying in the street that it was only my arm."

Kevin didn't go. He stayed. "Jesus. Who?"

"The group of guys who jumped me outside the bar." I was shocked to hear myself. I sounded calm, but inside I was shattered glass.

"A group?"

"I couldn't get Sean to go with me. His family was having a big celebration dinner for him, and then he was going out with some friends. We'd kept our relationship a secret, and we ran with separate crowds." My mouth still tasted foul. I licked my lips. "So I went alone up to Austin. It's not even half an hour away. I knew there was a gay bar there, and I wanted to go. It was my own personal celebration."

My gaze had drifted away from Kevin's; I forced myself back to confront his distress. Already he looked gutted, and I hadn't even…. My lips kept moving. "It didn't matter that I did it without Sean. He wouldn't have cared. We'd see each other a lot over the summer, and then we were going to meet in Dallas in the fall, where we'd each gotten teaching jobs. I thought we'd find an apartment together."

"But…." I could see Kevin didn't understand the connection. "But you didn't do that with him?"

"No," I said wearily. "I wasn't able to work in the fall because I was still all messed up. I didn't come here until the year after. That whole year Grant propped me up. He made me fit for working again. He made sure I applied for this job at Gunning and shoved me out the door when the time came, patting me on the back the whole time. He thought I was healed enough by then."

Kevin came closer and put his hand on my bad arm, the one that always felt cold. "You're not healed yet, are you?"

"No," I whispered, and I hated the tears that washed into my eyes. Hated that Kevin understood that when I hadn't until now. Angrily, I held back the tears.

"Being gay-bashed, run over…. Tom, anybody would take that kind of violence hard, it's no wonder—"

"That's not it."

"That's not what?" He frowned at me.

I turned away from him in my narrow galley kitchen. The refrigerator was to my left, the sink with its curtained window hiding the world was to my right. With Kevin behind me, I was trapped where I was.

That was okay. I could talk. It would only be telling a story. I looked at the clock on the wall, feet in front of me. Almost one o'clock. The second hand moved, the minutes would pass, and the years, they had passed behind me, hadn't they? Still, I remembered the attack like it was yesterday.

"I came out of the bar around one o'clock. Like a fool, I'd parked on the street, blocks away. No lights, no other people, but footsteps behind me, a bunch of them. I tried to pretend they didn't mean anything. I'd just got to my car when they came up behind me and knocked me to the ground."

It sounded so simple to say knocked to the ground. Nothing like how it'd really been: my racing heart, reaching for the car door, the fist coming out of nowhere pounding my face, the crunch of my nose blooming blood, another punch in the gut and doubling over, calls of *that got him, what a pansy, can't even fight, hey look, it's that guy from history class, he's been pretending he's normal* and then the roar of anger from all of them. Almost all of them. Five of them against me. I'd never been a fighter. Never been punched seriously. Never felt the shock of sudden pain that robbed me of thought.

I took a breath and went on, but it wasn't as easy this time as I got closer to the truth. "They were all drunk. Hell, I was drunk too. I had a hard time seeing who they were, but every time I got one of their faces in focus, I saw that it was somebody I knew from school. They must've been out in downtown Austin celebrating too. I guess one of them had the bright idea to go razz the gays. I don't know how they found the bar. When I was in rehab, sometimes I dreamed that Sean told them."

"He wouldn't have," Kevin soothed from behind me, senselessly. He didn't know, did he? But his hands were on me, flat on my back, on my shoulder blades, caring, and when did anybody touch me because he cared?

"They were out to beat up a faggot. The fact that they'd found somebody they all knew just made it sweeter."

I was in the gym locker room with him last month! God, disgusting! Get him, Andy, get him good.

"I tried to fight back, but I didn't have a chance. Every time I got back to my feet, they knocked me down. And kicked." I wanted to protect my side as I remembered how that had felt, to be helplessly flat with the concrete against my back, to see one of them draw back his foot and know I couldn't roll away before it got my ribs. "A lot of kicking when I was down, and it wasn't long before I wasn't in very good shape. I…. "

I wouldn't throw up again, I wouldn't. I could tell Kevin this, but not too much. Not that I'd choked on the taste of my own blood, and how I'd panicked when more of it dripped down into my eyes. But I could tell him this much. "I'd never hurt like that before."

I'd moaned there on the ground, rolling from side to side and praying they'd stop or that I'd die. But they'd kept at it and at it, going on and on…. And when they finally had stopped, it was only because they'd thought of something worse than beating me up.

"They hauled me up onto my knees and I couldn't stay up. They were saying something I couldn't make any sense of, because it was hard to hear anything, there was this ringing…. I fell down, but they got me on my knees again, with two of them holding me up by my arms. 'Somebody stick it in', they said, and I knew what they meant. Later on, I was grateful it wasn't rape."

Kevin pressed against me. "My God, Tom. That was rape, of course it was."

I barely heard him. I was back in that moment, what I'd tried to forget. It wasn't a story I was telling. This was real. This had happened to me. My tongue was thick in my mouth but I kept going. "They argued about it, who would do the deed, and then they stopped and there was this bare dick in front of me. Somebody grabbed my hair and pulled my head back, and I saw who it was. It was… it was Sean."

He'd been there all along. That pair of Adidas sneakers I'd seen when I'd rolled over onto my side, retching—those were Sean's. That voice I'd heard shouting, "You make me sick, fag!"—that had been Sean's.

"No!" Kevin choked out.

"He looked down at me, and it was like we didn't even know each other. He said…. He said…."

"It's all right, you don't have to tell anymore. Tom, don't."

But I had to get it all out. The things Sean had said to me. "He said, 'I thought you were my friend. But you're a homo. You're disgusting. Take it, bitch.' It was like we'd never… never…." I couldn't keep my tears in anymore. They spilled over my cheeks. "He used to love sixty-nining with me. That was his favorite thing. On Saturday night, we'd get drunk and pass out in his room, and when we woke up we'd—"

"Damn him!"

Even with tears flowing down my face, it was Kevin who was feeling it, not me. My anger from minutes before was gone. I was numb, transparent, without any substance of my own. It was better this way; had I waited all this time for someone to feel for me? "Yeah. Damn him. He just… shoved it… shoved it… in my mouth."

"Tom…." Kevin laid his head on my shoulder now, and he was practically holding me up with his arms around me from behind. "Honey, please don't."

I couldn't stop now. "Everybody was shouting and making bets… on how long it would take. I couldn't…. I kept seeing him over me, the look on his face, and I thought it couldn't be true. It couldn't be him fucking my mouth, but it was."

"He's the coward," Kevin spit out. "He was running with the crowd and got caught in it, didn't he? And he didn't know how to get himself out of it, even when it was you they found to bash. Oh, Tom, oh, hell…."

The salt of my crying had trickled into my mouth. "Afterward…. I've never known where the truck came from. I thought they were done with me. I didn't even know I was lying in the street and not on the sidewalk."

"Bastards!"

"The cops said I shouldn't assume that whoever attacked me also ran me over, but that never made any sense to me. It was them."

He drew back a little "Wait a minute. What do you mean, whoever attacked you?"

"I couldn't see them, didn't you know? It was dark, there were so many of them, and the cops didn't push me on it. I was just another faggot who got what he deserved, you know?"

"Fuck! You did that to protect Sean?"

"I did it to protect myself," I said harshly. "So I wouldn't have to testify. I couldn't do that. By the time I was well enough for them to question me, I'd decided that nobody would ever know what really…. I didn't want to think about him, didn't want to think about any of it, and I—"

"Wait a minute, wait a minute." Kevin didn't give me a choice, he turned me around to face him. "You said that you'd never told this to anybody…. So nobody knew about the rape? You mean since then you've never told—"

"Wasn't being run over enough? I was only another guy from the gay bar bashed in the night, with FAGGOT scraped into the hood of my car with a key. Nobody needed to know anything else. It wasn't like there was any evidence."

His voice shook. "You should have told, should have…. You needed counseling, help, some way to cope—"

"And then maybe I wouldn't be so messed up, is that what you're saying?"

"You were betrayed by your closest friend, for God's sake, by your *lover.* No wonder you—" He stopped abruptly.

I finished for him. "No wonder I decided that alive in the closet was better than dead on the street. And that I could do just fine going to Houston now and then. It was all I needed, until you came along."

"I *hate* Sean," Kevin hissed.

Kevin reflected me again, because I couldn't dredge up that same hatred, not now, though I knew I'd felt it before. I was too exhausted, too emptied.

"And now you know why I am the way I am," I said. "Why you and me together are impossible. I've got good reason for how I live. Now, will you leave?"

Kevin didn't answer out loud. Instead, he pulled me forward, wrapped his arms around me, and hugged me close.

I stood stiffly within his hold for a long time as he cried against my neck, because he was here when he shouldn't be, and he cared about me, and I didn't know if I could tolerate his caring, not about this. It was as if I'd have to walk barefoot across the shards of brokenness inside me to get to him, and I'd already been hurt so badly.

But after a while, sheer tiredness forced me to lean my head against his, and my hand inched up to clutch his shirt. I staggered against him and then rested within his hold. My eyelids drooped.

He whispered my name and spread his fingers in my hair. Swirls of images, feelings, sounds raced through my mind: the grunt that Sean always made when he came, that all those other guys heard when he gave it up to me on graduation night and flooded my mouth with bitterness; blinking my eyes open for the first time in the hospital, cushioned by the pain meds; the one and only time my parents came to visit me in the rehab facility, and after that Grant awkwardly explaining how busy they were; how empty my house seemed on the day I moved in with not much furniture, and how grateful I was to close the door behind me; the first time I received a thank-you note from a student, and then the time a parent told me I'd made a real difference in her daughter's life; the last song of the night at Good Times, when a dark-haired stranger came up to me and asked me to dance.

"God, Tom," Kevin husked. "I'm so sorry."

It was like coming up through water to hear him and to know that he was here with me. I'd told somebody. I'd told Kevin.

"I'm so sorry that you had to go through that, that it happened to you." He pulled back and took my face between his hands. "You've been alone with this for a long time."

"Now you know."

He looked so serious. "Thanks for telling me. It explains a lot."

I took in a deep breath. "My whole life. Kevin, I can't change. This is it. This is me now."

His hands on my face moved up over my ears, down to my neck, and back to where they'd started. "I love you."

God, I wished he'd stop saying that. He cut me each time he did. "It doesn't matter. We can't be together."

"You're exhausted."

"Awake, asleep, tired or not, it's always the same thing. I made a big mistake trying to date you. I didn't mean to lead you on. I thought…."

I really had thought I could, hadn't I? I'd thought that if I put boundaries on it, our relationship could be contained in one sharply defined corner of my life. But it had blasted past all my good intentions.

I should have pulled away from him, stopped letting him touch me, released him, but I couldn't. "I'm sorry. If I could…." This was killing me. "You know that if I could…."

"You can," he said, desperately. "Tom, you can, if you only—"

That did it, that gave me the strength to push myself away. "Kevin! Please! I can't. Get it?"

I saw him take that in, saw his devastation for a few seconds, and then the resolve returned to his eyes. He wouldn't have been Kevin if he'd listened. "I get that this isn't the time to talk about this. I'll go, but do you think you'll be all right?"

"I'm fine," I said.

Kevin grimaced. "Right. I've heard you say that before. Do you think you'll be able to sleep?"

"Just go, okay?"

"I'm…. Listen, maybe I should stay, just to make sure you'll be okay."

"You don't need to."

"But I want to make sure—"

"I've lived with this for years. I'm not going to kill myself, if that's what you think. It's… it's old news."

"No, not so old, I don't think."

Of course he was right, but I wouldn't admit it. "If nothing else," I dredged up, "the kids need me. Don't worry, I'll wake up in the morning and go to school."

"I need you," Kevin said flatly.

"Kevin, please. I just… I really want to be alone."

He gave up then and abruptly turned away. I followed him past my little table, through the front room, and up into the foyer. He put his hand on the doorknob and paused, turning to look at me.

"Good night, Tom. I…."

For a moment I thought he was going to try to kiss me. I couldn't let him; I'd never have the strength to make him leave if he did. His eyes focused on my lips, and he took a little half-step toward me, but then he looked into my eyes and stopped.

"Good night," he said.

The door closed behind him. I turned the deadbolt, and then I sagged back against the door. I had never felt so alone.

Ten seconds later there was a knock on the door. "Tom, open up," came his muffled voice. "We shouldn't leave your bag out here."

I unlocked the door and there he was, holding the bag out for me. “Think about it,” Kevin said. “I want to be with you.”

He did kiss me then, a swift, sweet pressing of his lips to mine that I had no ability to stop and no desire to ward off.

And then he really was gone.

DAMN you, Sean. I've done my best to forget you, and yet here you are, raping me all over again.

I struggled to find sleep that night. I'd resisted these memories for so long, had buried them deep, denied them life because I'd kept silent. But Kevin had yanked them out of the ancient sludge in my mind, and I overflowed with shame, rage, and loss.

I lay in bed with a blanket pulled up to my chin, kept my eyes closed, and struggled not to relive the worst moments of my life even as they danced brazenly before me: footsteps and dread creeping up my spine, the first blow that had stunned me, the brutality of Sean's thrusts. What I remembered most, though, was that I'd thought I loved him.

Anguish had driven me to hide in Gunning. Kevin had gotten it right. I'd been betrayed by the one I'd trusted most.

Under the sheet I rubbed my arm, trying to ease at least that ache. It was my constant reminder of the assault, which I'd tried to keep hidden from the world. But I hadn't hidden it from Kevin, had I? He'd cried for me. He'd hated Sean. For me.

See, Sean? Somebody's on my side. The best somebody.

Why was I letting myself think about Kevin? I couldn't have him. I couldn't have anybody. By sending him away, I'd lost all rights.

God, I'd been insane to do that. He could have been right next to me in bed. Not for sex this night, but to have him there, the only other person in the world who knew my whole story. Maybe I wasn't so weak after all. Knowing I'd regret sending him away for the rest of my life, but doing it anyway—that had to have been strong.

Even as I thought that, there was another part of me, a wiser, deeper part of Tom, who disagreed. Kevin wanted me. I wanted him. But I couldn't have him and live my life.

I closed my eyes, determined to escape into sleep, but I couldn't help but know I was stuck. Stuck with my aching arm and my house with the tree dying out back and the job where I pretended to be someone I wasn't, every day.

I JOLTED upright in bed, gasping, with *victim, victim, victim* resounding in my brain.

Christ! I sagged over my drawn-up knees and in the deep darkness held my head with both hands. I should have guessed the dreams would come back. I trembled, and my mouth hurt as if I'd swayed on my knees in the street two minutes ago instead of years past.

Kevin had been in my nightmare. He'd been watching it all happen, only he'd been tied to a parking meter. The whole time Sean had been going at me, I'd been impossibly watching Kevin at the same time, not knowing if he wanted to help me or join in hurting me.

And then the others had disappeared in a flash, and Kevin had revealed himself for who he really was. He'd stroked the hair back from my forehead and murmured, "You don't have to live like a victim."

In sudden, wide-awake anger, I pounded the mattress. "Yes, I do!" I hollered out loud. And then I stilled as I listened to myself. Who would say that? Nobody I knew. Nobody I respected.

ONLY long habit and my shrilling alarm clock got me up at six-fifteen to stagger into the bathroom. I tried not to look at myself as I shaved, but that was an impossible trick. The man staring at me from the mirror looked haggard and wrecked, as if he'd been on a week-long bender, or as if he'd lost the one he loved. Worse. As if he'd turned the one he loved away.

God. I missed Kevin the way I missed the strength in my arm.

I sagged against the counter and put the razor down. Wisps of white lather clung to my face here and there and, just out of view, flitting in and out of my imagination, were those five men who'd taken my life away.

Hello, Sean, I wanted to whisper, but I didn't. Only crazy people talked to ghosts from the past.

Happy now? Is this what you wanted for me?

EVERY move that morning was an effort. I wanted to go back to bed and sleep, the way I'd tried to sleep through my depression those months when I'd been recovering at Grant's apartment, when he'd instead rousted me out from under the covers and forced me into some sort of activity. I wouldn't have minded fortifying myself with some whiskey before I left my house, but I'd never gone to school drunk. I was stubborn enough to walk past the booze and get cereal and toast instead.

The pattern for the day was set as soon as I got to school. I held the door for the chemistry teacher, and she asked me, "What do you think the school board will do?"

It was a measure of my total self-absorption that her question came as a shock to me. I'd literally forgotten that the play might be canceled. But she reminded me that I needed to be on the watch for Robbie. I cursed under my breath and turned on my heel right in front of her, heading for the far wing of the school where his locker was as quickly as I could without breaking into a run. I imagined the worst, even though I told myself it was ridiculous to suppose that any of the kids would attack him the same way I'd been attacked.

When I got within sight of his locker I slowed down, because he wasn't around. But when I went closer, I saw that there were notes tucked into the crack of the locker's door, and a few books were piled in front too. I should have known. I squatted down to read the titles. One of them was the Bible and one was a paperback: *Can Homosexuality Be Healed?* I sighed and wondered that somebody in town should have that book, ready to be handed out at need.

But then, with a sort of wonder, I saw that next to the books were several envelopes, the kind that would have a greeting card inside. I picked them up even as kids walked by, immersed in the essential teenage talk for the start of the day, and as lockers around me were opened and then banged shut. One of the envelopes said *You go, Robbie!* On another was printed YOU ARE SO BRAVE, ROBBIE in block letters. The rest of them only had his name, but it seemed, unbelievably, that they held words of encouragement from castmates and friends.

"Hi, Mr. Smith," somebody said to me. I ignored whoever it was and concentrated on not clutching the cards in my hand so hard that I bent them. Maybe Robbie wouldn't be so alone. Maybe he'd have some support, the kind that was out in the open and couldn't be ignored, from people who understood who he was and what kind of help he needed. Maybe nothing earth-shattering and life-altering would happen to him, and he wouldn't be… damaged.

I really wanted to open those cards and see who'd left them, but I didn't. Instead I put them back where I'd found them and rose to check out the notes stuck halfway in his locker. Officially, the school should step in to deal with anything obscene or threatening, and I was a representative of the school.

More indications of acceptance: one girl had tied a pink ribbon around an artificial rose and wedged it into the crack. Somebody unnamed had gone to a lot of trouble printing out a beautiful photo of a rainbow over a lake. But there were also vicious words that made me wince at their crudity and virulence—words that last night I'd remembered being hurled at me, and that echoed in my ears. The drawings were worse. Three of them were definitely obscene; I crushed them in my hand and stuffed them into my pocket.

Young men could be cruel—and I had no doubt at all that these were done by fellow classmates who were male. Sean and the others had taught me about cruelty firsthand. There was a certain reflex that seemed to take over, especially in adolescents and especially in groups, when developing male sexuality was confronted with any other possibility but the preferred, dominant, hyper-masculine mode. Seek and destroy, denigrate and downgrade, threaten and attack.

I spent a moment wondering if it would do more harm than good to remove all of what I saw, and not only these few, when someone spoke to me. “Hi, Mr. Smith,” Angela Salazar said as she pulled a sweater from her nearby locker. “It’s a real shame about Robbie, isn’t it?”

I frowned, not knowing exactly what she meant. Had something happened to him? “What do you mean?” I asked sharply.

She shrugged. “Weren’t you at the meeting last night? I thought you would be. Shannon told me he told the whole place that he was gay.”

“Oh, that. Yes.”

I left the books, the cards, and the rest of the notes where they were, the good and the bad. Even though I wanted to, it would be impossible for me to protect Robbie from the fallout from his announcement.

The rest of the day was more of the same: chatter from everybody about what the board would do or chatter about Robbie. I let everybody else talk and mostly kept silent, even in the workroom or the lounge where teachers ate lunch. Teachers gossiped more than the students, I’d sometimes thought, and that lunchtime everybody was proclaiming when they’d first concluded Robbie was gay.

“From the beginning,” said the assistant principal, Neil Summers.

“That’s right, I knew it the moment he stepped into my algebra class,” said the math chair. “He was a real swish.”

“Oh, no,” Dottie Lansing submitted. “I thought he was, you know, one of the more sensitive types. Then I began to wonder when he took that role in the play, you know, the fairy one.”

I barely heard them. It was next to impossible to pull my thoughts from the dark hole they’d been in all day. I ate the disgusting enchiladas I’d gotten from the cafeteria line because I’d forgotten to bring a lunch and wondered why I’d gone to that bar in Austin. Why couldn’t I have done something, anything else? It was a well-worn groove in my mind—why this, why that—that I hadn’t revisited in years.

Why Sean? Why Austin? Why me?

Why Kevin?

I wanted to rip my thoughts away from the filth, but it seemed inevitable I'd have to live with my Sean memories now that they'd resurfaced. Kevin and I had barely made enough to count.

IT WAS good that the day wasn't a test day for any of my classes. I had to teach. My mind had to be engaged with the material and the students, with no choice to wander off into feel-mostly-dead land. If the kids didn't get the most amazing lectures from me that day, well, that at least I was able to forgive myself.

Halfway through the last class of the day, I roused enough to look ahead. Once the final bell rang I was going straight home, where I'd lock the door behind me. With any luck at all, I'd return to the pre-Kevin kind of weekend that I used to have. I wouldn't see anybody.

The loudspeaker crackled as I was giving out homework assignments. "Your attention, please," came Hiram's voice. "There is a meeting for all cast and crew members of the play in the Little Theater immediately after dismissal. Thank you."

Every single student looked at me. "Guess that takes care of that," Reuben Estaban said.

I abandoned hope of a quick getaway, of shelter and solace in a whiskey glass.

The Little Theater was crowded when I got there, with about thirty kids sitting on the floor, subdued, with a lot of slumped shoulders. Even the air in the room was heavy; discouragement was palpable. George, who I hadn't seen all day, was standing in front of them.

Okay. Time to act like a teacher and an assistant director, although it was difficult to square my shoulders and drag my thoughts from my personal hell. I went up to him and murmured, "Have you heard—" but he cut me off.

"Just wait, okay?" he said. "Is everybody here?" he asked the students.

"Johnny's not here yet. Neither is Mario or Layne."

Neither was Robbie, I saw, and that at least was enough to ring some internal alarm loud enough for me to hear. I stepped out into the hallway, looking, and then I trudged to the darkened auditorium, but nobody was singing or dancing there this day. Or getting beaten up. I suppressed the urge to go to his locker or look anywhere else for him and went back to where the rest of the cast and crew were waiting.

George retreated to his office, where we could see him through the glass wall typing something on his laptop. The kids besieged me with questions, but I couldn't tell them what I didn't know myself. I shrugged, found a chair in the corner, and waited. Then the students knew enough to leave me alone.

Finally George came back out. Like a dutiful assistant I got up to stand behind him in support. "I guess everybody's here who's interested in coming. So, could I have your attention please. I'm sorry to say that…."

He drew a deep breath but never got the next sentence out. Channing interrupted him by calling out: "Robbie! Steven! What happened to you?"

I turned to look at where Robbie and Steven had just walked in. My stomach flip-flopped. I took a few hurried, instinctive steps toward them, but the time for help was long since past. I should have gone in search of Robbie after all.

Robbie was a mess, with Steven only a little better. There was a killer bruise on Robbie's chin, and one eye was swollen and red, sure to turn into a monster black eye. The sleeve of Steven's denim jacket was hanging on by a thread, and his lip was split with blood spotting his flannel shirt.

But then I noticed: both boys were smiling. I stopped where I was, halfway to the door, perplexed.

"Hi, Mr. Keating," Robbie said, but really he was talking to everyone. "Sorry we're late."

"Yeah," Steven said, and a peacock could not have been prouder than he was. "There was a little something we needed to take care of first."

"Boys," George began. "You know fighting is against the—"

"We didn't start anything," Steven assured him. "But a couple a-holes were saying a few things about Rob, so—"

"And the play too," Robbie put in.

"Yeah, and the play. So we took care of them. We did it off school property, Mr. Keating, so you don't need to worry about that. You should've seen Rob here take them down."

"I didn't do anything."

"Sure you did, bro!" Steven tapped him with a fist on the shoulder, and Robbie's grin could have powered a small city. "You did great. Especially when Norman tried to get into it too."

"My mom made me take self-defense years ago," Robbie said. "But I was never much good at it."

"Sure you are. Anyway, you should see those other guys," Steven told the whole room with relish. "They're sorry they ever mouthed off about *Rent.* We laid them out."

Kids crowded around them, wanting to hear every detail, and the boys weren't hesitant to provide them. George made a move to wade in and break it up, but when he walked past me, I put a hand on his elbow and stopped him.

"No," I said softly. "Let them get this out of their systems. I think it's important."

Everybody knew that George had bad news, and so what Robbie and Steven had done achieved significance. The boys had fought for the honor of *Rent* and everybody in it, and they'd won. In some small, strange way, they'd vindicated everybody involved in the play by standing up against the abuse.

"Take that!" one of the boys from the chorus exulted as he pantomimed a right uppercut.

"Shows them what we're made of," a girl from costumes said, and a boy from scenery agreed.

"You can put us down, but you can't keep us down," Johnny shouted. The kids exchanged a series of high fives that could have been a choreographed dance, except it wasn't. It was genuine and so good for everybody there.

It was a wonder to me and an eye-opener. Nobody in the room seemed to care that Robbie had declared he was gay the night before; actually, the fact that he was gay tied him more closely to the play, the project that everybody had poured their hearts and souls into for months. Robbie had fought for them when he'd fought for himself.

Except he hadn't fought alone. Steven had been right next to him, and as I listened to the boys tell their tale, it seemed that it was Steven who had taken the initiative in, as he put it, "shutting up their trash-talking mouths." Robbie glowed through the telling, with his eyes riveted on the boy who had come to his defense.

See, Sean? I thought viciously. *That's the way it's done. Friends backing up friends.*

Finally George got the cast and crew to calm down, take seats on the floor again, and listen to the bad news.

"I'm sorry to tell you that the Gunning School Board has decided that *Rent* is not suitable subject matter for a high school play, and they have canceled all performances."

I was sitting on a chair behind George as he made the announcement, and I looked down at my fingers. This was what I'd wanted, wasn't it? But I couldn't feel good about it, even if now I thought I'd be safer. Safer... for what? For retreating to my house and locking the door against Kevin? The people who'd spoken at the meeting the previous night had won; their impassioned, frightened, ignorant views of my sexuality had carried the day. I was a man they had to protect their town and their children against at all costs. My fingers wanted to curl around something, to choke somebody, and to pound some sense into all of them as I showed them how wrong they were. I burned inside. But like always, I couldn't let anyone know why.

Even though they'd been expecting the news, many of the cast and crew were devastated. There were groans and a few tears, but mostly the kids were vocally angry, with jeers and catcalls. *Those bastards!* and *They don't get it, do they?*

Channing was the one who started saying *Let's do it anyway! We don't need them!* Her determination swept through the group. I saw face after face catch the possibility. Soon half of them were saying the same thing, all of them beseeching George. *Can we do it, Mr. Keating?*

Sure we can! Their naïve confidence broke my heart. Life didn't work that way.

George had to explain to them that it wasn't possible because we needed the board's approval for the play's budget; money didn't come out of thin air. Besides, he told them, nothing could happen in the school without the approval of the principal, and Mr. Watts supported the board.

After that the kids deflated. More than a few of them clustered around me, saying, *I just don't understand it. Mr. Smith, how could they do that? We've worked so hard.*

I didn't have any answers for them. The world was a shit place sometime. A lot of the time.

I couldn't fault George for the way he conducted this last meeting. He took the high road, insisting that everyone accept the board's decision. "That's the way it is," he said. George apologized too, telling them that even though the committee over the summer had approved the play, he should have realized that the community would have something to say about it. He didn't criticize the school board or any of the speakers from the previous night, and he didn't join the kids in their anger and lamenting, but disappointment was written in the bags under his eyes and the absence of his habitual sunny smile.

Finally everything that could be said had been said, by both the students and by George. I'd kept silent, mostly, still mired in the heavy quicksand of memory and fury and lost love that I'd been walking through all day. Besides, feeling the way I did about this production of *Rent*, I didn't have the right to speak.

"Go home and try to enjoy the weekend," George told them. "I'll pick another play over the next few weeks and you'll all—"

"You'd better get the board to approve it first," Sam said sourly.

"I will," George said flatly. "Don't you worry about that. I promise you that anybody who wants a role in the new play will get it, though of course I can't promise what kind of role that might be. But we're a family, right?"

"Right!" they all agreed.

"And we'll have a chance to work together again. We'll bring some other marvelous play to life on stage. There are other good plays besides *Rent*."

Some of the students shook their heads. "Not the same, Mr. Keating," Marie said.

"We would have wowed them," Channing agreed.

"And we'll wow them this spring with the new play, don't you worry."

"But *Rent* really meant something," Steven said.

George paused at that, but finally he simply said, "Yes, you're right. It did."

He was right. *Rent* meant that Mr. Smith's life had turned upside down. I never would have met Kevin a second time without it, and the wickedness of my graduation night I would have kept buried deep. Instead, my memories throbbed like raw wounds that had never healed. This was good? Why couldn't I have been left alone to slide unobtrusively through life, shunting my past to the side, averting my eyes, pretending?

Finally the students filed out. Robbie and Steven left together. I watched Steven sling his arm around Robbie's neck, in a friendly sort of way, but it was the warm look in Steven's eyes, and the returning gleam in Robbie's that suddenly blasted through my shaky pretense of Mr. Smith-as-usual. Anger rose in me, strong, and trampled on me where I hurt the most.

See that, Sean? God, I hated him. *Remember that? That's what we used to have. It was fucking good until you destroyed it.*

"Tom?" That was George, but I didn't turn around to face him. "You told me so, didn't you? I'm so sorry. I know you put so much work into the play, all those hours. Listen, I wonder if you'd—"

Wildly, I thought that if he asked me to help with the next play, or call the parent volunteers and tell them the news, I'd pick up one of the chairs and break it over his head.

Time for me to leave.

"I've got to go," I interrupted him. "I'll see you later."

I barely managed to get into my Miata without howling to the sky. *Damn you, Sean! Damn you!*

AT ONE o'clock on Sunday morning, I staggered out to my fenced, safe, unobserved backyard and tried to take my drunken anger out on the poor half-dead tree. With a shovel from the garage in my hand, I pulled back and let it rip, swinging it like an axe. The edge of it caught in the trunk with a *thud!*

"Fuck!"

I yanked the shovel out and tried again.

Thud! "You bastard!"

A huge slab of bark fell down to the ground. In the patio lights that had been shining for the past thirty-six hours, I could see the bare flesh of the red oak exposed, cracked and fragile.

Thud! The tree quivered under my attack.

Thud! The force of the blow traveled up my stiffened arms. "Coward!"

And again.

Thud! "Coward!"

I put everything I had into that last swing, and it was too much for me to stay upright. I overbalanced, lurched backward two steps, and fell onto my ass, right next to the gas grill I never used.

"I can't do it," I sobbed. "I can't. I'm the coward, not him."

I collapsed onto my back. Overhead, the few remaining leaves on the oak shivered in the cold breeze, but I didn't feel cold even though I was only wearing a flannel shirt in forty-degree weather. I was too tanked up to be cold. Too weary, too full of my own self-loathing.

I was just like Sean. As bad as he'd been. For years I'd thought I was strong, but now I knew I'd been weak. I'd thought I was adjusting to harsh realities, when in fact I'd been hiding from them.

My eyes stung, my fingers were numb, and I hated myself. How had I turned into what I despised the most? If I had a shred of self-respect, I would stand up and say, *Kevin Bannerman? Look at me. I love you. Let's....*

And there my imagination failed me. Let's do… what? Nothing seemed possible. All roads were the old roads, leading to the same impossible places they always had.

God, I was a wishy-washy, sorry excuse for a man.

I hauled myself up by pulling on the base of the barbecue. It took a while, because my head was swimming from the upended cans of Miller Genuine Draft that littered my house. I'd stopped off at the store on the way home on… on Friday, on the way back from school. It felt like months ago.

Once up, I wobbled past the tree and out into the shadows of the yard, headed straight for the honeysuckle that covered the back fence until I literally bumped into it. My nose scraped against the wood, but I barely felt it. Who cared? Not me. Not Kevin. He wasn't around. Why would he want to be?

Blinking, I kept myself up by leaning my good arm against the fence. All around, the night was still: no dogs barking, no cars on the street, and no conversation from the stars. There wasn't anything to distract me from my own muddled thinking.

Kevin had said that I'd been betrayed by my lover, and no wonder I'd gone into hiding. But maybe I'd done the same to him. I hadn't meant to, but maybe I'd passed the poison down the line: from Sean to Tom to Kevin.

The breeze picked up and whipped the hair back from my face, and I put up a hand as if I could ward it off—the more fool me. I felt like shit. I remembered the look on Kevin's face as he'd left. I'd hurt him. If he hurt half as badly as I did, he was down for the count, and I'd done that to him.

I wasn't much of a man. Kevin deserved a lot more than me. He deserved to be happy. To have somebody follow him when he left town in the spring.

Like a man compulsively probing a sore tooth with his tongue, I wretchedly considered that as I pulled honeysuckle suckers away from the wooden slats. Oh, but I wished I could do it. I remembered the happiness in Kevin's voice when I'd told him I'd go over to his house.

I wished I could have seen his face then. It would be even better if I could tell him, *Sure, I'll go start a new life with you.*

I spent a long time thinking about that. Me, Kevin, me and Kevin, Kevin's smile, his laugh, the times we talked. It occurred to me that he knew more about me than I did about him. A lot more. He'd always drawn me out, asked me questions, encouraged me to take one step after another and follow him.

Did that matter? I tilted my head and realized that I was sitting on the yellow grass with my legs spread out in a V before me. I didn't remember sitting down, but that was okay. What mattered was the injustice of not getting to know Kevin better. Not spending more time with him. Not making him smile anymore. Never making love with him again. Not continuing to live the life that I had started, ever so hesitantly, with him.

That wasn't my fault. That was Sean's.

Sean had taken control of my life, hadn't he? Every move I made was a reaction to the assault; it was as if Sean had been raping me every day for the past sixteen years.

Viciously, I grabbed a handful of prickly grass and yanked it up by the roots.

Fuck you, Sean. Thanks for ruining my life. Asshole. Motherfucker. You made me like this. Without you, I'd go off with Kevin in a second. Instead I'm stuck in this cesspool of a life.

After a while, there wasn't any more grass around me to kill. I managed to get myself up again, and into the house I went. The bedroom was way too far away, but the couch was right there. Down onto it I went, and I fell asleep.

THE sun was shining brightly through the open patio door, and the temperature was freezing. My head was pounding. I blinked against the light and groaned.

The telephone rang.

"Coming, coming," I muttered. I got up, slammed the patio door shut, and then stumbled into the kitchen toward the phone. Somehow I had the presence of mind to look at the caller ID before I picked up. Of course, it was Kevin.

I didn't answer, but I did reach out and touch the phone as if I might. It rang three more times before the line switched over to the machine.

"Hello, Tom, it's Kevin. I'm just checking on how you're doing. It would mean a lot to me if you called and let me know you were okay."

Okay? That wouldn't really be the truth.

"You haven't answered any of my calls, so maybe you've gone somewhere this weekend? Maybe you decided to visit your brother. Call me if you get this, so I can get some sleep. I… I won't bug you. If you want to talk… about anything, you know where I am. Call me, okay?"

I let go of the phone as if it were red-hot, or as if he could somehow see me and my indecision through the line, or as if I would be tempted to talk to him if I held on.

He hung up, and my first impulse was to snatch the phone up and call him back, not to tell him anything in particular but to hear his voice again. His just-for-Tom voice. I'd heard the caress in it—*If you want to talk*—and right that minute, I thought I'd tell everybody in town I liked men if only we could be together. Maybe stand up in front of Hunnicutt's congregation and make the announcement, if Kevin were in the back waiting for me.

I took a step backward in amazement as I realized what I'd just thought. Where had that come from?

Hesitantly, I reached for the phone and flicked through the history for the caller ID. I hadn't heard any of these calls; I must have been really out of it. He'd called Saturday afternoon, Saturday night, this morning, and a few minutes ago, when it'd been two twenty-one on a Sunday afternoon.

Warmth stole through me. Yeah. Kevin. I might not know as much about him as he knew about me, but a man revealed himself by his actions, right? These calls, the fact that he hadn't left a message for me until now, delicately respecting my privacy and my pain, that was who the man was.

My bladder reminded me of all the beer I'd thrown down my throat the past two days and how I urgently needed to piss, so away I went to the bathroom and did that and then splashed water in my face. I looked in the mirror and remembered that I'd seen Sean and the others in it on Friday morning, when I'd been wasted not from the booze but from misery and anger. Nobody was there now, and I was grateful for it. The tumult inside that had sent me careening into my yard with mayhem on my mind had disappeared too. In its place was a sort of watchful, expectant calm. I was hung-over, filthy, and in need of aspirin and a change of clothes, but I wasn't wild like I'd been the day before.

I spent a good fifteen minutes soaping up under the water, breathing deeply and trying to hold onto my newfound kernel of peace. Sean was still there, but the horror and the feelings of debasement weren't quite as sharp. Just sharp enough to hurt like hell, and that was an improvement.

I threw on jeans and one of my long-sleeved T-shirts and went out to the kitchen again. The table and counter—everywhere, really—were littered with empty beer cans, and I set about tossing them into a black trash sack. No way was I going to drink any more. I felt slightly sick to my stomach at the thought of downing another Miller.

Through the house I went, collecting empties, old newspapers, and the remains of fast food with determination. Compulsively I picked up everything I'd ignored since the weekend before, when Channing had found out about me and her father. And then I kept going, because the play had shifted me into survival mode. Or maybe it was that I'd been away with Kevin so much I hadn't had any time on the weekends to devote to house maintenance.

The table, the living room, the front room, the bathroom, the bedroom: I concentrated on going through them all with the sack that was mostly full by the time I was through. I went out into the garage to dump it… and there I stopped.

Kevin had said during one of our phone calls weeks ago that a man was known by his garage. Mine was a disaster, way worse than the house ever got. There was more crammed in there than a family of six should accumulate, but it was only me. Boxes on top of boxes, my old rusting bicycle, a forty-eight quart cooler missing its top, two folding lawn chairs covered in dust, fancy lawn tools I never used, my grandmother's handmade quilt faded and moth-eaten, and that wasn't even half of it. I never threw anything out, did I? Almost nothing here was useful anymore. I really should do some cleaning, have a yard sale, and make some money.

Though I didn't need any extra money now that I wasn't dating Kevin any more. The man was incredible, but he did like to spend the dollars.

With a sad sort of smile on my face, I went to the big trashcan and got rid of the trash from the house there, being careful not to scrape against the Miata while I did that. That Miata was my pride and joy. It was the one luxury I allowed myself, at least before that attractive, sexy-voiced banker had shown up at school.

I'd never given Kevin a ride; I wished I had. He would have liked it. It wasn't all that much, as sports cars went. Anybody really into Corvettes or Ferraris or the classic Triumphs would probably laugh at it. It was a poor man's sports car, but still a two seater with top-down, wind-in-your-hair exhilaration standard.

Except nobody ever rode in it with me. I rarely put the top down. I'd come close that first time out with Kevin, but even he'd realized that it was something I couldn't do, so we'd taken his Silverado from then on.

On a whim, I opened the door, poured myself into the driver's seat, and then pulled the door shut. My hands fit perfectly on the steering wheel, the seat molded to my ass just right, and I knew how well the car handled.

I was tempted to go get my keys and turn the engine on, to hear the throb of its power, and as soon as I thought that, another, darker thought jumped into my head. If I kept the doors down and breathed.... That was the way people committed suicide.

It wasn't the first time the thought of killing myself had teased through my mind, but it had been years since those worst days when I'd first moved to Gunning. My head thumped back against the headrest and stayed there as I remembered how difficult it had been to adjust to the small town, the careful way I had maneuvered through the innocent curiosity of the other teachers, and how tough it had been to decide what small part of myself I could show.

"I didn't do it, did I, Sean?" I said out loud. I'd had enough gumption to keep living. If I hadn't, Grant would have been devastated. I hadn't been able to do that to him after all the effort he'd put into getting me back onto my feet again.

Plus, I never would have met Kevin if I were six feet under now.

But what did my life matter if I didn't do anything with it? If I never made love with Kevin again?

Here in the car I couldn't smell the oil scent of the garage, and I couldn't tell whether it was windy outside. I was safe here, isolated, a king surrounded by the detritus of my life that, for some reason I didn't understand, I'd never gotten around to getting rid of.

I just didn't have the knack of letting go of the past. But… I wanted to. I wanted to hit the door opener, rev up the engine, and zoom out of there, away from the stale smell of beer in the house and the broken pieces of my tree on the patio and the figures who haunted the edges of my mirror. The only questions were: where would I go? And who would I take with me?

I WENT to school on Monday because that's where I always went. Even if it wasn't the safe haven that I'd always thought it was—how much of the real Tom did people know?—it was still my job, where people who weren't Kevin Bannerman needed me.

Before I left, I almost picked up the phone and called Kevin. He'd sounded so forlorn on Sunday night when he'd left another message. But what did I have to tell him, after all? That I was thinking about him. A lot. That would have been self-indulgent, and I didn't do that. Self-indulgent would have had Kevin dangerously staying with me the whole weekend. A man deserved to wrestle his demons in private.

"Screw you, Sean," I said, but the words meant nothing, because I left the phone where it was and went out to the Miata.

At school, a pass by Robbie's locker revealed no books, no cards, no obscenities, and no boy. But when I got to my classroom, he was there along with Steven, Johnny, and Channing. They all jumped to their feet as I walked in.

"Mr. Smith!" Channing exclaimed. "We've been waiting forever."

"No, we haven't, Chan, calm down," Johnny said.

"Well, we don't have much time before first bell," she said. "Mr. Smith, guess what we're doing?"

I placed my briefcase on top of my desk and shook my head. "I can't imagine. What?"

"We're going to do the play!"

I looked from one glowing, enthusiastic face to another—from Robbie's black eye to Steven's swollen lip to Channing's lost innocence to Johnny's steadiness—and sighed. "Look, didn't you understand what Mr. Keating explained on Friday? We can't do the play because—"

"Oh, it's not going to be here at school," Robbie said. "We're doing it at church."

"At church?" I pulled out my chair, sat down, and folded my hands in front of me. "Okay, you'd better explain."

"It's at my church," Johnny said. "First Christian Church of Gunning. They're really cool. My mom and dad are real involved there, and they asked Pastor Webster, and he said yes."

"Yes? To what?"

"To Wednesday night!" Channing exclaimed. "It's not the same thing as doing it six times at school, and we won't have all the scenery and costumes and stuff, but—"

"We're cutting the action way down, but it's still the play. We'll sing and all," Steven said.

I could hardly believe it. "Whose idea was this?"

The four of them exchanged glances. Robbie shrugged. "Well, I guess it was me on Friday night over at Steven's house."

"Yeah, we had a sort of party," Steven put in. "A sort of cry party. Not that we cried," he added quickly, "but we needed to, you know, uh…."

"We needed to complain," Channing said bluntly. "And we all talked about how we wanted to put on the play at least one time, even if it meant we did it in somebody's backyard."

Johnny took up the story. "So I said I knew a place we could use at my church, our social hall, but nobody believed me that Pastor Webster would go for it."

"Man, not after the way that guy from First Baptist came here right in the middle of our rehearsal! And that other fellow Thursday night, where was he from?" Steven asked.

"It doesn't matter," Johnny said. "There are all different kinds of churches, and there's plenty of folks who think live and let live is a good thing, and who would be way cool with a play like *Rent.* They just weren't the ones who showed up at the board meeting."

"They should have," Channing said darkly.

"Yeah, well, next time you can go door to door and get them away from the TV. Anyway, so I called my parents from the party and they said it was a good idea and they'd talk to Pastor Webster for us."

"And now it's all set," Robbie said, looking so happy. "We rehearsed some on Saturday, the eight of us, but then the whole cast worked all yesterday afternoon. We cut out everything except what we really needed, you know, some of the dancing and the props and all, and we set up a bunch of new cues, but it works. It'll be Wednesday night. Isn't that great?"

"It's our way of showing everybody we can't be stopped," Channing said with a definite nod.

"Yeah, that's right," Steven said. "They thought because we're in school and young that we could be pushed around. Well, we can't. My dad says a man has to know what he wants and go after it."

"Your dad's the bomb," Robbie told him.

"Yeah, he is. Anyway, just because some people are afraid of stuff like what's in the play doesn't mean we can't go on. We can do it ourselves without the school and the money."

"So, Mr. Smith," Robbie said. "We're spreading the word, but we don't think too many people will come. But will you? We know it can't be anything official because of the school board and everything, but will you come see us?"

I felt like I'd been knocked over by a wave from the ocean. These students, they were amazing. While I'd been shut up in my house alone all weekend, they'd banded together and found a way to make their dream for this play come true.

There was no way I could say no. Going to see them perform would be my last duty to the play, and then I could put it to bed, once and for all. Except… my relationship with Kevin was so entangled with *Rent*. If I went to see the performance at the church, I'd see him again, for surely he'd be there for Channing.

Hope rose in me, irrational though it might have been. I'd see Kevin again.

The kids' expressions had turned anxious. "Mr. Smith? Don't you want to—"

"Of course I'll bc there," I said in a rush. I stood up in a rush too. "I'm sorry I didn't say anything on Friday, but let me say it now. I'm so proud of all of you. For all the work you've done the past months, but now with this…. You've really got it all set?"

Steven beamed. "Well, we'll need to work some more tonight and Tuesday, but it'll be ready by Wednesday."

Robbie elbowed him in the side. "Yeah, if you stop going off key."

"Hey! Just one time!"

"It sounded awful. Don't do that Wednesday."

"Who voted and made you director?"

The warning bell rang, and all the kids grabbed their backpacks. "See you Wednesday, Mr. Smith!" Robbie called, and then they were gone, and my students for first period were pouring in through the doorway.

Those kids. They were like Kevin. They hadn't given up. The play was going to happen, even if not exactly in the form that was perfect, that had been planned for, or that had been practiced. But the essence of it, the truth of it: those kids were going to make it real even with the town and the board and the principal against them.

"Think about it," Kevin had said in my doorway, the last thing he'd said on that anguished Thursday night. *"I want to be with you."*

I remembered every nuance of his voice. Maybe…. Maybe his voice could be stronger than Sean's?

I had a lot to think about.

MY HANDS were sweating even in the cool of November, and my throat had constricted so I could barely swallow. I almost hoped that no one on the other end of the phone would pick up.

"Hello?"

Do or die time.

"Hi, Grant, it's Tom."

"Well, hi there, stranger."

"I know. We haven't talked in a while."

"That's okay. You're busy with that play you're working on. So, are you calling to say you'll be coming for Thanksgiving this Thursday after all?"

"Uh…." I hadn't even thought about that. Kevin and I had planned to go to Big Bend. When I'd called Grant to bow out of my regular trip for the holidays, he'd been out so I'd told his wife instead. I hadn't said why, and she hadn't asked. Cath was a great woman.

I slowly sat down in the blue velvet chair in my front room. Through the window, I could see my neighbor coming home from walking his dog. This Tuesday night was cloudy, windy, and cold. "I don't know. Things are in flux."

I could imagine his frown. "Why? What's going on? Is your arm acting up? Do you still have your pain medication?"

I had to give a small, indulgent, but nonetheless nervous smile. Grant would never stop mothering me. "No, the arm's okay. About the same. But…. Grant, do you have five minutes to—" I stopped, because I could hear two boys fighting in the background, with one of them hollering "Daddy!" That was seven-year-old Tommy.

"Hold on, Tom. Let me take care of this."

I waited while he told the boys to skedaddle, and that they'd find out what life was like without Nintendo if they didn't calm down. Then he said into the phone, "Wait a minute. Let me move over to…."

There was the sound of a door opening and then closing. "Okay," Grant said, and I heard him settle into his favorite recliner. "I'm in the study now. Talk to me."

I'd spent the past thirty-six hours thinking, screwing up courage I didn't know if I had, and trying to face what I'd long thought was inconceivable. I'd hurled abuse at Sean in my mind, and I'd done a lot of silent screaming. But at least I hadn't obliterated thought with the booze again or spent the night outside attacking the vegetation.

And then, sometime in the middle of last night, Kevin's guess that I'd gone to visit Grant had begun to make an awful lot of sense. I'd realized I had to talk to my brother. I needed to go back to the beginning and start there before I had even the smallest chance of moving forward.

"Do you remember…." My voice trembled. I couldn't begin that way. So I cleared my throat and tried again. "Do you remember my graduation night?" I could get through this. I could say it. "And how I was beaten up? Got this arm?"

"Of course I do," he said gently.

"I… I never really told you anything about that night."

"You didn't have to, and you don't now."

"I think I do."

The sound of him shifting in the chair came across the line. I could imagine him, my ginger-haired, lean-as-a-fencepost brother, with his serious eyes.

"I'm listening, Tom."

It would have been easier if he'd said he didn't want to hear anything, that it was too hard a memory. Well, it had been too hard for me. For sixteen years, it had been like concrete weighing me down. I'd decided the night before to crack it into pieces and then spent every hour since trying to talk myself out of it.

"I told the cops I didn't know who'd done it, but I did. They were students from school, all of them."

"You're kidding," he muttered. And then he said, "Then why didn't you—"

I cut him off. "There's more." I gripped the phone hard enough to hurt my fingers. Here it was. "Remember what was scratched into my car?"

I could barely hear his voice. "Sure I do."

"Grant…." I told myself he knew already. Of course he did, even if we'd never spoken of it, for my car had one day been returned to me with a newly painted hood and no explanations. "It's true," I said. "I'm gay."

He gave a long, quiet sigh. "I wondered if you'd ever tell me."

I rushed into more speech, as if delaying even a little would undermine my resolve. "There's something else I didn't tell the police. I was sexually assaulted that night."

"Oh, Christ," Grant said, low and heartfelt. "Oh, Tom. I sometimes wondered, but…. I'm so sorry to hear that."

"Yeah," I said, and I swallowed noisily. "It's been… difficult."

"Damn," he swore again. "And I was no help to you at all."

"What?"

"All this time I've wondered if you were gay and if there was more to that assault than the official police report. You changed so much after it, more than I thought you…. I'm sorry, Tom. I should have made you talk or talked myself, asked you…. But I didn't know how."

"I know, I know. I haven't known how either." Unaccountably, I found that my cheeks were wet. I dashed the tears away with the back of my hand. "But I had to say it now. It doesn't change anything about what happened, but—"

"Yes, it does. This is good that you're talking about it now, really good. You don't have to tell me, but…. Why now?"

I didn't have to answer that truthfully or in any way at all. Grant would understand if I didn't. But I hadn't called him to slide away from the truth, had I? This night was all about facing forward, no matter how difficult that was.

"I've met somebody." I didn't say anything more.

"Oh. Is he…. You haven't had someone special, have you?"

"No."

"I've always wished that you had somebody, little brother. I wondered if maybe you did and you just weren't telling us."

"No," I said, sighing and sitting back into the dubious comfort of the chair. "It's just been me here."

"So, this… this person you've met." I heard how carefully he said "person." "Is he pulling up bad memories? Is that why you've told me at last?"

"No. Yes. It's complicated. But he's—"

"You don't have to say anything more. It's your own private business."

"I know that. But I…." I stopped, because suddenly I didn't know what I wanted to tell Grant about Kevin when the truth was that I still didn't know for sure what I was going to do. "He's a good man," I found myself saying.

"I'm not surprised. Only the best for you."

I forced out a chuckle. "Grant, I haven't been alone all this time because I've been picky. I've been…." I finished with the only word that described the long, lonely process I'd gone through. "I've been recovering."

"Good," Grant said with sudden intensity. "That's the best thing I've heard all year. You keep on recovering, you hear?"

"All right."

"And anything I can do to be part of this and help, you let me know, okay?"

God, I did love my brother. "I will."

"You want to talk some more right now? We can talk as long as you want."

I shook my head. "No, I think… I think I've done enough tonight." I suddenly felt as if I could sleep for a week.

"All right, I don't want to push… except that's what I should've done back then."

"It wouldn't have worked."

"That's what you say. But… I am so sorry to hear about what happened to you that night. Hear me? I would have done anything if…. Well, wishing doesn't change anything, does it?"

"No," I said forlornly. "It doesn't." Still, it was good to hear him say it. I soaked it up.

"And I want to say thanks for telling me you're, you know, that you're gay."

"I should have long ago, I guess."

"And I should have asked you. But you know… you know it doesn't make any difference to us, right? You're still welcome in this house any day of the week."

Something tight in my chest loosened. "Thanks, Grant. I know, and I… I appreciate it."

"You're my brother," he said simply. "You want to go now?"

"Yeah. Let's call it a night."

"Okay. So, should we set a place for you at the table for this Thanksgiving?"

I just couldn't think past tomorrow night: the play, Kevin. I'd taken this step, and that seemed to clear the path in front of me, but I had no idea what I'd do next.

"I'm not sure."

"Okay, if you're here, great. If you're not, we'll miss you. Will you call me and let me know how you are in a few days?"

"All right."

"And maybe someday we'll get to meet this good man who's come into your life."

"I don't know," I said. "I really don't know."

CHAPTER 9
RENT

ON MY way out to the show on Wednesday night, I paused halfway through my kitchen and looked over at my reflection in the microwave door. The man looking back at me was pale and serious, dressed in my best navy blue suit, but at least his cowlick in the back wasn't sticking straight up.

"Come on," I murmured to myself. "Let's get this show on the road." Nervousness danced up and down my spine.

I stepped into the garage but stopped right away. One of the stacks of boxes I'd lamented over a few days before had toppled onto the floor. Three of the boxes had spilled open. Old newspapers I'd intended to read years ago, bills ten years old, ads, programs, all sorts of things spread out and disappeared under the Miata. I bent over and saw that they had reached so far under the car that they had reached the other side.

But I wasn't going to spend time picking any of it up. *Rent* started at seven-thirty. I had to get moving. So I got into the car, opened the garage door, and drove out, leaving tire marks on what I'd once thought was worth saving.

Although I'd never visited it, I knew that the First Christian Church of Gunning was in a quiet, residential neighborhood to the north of downtown. Old trees watched over the streets and modest, two-bedroom homes clustered close to one another. It wasn't the type of neighborhood that I'd associate with forward thinking, but then again, how was I to tell? Before this semester, I never would have pegged George as the type to want to direct *Sweeney Todd: The Demon Barber of Fleet Street* either. Danielle Robertson had been a surprise to me with her open-minded defense of the play, and so had the biker-man who hadn't tripped my gaydar, and definitely the kids who were going to put on *Rent* tonight. I'd never expected it of any of them.

As I drove close to Wellington Avenue where the social hall was, parked cars crowded both sides of the street. I didn't think that could possibly have any connection with the play. It was Wednesday night, and many churches held services then. There'd be a large group of worshippers in the sanctuary and then a small cluster of family members supporting the kids in their performance in the hall.

The church's parking lot was full, so I turned the Miata around. An open spot didn't come into view until I was more than two blocks away. I parked gratefully under a huge, spreading cedar elm that was stubbornly hanging on to a few of its leaves, and then I started walking back toward the church.

Perspiration prickled the back of my neck, but not because of the weather. It wasn't that warm, even if the night had turned unexpectedly balmy with the back-and-forth typical of weather in west Texas. Next week it might snow, but tonight the kids could have hosted the play outdoors without much problem.

No, I'd broken out in a sweat because Kevin was going to be at this performance. I was as nervous as a bridegroom and with far more cause. After six days of mourning and drinking and finally grappling with my memories, I still didn't know how much I could give him. As much as he'd asked for? In my isolated house, I couldn't imagine it. But being with Kevin had always changed things for me, and after each of our times together, I'd moved further along the path that brought me closer to him.

I shook my head and walked around a bushy, six-foot-tall pampas grass plant that had overflowed its landscape box. I needed to see Kevin and talk with him, of that I was sure. I owed him that. I'd dumped the sorry story of my life on him, shoved him out the door, and since then refused to answer his calls. Even I thought that was churlish. But Kevin had last called on Monday morning; maybe he'd changed his mind, and my desperate search for courage tonight would go for nothing. He'd ridiculed me Thursday night when he'd mocked how I'd insisted on leaving town for our dates. His patience had worn thin, and maybe it was still thin. I couldn't blame him. God, who would want to take up with a weak sister like me? All I'd accomplished over the past years had been securing my own safety. That wasn't much to offer a man like Kevin.

As I crossed the street, I reminded myself that he'd also said he loved me. The exact way he'd said it played through my mind—"Damn it, Tom, I love you. Listen to me, please"—and a sense of wonder tingled across my shoulders and down my arms. Even my bad arm felt the force of Kevin's words. He was the kind of man who meant what he said.

For the first time since I'd willfully resurrected the rape, I'd awakened this morning not obsessing about Sean but longing to see Kevin instead. Nothing had changed since then.

The social hall was on a little side street that could have appeared on a postcard for the town with its neatly trimmed bushes, edged walkways, and freshly painted walls. A small steeple announced the hall's affiliation with the church, and a few steps led up to the entrance. I paused and wiped my hands on my pants. There was a lot of noise coming through the double open doors. Voices rose and fell, but there was only one I wanted to hear.

Here goes.

The room was packed. Tightly spaced rows of folding chairs took up most of the hall; the fire marshal would not have been pleased to see all the people milling in the aisles. At least twice the number of people than had attended the board meeting crowded the room, far more than families of the cast alone could account for. The kids, peeking out from wherever they were waiting, had to be beside themselves with excitement.

But my heart sank. Maybe I wouldn't be able to find Kevin in this mess after all.

"Tom! Hey, Tom, over here!"

George was calling me. I scanned the room from where I'd entered from the side and finally saw his unmistakably beefy hand waving at me from the first row.

"Tom!"

"I see you!" I hollered, but I didn't know if he heard.

I began to make my way to him. It was slow going. Half the people there seemed to know me, but that wasn't surprising for a teacher who'd stayed with the school as long as I had. I endured pats on the back, acknowledged introductions—"Hey, Mom, this is Mr. Smith, my history teacher"—and fielded questions—"Do you know what play Mr. Keating has decided on for the spring?"—all the while searching for an athletic, dark-haired man.

As I got closer to George, I was able to see how the performance area at the front of the hall was set off by masking tape that defined a large rectangle, maybe twenty-five feet by fifteen. It was backed up by what appeared to be a typical church-hall kitchen with a long serving counter. The kitchen was blocked from view, though, by what looked like simple white bed sheets hanging down over the pass-throughs. That was the closest to our auditorium back at school that the kids were going to get: a makeshift curtain. The space certainly wasn't ideal for putting on the play.

I came at last to where George and his wife Jenny were standing. George looked like he was about to burst, like a proud father who'd been handing out cigars for the birth of twins.

"Can you believe this?" he asked me with a grin.

"There must be three hundred people here at least."

"I stopped counting at three hundred and fifty-seven," Jenny said. "There's probably a hundred more than that. This is wonderful. I'm so proud of you, George."

She clutched his arm and beamed at him, and then she turned his cheek so she could give him a quick kiss.

"It's not me," he said. "Just wait until you see—"

"Oh, start taking credit where credit is due. All these people," her arm swept to encompass the hall, "they're vindicating your choice of *Rent*. Enjoy it, George."

George looked at me and spread his hands. "What can you do with a woman like this?"

"Be glad you married her," I told him. "Listen, I'm going to try to find a seat. I'll see you at—"

"Oh, no, you don't," George said. "We saved one for you. You're right over there next to Kevin."

My mouth went dry as George gestured over his shoulder, to the rest of the row that he and Jenny had blocked from my view. Kevin was sitting there, looking at me with all his concentrated attention, and next to him was my seat.

Jenny gave me a little shove; she was as excited as her husband. "Go on, get going, it's only five minutes to curtain."

"They'll be late," George predicted. "Besides, we need to pack everybody in here that we can. I'll go tell the kids to hold off a while. They probably don't know about things like that."

He hurried off, Jenny sat down, and Kevin's gaze reeled me in. One moment I was with Jenny and the next I was settling in next to him, unaccountably unable to meet his eyes. We were too close, and I felt too much. I struggled to find the right thing to say.

I was saved by the man sitting on my other side. He held out his hand. "Sandy Patterson. I'm Marie's father."

I shook with him. "Pleased to meet you. I'm Tom Smith."

He nodded and then looked away, giving the impression of a man who'd said all he needed to say. Exactly the opposite of me.

"Hey," Kevin said.

"Hey." I glanced over at him and then away.

"Here's a program." He thrust it into my field of vision. "Layne was giving them out a little while ago, so I got you one before they ran out."

I took it but didn't even pretend to be interested in it. "Thanks." We were surrounded by parent volunteers. Anything we said would be overheard; any move I made would be observed.

His knee so close to mine filled my vision. He was wearing that sharp black suit I'd seen him in before, which worked with his fair coloring and dark hair. A slight imperfection in the fabric caught my eye, a nub on the outside of his left thigh. Under other circumstances—those weekends that had changed everything—I would have run my thumb over it and felt the solid strength of the man beneath. I still wanted to. Kevin was the sexiest man I'd ever gone to bed with. I could be happy making love with him for years and years to come. His masculine, finely controlled body, the way he looked at me, the way I was happy when I was with him…. Even though he hadn't told me Channing knew he was gay. Even though my situation at school was difficult. Even though Sean had crippled me both inside and out. None of that changed how my body responded to him. How my heart responded to him.

I shifted uncomfortably against the hard metal of the chair. How to get from *here* to *there* when so much was in between, and when I wasn't even sure where *there* was? "Uh…. How long have you been here?"

"I brought Channing, so I got here pretty early," Kevin said. "I wanted to get a good seat, so that was okay. But I was beginning to worry that you wouldn't make it."

"I wouldn't have missed this. I had to be here."

"Good," he said, and his voice was low and warm for all its habitual scratchiness. "I'd hoped you would. Did you see that your principal is here?"

"Hiram? You're kidding."

"No, I'm not. And you'll never guess who he's with. Mayfield."

"The president of the board?"

"None other."

I shook my head. It felt like an awkward gesture, staged and artificial. "That is strange. I don't understand it."

"The world's a crazy place, that's for sure."

"Yeah." I shifted forward so I was leaning with my forearms on my knees, my hands clasped between them. Kevin copied me. Our socially approved, suit-covered knees splayed out closer to one another; my elbow was an inch from brushing against his. We must have looked like we were deep in personal conversation, trying to establish a small zone of privacy. But we weren't private, and I was blazingly aware of that. Still, it felt so good talking to him that I needed to keep it going. "Uh, I know it's none of my business, but how is Channing doing? Okay?" I sounded so normal. I wondered if Kevin thought that too, and if he wondered if I were completely unaffected by sitting next to him. Maybe he thought I was the one who didn't care anymore.

Kevin shrugged where he sat hunched over. "She's all right, I guess. You know. And she's nervous about tonight, of course. When it's only one performance, one chance to get it right, that's nerve-racking. If she screws up, she can't fix it the next time."

"They'll do fine," I said without really thinking about it. I'd hardly focused on the fact that we were going to see the play tonight. Everything had been aimed at Kevin instead.

"I hope so."

I pretended to examine the piano set off to the side of the stage area. Carefully not looking his way, I asked, "How are you doing?"

I heard him take a measured breath. "I… don't really know," he said slowly. "It depends. More important, how are you?"

"I'm… okay. Better."

I watched his leg jerk a bit, as if he were restraining a larger movement. "That is really good to hear," he said with obvious relief. "Of course, Channing told me you gave a great lecture in class on Monday. And then again on Tuesday. You haven't lost your touch."

He'd been asking her about me. If he'd said that to me three weeks ago, even two, that news would have sent me into paroxysms of fear and anger. Now, it warmed me.

"If you believe that," I said ruefully, "there's a bridge I'd like to sell you."

He chuckled, a very small sound. "I haven't closed a single loan for the past week."

And then I looked over at him, and he was looking at me, and we didn't turn away from each other. I couldn't turn away from him. His lips parted, and then his tongue wet his lips, and then—

"Hello, ladies and gentlemen."

We both jerked upright and away from each other as if we'd touched a live wire. Having that moment of connection with Kevin destroyed was almost disorienting, and I blinked a few times to see who'd spoken.

Johnny stood in the center of the stage, wearing one of the headset mikes so his words were amplified. The crowd quieted slowly, people who'd been standing found their seats, and then finally silence took over, except for the wild rush of blood in my ears.

Somebody in the back started clapping before Johnny said another word, and of course everyone else followed. I was grateful to have something to pour my nervous energy into. I clapped loud and hard, and next to me Kevin was doing the same. Poor Johnny didn't quite know what to make of it, but he stood there taking it with an uncertain smile.

Finally everybody stopped expressing their opinion about the controversy that had surrounded *Rent*—because that's what the applause was really all about, even if Johnny didn't realize it—and Johnny was able to go on with his introduction. He thanked all the right people in the right way without saying anything negative about the cancellation of the show, and I saw his mother Danielle's fine hand in his words. I could imagine her typing furiously at her computer, creating the speech for her son. I'd come to understand she was one smart lady.

He announced that the show was different from how it would have been if presented on a real stage, and that he hoped everybody had brought their imaginations with them tonight so they could fill in the details of settings, costumes, and props. "We aren't really acting the play out," he explained. "We're mainly singing our way through the script, but we hope you'll like it anyway."

He took a step back and opened his arms wide. "And now, here's *Rent.*"

The rest of the cast emerged from the door to the kitchen as everybody applauded again. Each carried a high wooden stool. Johnny and Sam, who would portray Mark and Roger, put theirs in the center, while the other kids went and sat on their stools off to each side.

"Relax." Kevin had leaned close and was whispering to me. "They really will do fine. You have a lot to be proud of."

I hadn't known I'd tensed, but it would be better to watch this without my hands crushing the program into a ball. I whispered back, "You have a very talented daughter," instead of saying, "You are the most amazing man."

The pianist started the music, and the play began.

It couldn't compare with the production of the show I'd seen in Dallas. It couldn't compare with what the show might have been if George and I had been able to finish with the last two weeks of fine-tuning, or if we'd gone through the refinements of tech week and dress rehearsals. It was ragged at times, off-key at times, a little confusing at times, and absolutely splendid all the time.

The kids put their hearts and souls into it. Knowing them as I did, and sitting as closely as I was to the stage, I could see in their eyes the regret when each number passed—"One Song Glory," "Tango Maureen," "Will I?" They knew they'd never sing that song in performance again.

They'd come up with a workable way to change scenes; the kids went everywhere with their stools. When one scene finished and the characters would normally have exited the stage, they picked up their stools and carried them to the side, arranged them in a neat row, and sat down to watch. The characters who would play in the new scene came onstage, arranged their seats, and sang through their lines and the songs. *Rent* was one of those shows where one scene often flowed into another, so sometimes there were awkward stops and starts. There wasn't any blocking, no walking around, though they did the best they could to act from where they sat. I didn't know how effective it was in the back of the hall, but the kids were doing great from where I was.

I held my breath as Robbie and Steven took the center seats and began "I'll Cover You," the show's controversial love song. With the intricate blocking that George and I had come up with stripped away, it was just the two boys, turned toward each other, singing simply and powerfully. The audience went still, though a stir went through the hall the first time the boys sang the line "a thousand sweet kisses."

There was no doubt in my mind how Robbie and Steven would end the song: exactly as they had rehearsed it from the beginning. They came together in a sweet, soulful kiss and parted only to keep their hands clasped between them as they smiled at each other. It was either real or they were very good actors indeed. I would likely never know for sure.

Nobody got up and left. Kevin was perfectly still beside me. We'd kissed like that.

The big show-stopping group number, "La Vie Boheme," worked surprisingly well, with lots of energy flowing. The girls kissed in that scene, a quick peck, playful and amusing more than anything else, and I hoped JJ was there to see it. It could have easily been cut in this version of *Rent* the kids were giving us, but I imagined that Channing had insisted. After that, act one quickly came to a conclusion. The poor pianist, who had played for more than an hour straight, stood up and announced, "We'll have a twenty-minute intermission now. We're selling soft drinks and snacks from the kitchen if you're interested."

The typical between-acts chatter began, people stood up to stretch their legs, and Kevin looked over at me. "See? Nothing to worry about."

"Channing was excellent," I said sincerely.

"Thanks."

A line was forming for the intermission sales directly in front of us. There was no way we could talk meaningfully. Abruptly, I stood up and looked down at him. "You want to go outside and get some fresh air?"

He got up right away. "Lead me to it."

We managed to walk right past George because he was surrounded by well-wishers. Mostly smokers went with us outside, and they congregated on a grassy plot immediately to the left of the doors. I stuck my hand in my pocket and walked further down the street to the right. Kevin, for once, followed me instead of the other way around. I stopped next to a row of crape myrtle trees that were dormant and bare for the winter. Nobody else had gone so far away from the hall, and we had privacy. Maybe it would look peculiar, the two of us apart from the crowd, so intent on each other. Undoubtedly it did. Maybe it looked… suspicious. But I couldn't help that, could I? I had to talk to Kevin.

I turned to him. We stood in muted shadow, the streetlight half a block away. Everything had a tinge of unreality imparted by dark skies and indistinct edges. Was this real? Kevin and me facing each other? If Kevin had his way, this was how we'd always be: going to plays together, supporting his daughter together, leaving together and weaving a shared life we could call our own… but also out in the open, subject to scorn and attack.

I'd given up any prospect of a shared life with anybody the day I'd awakened in the hospital. The danger had always loomed too high; I would not risk a repetition of what Sean and the others had done to me. And yet… here was Kevin, tempting me.

Nothing seemed clear except that I needed to apologize.

"I'm sorry I didn't pick up when you called," I said. "I should have called you back."

Kevin searched my face. "I wish you had. I was really worried about you."

"I'm sorry about that too. I never meant for you to—"

"Tom, stop that," he interrupted me. "Of course I'm going to worry about you. It comes with the territory."

That did stop me. I'd stupidly fretted about him driving home on Thursday night and upending his truck in a ditch, hadn't I?

"Listen," Kevin said. "I've got my own apologies. Since we're not fighting now, will you listen to me? Please?"

"You don't have to ask. Of course I'll listen."

"I said this before, but I want you to hear me. Really hear me, okay? For the third time, I'm sorry that I didn't tell you Channing knew about me. I'll admit that I was afraid I'd scare you off if I did, but I should have counted on your own strength."

"And on how I feel about you," I said quietly.

He took a step closer. A dried leaf crunched underfoot. "Should I have counted on that?" he asked in a whisper.

We were too close to each other. The truth of how I felt about Kevin rose up in one huge, complicated rush. "Yes," I told him.

He closed his eyes, and when he opened them again there was more of the old Kevin there, from before I'd turned away from him. "Do we still have a chance?"

Everything in me wanted to say, "Yes!" To scream *yes*, to break away from my old fears and go with him. But I just wasn't sure I could do it.

Maybe he saw the hesitation in me, because right away he said, "No, don't answer that. I have something else that's been really bothering me that I need to say to you, okay?" He ran a hand through his hair, that gesture that I'd grown accustomed to from him. "Back at my house, remember the porn we watched?" He quickly looked around, but nobody was close to us. His voice quieted until I could barely hear him, and he kept his gaze down to the street. "There was that scene, that one where…. One guy was taking it in the mouth. And I said…." Kevin swallowed audibly. "I said I really wanted to do that to you."

He looked up to me again. "You hadn't told me about what had happened to you then, so I didn't know how you must have felt when I said that. It must have been…. I'm sorry. I didn't mean to…. Tom, you've got to know I would never want to hurt—"

"Mr. Smith!"

Two girls came racing toward us from the social hall but I barely noticed. What Kevin had said reverberated as loudly as a thunderclap inside me, and I couldn't pay attention to anything else but my astonished thoughts.

I hadn't associated Sean with that scene in the movie. I'd wanted Kevin to fuck my mouth. Nothing else had mattered to me but him.

"What do you need, girls?" Kevin asked when I remained silent.

"The play!" one girl said. "You don't want to miss it! Everybody's going back in." She bounced like a puppy and waved toward the doors. "Come on."

Kevin glanced at me and said, "Of course. Mr. Smith wouldn't want to miss the play when he's worked so hard on it, and my daughter would have my head if I skipped a second of it. Come on, Mr. Smith, let's go."

This time he led the way. I followed, still thinking furiously about what he'd said as we walked inside, through the settling crowd, and to our seats. I scarcely paid attention when the kids began "Seasons of Love." I was caught in my own personal wonder.

When Kevin had said that he wanted to fuck my mouth the same way the actors in the porn DVD were going at it, I hadn't thought of Sean's attack at all. Not for one second. Kneeling before Kevin and opening for him, letting him shove it in and take what he wanted from me… that had turned me on. I'd wanted to do that with him. I still did.

Sean hadn't been there in Kevin's house that day with me. Only Kevin had.

Warmth spread through my gut. My God. Only Kevin had mattered.

On the stage, Angel was dying, and Collins was remembering their love, but I was suddenly realizing how different a man I was now than the just-graduated victim Sean had left in the wake of the attack. I'd lived hard years since then, and maybe some of what I'd done here in Gunning had been a mistake, but from where I sat it all seemed necessary.

I really had been healing, just like I'd told Grant. Maybe not consciously, but I must have been. Otherwise I wouldn't have had sex with Kevin in Houston a second time. I wouldn't have wanted Kevin to take my mouth without immediately relating it to Sean. And I wouldn't have finally been able to tell out loud what had been done to me and to spend the past week coming to terms with it.

Maybe I was… healed enough for Kevin.

Rent swirled around and over me, in front of me and through me. Scenes I'd helped create, songs I'd helped shape, lines that I'd helped make clear suddenly became a part of the whole, when before they'd been separate, meaningless, and without context.

Mark and Roger began singing "What You Own." Roger had left New York for Santa Fe, and there he was at last finding his muse and writing that one song he longed to compose. Mark turned down the TV job that had kept him away from his own film project and vowed to devote himself to his own vision. They were each uncertain, groping for answers, and the world kept batting them down, but they were trying their best to build the lives they could see for themselves. Wasn't that what *Rent* was about? I'd let Sean bury the life I'd wanted, and I'd crafted a poor substitute for it. But now I'd changed.

What did I really want?

Act two seemed to zoom by in about five minutes. Soon the kids had sung their way almost to the end. It was Christmas again, and a full year had gone by from the first scene. Mark was ready to show his film, Roger was back in New York and had completed his song for Mimi, but Mimi couldn't be found. Collins showed up with lots of cash, hijacked from an ATM he'd reprogrammed to disgorge it to anyone using the password "Angel."

Maureen and Joanne arrived, supporting a near-death Mimi, whose heroin addiction was about to claim her. She seemed to die as Roger sang "Your Eyes" to her, but then she suddenly revived. "I was heading for this warm, white light," Mimi said. "And I swear, Angel was there. And she looked good! And she said, 'Turn around, girlfriend, and listen to that boy's song'."

And then all the main actors, and the supporting ones, too, came off their stools, faced the audience with linked hands, and began to sing the finale for the show.

"Will I lose my dignity," they sang, and their voices soared. I could hear Channing loud and clear, and Marie, and Johnny and Sarah and all of them, separate and together, and wasn't that the best way to live? "Will someone care? Will I wake tomorrow from this nightmare?"

The girls sang different lyrics than the boys did, the words weaving in and out, creating beautiful interlocking and yet distinct melodies. But I knew all the words, even if they hadn't had much meaning for me before. I'd memorized them over the months that had started with me arguing with George in the school hallway, that had grown as I'd climbed Enchanted Rock with Kevin, as I'd relived the agony of being attacked, and as I finally came to… this day.

"The hand gropes, the ear hears, the pulse beats, life goes on," the girls sang, but it was the boys I heard best. "There's only now, there's only here," they sang, and I saw that Robbie, the different one, stood between Steven and Preston. They sang this first time, this final time together, telling the message that *Rent* had to give and that each of them had learned.

I had never been so proud in my life. Or so moved. I'd helped create this.

"Give in to love or live in fear. No other path. No other way."

"I die without you," the girls told us.

"No day but today," the boys proclaimed.

At last the girls' and the boys' lyrics merged, and the sound they made filled the hall. Everybody around us was on their feet already. I was on my feet, although I hadn't known it.

"No day but today."

The voices rose, blended, made sweet beauty for one last note, and then *Rent* was over.

THE crowd kept the kids on the stage for what seemed like a very long time as they applauded as enthusiastically as if they had been privileged to watch a Broadway hit. All the actors and the crew who had helped out, and definitely the pianist, took bows. Robbie was flushed bright red, and Channing's smile glowed.

"Bravo!" someone shouted.

"Bravo!" agreed Sandy Patterson next to me, and plenty of other people let loose with the same. I wondered if Hiram were shouting, or Mayfield.

"Those idiots," Kevin growled next to me. "We could have had six performances like this. Idiots!"

Finally Johnny Robinson stepped forward and made calming-down motions with his hands. "Thank you, everybody, for your support. We have a special presentation to make." Marie and Channing ran back into the kitchen. "We'd like to thank our director, Mr. George Keating, for all his hard work, his inspiration, and his help to us every day of rehearsal."

The girls came back out carrying an enormous bouquet of flowers.

"Mr. Keating, would you come forward please?" Johnny asked, very formally.

I'd never seen George look bashful before, but he did then. The girls thrust the flowers into his hands, and he looked like he didn't quite know what to do with them.

"Everybody…." Johnny said to the cast. "Now."

“Thanks, Mr. Keating!” they all shouted.

“And we’ve got a little something extra for you. Here.” Johnny tried to give George an envelope, but he had a hard time taking it with his hands already full.

“Jenny,” he plaintively asked, “would you come get these?”

The audience laughed, Jenny took the bouquet, and George was able to open the gift.

“From the cast and crew of *Rent,”* he read aloud. “With thanks for the memories.” Then he turned his head to see what else had come in the card. He looked up, startled. “I can’t take this!”

“Sure you can,” Kevin said from where he was standing next to me. “You’ve earned it. Enjoy it.”

“Well….” He tucked whatever it was back in the card. “Thank you, everybody.”

Johnny stepped forward again. “And we’d also like to thank our assistant director, Mr. Thomas Smith, for his hard work and dedication and help. And the art director Miss Tiffany Davis, who worked hard on the scenery, even though we didn’t get to see it tonight. And all the parent volunteers too. Everybody… now.”

“Thank you!” the kids yelled in chorus.

“Thanks for coming, everybody,” Johnny finished with. “Good night!”

The kids waved from the stage, and then they were mobbed as family and friends rushed up to them.

I stayed back and watched it all with the strangest feeling in my chest. The high from the last song lingered; I could still hear the kids singing together. I had no one to share the moment with, because that’s how things were with me, but I could still smile to see Kevin and Julianne fussing over Channing, and Mr. and Mrs. Sutton beaming as Steven’s mom took a picture of them with Robbie, and George receiving congratulations like a seasoned impresario. Everybody was happy. I was too.

“Mr. Smith?” Johnny had come from the stage area to me.

"You were wonderful," I told him. "You all did so well. I'm very proud of you."

"Thanks. We got you a little something too. Here it is."

He offered me an envelope and then said, "Channing said you wouldn't want any flowers or fuss. Girls usually know about those things, so we went along with her. Hope that was okay."

I had a little trouble getting out, "That's fine. Thanks." I guess I hadn't needed to ask her to keep quiet about her dad and me after all.

"Well, aren't you going to open it?" Danielle asked. Somehow she and Kevin were back from the stage, and a few of the kids were too.

"You really didn't have to get me anything," I said as I slipped my finger under the flap.

"Oh, yes we did," Steven assured me.

Inside was what had been on the card for George, handwritten: "From the cast and crew of *Rent*. With thanks for the memories." It looked like everybody had signed it and left small notes.

The card also held a Visa gift card for two hundred and fifty dollars. I was shocked. "You can't do this," I said to everybody. "There are rules about teachers accepting gifts."

"Already cleared with the school board," Kevin said briskly. "The parents all wanted you to have that, so accept it with grace."

I couldn't help it. I laughed out loud. Grace hadn't exactly been in my vocabulary the last little while.

I thanked everybody around me, but nobody wanted to accept much credit. All the students slipped away; they went to stand by the door where people were exiting. I couldn't blame them. That way they got to thank the audience for coming and the audience got the chance to tell them how great they'd been.

Soon the only people left in the hall were the cast and crew and those most closely connected with them. George came bounding toward us from where he'd stood at the doors too, and he called, "Cast and crew of *Rent*, gather 'round!"

The kids came back to the stage, which still had the stools pushed back against the kitchen wall, and circled George. The rest of us stood back and listened.

He put his arms around the shoulders of Preston and Marie, who were standing to either side of him. "I can't tell you all how very, very proud I am of you," George started. "You gave an excellent performance under difficult circumstances. Who came up with the idea of sitting on the stools and moving them with each scene?"

Sam raised his hand. "Me! I saw something like it on PBS."

"It worked very well. The cuts you made, the transitions you provided, the way you acted while you were singing even though you couldn't move…." He lifted his shoulders. "What can I say? It worked.

"But more importantly, you accomplished this together. You didn't have parents holding your hands or teachers smoothing the way for you. We had the show canceled by the board, and that was a blow, but you didn't let that keep you down. As you could see from the reaction of the crowd tonight, they respected you for just putting the show on, as well as for your performances."

He looked around the circle, slowly, starting with Preston and moving on to Sam and Sarah, and then all the way around until he ended with Marie next to him. "Very well done, all of you. I'm immensely proud of you."

Everybody clapped, including me and Kevin, who was standing next to me again.

George looked over the kids' heads and said, "Mr. Smith? Would you like to say a few words to the cast and crew?"

For a moment I hesitated. I shouldn't say anything, should I? I should let everybody go home to some well-deserved rest and celebration. I should keep my mouth shut and retreat the way I'd always retreated.

"Yes," I said. "I would."

I left Kevin's side and went into the circle the kids made, deliberately standing next to Robbie, who was next to Steven. Those two were together all the time, weren't they?

"You two were very brave," I said, and everybody heard me. "I'm proud that you kissed at the end of your song." Then I addressed Channing. "And you and Marie too."

I included everybody in what I had to say next. "I didn't always feel that way, did you know? Mr. Keating and I had some heated discussions about those kisses. He was always for them, but I was very concerned that they would cause problems. I guess I won that round, though I wish I hadn't.

"As a matter of fact, I'll confess something else. I wasn't enthusiastic about *Rent* at the beginning. I only agreed to work on it because Mr. Keating asked me to, and because the committee wouldn't let the play go on without me being there to help."

Murmurs of dismay rippled through the group. George looked as if he was afraid of what I'd reveal next.

"But a funny thing happened as soon as we got started. Good things began to happen to me. The world doesn't have enough good things, so I… appreciated them."

Kevin on the golf course, being proud of my putting. The long, slow, and surprisingly painless slide of his cock into me. Pulling him close and dancing with him in the cabin. His tears against my neck as he cried for me.

And there he was, standing behind Sam, watching me with the hint of a smile, with a sort of intent pride—for me—that I wanted him to have all the time. If I didn't have much to offer him yet… that could change, couldn't it?

"Some not-so-good things happened too. You all know about that. You've seen how the give and take of an open society works, I guess." I shrugged. "And at least you've been to your first school board meeting."

"My last one!" Preston mock-growled. Everybody laughed.

I waited until they quieted and I had their attention again before I continued. "But what I wanted to say is that… I learned from this play. I think you have too. There are still plenty of people in this town who are dead set against what you did tonight. This performance didn't change that. You knew people were against you, but you believed in what *Rent* has to say and in the friendships you've made during rehearsal. You wanted it to come alive at least one time. You didn't know that anybody would show up to see you tonight except your families, but still you did it."

I looked at them the way George had, seeing the not-quite-children, almost-adults, and I wanted to be a teacher for the rest of my life. I was born to teach; there wasn't anything better. "What you did, all on your own, was extraordinary. Remember what you accomplished tonight when you run into rough patches in your life, because everybody does. You can… get through it. You can find some way to make it good again."

I smiled, because a lump had lodged in my throat, and I was very, very glad that George had asked me to help him direct *Rent*. "That's all. Sorry to get so serious on you. Tomorrow's Thanksgiving. Have a good day. Enjoy these next four days off. You've earned them."

"Happy Thanksgiving, Mr. Smith," Channing said, and then she came over and hugged me. I was startled and didn't quite know how to react, but then I gingerly hugged her back.

George clapped me on the shoulder, my bad side, and that sent a ripple of pain down my arm. "Tom, it's been a pleasure working with you."

"And with you, George," I said, and I really meant it.

"Hold on a minute," Danielle said. "I want a picture of the two of you. Could you stand there and shake hands?"

We did that for her while everybody watched, and she snapped the picture.

"Good," George boomed. "So, tell me, what will you be doing tomorrow for Thanksgiving? Going to your brother's like you usually do?"

It was only my imagination that everybody stopped breathing while they waited for my answer. Not everybody was watching and listening. Directly over George's shoulder, though, Kevin was. The hope on his face was excruciating.

"No," I said as steadily as my shaking world would allow. I trained my eyes on George and kept them there or I wouldn't have been able to say a word. "I'm not. Kevin and I are leaving tomorrow for a trip to Big Bend."

Said. Done. Acknowledged. One more trip out of town over a weekend for us, but openly. "We're taking my Miata," I added.

George's eyebrows rose, but then he smiled, and it was a genuine smile. "You are? You and Kevin? That's great! You'll have a good time. When do you leave?"

I risked a look at Kevin. Oh, yes, it had all been worth it. Kevin was trying so hard to act nonchalant, but I knew this man now, and I saw his joy.

"Kevin?" I asked. "When do we leave? Five a.m.?"

He groaned and clapped a hand to his head. "Have pity on an old man. Six?"

"We could do seven, but only if we stop for breakfast at that little café in San Angelo."

He drew closer to me. "It won't be open on Thanksgiving."

I took a step closer to him. "We'll have to figure something else out then."

George turned away to pick up his flowers. Danielle got busy taking the makeshift curtains down from the kitchen. Sandy started pulling up the masking tape from the floor. The kids were picking up their stools as keepsakes to bring home.

Nobody here cared.

"We could eat before we leave," Kevin suggested, and his eyes danced.

I wanted to keep them dancing. I wanted… to be free. "At my house," I said deliberately. "Drive over and we can leave from there."

I'd wondered how Kevin had looked when I'd told him I would spend the weekend at his house. Now I knew, ten times over.

In some other universe, or maybe in Texas a hundred years from then, he would have grabbed me in a hug and kissed me, and we would have laughed out loud, because he didn't have to push me anymore.

Kevin had seen a place for the two of us together all the way back when he'd asked me to tour Houston with him for just a day. He'd been in that place, somehow, in a way that I still didn't understand, from the beginning. And now I'd finally caught up with him. I wasn't walking behind.

But this wasn't a hundred years from now. This was Gunning, Texas, in 2008, and freedom only reached so far. So instead, Kevin looked up at the ceiling and grinned. I watched him. My confident Kevin.

"That," Kevin said, and he looked back to me, "sounds like a very good idea."

CHAPTER 10
LEAD ON

FOUR of us were the last to leave the social hall. George, Jenny, Kevin, and I made certain everything was put back where it should be before walking out into the night together. Outside, on the sidewalk, George shook my hand one more time, I congratulated him on the play's success, and he and Jenny turned away to where they'd parked their car in front of the church.

"Where are you parked?" Kevin asked.

I still felt slightly giddy from all that had happened. I hadn't let myself imagine that I'd walk out of that church hall with Kevin so securely by my side. Anyone talking to him the past half hour would have assumed he was happy about the way Channing had done so well in the play, but I knew the smile that hadn't left his face was for me. For us. I might have been doing a little smiling myself. I'd really done it. Maybe nobody had noticed but Kevin—and George—but in my own very small way I'd taken a huge step toward a new life. I had one foot out of my own personal closet and one foot still in. Even so, I'd never thought I'd get this far.

Waving down the street, I said, "I'm that way two, three blocks."

"I'm here in the lot," Kevin said as happily as if that were the most fortuitous circumstance there could be. "Come on, I'll give you a ride to your car."

My feet were in perfectly fine shape, but riding with him would prolong the time until we said goodbye. Suddenly, I was desperate for alone time with my lover.

"All right," I said. "Lead on."

Shutting off the rest of the world when we slammed the doors of the Silverado was the best thing. We were the last vehicle remaining under the security lights, and George and Jenny had disappeared around the corner.

Kevin started the engine, but then he turned in his seat toward me. The outside lights didn't reach into the pickup; his face was shadowed, but still I knew the slope of his cheek, the curve of his eyebrows, and the desire in his eyes. He laughed softly. "I want to kiss you in the worst way right now." His hand reached across the console between us, not quite touching me.

The temptation to kiss him right then was overwhelming, and I actually swayed toward him before I caught myself. I grabbed the edge of the leather seat instead. I might have wanted nothing more than to connect us in whatever ways were possible in the restricting front seat of his truck, but we couldn't. The church parking lot wasn't really private, not like his house. Or mine.

Frustration raced through me. "Fuck," I said directly in his face.

His smile grew. "That too."

"Kevin…."

He did take my hand then. He had strong, capable hands, a man's hands. Feeling his palm against mine did nothing to calm me down.

"Tom," he said, and sudden wonder enriched his voice. "Thank you. I wasn't even sure you'd talk to me but now…. Four days together. Three nights with you." He shook his head. "I wasn't hoping for that because it seemed like too much to ask for."

Thursday night, Friday night, Saturday night together: that's what he meant. But…. It was ten-thirty p.m. on Wednesday, the day before Thanksgiving. Yes, we had the long, four-day weekend in front of us, but I wanted more.

Were we going to just say goodbye and drive away from each other? Today was the most important day of my life. I wanted to celebrate what I'd done, and I wanted to keep walking forward.

"More," I croaked. I stroked the back of his hand with my thumb. "Let's…."

"What?"

"Spend the night with me. Come back to my house."

His breath caught. He tightened his grip so fiercely that it hurt, but I wasn't going to pull away. "Do you mean it?"

"Please. Yes. We can go back to your place tomorrow morning and get you changed and get your camping stuff, but tonight…." I slid my hand up inside his sleeve, feeling the fine skin at his wrist, his shuddering pulse. "Don't make me go back home alone."

Kevin jerked away from me and reached to put on his seat belt. "Right now. Let's go."

I tersely directed him to where I was parked, and he answered with mere nods; neither one of us wanted to talk right then. We had a lot to discuss, but not now.

I slammed the door of the pickup and got into the Miata in a hurry. It couldn't go anywhere, though, until the Silverado pulled away. I looked up from my low-slung sports car seat to find him looking down at me from the high perch of the truck. He rolled down the window. "Last one there is a rotten egg."

He gunned the engine and was gone.

I still made it to the house first because I knew the shortcuts. Even so, I had just managed to park in the garage, get that door down, and race through the kitchen to the front when the bell rang.

I fumbled with the deadbolt and the knob, but then the door opened, I stepped back, and Kevin came into my house. Standing within the still-open door, and with his hand on the doorknob, he said with wonder, "You said we were going away for the weekend together in front of everybody. Are you really the Tom Smith I know?"

Maybe more like the Tom Smith I was meant to be, or the outline of him. I nodded a few times and then managed to say, "It's me."

He took a step inside and closed the door by leaning against it. The lock caught with a loud *snick*. "Have you…. Are we going to…. Tom, don't lead me on." The look on his face broke my heart. "I can't take it if…."

"Come here," I told him, but I was the one who stepped toward him and pulled him into my arms, away from the door, and pressed against his solid strength the way I'd been wanting to since I'd seen him looking at me with such need at the play. He clutched at me, and I kissed his cheek. “Don’t worry,” I whispered. “We’re going to work it out, okay? I… I’m going to make it happen. I’m not going to let you get away, no matter what.”

He drew a deep, long breath and then pulled back to take my shoulders. I couldn’t look at him enough. My gaze darted between his lips and his eyes.

“You are incredible,” Kevin said. “I knew it. Nobody else would be able to…. In a week, only a week, you’ve been able to reconcile all that you told me about? To deal with it somehow? You were wrecked that night. Hell, I was wrecked, and I’m not the person who’s been living alone with that for years. Are you really okay?”

“I just needed….” The span of years, sleeping with many nameless men, the increasing weight of my isolation in Gunning, a high school production of *Rent* and, finally, someone I could talk to. Someone who could pull my pain out of me. Someone I could love.

“You,” I said. “I just needed you.”

The youthful fool I’d been had thought I’d known love with Sean. Since then I’d given up on the idea and arranged my life so I’d never come close to it. Then Kevin had crept up behind me, and there it was, so unexpected I’d barely recognized it when it arrived.

Love was in Kevin’s eyes as he looked at me now. Love had been in the way he’d held me the week before in my kitchen, and in his calls, and in how he wanted me to leave Gunning with him. I didn’t understand why, because I was an ordinary man, but I felt it.

I took Kevin’s face between my hands, and I wanted to say it back to him, but I couldn’t. That was okay. I tilted my head, went closer, and finally touched my lips to his in the gentlest, barest contact. I closed my eyes, feeling it, how close we were to diving down into each other: into lust, into sex, into the messy, wonderful challenge of us together.

He sighed and murmured, “Kiss me,” and so I did.

I hadn’t kissed anyone this meaningfully—my whole heart in it—since college, and those kisses had been but a pale shadow of what I gave to Kevin and what he gave to me. We spent minutes there in the foyer, erasing the memory of the last time we’d stood there together, deliberately and slowly feeding on what we had to give to each other with lips and tongues and roving hands.

But then it was time to move on. I tried to pull away, got caught in him again when he brushed the tip of his tongue against my upper lip. It took a few minutes before I managed to part us even a little.

"You want a tour of the house?" I asked, out of breath, and amusement appeared in his eyes. I moved my fingers through his short hair, loving the way it tickled my palms.

He chuckled and kissed me again. "No."

"You want a beer?"

"I think I'm drunk on you already."

"You want me to drag you to the bedroom?"

"Tom. Take me to bed or we'll be arm-wrestling to see who does the dragging."

When I flipped on the overhead light, the bed was the way I'd left it, with the sheet a chaotic mess and the blanket trailing onto the floor; sleep had eluded me for half the night as I thought of seeing Kevin at the play. I didn't have fancy mirrors in my room, and it was small for a master bedroom, but everything we needed was there: One mattress for two men.

I undressed him in a wild rush, batting away his attempts to get to me because I needed him to be nude before me while I was fully clothed. When I finally worked his pants and briefs down off his legs and he stood naked, he took a step back. With his fingers along the underside, he lifted his cock, as hard as I'd ever seen it, the head of it purple and firm. "See what you do to me?" he said. "I'm thirty-seven and you drive me crazy like I was seventeen. I've jacked off more since I've met you than any time in my life."

I moved toward him but he quickly shook his head and held out his hand against me. "You get none of this until I see you." In his sex-drenched, raspy voice, he said, "Get undressed."

There was a time when I hadn't liked being ordered around that way by him, when I hadn't trusted him, when I'd feared my own responses. But not now. With his eyes following my every move, I took off my suit jacket, threw it onto the dresser, and felt like a porn star.

When I unbuckled my belt and unzipped, Kevin licked his lips, and I became impossibly harder. Off came the pants and my briefs, shoes and socks, and I stood there in my white dress shirt with my cock poking through the opening. My hands went up to my tie, but Kevin stopped me.

"No, let me do that."

He came to me with the smooth walk that had attracted me in the first place, like a panther silkily stalking me and making me love it. "Lift up your chin," he told me, and I caught my breath. He could ravage me with words alone. It was like being told to turn around and bend over because I was going to get the fucking I deserved. His fingers brushing my neck, busy at undoing my tie: my cock lifted and pulsed. The sexiest thing anybody had ever done to me. He was so close. His nostrils flared, his eyes were so alive, and if I moved forward mere inches our cocks would brush against each other.

"Kevin…."

"Just a minute."

"I need you."

"You'll have me. But I've got to do something first."

I willed myself to patience and rested my hands flat against his chest to stop myself from throwing him down onto the bed. His skin was warm.

The tie came slithering off my neck, and he simply dropped it to the floor. He reached for the top button of my shirt but paused to devour me with his eyes. My fingers curled in his chest hair as I was seen, and as I looked in turn. Kevin was a beautiful man.

"Love you," he said quietly, matter-of-factly. "You're going to have to get used to me saying that." He finished opening my shirt and pushed it off my good arm, leaving only the scars on my left arm covered by cloth. Kevin left the shirt that way, took my hand, and pulled me over to the bed; he pushed me down so I'd sit on the end of the mattress. He knelt in front of me, off to the side, and slowly pushed the hanging shirt off my shoulder.

He did it slowly because, after a few inches were exposed, he stopped to press his lips to my skin at the very top of the worst scar left from the surgery. Unmistakably. Deliberately. He kept his mouth there.

The entire world shuddered, tilted, and then stopped: my heart, his lips.

I stared down at him, at his mouth moving against the evidence of my long-ago shame. Our faces were close as he lifted his eyes to mine.

"Kevin," I breathed. "You don't have to—"

"All of you, Tommy. All of you."

He inched my sleeve a few inches further down and held it in place. There, laid bare, was the next puckered remnant of hate, and misunderstanding, and Sean's cowardice, and Kevin bent to give his healing touch, lapping at it with his tongue. I trembled to see it. The rest of the room narrowed to that: Kevin at my arm.

I leaned down, kissed the top of his head, and rested my cheek against him, blinking for what he gave me. I embraced him with my good arm, and I felt more than heard him sigh as he twisted a bit and laid the side of his face against my bicep.

"Don't hide from me anymore," he said even more hoarsely than usual.

My throat tightened. "I'll try."

"Am I hurting you?"

"No," I told him right away, low and forcefully. "You are not hurting me." Even though the bone-deep ache would never go away, and shattered nerve endings would always fire.

"I don't believe you."

With a finger on his chin, I brought his face around to mine. "Thank you," I said. I brought us together, and his mouth promised everything.

He went back to my arm, and I let him. He inched down past my elbow, past the wrinkled white flesh and the flared red line that had never faded, licking and sucking and kissing until my whole arm tingled. I hadn't ever been touched like that.

Down to my wrist, thankfully uninjured, but still there Kevin paused and spoke to me in a way that I would never forget, on his knees, joining me in my journey toward wholeness.

The moment finally came when Kevin released the shirt he'd been holding all this time against my skin. It dropped to the carpet, and I grabbed Kevin right away, pulled him against me, and fell back against the bed, taking Kevin with me as my cover. My erection had diminished as he'd spent time filling up the rest of me, but I didn't care. Having his weight on me, holding me down here in my own bed, was my unacknowledged dream come true.

He didn't stay on me for long. Kevin slithered down to suck on my left nipple. Then he bit my right one. He went back down onto his knees on the floor between my spread legs, but he pressed against my hips to keep me from sitting back up.

"Stay there and enjoy this."

The overhead light fixture blurred in my vision as he took my cock in his mouth and set about making me hard again. It didn't take long. Yellow light cascaded down on us, on Kevin's bent head, and on me. When he rolled my balls in his hand, my heart pounded. When his fingers strayed into my butt crack, hinting at what he wanted to do without doing it, I hissed in frustration. When he carefully scraped his teeth against my shaft, I grabbed at the sheet.

His breathtaking, noisy sucking.... I threw my arm over my eyes and gasped for air. Another minute and I'd—I was so close to—If he didn't quit—

Awkwardly, I forced myself up onto my right elbow and looked down at him. "Stop! I don't want to come alone. Come up here."

His lips were red and puffy, his skin flushed, but he released me. In a frenzy to get to him, I seized him and wrestled him down to the mattress, gave him a sloppy, all-tongue, open-mouthed kiss. But I quickly tore myself away.

"Wait," he objected, but I flipped myself on the bed so that we nestled close, head to toe on our sides, and his cock was waiting for my kiss.

"Yesssss," Kevin hissed.

I felt his hand circle the base of my erection, and then his moist lips covered me.

We'd tried this only once before. The second time in Houston, the morning that I'd relented and had breakfast with him, we'd tried sixty-nining. He'd finished way before I had and my own orgasm had been forced and awkward, which was why I'd avoided doing it with my sex partners; it never worked, was never right, never had the same feeling as when Sean and I had done it as stupid college kids.

Everything was different now. At that moment, it hardly mattered if we came together or one right after the other or minutes apart. What mattered was how incredible it felt as I took Kevin in while his mouth was on me. The confusion of you're-sucking-me, I'm-sucking-you, I'm-sucking-myself swamped me. For long seconds, for minutes, we fell into a joint rhythm.

I couldn't tell the two of us, separate men, from the one-of-us we were creating together on the bed. We breathed together, touched together, licked together. Pre-come coated my tongue, and I knew he was close. Kevin fingered my asshole, I gasped, and I was close too.

"Yes, do it," I choked out. He did. I abandoned his cock and reveled instead in his finger sliding inside me, while he worked his throat muscles against me. I had no chance, but I didn't fight it. Everything—me, Kevin, *Rent*, Sean, my one exhilarating step away from my past—compressed into a bright diamond about to explode. "God, yes! Here… here…. Take me!"

I grunted, stiffened, held it, held it, and finally, in one second, the world expanded past my knowing: all was possible, and I came. I could not help but thrust into him, trying to follow that flash of the future. Kevin took me with ease, opening and swallowing as I poured my coming down his throat.

I didn't even wait for the last glow to start to diminish. I aimed to give to him what he had given to me, and the same as I had, he allowed it to happen. He tilted back onto the bed with his arms spread out to either side, and I followed him, my mouth always full of him. Within a minute he was bucking up uncontrollably.

"Oh, Tommy, oh, yeah, that's so good. So…. Here I come! Right now! Uhn…."

It felt as if I were coming along with him; though my body was sated, my mind was still flooded with Kevin's light. I gulped him down, and it was so good.

I stayed on him even as he came down from the high, even as he relaxed and started to soften, even when he reached down and rested his hand on my head.

"Come here with me," Kevin said.

Carefully I released him and crawled up the bed to where he was waiting for me with open arms. We settled on my one pillow, with me on my right side as always, and he rubbed my top scar with his fingertips.

"Someday," Kevin said, "I want to sixty-nine with you so we both come at the same time. What do you think?"

Already I was fading. The night, the week, my life was too much for me to stay awake. "Yes," I said with my eyes closed. "The mirrors in your bedroom… and that. Let's do it all someday."

THE sound of a car door slamming opened my eyes. My next-door neighbors were coming home from a late-night party or a bar closing. I listened to them in the deep darkness until it was quiet again. Kevin's breathing next to me changed.

"Are you awake?" I whispered.

He drew a hand across his forehead. "Yeah," he said thickly. "You okay?"

"I'm fine." But there was something I had to say. I rolled over until I was mostly on top of him, looking down on him. His face was barely visible, but I felt his breath on my skin and the way he held me in place. His hands on me.

"I'm not incredible, like you said," I told him softly. "No, no, listen to me," I said when he immediately opened his mouth to contradict me. I pressed a finger against his lips. "I'm still all messed up inside about being attacked. It's still there." Sean was still there, my hatred of him, my fear, jumbled with the good memories of what we'd shared, but I couldn't bring myself to say that out loud.

Kevin soothed me by stroking down my side. "That's all right."

"I'm not over it. I don't know that I'll ever be over it."

"But maybe you can go past it, right?"

"Instead of being stuck where I am. That's what I'm going to try to do. But I can't pretend it'll be easy or pretty. I know what I want to do with you, but that doesn't mean I'll be able to do it."

"I think I'll take my chances. From the day I met you, you've been putting yourself down. Maybe it's time to stop that."

I bit my lip and then let it out. "What do you see in me?"

"I wish I could turn you around to look in a mirror and introduce you to yourself."

I bumped his chest with my chin. "Idiot," I said fondly.

"You might be a teacher, but you're dumber than dirt about some things." He guided my head down against his shoulder, and the rest of me slipped off him onto my side. I lifted one leg over his and relaxed against him. "We'll figure things out as they come along, okay?" Kevin said. "Do you think you could sleep like this?"

I swallowed at the marvel of this night: this man wanted me so close, and I had grown so that I wanted Kevin just as much.

"I've never slept like this," I said. That wasn't true. I had slept with Sean this way, but Kevin was not Sean, and I was not the man I used to be. "But we can try."

"Exactly."

I felt his lips against my hair and his arms around me.

"Good night, professor."

It took but a minute for Kevin's breathing to even out, and I knew he was asleep. I stayed awake a little longer, thinking… and touching the happiness at my core. I could barely allow myself to express it even in my thoughts, but Kevin and I had a future together. The only thing I shared with Sean was my past.

Languidly, indulgently, I rubbed my cheek against Kevin's shoulder, feeling myself sink deeper into the mattress as sleep inched closer. Sean would be thirty-eight years old now, like I was. Funny, I'd never thought about that. In my mind, he'd always been that careless, carefree twenty-two-year-old. During that long-ago phone call, I'd wished him a shitty life. Is that what he'd had? Had he been consumed with guilt the way I'd been consumed with rage and fear? Had that one night twisted his life the way it had ruined mine?

Sean? You're fine, aren't you? You weren't going to let a little something like raping your best friend and lover stop you. I bet you've laughed your way through life, have lovers and friends and smiles all around. I'm the one who's had the shitty life.

I'm done with it now though. Here, take it back. I don't want it anymore.

That felt… right. I thought I could sleep then, and I did.

IT WASN'T until we were halfway to Big Bend, driving across the arid west Texas landscape, that Kevin and I started talking seriously.

"I know you couldn't say last night with everybody around," I said into the comfortable silence that had fallen between the two of us. "But how's Channing really doing?"

Kevin took his time answering, but that was all right. Every moment since he'd walked into my house last night had been all right. Driving with him west along Interstate 10 had been relaxing; Kevin was easy to talk to. It'd been reassuring; our intense compatibility was real. And it'd been liberating; I'd taken the wheel of the Miata with him in the passenger seat and driven through Gunning with the top down. The world had not ended. Instead, it felt as if the world were opening up before me with every mile that passed under our tires.

The highway was practically deserted this early Thanksgiving afternoon, since everybody was off at Grandma's house eating turkey or glued to the TV for the football game. Kevin and I had gotten a much later start than we'd bragged about the night before. It was past ten before we even dragged ourselves out of bed to share a shower. Packing had been problematic. There was no way we could get the camping gear we'd need into my car's tiny trunk. I solved that by going online and making us reservations at the Chisos Mountains Lodge, the only motel in the park; I didn't want to try to make love with Kevin in a tent in a crowded campsite anyway.

Then there'd been breakfast in my tiny kitchen and the drive over to Kenneton, and so we were still on the road. I didn't mind, and I knew Kevin didn't either.

We drove under the brightest blue sky with the Miata cutting through the air, creating its own wind on a windless day. The flat land stretched all around us, hardscrabble ranch land that was mainly scrub brush and the occasional ravine to show that spring rains did sometimes visit here. A few cows kept us company as we zipped by, going an easy eighty toward the haziest hint on the horizon that proved some sort of mountain range waited for us.

"She hasn't decided what to do yet," Kevin said. "It's early days, so she has some time."

"What do you want her to do?"

"It hardly matters what I think, but…. She and JJ made a mistake. I think they should own up to the consequences of what they did, and she should have the baby. Then she should give it up for adoption. But I'm not sure that's what she and Julianne will decide. It's really not up to me. I won't be around much after I move."

He gave me a significant look and reached over to rest his hand on the seat behind me. His fingers danced along the back of my neck. "And that brings up an interesting subject, doesn't it?"

I glanced over at him, at his stylish sunglasses and his navy blue jacket zipped over a white T-shirt. Kevin looked like a rock star. "You want to talk about that now?"

"Yeah, I do. What are you thinking about? Will you come with me?"

The last time he'd asked me had been wild and impossible. This time Kevin asked as if he confidently knew the answer already.

We drove past what looked like an abandoned, broken-down church that hadn't been painted in fifty years. It was out in the middle of nowhere.

"I have a contract with the district," I said. "And more than that, an obligation to the students and my fellow teachers not to abandon them in the middle of the year. Plus…. You and me. It's a big change for me."

"I know," he said soberly. "It's going to take some time for you to get used to…."

"Not being afraid," I said flatly.

"To get used to living the life you want to live."

"If that's how you want to put it. I'd rather not beat around the bush."

"You need to get more comfortable with the whole idea and see how far you can go with it."

I nodded. "I do. I need to take this at my own pace." One drive around Gunning with Kevin did not create liberation. I was realistic enough to know that. This was going to take a while.

"I think maybe George knows about me," I said thoughtfully. I'd been slowly accepting that fact over the past weeks. And if George did and Channing did, then others probably did too. Or they guessed. No one had treated me any differently this semester. That was hard to believe, because I'd feared the repercussions of being outed for so long, but it was true. Maybe I could get used to… being known.

"Are you okay with that?" Kevin asked. "George knowing?"

"Yeah," I said. "I think I can cope."

"Good. You know, I'm sure two of the guys at the bank know I'm gay, and so far it's been all right. Even so, I still want us to move somewhere else and live openly from the beginning. Do you understand why I want to leave? How I don't think we can do it here?"

"I couldn't do it here," I said, shaking my head. "I couldn't. I don't have a problem with moving. I need to get out of Gunning and start over again."

"So, when? End of the school year?"

"Early June. Can you wait that long?"

He tugged on a strand of my hair. "I've waited thirty-seven years to meet you. A few extra months before we head out together won't make me sweat. You know, this is a lousy economy for both of us to be looking for jobs."

"I know." I smiled over at him. "We're crazy, aren't we?"

"Certifiable."

"I want to teach wherever we go. So, get the job first, and after that...." I shrugged because I didn't know what else to say. How a gay man went about living that kind of life, I didn't know. But I'd try.

"Any ideas about where we should go?"

"A few."

"Where?"

I stretched my left arm to relieve the strain of driving for hours and then rested it again on my thigh. I still felt Kevin's kisses on my scars. "I hate to sound so predictable. I'm a cliché. To one of the coasts? I'm ready to try a big city, I think."

"Perfect. Me too. Which one?"

I lifted my shoulders. "Take your pick. I don't think I'm crazy about New York. Too big."

"We need to do some research."

"Right. Los Angeles? I like the idea of living by the water. That would be new."

"How about Boston?" Kevin asked.

Where a Massachusetts-styled Prop 8 had never passed and presumably gay men and women were... comfortable. If people like Kevin and me could marry there, then surely life would be easier for us. I nodded. "That sounds good. It's about as far from Texas as we could go."

"I like the idea of Boston. Great seafood, by the ocean, lots of history. I bet they could really use a history teacher like you."

"Let's keep an open mind but start by looking there."

As easily as that, we agreed. I had six months to learn how to navigate my way in a new world. I didn't think it would be easy. But I did think it would be worth it.

ON SUNDAY morning, our last morning at the park, we got up way before dawn and drove down from the high Chisos Basin, where the lodge nestled, into the Chihuahuan desert. No other cars paced us or passed us on the road that cut through Big Bend; our headlights led into splendid, natural isolation. The stars overhead were still bright. Kevin drove, so I pitched my head back and feasted on the sight. Civilization was far away.

"Beautiful," Kevin said, not for the first time.

"Hmmmm."

"Maybe we should become park rangers and live here."

I smiled to myself at the thought. Kevin would look great in a ranger uniform.

The day before we'd climbed Emory Peak, the highest point at Big Bend. It'd taken us seven hours to make the round trip. My legs still ached from the last fifty feet of the climb, which had taken us over torturously jumbled rocks to the top, but the effort had been worth it. As Kevin had said, most practically, why hike all that way only to fall short because the rocks wanted to stop us? We'd easily seen into Mexico from the summit. Layers upon layers of mountain ranges stretched as far as we could see into the mist, repeating themselves endlessly, as if they went on forever.

Now Kevin was taking me to one of his favorite places to view the sunrise. Big Bend was huge, one of the biggest of all national parks. Already we'd driven forty minutes, first along the paved road and then along a dirt one, past the usual paths that tourists regularly hiked and into the wilder reaches that the rangers and the animals knew.

"I found the best place to see the sunrise with my dad when I was twelve, right before we left for Little Rock," Kevin had told me before we'd fallen asleep the night before. He hadn't needed to say it was special to him; I could hear it in his voice.

He parked along the side of the road and shrugged into the Camelbak. He prized it, I think, because Channing had given it to him. I stuffed a plastic water bottle into my pocket, and we found the faint trail that disappeared into the wilderness.

Kevin led. I followed behind him. Flashlights lit our way because there still wasn't even the hint of light in the eastern sky. The dirt under our hiking boots was hard packed and made for easy walking even in the dark, but after a while it became softer and sometimes slid out from under our feet. Low desert plants surrounded us, and I was careful not to brush against any cactus.

I kept my eyes open for mountain lions, although it wasn't likely they'd be prowling in the open desert. You never knew, though. We'd come across unmistakable footprints along the banks of the Rio Grande River on Friday.

Kevin stepped softly in front of me, and I had confidence that he wouldn't get us lost on the day we had to drive back home. He knew Big Bend well from living so close to it as a boy. On Thursday afternoon, after we'd arrived, we'd driven all over the park, showing each other the places we remembered from our visits when we were younger. *That's where my sister and I saw the bear. Here's where we came across a pack of javelinas. I found a tiny fossilized bone by the river. Do you know about the archeology dig? It's over on the other side of the mesa.*

Half an hour of walking took us to a ridge that rose from the desert floor perhaps forty feet. By then the sky was brightening and dawn wasn't far off. We scrambled up to the top, an easy climb, and sat down cross-legged, side by side, facing east.

I wasn't immune to the symbolism. Probably Kevin wasn't either. A new day trembled on the edge of being as we watched. When the first sliver of sun appeared, Kevin put his arm around me, and I leaned against him.

We watched in silence for a while. The stars disappeared. The desert appeared. Tonight the cycle would reverse itself, and then it would repeat in the morning. Over and over. I couldn't sit within the midst of that reality without knowing how incredibly lucky I was to have broken the cycle that had defined my life.

"Tell me something about yourself," I said. "Something I don't know already."

"Like what?"

"I don't know. Anything."

He turned to me, his eyes serious, and he took my hand to hold between us. "All right. I'll tell you this. I fell in love with you from the start. Right away. Did you know that?"

I shook my head, but on the edge of my thoughts I realized maybe that wasn't so much of a surprise. "Really?"

"Yeah," Kevin said roughly. "I don't even believe in love at first sight. I barely knew you, but there you were, and there I was, and I was a fool for you right away."

"You mean in Houston, right? The second time?"

"Right."

"You hid it well."

"I might have been besotted, but I wasn't a total idiot. You were so hard and fierce on the outside, and I could see there was this… this neediness in you, but you weren't admitting it, no way, no how. I think that's what first caught my attention. That combination of strong and vulnerable." He drew a breath. "You were so tough on me, leaving the way you did. I cursed your stubbornness all the way home."

"I regretted leaving you like that before I was twenty miles away."

"And then there you were at Channing's high school. I thought I'd died and gone to heaven to see you there."

"I sometimes wondered if you maybe had found me. You know, tracked me down?"

The rising sunlight caressed his face. "I would have if I could have, believe me. But I didn't believe you when you said your name was Smith."

"Just an ordinary name."

He let go of my hand and stroked a thumb across my cheek instead. I couldn't believe that I would have the pleasure of looking into his eyes like this from now on. "Now you do it," he said quietly.

I was losing myself in him, in the sight of him. "Do what?"

"Tell me something I don't know about you."

That was easy. The words had trembled on my lips for days. "I love you."

His smile warmed me more than the sun ever could. He'd warmed my arm, after all. "I know that."

"But I haven't said it yet. I love you."

We came together in a kiss. Not a passionate kiss, not one that made promises, but a kiss filled with the moment: I loved Kevin. He loved me. Here and now, today.

"Give in to love or live in fear," the kids had sung in the finale to *Rent*. "No other path. No other way."

For years JENNA HILARY SINCLAIR approached creative writing as if she were looking over the edge of a cliff—the view was terrifying but seductive. She couldn't comprehend how anyone could compose a complex plot and have the patience to put it on the page. But one day she sat down, picked up a pen, and much to her astonishment, a novel began to take shape.

Since that day, Jenna's been in an exhilarating free fall. She lives her own life plus the lives of her characters, searches for the answers to the most important questions—What is love? Where is courage? Why is there fear?—and has a wonderful time writing gay romance.

Jenna is fiercely in favor of GLBT rights, kindness, keeping promises, and mountains. She lives in the Great American Southwest with her beloved husband, two cats, and a hundred characters dancing in her head. Some of them dance together. She hopes the music never stops.

You can visit Jenna's blogs at http://jenna-hilary.livejournal.com and http://jenna-smiling.livejournal.com.

Other titles by JENNA HILARY SINCLAIR

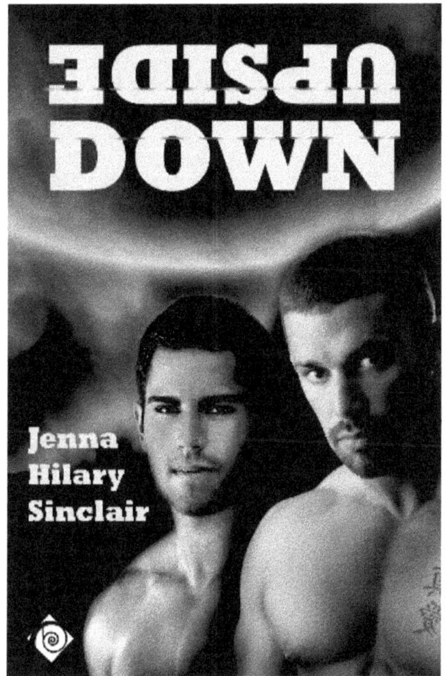

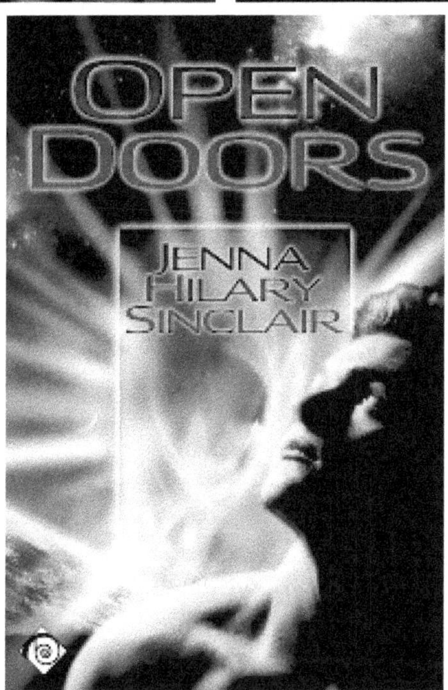

http://www.dreamspinnerpress.com

Dreamspinner Press
For more of the best M/M romance, visit
Dreamspinner Press
www.dreamspinnerpress.com